Adam Tideborne and the Greatsword of War

Joshua Stevens-Shachar

TO RUMAISA,
THANK YOU SO MUCH FOR BUYING MY BOOK, I HOPE YOU ENJOY IT AS MUCH AS I ENJOY SPENDING TIME WITH YOU!

Josh

Acknowledgments

To my mother who has always wished the best for me.
To Dylan for being my second mind.
And to every Interactor who has ever brought a spark of magic into my world.

1. The Endless War 5
2. The Portal 23
3. A Spark of Magic 40
4. First Breath of Fresh Air 57
5. A Criminal Amongst Heroes 71
6. A Feast Fit for the Gods 84
7. Brown Fairies 102
8. Hunted by a Monster 116
9. The Cherry Blossom Tree 132
10. Team bonding 147
11. Magic is Power 163
12. Flame Spell 179
13. Confessions 193
14. The Qiqirn 209
15. Two Beings at the Start of It All 228
16. A Bakunawa in the Cosmic Sky 231
17. The Perfect Mentor 248
18. Storytime 267
19. Learning from the Best 279
20. Crux of Life 298
21. A Heroes Downfall 314
22. Charon's Disciple 327

23. Another Funeral 340
24. Adventure Time 358
25. Honour and Treasure 371
26. Let the Dead Be Forgotten 384
27. The Fourth Strain 399
28. Epilogue 405

1. The Endless War

Adam had just taken a nasty fall. He would have manoeuvred around the chunk of rubble with ease any other day – even when his head was filled with fantasies about being a hero – but today the large piece of jagged stone had held its ground against Adam's foot.

Instinct had taken over and his hands came out to protect his head as he fell down onto the sharp pieces of glass and dark grey stone scattered across the ground, not that it mattered. As he stood up, wiping the filth from his hands and removing a few pieces of glass that had lodged in his palm and right arm, the nanobees inside of him would already be mending his injuries. By the time he reached school, it would be like the fall never happened.

There were few things that those microscopic pieces of technology inside of everyone weren't capable of fixing. Science and medicine had conquered just about anything that could affect the body... at least on Earth.

This had been the very thing that Adam had been so absorbed in that made him trip on one of the many pieces of rubble he passed every day. Specifically, he had been thinking about how boring Mr Smithers' long life had been.

All of his one hundred and seventy years of life had been spent on Earth. Mr Smithers had been around to see the Endless War destroy most of the planet, he would have heard about the last animal dying, he would have seen the last plants die out. And he had nothing to show for it. He had spent the first part of his life fighting on Earth and then when the portal opened, he stayed on this wasteland, wasting away his life watching old shows and films.

Adam had no intention of spending that many years alive. Today would be his last day at Kiwi High, and tomorrow would be his last day on Earth. Adam would experience what Mr Smithers had always been too afraid to do. Tomorrow would be Adam's first day in Elysium.

Adam didn't look it with his round babyface, small nose, and short stature, but he had finally turned seventeen. So, in just over twenty-four hours when the colossal stone gates opened – as they did every year – he would finally be eligible to go through them where the holy portal awaited him.

As he made his way deeper into the heart of his town, fewer pieces of rubble and debris blocked the now visible path and the many smooth stone-grey factories towered over him. It felt as if he lived on a landfill, not that anywhere else on Earth was in better condition. Adam imagined that if the air wasn't so thick with pollution, the sun, which he could barely see through the dark grey sky, would cast great shadows onto him.

Shaking his hands over his curly brown hair helped keep the little pieces of ash that filled the sky from getting stuck in it. He then went back to fiddling with the small streak of blonde hair hiding in his nest of brown just above his right ear.

The blonde had always been part of his hair and was slightly softer than the rest, and so he had grown used to playing with it subconsciously whenever he was thinking.

With only a few turns left, Adam passed the dull faded houses at the centre of town which belonged to the people who had jobs, each identical to the next and just like those on the outskirts. Every house had a screen in each room to watch, read, or play any piece of media since the dawn of technology. It kept them happy, those who were content with doing nothing of interest with their lives, like Mr Smithers.

A few minutes later, Adam reached Kiwi High. The building had an identical concrete-cube structure to their hospital, where Adam had spent his time as a baby after his parents sent him to Earth alone after his birth.

The school had a grid of thick windows that allowed students to see outside into the desolate world as they learnt about the past and about Elysium.

The hundred or so students of the town were all filing into the building where a special kind of spark scattered through the halls.

Most of the younger students were moping about looking miserable, whilst everyone else had fresh invigorated energy. Students who were always quiet and moody whistled as they walked through the bland halls, heads held up high, taking in the school they hated so dearly. It was easy to tell who was of age and who wasn't. Who would be leaving to explore Elysium and who had to stay behind.

Adam bounced around with Kaya the moment they saw each other, as if they were kids at the end of a Christmas movie opening the presents they had wanted since the opening credits, their excitement pouring out of them.

Kaya Marley was lanky with thick black dreadlocks and a wide rugged face which made it look like he was a few years older than everyone else in his year. Compared to Adam, it looked like there were five years between them even though they were the same age. He already had a decent amount of stubble growing in patches on his chin and above his lip.

The two first met when Kaya's mother decided to help out with the overcrowding at the hospital and offered to take Adam into her home when he was two, giving him a place to live and be raised for his childhood.

Their first lesson of the day was maths and it immediately turned into a conversation about what people were desperate to experience in Elysium.

'I don't really know what I'm excited for. I think it will be cool to use magic. I don't mean anything too dangerous, just something that can make me stronger,' Max said quietly after Alycia had spent the last five minutes talking about how she couldn't wait to wear anything other than the dark blue clothes the fabric factory massproduced.

'Magic is definitely something I want to get good at,' Olivia added, resting her hand on her round freckled face. 'But there is so much we don't know about it. The portal's only been open for twenty-one years and the Endless War was fought there for like half of that. I can't imagine we know all that much magic. See, that's not a problem when it comes to seeing all the adorable creatures out in the wild, because they are just wandering around, living their best lives.'

'It took seven years for the war to end in Elysium, that's a third. Come on, Olivia, we're in maths class, get your numbers right,' Kaya teased. 'And of course, you would care about creatures. That's got to be one of the most boring things to care about. We already know all about them, and they don't do anything. All they're good for is being made into food, which is so obviously the best thing about Elysium. I can't wait to stop eating these damn tablets and taste some real food.'

'I can't believe you would say that!' Olivia said in the same annoyed way that Kaya always managed to bring out in her. 'In the next couple of days, we are going to see creatures and nature that have been extinct for hundreds of years and you think that's dull! That's not even mentioning the hundreds of magical creatures we've only read about in fairy tales that are now thriving in Elysium. How can you think that's boring?'

'Just can,' Kaya stated with a loud, fake yawn.

Adam thought it best to jump into the conversation before Olivia inevitably started hitting his best friend. 'I just can't wait to get out there and start making stories, we've spent all our lives watching them on the screens and hearing about all the things people have done in Elysium. I just can't wait to stop being a spectator to all this. I can't wait to be like a real hero.'

'I bet it'll be easy for you to be a hero,' Olivia said, turning back to look at Adam. 'If the stories of your parents are even half true, they'll take you on crazy adventures in no time. Just make sure you put in a good word for me, would you? I've always been nice to you, remember.'

Adam shrugged, joking like he was thinking about putting in a good word for her, as an uncontrollable smile spread across his face and flooded his body with excitement at the thought of finally meeting his parents.

'Oi! Don't try and leech off him, and anyway, what do you need a good word for if all you want to do is pet a cow?' Kaya argued.

With this, Mrs Blake finally decided to put a stop to the conversation. 'Everyone, stop! I know you are all excited, but you need to remember that it is incredibly dangerous through the portal. Most people don't survive the three years at that awful training camp. You are going there as fodder to throw yourself out into the world to find all the horrors it has, whilst trying to survive any attacks from monsters. There's still the choice to stay behind and live a safe life.'

Mrs Blake was always trying to deter students from going through the portal. She had gone through herself, not long after it opened, to help fight, but after years of war, she chose to leave Elysium and come back to Earth, deciding to stay even after the Ascensionists had been defeated. She was the only person in their town who had seen Elysium and come back but she never spoke about her time in the other world, except for talking about how dangerous it was.

'What do you miss most about Elysium, Miss?' Olivia, like the rest of the class, chose to ignore Mrs Blake's constant warnings.

'Look, I'm sure all of you will find out everything tomorrow, you don't need me to talk about it,' Mrs Blake protested, crossing her arms.

'Oh, come on miss,' Kaya whined. 'You don't have to tell us any stories. Just the one thing that you enjoyed about the world.'

'No, I... I really shouldn't. There's no reason for me to do such a thing.'

'Please, Miss, it can't do any harm,' Adam pleaded.

Mrs Blake's eyes started to gloss over as she stared off into the distance. It was clear to Adam that she was thinking back to her time through the portal, she looked just like he did when he thought about his future, and although she was currently standing in a school classroom, all she could see was Elysium.

'The colour,' she finally said. 'The only thing that I truly miss about the other world was how colourful it was. The sky, the land, the fields of grass covered in flowers. It was all so splendid. Even at night, the way that sky made me feel like I was somewhere special. Here on Earth, everything is grey or blue, unless you're looking through a screen. There, that's it. No more questions.'

'But then if it was so beautiful, why did you come back to Earth?' Kaya was pushing their luck now.

'Well, you see, Kaya. After everyone you have ever loved dies a cruel painful death, it simply doesn't feel deserved to have any colour in your life anymore.' Mrs Blake sniffled, and hastily left the classroom as she pulled a used tissue from her sleeve.

'What did you do that for? You made her cry!' Olivia shouted, punching Kaya's arm with her right fist where she had two silver rings.

'I didn't mean to make her cry! I just wanted to know why she came back, we all did. How was I meant to know that would happen?'

Kaya and Olivia continued to bicker until Adam dragged Kaya out of the room as the lesson came to an end.

'Why is she so annoying? I don't know what's with her, she's always trying to pin things on me!'

'I mean, you know what they say about stuff like that. Has she also been pulling on your hair and leaving you little notes?'

'Oh, shut up!' Kaya smirked, as he pulled on his dreadlocks. 'You're only saying that because you're mad that I'm the main character.'

'What do you mean, main character? You barely pass as a sidekick! I'm obviously the hero. I've got the skills to be one, and I have my own unique thing like all proper main characters have.'

'You can't seriously think that bit of blonde fluff is anywhere close to getting you the main character status?' Kaya laughed.

'You know what, at this point, I don't even care if I'm a background character. As long as I'm in Elysium, I don't care.'

'Same here. I mean...' Kaya trailed off, watching something just past Adam's shoulder. Adam turned around in time to see two identical twins attacking a younger student who was curled into a ball.

'HEY!' Adam shouted.

The twins turned around. It wasn't possible for someone to be fat or too skinny in a world where the only food was white flavourless wafer-like tablets. However, nothing could be done about genetics. The Shark twins had won some kind of lottery with theirs, as they were both well over six feet tall, making it easy for them to scare anyone they wanted. Even Kaya was a good few inches shorter. One was called Bruce Shark and the other Eddie Shark, not that you could tell the difference.

They were exactly the same height, their faces square and stupid-looking with their identical smooth wavy black hairstyles the same length, and like everyone else, they wore the same dark blue clothes.

'Oh, I can't wait to finally destroy you two,' Bruce said in his deep voice, cracking his knuckles, immediately forgetting about the younger student he had been attacking.

'We're gonna break you both so bad, they'll have to bring you through the portal in a coffin,' Eddie said in a barely higher tone.

Adam couldn't be bothered to talk back to the twins, they had been through it all already. The four of them had been enemies from day one at Kiwi High when Adam and Kaya stopped the twins from attacking their first victim, leading to a near-daily battle of justice.

As usual, Bruce went to attack first, throwing his entire body behind one full-power punch at Adam. After years of fighting, Adam and Kaya knew exactly how to exploit the twins, and this first punch always left Eddie in an awkward spot.

Adam dodged to the left of Bruce's fist with ease, as Kaya kicked off the concrete wall to land a punch on Eddie's face. By the time Adam was clear of Bruce, Eddie had stumbled directly toward him, and in his dazed state, he could do nothing to stop the flurry of punches that Adam and Kaya delivered, dropping him to the floor.

Adam and Kaya had plenty of opportunities to improve their fighting skills over the years. The Shark twins weren't the only bullies at Kiwi High, but they were the only ones ignorant enough to keep trying after Adam and Kaya had been through with them.

In a surprising break from tradition, Bruce picked Adam up from behind in an attempt to slam him down onto the ground. He raised Adam higher and higher into the air and no matter how hard Adam tried to escape the giant's clutches, his fury was too fierce to break.

Thankfully, Kaya was quick to find a way to help. The trick with the twins was that they were tall, which meant that they could reach a lot farther with their attacks. It also meant that they were a bigger target to hit and so as Kaya threw himself like a wrecking ball into the back of Bruce's legs, it forced him to collapse to the floor like a demolished building.

Bruce tried to get back up but was swiftly brought back to the ground. Eddie, who was still out cold, would come back around with his injuries healed in ten minutes at most. Still, Bruce tried again to get up, believing he would be able to take the two on. Once again, Adam made him drop to the floor.

'I'll kill you!' Bruce screamed as the two started to walk away. 'You hear me, Adam! You're dead!'

'Oh no, I'm really scared now,' Adam remarked. 'How many times have you said that now?'

'Gotta be in the hundreds.' Kaya shook his head.

'This is the last time you get in our way, watch your back because you're a dead man!'

'Are you really this stupid?' Kaya asked.

'Yeah, how is killing me going to do anything? You kill me and then within hours, my nanobees will fix me up, or the hospital will revive me and then what? You'll get banished from the town and probably won't be let through into Elysium. If that's really your plan, then by all means kill me.' Adam goaded stretching out his arms and puffing out his chest.

Before Bruce could say another word, the student he had been pummelling kicked him in the head whilst he was down, knocking him unconscious like his brother.

As if he hadn't done anything, the younger student thanked Adam and Kaya for helping and made his way to his next class, his injuries numbed and healed.

'You worried about what Bruce might do to you?' Kaya asked as they made their way to their next lesson.

'I'll be fine. He hasn't got it in him to do anything more than a light beatdown that nobody can really feel,' Adam said with a shrug.

Sitting down for History and Ancient Folklore, they continued talking about what they wanted to do in Elysium with the rest of the class when Mr Darby slammed his hands onto the table, making everyone jump.

'You are still on Earth! Most importantly, still in my classroom, and so you will treat me with proper respect!' He shouted, his veins popping out of his head as they so often did whenever he grew angry.

'But it's the last day. What does it matter?' Kaya asked.

Once again Mr Darby slammed his hands onto what must have been his seventh desk. 'How many times do I have to tell you, Kaya! You call me sir! There may not be much that I can teach you, but it is vital that you understand the deadly world you are about to enter.'

'We already know all about Elysium, sir, at least as much as we can,' Alycia said, trying to warm up to the teacher in the hope he would let them continue to talk.

'Then tell me who Gonti is.'

'He was the leader of the Ascensionists, sir,' she responded.

'Were the Ascensionists the only enemies in the endless war?' He asked the class.

Adam had read through their history books dozens of times and was ready to recite a perfect answer.

'No, sir. Throughout the war, there were seven main armies fighting against each other to rule Earth. Then when the portal opened, the war evolved. All sides had to choose to fight with or against the newly formed Ascensionists. The threat of a world-ending event brought the portal to open on Earth and it was their belief that another event like it in Elysium would grant them a portal to heaven, so they did everything they could to destroy Elysium.'

'And how did Gonti manage to become the leader of the Ascensionists?'

'After a year of fighting in Elysium, Gonti became one of the most powerful people alive as he was the only one to learn necromancy magic, letting him rise in the ranks and become their leader,' Olivia answered as she gave a dirty look to Kaya.

'What brought about his downfall? Who brought peace to both our worlds with the end of the endless war?'

'Micholesh,' Kaya said with confidence, keeping eye contact with Olivia.

'Wrong,' Mr Darby said, glad that someone had answered incorrectly.

'I'm right though. Micholesh led everyone to defeating the Ascensionists, and is now our king.'

'Wrong, wrong and wrong again! Micholesh was not always our leader. Their downfall was caused by a lot more than just a single person. And unlike Gonti the Necromancer, Micholesh goes by no title. He does not accept the title of king, ruler, or ender of the endless war, he asks us to simply call him Micholesh. You all clearly have not learnt enough. I want you to open your books and search for the correct answers that Kaya has failed to understand.'

The whole class groaned as they took out their books, sitting in silence for the lesson. Nobody cared to read what was in their exercise books, they had all read them front to back more times than they could count. Instead, everyone let their minds wander, imagining what their new life – the one they had been dreaming of since the day they heard of the holy portal – would look like.

As the school day came to a close, there was a ceremony for the year's leavers. A small celebration of their time at school and for every student, except two who had decided to stay on Earth, a celebration of their last full day on the planet. Nobody stayed for too long. It wasn't like prom in a coming-of-age movie, there was no food or drinks other than water and they hadn't bothered to play any music to keep the students entertained. So, after a long hour, everyone found themselves saying their goodbyes and walking home.

School had been interesting enough for the last five years, but learning about life on the other side had lost its novelty. Communication between worlds was scarce, only happening when the gates opened for a few hours every year, and so Adam was never sure how accurate the information he had been taught was.

His town was only one over from the one which held the portal, but even then, the information took a long time to reach them and would have been told through several different people all changing and forgetting small details.

Every single year, he went to the town over and watched everyone come in and out of the portal. There were only ever a few people coming from Elysium because they no longer wanted to live there, or because they were no longer allowed to stay there, or like Adam, the children and babies who had been sent alone – so that they could grow up in a safe world.

Adam had waited every year for his parents to come and bring him back to Elysium. No matter how many times he was certain they would, they never showed. His earliest memory was when he was three, standing in front of those overwhelmingly large gates, certain that now he was no longer a baby, his parents would want him back in Elysium.

On those lonely nights, he would remember screaming for them through the portal as the gates came to a close, crying louder than that deafening grinding noise they made as they scraped against the ground.

Over the years, he had grown to accept that they had sent him to Earth so that he was safe, and he made sure to train as much as he could to prepare for Elysium, so that they could see he could make them proud.

Making his way out of the school for the final time, Adam went over his plans with Kaya. In the morning, there would be the rusty metal bus waiting to transport them. It wasn't a long ride but it was the only way to get there, and like every year, there would only be one to take them there. Once the portal gates closed, it would then drive anyone back.

Adam and Kaya planned to meet on the edge of the town where the bus waited at nine o'clock, an hour earlier than when the bus would leave, just so that there was no way of them missing their ticket off the planet. The portal gates would open at eleven o'clock on the dot and close exactly two hours later.

The two of them made their way back to Kaya's house. Adam spent a couple of hours saying his final goodbyes to Sharon and David, Kaya's older brother and sister, Damian, Julie, and Mackie, the younger siblings, and of course to Rita and Junior for being his Earth parents until he moved out of their house when he was twelve.

It was a surreal feeling knowing that he may never see some of them again, and the next time he would see some of Kaya's brothers and sisters, he would be settled into Elysium years in the future. As evening came, Adam decided to head back to his own house to let the Marley household have one more night with Kaya before he left them.

Being all alone in his own house on the outskirts of the town, Adam resorted to spending his evening watching his favourite films from the early 2000s – the platinum age of media, as he called it – for the final time. Sending any kind of technology through the portal would always vaporise it, and no matter how hard they tried in the early days, nothing technological seemed to work on Elysium.

Not wanting to stay up all night, Adam made his way to bed, where he struggled to fall asleep, thinking about what he would say when he finally met his parents. For so much of his life, he had been furious with them, yet as he finally slipped into sleep, he was giddy with joy to be with them. The people that throughout his entire life had only given him one thing, his name. Adam Tideborne.

2. The Portal

Adam awoke early the next morning. No dawning sun shone through his windows nor did any birds chirp to tell him that it was a new day. Only his phone gave him the time. After eating his morning tablets, he spent around an hour walking around the house not knowing what to do.

It was too late to watch one last movie or play one last game, so he resorted to taking in the house that he had spent the last five years of his life in. There was a sickly feeling in his stomach that he hadn't experienced before, as though the anxiety and anticipation were so strong that the nanobees had to swarm around in his stomach to keep him grounded. Deciding that it would be better to pace around by the pick-up spot instead of his house, Adam set off on his journey.

Only a few minutes from his house, he ran into the last two people he wanted to see. Emerging from behind a large piece of rubble were the Shark twins. Without Kaya by his side, Adam started to worry.

'Well, well, well, look who it is,' Bruce said as if he hadn't been waiting for Adam.

'It's over for you,' Eddie added.

'See, Adam, we don't want to have to deal with you for the rest of our lives, always getting in the way of what we want to do, and we've been thinking about how we can stop you.'

'Yeah, we have!' Eddie chimed in again.

'We realised that if you never made it through the portal, nobody would care, and our problems would be solved, and that's exactly what's going to happen.'

As Adam had been expecting, they both went for him. He managed to dodge Bruce, but Eddie grabbed hold of him before he could escape.

'There's a couple things we could do here.' Bruce had a horrible smile on his face. 'We could knock you out, but then there's no way of telling when you would wake up. We could hold you here until the bus leaves, but then obviously we would miss the portal, no can't have that.'

Whilst speaking, Bruce searched through Adam's pockets who wriggled around, trying desperately to escape Eddie's bear hug. It didn't take long for Bruce to find Adam's phone, which he used to send a message to Kaya saying that he couldn't wait to get the bus and had walked it all the way to the town over. After the message was sent, Bruce dropped the phone on the floor and crushed it with his boot.

'There, that should be enough to make sure he doesn't come looking for you. Now, where were we? Oh yes, in the end, we just decided it would be easier to simply kill you.'

Bruce pulled out a piece of sharp metal from his pocket and – ignoring Adam's desperate pleas – stabbed him in the stomach. Bruce took the makeshift knife out and Adam glanced down to see it covered in blood. He watched in horror as Bruce stabbed him again and again.

Once Bruce was done, Eddie shoved Adam's pale body down to the ground. He tried to lift himself back up but he didn't have enough strength, a pool of blood leaking out onto the filthy ground growing as he struggled more. The twins ran off, throwing the piece of metal into the distance, whilst Adam was unable to move or call for help, choking on his blood, until, as hard as he tried not to, he slipped out of consciousness.

# #

As Adam's eyes flickered open, a kind-faced woman swam into view above him, dabbing his head with a hot towel.

'Hello Adam, don't worry. Everything is going to be just fine,' she said in a gentle, soothing voice.

'I need... I have to get to the bus.' He sat up quickly and realised that he was in the hospital, on the other side of town from where he needed to be.

'I'm sorry, dear, but I don't think you're going to make it in time. You should spend a little longer in bed so that your wounds can heal properly. If you can remember, would you mind telling me what happened? Did someone attack you?'

'It doesn't matter.' Adam didn't care what she said, he had to make it. He couldn't wait another year.

'You can't seriously suggest that you're going to try and get there in time. It leaves in what...' The nurse checked her phone. 'Fifteen minutes. It's going to take twenty to sprint there in a healthy state. I'm sorry, dear, but it's not possible. Please lie back down.'

Still, Adam chose to ignore not only the nurse but basic maths. He stumbled out of the cheap spring bed and started to make his way to the exit, holding his aching stomach, knowing that without the nanobees, he would be in agonising pain.

In old movies, running out of the hospital was always a dramatic chase usually followed by gunfire, but his escape was just a light jog followed by the nurse's echoing concerns. Without thinking about anything other than getting to the bus in time, he moved his jog into a sprint, trying to ignore the pain as he bolted towards his destination.

Adam was an excellent sprinter, probably one of the fastest in the town. The problem was he was only good at short distances, he couldn't go more than a couple of minutes at full speed before he had to stop to catch his breath. But he knew there was no time to stop so he kept on moving as fast as he could.

Normally, nanobees would work to numb pain from the person, but Adam discovered after seven minutes of constant sprinting that even they would not hold back the agony intending to stop Adam from causing any more self-harm.

With the nanobees working to stop him running, each ragged breath Adam took made it feel like he was choking on the air around him, and it felt like his stomach was being stabbed all over again. Still, Adam did his best to ignore the overwhelming torment, determined to reach the bus.

Fifteen minutes later, in more anguish than all his past experiences combined, Adam had made it to the edge of town. It was like his body was on fire, but it was worth it because he could still make it in time. There were only a few more turns until he was there.

Then, he heard it. A great whistling noise and over some mounds of rubble and dilapidated houses, he saw a large cloud of black steam billowing in the air. He almost tripped as he turned around the last corner to see the great metal monster driving away, roaring as it went.

He'd missed it. He was in so much pain and it was all for nothing. He had failed. The thing he wanted most had slipped from his grasp. There it went, the stupid metal bus, carrying all the town's hopeful souls, as he was left to drop onto his knees, gasping for air in between his screams of rage.

Adam slammed his fist into the ground over and over again, he had given it his all and had come up short. He knew how easy it would be to just lay on the ground and let his sadness engulf him, but then deep inside, past all the misery, his soul still kept a tiny flame of hope from burning out, keeping him from giving up, telling him that it wouldn't make for much of a story to accept defeat and roll the credits.

I can still make it, he told himself.

The bus wasn't the portal, after all. It was only one way to get to it. The gates to the portal would close at one o'clock exactly. Adam checked the large clock on the fabric factory's wall to see that the time was one minute past ten.

He knew how it felt to run at full speed for fifteen minutes, how much agony that caused him. It seemed stupid to even think about running to the portal, and there was no way of telling if it was possible to make it in time, but he had to try.

So, having barely caught his breath, Adam started to walk, then jog, then sprint towards the now speck of silver in the distance. His parents were heroes, they had gone on numerous adventures. This was simply his first adventure, something that he could tell his parents about when he met them.

The road was dirt where there was no debris. On either side were fields of scrap that had been thrown out by the city, waste and garbage no longer needed by the factories. As far as he could see, it was just a never-ending stream of waste, with two large tracks carved into the floor by the bus that was now nowhere to be seen. It would have been easy to think that there was no end. That he would just run the path for the rest of his life, with only the sound of his controlled breathing and the beating of his footsteps against the dirt to keep him company.

He could see things thrown out after the war hidden in the debris – weapons, armour, and stacks of defused missiles, all tossed to the side. Around forty-five minutes in, his tiredness and pain became so extreme, the world started to spin around him.

With each breath he took, it felt like he was swallowing razors. This was the first time Adam had ever felt something so fully. Though the pain made him want nothing more than the sweet release of death, he continued to push forward.

Even though it was hard to run straight, he was able to stay on the path, willing himself not to fall into the walls of scrap that had been building up the further from civilization he progressed.

In his state, Adam started to hallucinate. He was sure that he could hear some kind of parade behind him, with the beating of drums, and the songs of support all for him. They were cheering him to carry on, to not be defeated by the endless road. The little pieces of ash falling from the sky turned to confetti, pushing him towards his victory. It was bordering on insanity, but it was what he needed to keep moving.

Time itself felt like it had evaporated. With his phone broke, he had no way of checking how long it had been, not that he would have been able to read it anyway. The hallucinations had long since been smudged away. His vision was now completely blurred. All he could see were two jagged walls to his sides with the block of smoke ahead of him, which he refused to stop chasing at full speed, like a zombie chasing after a group of humans.

Eventually, Adam noticed that the walls started to lower, and he started to believe that he was almost there. In his mind, he had been running a truly endless path for all his life, that there was simply no life before he had started to sprint.

He could just make out a city in the distance, he hadn't gone mad. Adam still didn't slow down to catch his breath. He knew that the moment he stopped running he wouldn't be able to start again.

Adam darted past a long line of rusty silver buses as the dirt path turned to concrete. He could remember where the portal gates were and, with energy he was plucking from the filthy air, he made a full turn for the first time in almost three hours of non-stop sprinting. It was a strange sensation that almost made him trip and fall over.

Then he heard something again that brought a blow to his heart. The sound of two immensely heavy gates grinding against the floor as they closed.

Adam forced himself towards the noise, bargaining with his body that the moment he reached the portal, he would allow it an eternity of rest. It was the final stretch and as long as he could make it, all would be good.

A few more turns and then he saw it. Two stone gates the height of the factories closing in like a door on hinges. Adam was sure he could make it. They were closing slowly and there was still a sizable gap for him to fit through. He could just make out a light coming from behind the gates, a wonderfully bright golden yellow glowing as potently as the sun.

In the span of a few hours, it felt like everything had tried to break Adam; first the Shark twins, then time, and finally, fate. There, in the middle of the road, was a screen that someone had thrown out as they left Earth, which Adam crashed into.

Whether it was the impact of his head smacking onto the hard ground, or his body finally being able to rest, Adam passed out again, his body skidding and rolling across the floor like he was on ice.

For the second time that day, Adam woke inside a hospital, the same kind of bed supporting his exhausted body, but with a different person watching over him. This man was only a little taller than Adam, but his bulging muscles were larger than a superhero's. Protecting his body was a deep emerald green cuirass, made from leather. It looked similar to what a great fighter would wear, like Thor or a Roman warrior. His head was covered with long fiery red hair along with a great bushy Viking beard. His arms were exposed, showing off a pair of bulky arms, that looked like they could pick up the world and rest it on the man's broad shoulders. The only way someone could get as mighty as that was by living in Elysium.

'I missed it, didn't I?' Adam asked.

He was too tired to try and cry, but an overwhelming amount of defeat took hold of him. He already knew the answer.

'Afraid so, kid, but try not to worry about that right now. You're Adam Tideborne, aren't you?' The man's voice was deep but oddly warm, making him seem like a friendly lion.

'Do I know you?' In any other moment in time, Adam would have been interested beyond reason that someone from Elysium knew him, but now it was all he could do not to turn his back to the man.

'No, but I knew your parents. Casper and Amber Tideborne, two of the greatest people that I ever knew. Thought you were their son when I saw you fall, you look just like Casper had hoped. Then I noticed the blonde streak behind your ear when I carried you here, just like Amber had, and I knew for sure.'

In his despair, the anger that he had from hearing about the incredible things his parents had done without him started to build up once again. Adam could feel a fury building up within him as the reality of everything started to set in.

'I know you must have some feelings about your parents, what with how they sent you to Earth, but believe me, it was for the best.'

'For the best?!' Adam stared at the man with disgust. He could snap Adam in half, but he didn't care. 'I have waited for my parents to come back *every year*. I've had to accept that my own parents don't want me! *For the best?* Do you have any idea how hard it's been?'

'You don't understand what it was like, kid. It was safer this way. They wanted to be there for you so much, but they couldn't come with you to Earth. We needed them too much to win the war. But they had to make sure you were safe. I know it was the most difficult decision they ever made. They doubted that choice every day, but your dad, Casper, he died a hero's death before you'd even turned one, and Amber... She just couldn't face watching you die too.'

'My dad... he's dead?' Adam's world slowed for a few moments but he snapped out of it. 'That's not good enough! Even if my mum was scared to bring me back, she could have still visited me.'

The man shifted his weight several times in the chair as he ran his hand down his beard. 'I'm sorry to tell you, but your mum... She's also passed.'

'What?' Adam couldn't keep the pain in his voice at bay as hot tears forced themselves down his face, his heart pounding in his chest.

'She wanted to take you back after the war had ended, but Gonti was still at large, and she needed to know you would be safe in Elysium. Micholesh and his army had wiped out pretty much all the other Ascensionists, but he was still a great threat alone. Then ten years ago, we managed to kill Gonti, but he... he killed her too. I'm sorry.'

Adam slid down the bed and stared at the ceiling. Everything had fallen apart. All that time he had spent training to be with his parents was for nothing. They had died and he never had the chance to see them, to show them how good a son he was. To be part of their family.

'It's my fault. Someone should have taken you back to Elysium when your mum passed and I could have been the one to do it.'

'Doesn't matter anymore. I don't know why you didn't go back through the portal; you should have just left me behind.'

'I said don't worry about getting to Elysium. How did you end up on the ground anyway, the buses were all here hours ago?'

'I ran.'

The man laughed heartily at this. 'You ran! From how far.'

'The town over,' Adam said through gritted teeth, wiping away the tear stains from his face now that they had stopped falling.

At this, the man laughed even more. If he was anything like the rest of the people on Elysium, laughing at others' pain, Adam felt that he was better off on Earth.

'Incredible, you truly have Tideborne blood in you.'

'I don't want Tideborne blood in me,' Adam snapped. 'I wanted to be brought up in Elysium, or at least be brought up by my parents!'

The man stopped laughing and looked guilty. 'Look, I know it can't have been easy, but your parents were vital to winning the war. They were some of the best fighters I've ever seen, and I don't doubt you'll be just as incredible. You'll be incredible with helping us explore the Wildlands. Now come on, I've kept you waiting for long enough.' The man stood up and started to make his way out of the room.

Even with his resentment towards the man, Adam followed the fire-haired warrior out of the hospital. As they stepped outside, the man struggled to place a breathing mask over his face, allowing him to breathe the polluted air, like what the nanobees did for Adam, just without the other several million functions.

'The name is Gerard Gamble,' Gerard said through the mask that muffled his voice, walking towards the closed gates, as though he had somewhere to be and hadn't gotten himself stranded on Earth.

By now the streets were empty. Everyone had gone back to their homes and all the buses would have taken everyone back to their towns. It pained Adam to see the gates, having been so close to his new life. However, to Adam's surprise, Gerard removed a small remote from his pocket and clicked it. The gates immediately started to make that loud noise again as they opened.

'Someone has to open the gates every year and I was chosen to do it! Apparently, I've been getting in the way of the investigation!' He shouted over the noise.

Adam's mouth was open in awe. He had barely paid attention to a word Gerard had said, he was so starstruck by the beams of golden light starting to shine on him. Finally, some good luck. He didn't care how easy it was to open the doors, he had been through enough that there could have been a secret entrance nobody had ever noticed and he wouldn't have cared. He had never been so grateful to have met someone, except maybe Kaya.

'Come on! We can slip through now, there's no point deafening the entire town any longer!'

The pair of them wiggled through the gap in the gates as people in the houses close by started to peek out of their doors to see what was happening. Gerard pressed the button on his remote again and the doors started to close once more.

Surrounding them were concrete walls as high as the gates, with a small heavily fortified metal box attached to one wall, that Gerard headed over to and placed the remote safely inside.

The room was mostly empty with the portal hovering in the very centre. Adam had never managed to get this close to it. It was like yellow ink constantly mixing with splashes of water spiralling around in the air, emitting a light so bright that when the gates closed, the room became no darker. It was almost as tall as the ceiling and as wide as a dozen people.

Small golden bubbles roamed around the substance, each growing and shrinking in size as if being pushed back and forth through the thick liquid, but as Adam walked round to see the other side of the portal, he found that it was flat with no bubbles and produced a lot less light. After looking at it for so long, he found that his eyes started to hurt and when he looked away, he could still see the afterimage of the portal for a good minute.

Adam had learnt that before the portal spawned into existence, the area he was in now used to be called the Box. It was a place where a weapon was kept, one that when activated would send a shockwave across Earth that would shut down the brain of every single person, killing them without fail.

The idea was that if another world-ending event was going to happen like a meteor shower or nuclear missiles, it would be kinder to wipe out the last living race in an instant than put them through any more unnecessary pain.

Two people at a time were assigned to live in the Box for most of their life. Their only responsibility was to be ready to activate the weapon. However, one of the more violent armies in the war found out about the box and managed to activate the sirens inside, intending to end the world's suffering once and for all.

Nobody ever found out what happened when the two residents believed that they needed to end millions of lives. All that is known is that they received the order and then nothing happened. Everyone who knew about the Box and that the weapon was to be activated braced themselves for a death that never came.

After a couple of terrifying days, they went to check on the Box and found the weapon destroyed along with everything else inside, except for the new portal which swirled around in the aftermath. Both residents were nowhere to be found. Once all factions found out about the miracle of the new world, the fighting spilt into Elysium almost immediately.

There was a metal plaque on the wall next to Adam that read:

Hope Husk & Ron Steward,
Your sacrifice will always be remembered, and your gift will always be embraced.

Gerard had waited for Adam to finish reading the plaque before he continued to speak.

'Before we go through, there are a few things that need to be done. I'm not an official disciple of Charon, but I've been around long enough to know how it's done. I need you to raise your right hand and repeat after me.' Adam lifted his hand as instructed. 'I swear on my life, that as long as I am in Elysium, enjoying all of its gifts, I will protect and respect the land and all that encompasses it.' Adam repeated the oath. 'I will only attack those that intend to harm, for my survival, or if it is necessary to save Elysium. Above all, I will never take advantage of the gifts given to me and use them for evil. Doing so would disgrace all that I and Elysium stand for.'

Adam finished reciting the oath. He had never needed to take an oath before. In his head they were just words, but now after being completed, it felt much more like a promise that he would vow to keep.

'That oath is in place so that we do not repeat the war that destroyed almost all of Earth and too much of Elysium. When you're ready, you may step into the portal. Know that by doing this, you are sealing your oath. Any augmentations to your body will be destroyed by the portal. This includes your nanobees. This means that from the moment you enter Elysium, you won't be aided by anything you weren't born into this world with.' Gerard finished his warnings and stepped back to allow Adam to go into the portal.

Adam checked his stab wounds and they all felt fully healed. He couldn't see any scars or indications that he had been injured, and he felt perfectly fine. Deciding that his nanobees had done their final task, Adam stepped towards the portal.

As hard as he looked at the blinding light, he couldn't see anything through it. There was no point in waiting anymore. He stepped forward into the magical liquid.

He wanted to see what happened whilst he was in transit but found that it was impossible to keep his eyes open as the blinding light burnt his retinas while he was transported through to Elysium.

3. A Spark of Magic

Adam felt as though he was falling in every direction, a mix between zero gravity and being submerged in water. He started to experience a strange tingling sensation, and he knew, as the tingling increased into a burning pain, that his nanobees were disintegrating from his body.

He wasn't sure when he had left the portal, but after a few minutes, he noticed that his hands were pushing against a cold stone floor, his head spinning as his eyes adjusted to the lack of overwhelming golden light.

He was a little let down to find that, once he regained his vision, he wasn't anywhere special. The portal was behind him, appearing the same as it did on Earth, illuminating the room that, in most aspects, was the same as the Box, except the smooth concrete walls were much lower. A thick metal door was closed on the wall in front of him and looked as though it could withstand the full force of a stampede.

'Now, kid, it's time for the fun to start. This shouldn't take too long and then we can catch up with the others,' Gerard said, having just come through the portal. 'They should still be in processing. We didn't come through that much after they did.'

Adam hadn't paid much attention to what Gerard had said, being far too interested in a floating ball of light that he had noticed in the corner of his eye, hovering behind his right shoulder. Whichever way he turned, no matter the speed, the ball of light would always stay in the very corner of his vision.

'I'm guessing Hope has presented itself to you? I can't see it myself, only you can.'

Accepting that he wouldn't be able to focus on the thing, Adam tried to grab it, only to find that his hand passed through as though Hope was nothing more than a light flare, but the ball pulsated with a strange glow that could only be described as magical.

'Isn't Hope the person that went missing in the Box after the portal was created?'

'Yes, it's named after her, but we don't really know what that ball of magic is. However, we do know what it does, and right now, it'll be analysing you to see if you are worthy of the spark, which everyone almost always is, and then it will give it to you.'

'Hope is going to give me the spark? I'm about to be able to use magic?' Adam asked, so excited that the sadness of his parents' deaths continued to be suppressed.

'Exciting, isn't it? Now, I will leave you alone to experience this so I can find ol' Disciple Maria, and make you a registered citizen.'

With that, Gerard opened the metal door with ease and left Adam alone with Hope.

Adam had given up on trying to interact with it, allowing Hope to hover like a guardian angel over his shoulder. For a while, nothing happened. Adam thought he could feel the ball of light scanning inside his head. He kept on getting a tingling sensation moving around his brain and down the back of his neck, making his hairs stand up.

The longer Adam waited, the more he started to worry that he wasn't worthy, that he wouldn't be able to use magic. He started to pace around the room, trying not to think about a life where he was one of the only people in Elysium to not have any magic in them.

Then, all of a sudden, as Adam made his fourth lap of the room, the light that made Hope turned from white to a deep blue, which then faded away. Adam didn't know if something had gone wrong. He didn't think anything new had happened to him. It certainly didn't feel like he could now do what was once thought impossible. Not knowing what else to do, he exited the room through the door that Gerard had left ajar, wanting to test as quickly as possible if he was worthy.

Compared to Adam's dreams of Elysium, the hall he found himself in was rather bland. A long cream corridor with heavily secured doors lined along it. Although, behind these doors Adam assumed were artefacts or scrolls that were strong enough to kill everyone on Earth.

Standing on the other end of the hall, Gerard was speaking to someone. Unlike Gerard, who was dressed for combat and manoeuvrability, this person was cloaked in a tattered white garb that covered all of their body. It reminded Adam of what a church clergyman would wear, only the material was deliberately ripped and frayed.

They also held a long wooden stick as tall as themselves. From the side, the only part of the person not hidden by the garb was their long frayed black hair that came out of their hood and fell down to the collarbone.

Their conversation seemed important, but Gerard quickly noticed Adam and beckoned him over.

'Ah, Adam, how did it go? I was just telling my friend here all about your trek across Earth. Rather impressive, isn't it, Maria?'

Adam walked down the hall to meet with Maria. Under the hood, she had a harsh, rough face, that had presumably never wrinkled into a smile in her long life.

'Pleasure to meet you,' Adam said, extending his hand.

'Gerard is barely a friend. I owe him two favours, and I am thankful for no longer being burdened by one of their weights.' She ignored Adam's hand, speaking with a dry, strict tone. 'If he had not called on this favour, I would have sent you back to Earth. I do not care if you are a Tideborne. No matter who you are or what you went through to get here, you failed to make the time allotment, and shouldn't have been allowed through the portal to Elysium, especially considering a disciple of Charon like myself did not read you your oath, nor did we see you testify it. Nevertheless, a favour is a favour, I cannot go back on my word, irrelevant of how much I wish to.'

Adam felt stupid keeping his hand out so brought it back to the side.

'Ahh don't be so hard on the boy, I doubt it was even his fault that he missed his transport,' Gerard said, patting Adam on the back with so much power, it pushed him forward a few steps.

'There is no point in hearing excuses. The deed is done. I am obligated to let him stay. Before you get ahead of yourself, child, thinking I will be kind to you, I want you to repeat the oath back to me. They are the most important words you will ever say in your life. I expect you to have them memorised.'

'Oh, come on Maria, there's no need for this just because he's Amber's –'

'I swear,' Adam had his hand raised, 'to always protect and respect Elysium. I will only harm that which intends harm, for the sake of mine or someone else's survival, or to protect Elysium. I will never use what is given to me by the world for evil. Doing so would disgrace all that I stand for.'

Gerard clapped his hands and let out a hearty laugh from behind his beard. 'See, what did I tell you? This isn't a mistake.

Adam here is going to do great things. I can sense it. The son of Casper and Amber Tideborne. You know, Adam, Maria fought with your mother on many occasions. They also battled other things when they weren't at each other's throats!' Gerard laughed at his own joke, as Maria stared daggers at Adam.

'Gerard, I have done you your favour, I ask for you to leave so that I can continue guiding these children through Elysium.'

'Fine, I need to report back to Micholesh anyway, he'll be wanting to know everything has gone well and I can check if there have been any updates with the investigation.'

'I don't see how all has gone well, you opened the gates after the allotted time, and you have broken the very rules Micholesh set in place to protect this world and the other. Since the gates were made, they have opened at the same time every year and you decided to change this because you wanted to break another rule by bringing someone through the portal without my guidance. You have made an effort to be the absolute worst as guardian of the portal, and it pains me that Micholesh assigned you the honour.'

Gerard gave a sigh. 'I didn't want to go to Earth in the first place. Something can't be an honour when you are ordered to do it.'

'I am ordered by Micholesh to protect this world and it is an honour. I am ordered by Charon to guide those through Elysium, in the same way that he guided the souls of the dead across the river Styx and it is an absolute honour to do so,' she lectured.

Gerard turned away from Disciple Maria and rolled his eyes at Adam as he started to walk down the hall. 'I'll catch up with you later, kid. For now, just relax, you made it.'

As he started to walk away, Maria gave him another scolding look. 'And where are all the books you were supposed to bring from Earth? They have spent a year gathering all that knowledge to give to us.'

'Damn it, I knew I forgot something. Must have left it in the Box.' He groaned as he turned around and jogged back towards the portal.

Without Gerard and his flaming hair, the hall became even more bland, like Adam was back at school and was being told off by a teacher for fighting in the halls. This dullness was made all the worse by Maria in her boring plain white garb.

'Go through that door and join your other initiates,' Disciple Maria had pointed to the double doors to their right, 'and I expect you to follow the other Disciple's instructions without question.'

'What investigation is going on with Gerard? Is there anything that I can help with?' Adam asked politely, wanting to do something to help Gerard for saving him from another year on Earth.

Quicker than he had ever seen someone move, Disciple Maria slapped her wooden staff down hard onto Adam's hand.

'How dare you ask such an invasive question!' Disciple Maria shouted.

'I'm sorry, I just wanted to help!' Adam shouted back defensively, trying to ignore the pain.

Again, she slapped her staff onto his hand.

'You shall not ever raise your voice at me, boy!'

Without the nanobees' numbing effects, Adam's eyes had started to water. He couldn't believe it would sting this much when something as simple as wood struck his hand. Being stabbed hadn't been as unbearable as this.

The pain kept going long after he had been hit and instead of healing, a thick red line started to flare up as the stinging continued. Not wanting to get struck again, Adam stayed completely silent, as he rubbed the back of his hand to try and ease the pain.

'That's better. I hope you have learnt a lesson to never disrespect me like that again.'

'Yes, ma'am,' Adam replied rubbing his aching hand.

'Good, you used madam. You may also call me Disciple Maria, not that I expect to be seeing you anytime soon. Now leave before I strike you again for wasting my time.'

Not wanting to experience that pain again or be in her company anymore, Adam quickly went through the door she had gestured to.

The moment Adam walked into the room, he was caught off guard by a sea of dark blue clothes. He'd walked into an open area, like a school cafeteria in teen rom-coms, filled with hundreds of people sitting around large circular tables talking excitedly to each other.

At the end of the room was a long desk with several neat stacks of papers on them. Another Disciple dressed in the same tattered white robes as Disciple Maria went through the stacks of documents, explaining things that Adam couldn't hear to four newcomers.

Adam had never seen so many teenagers all in the same place before. He scanned the room for Kaya or at least a familiar face, but as everyone wore the same thing, it was a challenge to work out who was who.

After a short while of searching, Adam finally managed to find a table that had people from Kiwi High. After looking around in that area, he saw his friend frantically arguing with Olivia.

'Give it a rest, Kaya, he didn't make it through, there's nothing anyone could do. Would you please just sit down and stop!' Olivia said, clearly fed up from an argument they had been having for hours.

'How can I stop! Something went wrong! I knew it didn't feel right that he walked to the portal without me. I bet it was those bloody twins! I don't want to wait a whole year before I see him again!' Kaya was beyond consolation, pacing around like it would achieve something.

'Come on, like I'd ever miss the portal and let you have all the fun.'

Olivia and Kaya gasped as they turned to see Adam.

'Oh, thank God,' Kaya breathed with relief, as he wrapped his arms tightly around Adam. 'What the hell happened to you? I've been worried sick over here!' He said, pushing back and punching Adam on the arm.

Adam explained everything that happened to him. He had reached the part where he first met Gerard when he was interrupted. Some strange golden glass-like material had started to appear in the air. Everyone's conversations came to an abrupt end as they all looked up to the space above the Disciple, who was muttering words whilst holding his hands up towards the contorting crystals that were each forming into a letter. Within seconds, the strange glass material shone four names.

MAX AGLET – OLIVIA LEAF – JAIDEN HUTCHINSON – REBECCA PARKER

'I guess we're up, Max,' Olivia said, standing up. Max had been silent all the time Adam had been there and had now gone a shade green in the face. 'I'm glad you made it, Adam. Kaya would have been a nightmare if you hadn't.'

'What was that glass stuff?' Adam asked as it shattered into tiny little pieces, which dissolved into the air.

'Magic. I have no idea what else that stuff can do, but I can't wait to get the hang of some spells, so we can get back at those Shark twins for what they've done.'

Every movie Adam had ever watched that showed someone getting revenge would always end with the conclusion that it was bad and never worth it, but he didn't care. His heart was shattered from finding out both his parents were dead and now it felt like he had no place in the world. He had never understood how much he wanted to experience his so frequent dream of being with his family and now that he couldn't be with them, he wanted to hurt someone to help take the misery away.

'You're right, they won't get away with what they did. We can deal with them later though, right now I want to know what I've missed?' He pushed down the rise of hot anger and pain in his chest.

'Not that much. We all had to go through the portal one by one and then Hope presented itself to all of us. That was fun but it took a while, and after that, we were told to wait in this room till our names were called. I thought you were already here when I went through the portal, and they wouldn't let me go back to Earth to find you,' Kaya explained as he rubbed the back of his hand subconsciously.

'Don't worry about it, I know you did everything you could. Why did they only call up four people, wouldn't it be quicker to just make a long line?'

'Oh yeah, I completely forgot about that! We are all put into teams of four.'

'We were never told about any teams in school!' Adam knew there were things left out of his education that hadn't made its way back to Earth, but this and Hope felt like the people in Elysium weren't bothering to give him a proper education.

'I know that old mean woman said we would do everything with our teams.' Kaya had quickly looked behind him after saying this, scared that Disciple Maria was behind him. 'Teams live with each other, they train together, are tested as a group, go out into the Wildlands together, and each one is even given their own animal totem thing. It's only whilst we're students though, we'll be strong enough in three years to go around by ourselves if we want.'

At first, Adam became excited at the idea, but after looking around at the hundreds of other students, something occurred to him. 'That sucks. What are the chances we are together? I didn't sprint all the way here just to spend the next three years with people I don't know.'

'I thought the same thing, but apparently, the Disciples consider that kind of stuff. I've already hounded them to put us together, and they said they try to put at least two people from the same town with each other.' Kaya raised his head with everyone else to see the new names starting to form above in the same golden glass material as before.

As relieved as Adam pretended to be, he wasn't so sure about their chances. Adam knew how Kaya could be when he badgered someone and he may have ended up ruining their chances of being together rather than making it a sure thing.

To move Adam's mind away from everything going on in his head, the two started to speculate about all the kinds of magic they would learn. As Kaya spoke animatedly about wanting to learn how to make time slow down, a girl with a small mousy face, sharp high nose, and bushy eyebrows walked over to them, taking a seat next to Kaya. Her long shaggy black hair hit him in the face as she turned to face him.

'You can't slow down time,' she cut in. 'Don't you know it's impossible to manipulate time? Whilst a great deal of things are possible in Elysium through the use of magic and artefacts, the world still has to obey some kind of physics.'

'Huh?' Kaya had a confused ogre-like look.

'Physics. It's how the world works,' the girl replied slowly as if Kaya were hard of hearing.

'I know what –'

'Sorry, I completely forgot to mention my name. It's Amelia, Amelia Watts.'

Amelia had a posh-sounding accent. One that would have been much more pronounced if everyone's accents hadn't been roughed down over generations away from their relative's home country.

'I don't care –'

'How do you know what spells can be cast in Elysium?' Adam asked, trying to avoid another Olivia situation. 'We weren't taught anything like that in our school.'

After paying attention to Amelia, Adam noticed that she was incredibly small, even smaller than he was, which was a rare thing to see.

'Neither did mine, but I found a couple of people in my town that used to live in Elysium. From them, I learnt that scrolls found in the world have taught us three types of magic. Elemental magic is pretty self-explanatory. Life and Death magic is all to do with controlling nature and life cycles. And Enlightenment magic, which is the strain that makes that glass substance we keep seeing and has the expected potential to do a lot more. None of those allow for time to be stopped. They are all much simpler than that. Of course, there are costs you have to make to cast each strain, but I'm sure we'll be told more about that soon.'

'Wow, well, I guess you got lucky that you had people in your town willing to talk about being in Elysium. Our teacher only told us that it was colourful,' Adam responded.

'For your information, they weren't just handing out that knowledge, it took me years of doing favours and helping them out just so that I could persuade them to give me the smallest nuggets of information. Then even those small pieces of information were worth it because now I have an edge against everyone else, which should mean that I'll pick things up quicker than others.'

'And I'm sure everyone is going to care,' Kaya said sarcastically.

'It's annoying that we need training to cast magic,' Amelia continued. 'No matter how hard I try, I can't seem to make anything happen. There's no point worrying about that now though. There are still plenty of things to see once we are done getting processed. I can't wait for my name to be written so I can get out of this boring room.'

'And I can't wait for this conversation to be over,' Kaya whispered under his breath.

'It was nice meeting you. I should move on to the table next to us. I've been trying to find people who know something about the world that I don't so that they can teach me about it. I'll see you two around.'

'Wait, what did she mean by that? Does she think we're stupid or something? Just because she knows a thing or two doesn't make her special,' Kaya argued, watching Amelia walk away.

'She wasn't that bad, and she's as prepared for Elysium as we are. She knows the basics, and we know how to fight.'

It occurred to Adam that neither of them had told Amelia their names.

'I feel bad for whoever has to be on a team with her,' Kaya exclaimed.

'Well, now we're definitely going to be on a team with her, aren't we.'

'No, no, no that one doesn't count,' Kaya whined.

'Of course, it counts. You know the rules. If someone says, '*I'll be right back* –"

'They'll be dead before seeing them again.'

'And when someone lays out a perfect plan that seems fool proof?'

'The plan fails.'

'And when someone says they feel bad for whoever has to spend time with a person...?'

Kaya gave a long-resigned sigh. 'They spend time with the person. But this is real life. I'm sure that won't happen.'

'Saying you're sure something won't happen will always mean that it happens.'

'Damn!'

Hours went by as Kaya and Adam waited for their names to be called. The anticipation of whether they would be in the same group started to make them feel sick. Having waited for several hours, the room had mostly cleared, and still, they hadn't been called up.

Kaya had been resolute in thinking the two would be together but had now started to get uneasy as he watched the room go from a hundred people to a couple of dozen, with Amelia still being left without a group.

Eventually, only eight people were left. By this point, they had all moved to the front of the hall to the tables opposite the desk.

'The next four to come up are Ludvig Knight, Zoe Stevens, Megan Vice, and Brendon Fear.' The Charon's disciple had stopped using magic a few announcements ago as there was no need to do so.

After a few minutes, Adam, Kaya, Amelia, and the last person waiting were beckoned over so that they could finally be processed and head out into Elysium.

4. First Breath of Fresh Air

The four remaining teenagers made their way over to the desk, which now only had a few sheets of paper on it. Adam looked over at the last member of his new team. Her skin was light brown, and she had long smooth black hair which her pointed ears poked out from. It was clear that she was a follower of the Old Ways, with thin yellow lines painted on her face in circular patterns most prominent around her forehead, flowing down the side of her thin cheeks.

The Disciple glared at each of them before speaking. 'Before we process you, Disciple Maria wanted you to know that you have all waited until the end of processing for a reason. In fact, unlike every other group that has been selected today, you four have been chosen not out of your predicted ability to work effectively together, but your collective ability to burden her.'

The Disciple then pointed to Kaya. 'You continuously slowed her down trying to stall, for you.' He pointed at Adam. 'Who shouldn't be here at all. Then you.' He pointed at Amelia. 'You wouldn't stop asking unimportant questions, again slowing her down. And you–' This time, as he pointed at the follower of the Old Ways, his finger shook with rage, '– you committed the worst act of all. For what you said, you should deserve a much higher punishment.'

Adam, Amelia, and Kaya all looked over at this new member in surprise. What could she have possibly done to merit such anger from the man?

'I can't pronounce what is bound to be an idiotic ancient name. So, for the sake of knowing what it is so that we can mention you personally to Micholesh, can you tell me your name? That is, if you haven't taken some vow of silence.'

'My name is Iosefka,' she said, unfazed by the volley of insults. 'Phonetically, that's You-Sef-Ka. Just so that you can say it right if you ever feel the desire to curse me with your ludicrous rituals.' Iosefka gave a wide smile, showing off a large set of bright white teeth.

'Watch your tongue, young lady. If you're not careful we will curse you with the might of all the Gods, from Zeus to Hades, and it will be far worse than anything your imaginary God has ever done.'

'My *imaginary* God created this entire world, that's more than all of yours have ever done.'

'Sure, it is, you stupid girl. Now, let's get this done quickly so that you can all leave, go out into the world, and die before the month's end. I doubt you'll even set foot in the Wildlands with the incompetence the four of you have shown.'

The next few minutes were spent going over their ages, places of birth, and other formalities so that they could all officially be citizens of Elysium. Once everything had been sorted and filed away, the Disciple accepted that he would have to speak to them again.

'You will be given a short tour around the Capital, which is the city below the mountain we are on.'

'We're on a mountain?' Kaya blurted.

'You idiot, of course we are on a mountain. We are inside the Sanctuary, which is on Mount Ida, which makes it the safest place in any of the worlds.'

Kaya had backed off a few steps, eyeing the wooden staff next to the Disciple, but it seemed this Disciple wasn't as keen to use it as Disciple Maria.

'As I was saying, your tour will conclude at the Pantheon where you will attend a feast welcoming all those from Earth and to celebrate the first-year students who have made it back from their first mission out into the Wildlands.'

With great anticipation, the four left the hall through a set of doors behind the desk, where they were found an exhausted Disciple, red in the face with sweat gleaming from his large forehead and bald head. The man was using his long wooden staff to lean on as he took deep breaths, trying to regain some energy.

He was over six feet tall and looked even taller than the Shark twins with a larger stomach that stretched out his garb. His bulging eyes locked onto the group as they approached him and they were surprised to find him smiling at them.

'You four all good?'

'Are you good?' Kaya repeated back to him.

The Disciple chuckled as he pulled himself upright. 'I'll tell you something, I could do with the portal not being all the way up this bloody mountain, it's a real pain having to drag myself up it all day for these tours.' The man then cartoonishly looked around with his wide eyes popping out as he checked that nobody else was around. 'Probably shouldn't have said that. Oh well, my name is Peter and I'll be honest with you four, it's been a long day so what do you say we just skip the boring stuff so we can all sit down and enjoy the feast?'

'That sounds like a great idea, that's very kind of you, sir,' Amelia said, apparently wanting to be back in the Disciple's good books.

'Don't mention it,' Peter said with a shrug as he started to lead them through yet another set of doors into another hallway before slowing down and looking at them seriously. 'I want to make it extra clear when I say don't mention it, I mean don't tell another person that I've skipped some of the stuff. If someone asks you what you thought about the Mausoleum of the Gods, you just tell them that's where all the artefacts that are too powerful are kept and where Micholesh lives and works. If they look like they want to hear more about anything you don't know, just make it up. If I'm helping you out by getting you to the feast before all the food runs out, then you have to help me out if needed.'

'But, will we have another chance to visit all these places on the tour? It's just that I don't want to miss out on anything important that the other initiates would have experienced,' Amelia whined.

'Yeah, of course, don't worry about that, there will be plenty of time to go around the Capital once you complete your first challenge at Camp Paragon,' Disciple Peter said with a wave of his hand as he opened the door to an even longer hallway.

'What challenge? Is there anything you can tell me about it?' Amelia pleaded.

'Couldn't even if I wanted to. They change it every year and all the Disciples have been far too busy trying to find Gerard's artefact to hear about what's going on over at the training camp.'

'Is that what the investigation is?' Adam asked.

'Zeus, what am I doing?' Peter said in anger. 'Forget I said that. I'm too tired to think straight. I really shouldn't have told you that, make sure you keep it to yourselves. Come on, we are almost at the entrance.'

Having gone through so many doors and almost identical hallways, Adam's head was spinning from confusion. It was like a maze and he had no idea which way he would have to go to make it back to the portal. But he guessed that was the point.

It was obvious when they had reached the entrance as they were met by a massive circular door, made of a strange jagged dark indigo stone the size of a bell tower clock. Five well-built Charon's Disciples were guarding the door, sweaty and red in the face from a day of having to open the massive door.

'This is the last group, brothers. I'll be back before dawn. Once the feast is over, of course,' he said with a wink.

The Disciple guard who appeared to be in charge gave a nod. 'Very well, but I'm not covering for you. It's on your own head.'

'Don't worry about it, I'll be fine. Do you want me to bring anything back for you?'

The lead Disciple seemed to think about the question for a few moments before shaking his head. 'No. Thank you, I'll see you at dawn. Disciples, open!' He shouted to the others who seemed to be wishing Peter would bring something back for them.

The Disciples grunted and pulled on the heavy door, and slowly it opened out into the world.

A soft warm breeze managed to slip through the growing gap, and it felt like an angel was blowing onto them, washing their sins away, bringing peace to Adam's body. His muscles relaxed and his mind enjoyed a wave of tranquillity.

They could hear the faint noise of what must have been a waterfall, its flowing water crashing down the mountain in an oddly elegant way, sounding as divine as a mermaid singing in their ear.

Adam could just make out what was outside. The cleansing moonlight breached through the door and all four of them gasped as the holy rays brought them through into Elysium.

Immediately their eyes were drawn upwards to the night sky where millions of stars were scattered and overwhelming waves of dense smoke moved like ink in water through the black velvety universe. Dark purples, deep blues and crimson reds, all melting together, forming flawless works of art.

Colossal planets hung so far away, some with extravagant rings and others having craters to add to their beauty, each one made of a magnificent mixture of colours. Fluffy white clouds hid calmly behind the veil of the cool night, acting as the last brushes on the canvas that Adam believed to be of heaven.

With a lot of resistance, he managed to tear his gaze away from the sky. The door had now completely opened and Disciple Peter ushered them out. As they tripped into the open air, like a puppy walking into a wall too distracted by a butterfly, their eyes feasted whichever way they gawked.

From atop Mount Ida, they could see so much of the world, even during the night. To Adam's left blossomed a lush, seemingly endless forest packed with monstrous trees that blocked any clear view inside, like a layer of armour protecting all within. He noticed small flecks of red flying around in the distance like they were swimming around in a sea of black and green. His heart pounded, realising that he was looking at the first living creatures in his life other than humans. It was far too distant to work out what creature it was, but it lived and knowing that sent goosebumps down his neck.

As Adam moved his head to the right, the forest started to shrink and its defences weakened as a swamp became visible. This swamp, visible only from the moonlight reflecting on the murky water, was smaller than the forest and paled in size to the ocean next to it.

The parts of this sea connected to land were calm, it was so still that it acted as a mirror, and once again, he struggled to take his eyes from even the reflection of the sky. The farther Adam looked, the deadlier the water became. Flashes of lightning lit up the raging sea that Adam was otherwise blind to in the night's darkness.

Another flash of lightning lit up an area just enough to illuminate a silhouette of some massive being emerging from the water, thick tendrils writhing up towards the sky as if they were trying to pull the moon to the depths. The size of just its tendrils breaching from the ocean made Adam wonder how horrifying it would be to try and survive the waters on a simple boat. By the time another flash of lightning came, the monster had disappeared, but he would never forget how scared he felt staring at it all those miles away.

Adam continued moving his head to see all that he could, wanting to move away from the thought of drowning. Cutting the rest of the ocean from his view was a range of mountains. None were as tall as the one he was currently standing on.

'It's just like how I imagined and so much more.' Amelia couldn't stop smiling as she took it all in.

'Thank you, God, for giving us such a graceful gift,' Iosefka said.

'Right.' Disciple Peter clapped his hands loudly, getting everyone's attention. 'You've all had enough time to take in the world, it's time for me to tell you everything important.'

'This is just the coolest thing ever. Adam, did you see the sky?' Kaya asked, tapping Adam on the arm, without taking his eyes off it.

'Yeah, I know, can't believe we've had to stare at smoke all our lives when this was waiting for us.'

'I was just like you all when I first arrived, and trust me, it will keep getting better.' Peter looked up at the sky like everyone else, his thick strong hands on his hips. 'Now as you have all seen, the sky above us is spectacular. We believe there are twenty-three planets other than Elysium, but we don't know if any of them have life. The technology needed to find that out is out of our reach and will be for a very long time. The mountains to our right are where we get all the minerals and ores we can't create through magic, mainly obsidian, which is what the door you have just gone through is made from. It is a material that absorbs and counteracts any form of magic and so is an excellent form of defence.

'Moving on, I'm sure you can see the Ocean of the Damned in the distance. It has barely been ventured into, as even with legendary artefacts that help you in water, it would be almost impossible to traverse without a certain chance of death. The swamp that you can barely see has been named the Devil's Bog. It is filled with most of the worst monsters we have encountered so far. After your first year of training, you lot will most likely be spending your time in the Wildlands, that is what you have come to this world for, after all. I am sure you have been told that this feast is also for those first-year students who have returned from their first expedition in those Wildlands. Now if you all come a little closer to the edge, you can see the Capital below.'

As they moved forward, Adam glanced behind him so he could get a good look at the building and found that he had just left an immense Greek temple made from marble, taking up all the space on the mountain, an impenetrable fortress protecting the most important thing in Elysium.

Adam made it to the marble barrier at the edge of the mountain and touched the cool smooth surface with his hand as he leaned over. The drop was almost completely vertical and he started to feel lightheaded at the thought of falling down to the bottom. He had to step back away from the edge so that the world would stop spinning.

Having lived a life on the ground, he had no idea how terrifying heights could be. He had to fight against his instincts to head back to the barrier, where he tried not to look directly down. Adam was thankful that the Capital was large enough that he didn't have to look too far over the barrier to see it.

Long streets lit with a warm light filled the city like a spider's web made of gold. The cobbled streets turned randomly into each other, creating turns and crossroads in what appeared to be no discernible pattern. Black steel lampposts shone their golden halo flame to help guide the wandering citizens to their homes. Each cluster and line of houses displayed its own unique style.

Medieval-style homes made from light brick and wooden beams could be seen on the outer sections of the city. Towards the inner part of the city, an old Victorian style dominated. The closer the house to Mount Ida, the more expensive looking they were. The ones as close to the base as Adam dared to look appeared to be full mansions.

The waterfall flowing down the side of the mountain created a river around the left side of the Capital. Adam couldn't wait to spend the rest of his life exploring everything it had to offer.

'... And that over there is the Mausoleum of the Gods that I mentioned before,' Peter explained.

Adam had been completely in his head and missed all of the information about the Capital. He had to stare straight down to see the Mausoleum of the Gods. It was easily the largest of all the buildings down below, a strange mixture of a palace and a stone castle.

'Almost all of the fighting from the endless war took place behind us, on the other side of Mount Ida, which is what we will be seeing next before heading down to the feast.'

Peter led them around Mount Ida, where they passed other Disciples, all dressed in the ripped white garb and holding a wooden staff, each the same height as the wielder. All of them scowled at Iosefka as she walked past them.

'What did you do to make Disciple Maria so angry at you?' Adam asked Iosefka once they were clear of any Disciples other than Peter, who was out of earshot answering Amelia's bombardment of questions.

'Oh, she started to drag my religion and beliefs through the dirt, and so I said a few unsavoury things about Hellenism. I mean, it's completely ludicrous. Grown people believing in stories made for Greek children thousands of years ago. Tales to make sure they didn't go out at night or misbehave, and these Disciples have the audacity to think it's gospel. That the holy portal and all of Elysium were the work of Zeus, Poseidon, Hades and the lot of them. Solely because some of their stories have been put into this fantastical world by the one true God.'

'I bet she took that well,' Kaya said.

'No. No, she did not,' Iosefka admitted, rubbing the back of her hand, which the other two also started to do, thinking about their first encounters with Disciple Maria.

'We haven't been properly introduced yet, have we? I'm Kaya.' He extended his hand.

'Nice to meet you.' Iosefka shook it and then did the same with Adam. They then turned past one more pillar where Peter was waiting for them, looking at the place where part of the war had been fought.

'As you all know, the war destroyed Earth. Its wildlife and nature were completely eradicated, leaving only humans to continue fighting. When the war funnelled into Elysium, it brought more bloodshed than the four of you could ever imagine. This land was once a wonderful meadow filled with millions of mystical flowers and a forest filled with kind magical creatures in the distance,' Peter explained.

All any of them could see was now a wasteland. The few patches of grass that were dispersed over the land were blackened by fire or withered to death. The gaping dips and craters the size of dragons stopped most of the land from ever regrowing life. The dirt that was surely once rich in nutrition had turned grey, like the soil itself had perished from all the relentless damage.

The bones of monsters and humans were deserted all around. Arrows and swords lodged into the bone, with more skeletons than there were stars in the sky. In the far distance, Adam could see what looked like a hydra's skeleton, sunken into the ground so that only a couple of its heads could be seen, as though the ground had turned to quicksand. All across the land remained the remnants of the carnage, the aftermaths of different spells, broken weapons, and mounds that had been made for cover created from rocks and dirt. There was no sign of any mystical flowers nor could Adam make out a standing tree that hadn't been burnt or sliced to pieces.

'This can never happen again,' Disciple Peter said in a deep pained voice. 'This is the result of a single battle, one of the largest ones we had, but this is just a small fraction of the damage we caused to the world. As a race, we must make sure not to follow in the path of our ancestors, waging war and destroying all that is perfect. Remember this battlefield. Be grateful you never had to be part of it, be thankful that it has stopped. Make sure to maintain the peace for as long as you live. Keep your oath.'

5. A Criminal Amongst Heroes

The long walk down the mountain was made so much worse by the hunger and thirst that had now consumed all four members of the group. Not only had they not had any tablets since morning, but the knowledge that real food was waiting for them made their desire only grow.

'Couldn't you have just used some kind of magic to send us straight down to the bottom? We would have been at the feast already if you had,' Kaya groaned as his stomach rumbled.

'No can do,' Peter responded, shaking his head. 'The mountain has just about every possible defence you could image, and even if it didn't, this descent is a great way to get your body running properly without your nanobees.'

It was hard to complain, even with how hungry and exhausted Adam was. Whenever he started to struggle, he only had to look off in any distance, and he found that his excitement returned, and with it a new rush of energy to keep him moving.

'Disciple Peter, I have tried as hard as I can to learn everything I could about Elysium but there is barely anything about what happened once the Ascensionists fell. There are even people on

Earth who believe that Gonti died when the war ended but I know he went into hiding and was found later.' Amelia said this like she was asking a question without actually asking one, having spent the last ten minutes hounding Peter about what he knew about the Endless War when it moved into Elysium.

'I'll be honest, there's not much that I can add. Gonti spent about four years in hiding. During that time, we built up the Capital and started to build a proper society. Then we found Gonti. He was killed and then the world prospered even more.' Peter had simplified his answers more and more over the last half-hour.

'Another thing I wanted to ask—'

'Why are we put into groups of four?' Kaya asked, cutting Amelia off. 'Couldn't we just have groups of three instead?'

'Haha, afraid not. Micholesh decided long ago that groups exploring Elysium should be in four. It has been tradition ever since the first team of four killed Gonti.'

'Why didn't you say that when I just asked about that?' Amelia whined.

'It slipped my mind is all,' Peter said, using his staff to help him down a short drop with a grunt. 'Micholesh himself, Disciple Maria, Gerard the Unstoppable, and Amber "Valkyrie" Tideborne were the ones to track down Gonti the Necromancer.'

Adam had not been expecting his mother's name to be thrown about so casually. It caught him so off guard that he found his eyes glazed over and the world span a little.

'Hey, Tideborne!' Kaya shouted in excitement. 'Adam, that'll be your mum.'

Everyone stopped moving and stared at Adam.

'I can't believe you never told me your mum was Amber Tideborne!' Amelia's eyes were wide open.

'Why do you care who my mum is?' Adam asked defensively.

'Your mum was the one worthy of wielding Excalibur. She was one of the most powerful people in Elysium.' Amelia took a few steps closer to Adam, inspecting him like a lion stalking its prey.

'She also used to lead me and the other Disciples before Disciple Maria,' Peter said, staring at Adam like he was some special artefact.

'That's great, Adam.' Kaya gave his friend a happy nudge. 'When we meet her, you can mention a thing or two about Maria, maybe that'll get her to be a little nicer.'

'She's dead.' The words felt like fire coming from Adam's mouth, burning every part of him once they had been spoken.

'Yes, she... she died taking down Gonti,' Peter added.

'Oh.' Kaya placed his hand on Adam's shoulder and brought him in for a hug. 'I'm so sorry. Maybe you can still meet your dad?'

Peter gave a sad sigh. 'I'm afraid to say–'

'He's dead too,' Adam said bluntly, wiping away at his eyes, lightly coughing trying to clear his throat, which had tightened like the hug Kaya was giving him.

Adam felt someone's hand softly rest on his shoulder.

'I am so sorry for your loss,' Iosefka said. 'I have not known you for long but I am sure your parents would be proud to see the person you are now.'

'This is great!' Amelia blurted. 'Your name carries so much weight and with that, this team already has an edge over the others from Earth, and it probably even puts us past the teams born in Elysium!'

Amelia's smile immediately fell when everyone glared at her in disgust.

'What's the matter with you?' Kaya looked like he was ready to throw Amelia down the mountain.

'Er – I mean, I'm so sorry for your loss.' She quickly walked over and placed her hand awkwardly on Adam's shoulder.

Slowly, Adam started to feel better. It felt good to accept that his parents were gone. Saying that they had died made it real, and now that it was out in the open and not buried within, he found that his mind wasn't so numbed and pained.

As they made their way lower down to the city, the noise of the crashing waterfall grew, but was washed out by the noise from within the Capital, conversations and chatter filling the streets even in the late hour. By the time they reached the bottom, all of them were sweating profusely, something they had never experienced before.

'You can smell the food from here. Oh, Dionysus, I hope there's some good meat this year. Now I'm sure you've worked out that I'm not really meant to go to the feast but it shouldn't be a problem so long as I wait around the market for a little and sneak into the Pantheon in about an hour. So, we can call this the end of the real tour but you can have a look round the Capital if you feel like it. The Pantheon isn't far from here, just head down that road.' Peter gestured down a long main road with massive houses on either side.

They all gave Disciple Peter their thanks and he shook each of their hands before sneaking off down a thin alleyway that barely hid him, given his large stature and bright white clothing.

As the four started to walk down the road Disciple Peter had gestured towards, they had to lean on every wall and lamppost they could just to support their exhausted bodies.

However, their lust for food and water dissipated for a while as they wandered around the town, exploring as much as possible, their eyes becoming hungrier than their stomachs. They walked down the cobbled streets, commenting on all the small differences in the houses. One had vines wrapping around the front wall made of a dark brick, another had a couple of apple trees growing in the front garden along with a wonderfully bright selection of flowers lining the fence.

Cosy taverns advertised their fresh food on wooden floor signs set up around the town square. Most of them seemed to be closed for the main feast but a few remained open, their warm lights from within spilling out onto the dark cobblestone.

The four of them stood transfixed, looking in on the bustling crowds within, drinking merrily after a long day in the magical world. Adam imagined that they were all telling stories of great foes they had vanquished in the Wildlands and God-slaying artefacts they had discovered.

The few groups of friends and families heading home that the four walked past smiled and welcomed them to Elysium. Almost all of the people they saw wore similar clothes to sitcom shows during the 21st century – jeans, dresses, and jackets, in all kinds of styles and sizes that the era of fashion had used. Adam noted that most of the people they had seen dressed this way were wearing suits or particularly beautiful clothing for this celebratory evening. It reminded Adam of how characters would dress for a wedding when one of the main cast were getting married. It was comforting to feel like he was inside an episode.

There was the occasional group dressed more like Gerard, ready for battle, except their armour was never so unique. Adam and the others had the chance to talk to one group of four who were preparing to leave for the Wildlands. They appeared only a few years older, their bodies protected by armour old knights would have used, and it was clear the strong defence came at the cost of a heavy weight as they took the opportunity to all sit on a low wall whilst talking.

Their helmets, carried at their sides, were the only unique piece that distinguished who was who in the midst of battle, except for the few nicks and dents in each person's metal that they hadn't managed to fix.

The young knights didn't chat for long, but they advised Adam, Amelia, Kaya, and Iosefka to focus on training as much as possible whilst at Camp Paragon. They all said they wished that in their first year they had spent less time enjoying what Elysium had to offer and more time working to get fitter and stronger.

Adam noticed that they all had a small bird engraved into the chest piece slightly above where their hearts were and he was about to ask what they were for before the young knights took their leave.

After almost an hour of wandering around the Capital, Kaya started to whine that he was starving, but the moment they all decided to head to the Pantheon, a middle-aged man with dark grey hair and grey wiry stubble stumbled through the town, grabbing their attention.

The man had a dirty face, which he tried to wipe with the sleeve of his oversized dark brown sweater that had several rips and holes in it, not precise and deliberate like the garbs of the Disciples, more like he had just fought a bear.

What stuck out second-most with this strange man was that he appeared to be completely blind. His eyes were covered with the same golden glass material that was used to write the names of people in the Sanctuary, a form of Enlightenment magic as Amelia had said.

Whilst this was a strange and sorry sight, it was nothing compared to the thick obsidian chains that were attached to his wrists and legs, thumping together loudly as he moved. As he struggled to hold himself up, people who walked past gave looks of disgust, as though he was some vile creature they didn't want plaguing their streets.

As he came closer, walking without checking if anything was in his way, his hands hanging at his sides, swaying uncaringly – like it didn't bother him that he didn't know where he was or where he was going – they could hear that he was singing in a hoarse voice.

'There is no balm in Gilead,
To make this wounded whole;
There's no power in heaven,
To cure this sin-sick soul.'

Then before the man could sputter another line, he tripped over his chains. As he started to fall, Iosefka leapt forward fast enough to catch him.

'Oh, dear. I suppose I should say thank you; I should have been more careful, I've been in these for so long now, and I still forget they're there sometimes.' His voice was gravelly and harsh, giving the impression that he didn't speak very often.

'What you were singing? It's similar to a hymn that I know. Do you follow the Old Ways?' Iosefka asked, helping the man back up.

'I *used* to follow the Old Ways; been a long time since I've given a proper prayer. It's easy to lose your faith in this world, many tend to lose sight of their beliefs here with so many temptations. Be sure to keep yours as close to you as possible.'

Adam completely missed the shock of horror on Iosefka's face. 'Why are you in chains?'

'You want a lot of information from me, and I'm getting nothing from you. Why don't, I'm guessing there are four of you, all tell me your names. It is nice to know who is kind in this world.'

Kaya, Amelia, and Iosefka spoke kindly as they introduced themselves, seeing him as a frail man who struggled to walk up a hill, but Adam felt off about him. It couldn't be an innocent reason for why he was in chains, and why his vision had been taken away.

'I'm Adam Tideborne,' he said last watching the man carefully.

In hearing Adam's name, the man seemed to raise himself unconsciously. Almost like he was hunched over on purpose to appear weaker, and hearing the name had reignited something inside him. Even his face hardened slightly, the old pitiful innocence turning to something a little more sinister. Yet it made him look years younger. The reaction only lasted for a few seconds before he played it off as a harsh cough, quickly returning to his weaker-seeming state.

'It's nice to meet you all,' he said, looking in the direction of Adam's voice. 'So, what everyone here in the town will tell you is that about sixteen years ago, I tried to overthrow Micholesh and take Elysium as my own. As punishment, my eyesight was taken from me and I was forced into these Prometheus chains, a lovely bit of crafting that makes it so that I can't use any magic, no matter how hard I try. This punishment also came with the whole world growing to hate me for trying to kill Micholesh, and by many people's beliefs, my punishment should have been death.'

'But then what really happened? If that's just what the people of the town would tell us, surely there's more to the story,' Adam probed.

'Quite observant, aren't you, Adam Tideborne? Unfortunately, what I know is information that will cost a lot more than simply telling me your names, but I think it's time for me to get back to where I belong. Iosefka, thank you so much for catching me, I owe you. Just something small though. To the rest of you, I hope to hear you sometime soon.' With that, he continued blundering up the hill, his obsidian chains rubbing against his clothes and skin harshly as he went.

Continuing their walk towards the feast, Adam could tell that the interaction with the shackled man had rattled Iosefka, who was lagging behind.

'Is everything alright?' He wanted to help her, the same way she had shown kindness towards him when finding out about his parents.

'I don't understand how a follower of the Old Ways could stop believing in it, and he said that lots of people stop following in Elysium. That just can't be,' Iosefka responded.

'Don't worry about it, I think he was just trying to get to you. I'm sure we are going to see plenty of people that follow the same religion as you do,' Adam said, wanting to cheer her up.

'Yeah, he doesn't know what he's talking about. What does he know? He can't see anything,' Kaya added, which put a smile on Iosefka's face.

'I'm sure you are both right, thank you.'

Not long after departing from the blind man, the group found the feast in what seemed like a replica of the Roman Pantheon, which gave reason to its name. Its smooth stone pillars were so large that three people the size of Disciple Peter would not have been able to stretch themselves around them. These pillars – three at the side with eight at the front – held up the grand entrance of the Pantheon, which was triangular at its front, and formed a pediment that glowed with that deep golden glass strong enough to light the field of grass that rested outside.

The golden text read: FEAST FOR ALL.

People of all kinds were scattered outside. Those who had come through the portal wearing the drab blue clothing of Earth ate with their new teams on the cool silky grass that swayed in the night's breeze. They all stared up at the mesmerizing sky, talking to one another about their lives in between bites of food that they wolfed down.

Also at the feast were long-term residents of Elysium, leaning against the stone pillars, listening to students who had just finished their first expedition into the Wildlands. Adam could overhear them talking about all the challenges they faced with so much energy and excitement that it made Adam want to run straight into the forest to experience it as well.

'Before we head in there, I want to make sure you're good,' Kaya said, placing his hand on Adam's shoulder as the other two made their way to the entrance. 'It must hurt hearing about your parents.'

'I'm fine.' Adam shrugged, turning away. 'Your parents raised me a hell of a lot more than mine ever did. You have always been my real family, and you always will be.'

'That means a lot, but come on, you're downplaying how much you wanted to meet them. I've been with you almost every year the portal gates open. I know how much you wanted to meet your mum and dad.'

'I'm not going to pretend like it didn't suck hearing that I would never meet them but there's nothing I can do about it.' Adam found that it was harder to get his words out than normal.

'But what are you going to do now? I know that meeting your parents has been one of the main things driving you. I don't want you to fall apart now that they're gone. I want to make sure you can be the main character.'

'You're saying that I get to be the main character now?'

'At least alongside me,' Kaya replied with a grin.

Adam smiled back, grateful to have Kaya in his life. 'Don't worry, I'm not going to give up this easily. In fact, I know exactly what we are going to do to be heroes.'

'What's that?' Kaya asked, his eyes growing a little larger in excitement.

'We are going to find Gerard's artefact for him. He helped me and by the sounds of it, he could do with our help to get it back, and I bet that blind man has something to do with it.'

6. A Feast Fit for the Gods

Starving Adam and Kaya joined Amelia and Iosefka up the few steps leading to the entrance of the Pantheon, which was made from two overwhelmingly large doors. Unlike the portal gates on Earth made of thick dark-grey concrete, these silver doors were covered with carvings depicting moments of the war within Elysium.

Stories of battles being won against insurmountable odds. Artefacts slaying monsters and armies fighting against hordes of the undead. The very bottom of the left door depicted a silhouette of what must have been Micholesh atop a mound of bodies, holding a strange black cubed rock. Victorious. The moment that he ended the war spanning generations. Adam, Amelia, and Iosefka wanted to continue examining the engravings on the beautifully crafted doors, but Kaya dragged them inside.

They found themselves in a great dome-like structure. The top was open, letting in a beam of moonlight into the centre of the room where dozens and dozens of tables were lined with all kinds of food. From an array of tender meat on one table to heaps of bright fruit and vegetables on another, over to a table covered with bowls of potatoes, rice, and noodles. Huge cauldrons sat steaming on open flames, each filled with soups, their delicious smells wafting through the cool night's air.

The hundreds of people in the room all spoke to one another noisily. Their conversations echoed all around the large dome structure, making it feel like everyone was speaking to everyone.

Before Adam had the chance to eat anything, he saw something far more important. At the back of the room sat a grand table, on a platform raised a few feet higher than floor level so that all that sat at it could see over the crowd and look down at all those below.

About half of those seated were in armour more protective than Gerard's, all in pristine condition. Their gleaming polished metals against the moonlight made them look like angels. The other half of the table dressed in equally fancy fabrics, bright loud colours, and often an animal crest embroidered on their proud chests, like the bird Adam had noticed on the students before. They all drank from crystal and golden goblets encrusted with opalescent jewels.

Disciple Maria was one of two that didn't wear clothes like the rest. Her white hood down, revealing a bored and impatient face. Slowly, she picked at her food with her wooden fork. The other sat on the furthest end of the table and was dressed even worse than the blind shackled man.

This member of the high table ate like an animal starved for food, ignoring his cutlery, using his filthy bare hands to wolf down the plate of meat in front of him. Scratches and bruises covered his filthy face. Since he didn't wear a shirt, Adam could see the deep scars across the man's chest and arms. Glancing underneath the table, Adam could see that he was barefoot, his soles black and hard. Thankfully the man had brown trousers on, but they had been ripped and poorly patched back together with slightly different shades of brown so many times, they barely covered his legs.

Adam had no idea what this person did that granted him a chair on this high table, but it must have been something incredibly important. To allow such a feral-appearing person to dine with people of such importance seemed more like the set-up for a punchline than anything else.

However, the person that attracted the most attention from Adam was sitting at the centre of the table next to Disciple Maria, in a chair slightly higher and grander than the rest. Talking to a furious Gerard was Micholesh, ender of the endless war.

He sat with a fist covered by his other hand resting under his gaunt face concentrating on Gerard, who was animatedly complaining about something. He had a deep crimson scar in the shape of a crescent moon that started at the left side of his forehead and made its way in between his left eye and large nose that appeared to have been broken on numerous occasions. His eyes scanned the room like a hawk, precise and piercing.

Because he had fought alongside Disciple Maria and Gerard, Adam had expected Micholesh to be around the same age. However, he was much older than the two next to him, his body skinny and fragile, his face dishevelled and hardened, and his wispy white hair did nothing to help him look younger.

Ignoring the pleas of Iosefka and Kaya to sit outside and start eating, Adam and Amelia both made their way towards the high table, entranced by the sight of Micholesh. They had such a strong desire to introduce themselves, it felt like they were cartoon characters floating through the sky following the smell of freshly baked pie.

Adam assumed Gerard had received bad news about his missing artefact. His face was almost as red as his hair and spit flew out of his mouth with every word. Being the leader of the world, Adam was amazed that Micholesh was sitting so calmly, not interrupting Gerard's meltdown or appearing in any way disrespected by how he was being yelled at in front of so many people who were purposefully not paying attention to the high table.

'You know what, maybe it would be better if we came back later,' Amelia suggested, staring at Gerard.

But it was too late to turn back, Micholesh had lifted his finger towards Adam and it was enough to silence Gerard, who beckoned the two of them over.

'Adam, how are you finding the feast?' Gerard asked in a fake calm tone, his voice echoing down towards the two, his powerful voice helping to cut through all the other conversations.

'It's incredible. I just wanted to come over and thank you, Micholesh sir, for letting us into Elysium and giving us this feast.' Adam had bowed his head a little, not sure if he was meant to be giving Micholesh the same respect as old kings, but he thought it was wiser to do so than not.

'Don't worry about it, I love any excuse to have a feast. Don't call me sir though, Micholesh will do perfectly fine. Come over closer so we can have a proper conversation,' he said cheerfully.

'Are you sure? I don't want to interrupt anything.' Adam looked over at Gerard, who still had veins pushing out of his forehead.

'Certainly, Gerard can let his emotions run wild, but there is nothing to be concerned about,' Micholesh said with a wave of his wrinkly hand.

'Nothing to be concerned about!' Gerard shouted, his fury immediately flaring back up. 'My greatsword has been stolen! Do you not realise how terrible that is? It could mean the end of our world!'

'What?!' Amelia blurted out.

'You're overreacting, Gerard, it will all be fine. I'm sure it is just some silly prank by one of the younger students. You of all people should know how they like their jokes. You are the one that taught them to be so mischievous after all.'

Adam was very glad to be hearing more about the investigation, and now that he knew how important it was to retrieve, there was no doubt in his mind that he would find it for Gerard to help save the world. He was certain that this is what his parents would have done if they were still alive and he felt it was his responsibility to carry on their legacy.

'Nobody would be stupid enough to take away my greatsword, and how do you explain the burn marks around my house, and how would you expect any student to pull off something like that, only the fiercest warrior in the world can wield it, only I can wield it!' Gerard slammed his fist onto the table, making everyone around jump except for Disciple Maria and Micholesh.

'As I said, no matter who has taken it, Disciple Maria is going to join in with the investigation and she will send out her Disciples to find it and return it to you.'

Disciple Maria gave no indication that she had heard her name or that she would do as requested, staying bored in her chair, slowly eating some chicken.

'That's not good enough!' Gerard yelled before storming away, exiting through a door behind their table.

'Will he be alright?' Adam asked.

'He'll be fine, just has a short temper is all, and he is rather fond of that greatsword of his.'

'What makes the greatsword such a powerful artefact that it makes him think that someone could destroy the world with it?' Amelia tried her best to sound casual.

'Have you two seen any magic yet?' Micholesh said, acting as if Amelia hadn't spoken.

'We have seen a little bit of Enlightenment magic and it truly is incredible,' Amelia replied, red in the face, worried that she had accidentally offended him.

'Only a little bit? What's the point in coming to Elysium, if you don't get to see anything of interest? Here, watch this.'

Micholesh stood from his seat and made a few motions with his hands like he was fighting the air before shooting his palms out towards the sky. Two blasts of fire came from each of his palms like he was a dragon. The whole room turned silent to watch the display of magic and all cheered and clapped after he had finished.

'That was awesome.' Adam could still feel the heat from the fire that had left the room through the skylight.

'Thank you, thank you. Now I must say, Adam, I had quite the fright when I first saw you a few minutes ago. I thought Gonti had resurrected and brought your father back from death. You are the spitting image of him.' Micholesh's face turned grave and his jaw clenched. 'Of course, if that did happen, it would have been a horrible sight. There wouldn't be a healthy warrior standing before me—one that appears to have all the strength and courage of their parents—but a monster, a deadly rotting corpse taken away from their rest to do another's bidding.'

Micholesh then stared off into the distance so intensely that it was like he too was a corpse being controlled by Gonti. But then with a shiver down his back, Micholesh's smile grew back as his body relaxed.

'Well, that turned rather dark, didn't it? Sorry about that, sometimes bad memories come flooding back and I find it is always better to let them pass through than to try and fight against them. Adam, I know you never knew them but you should know that your parents were good people. It was an honour to have had them fight for me. Without them, the world would still be at war. Of that I am certain.'

Adam didn't know how to respond after all that Micholesh had said and done so just stood there and nodded. After a few moments of silence, a strange white glove crawled onto the table by itself.

'What's that?' Amelia asked, making Adam jump, having completely forgotten that she was there.

'Oh, this.' Micholesh held out his hand and the glove used all of its fingers to jump across the table onto it. He looked over at Disciple Maria with a childish grin on his face, as she rolled her eyes, knowing what was about to happen. 'This is my helping hand.'

'Not once have I ever heard someone truly laugh at that joke,' Disciple Maria said with a scoff, leaving her seat and walking away.

'Don't worry about her.' Micholesh laughed, dropping the glove back onto the table where it started to moonwalk, using two fingers as legs. 'It's an artefact that I found on my travels. I named it Patches. Since I found it, it became somewhat sentient and obeys my commands, but I mostly just let it wander around. I find it rather soothing.'

'Can I ask how rare it is to find them, sir? An artefact, that is?' Amelia asked, mesmerised by Patches, which had now started to flick bits of food off the high table.

'Again, don't call me sir or any title, it's just Micholesh.'

'I am so sorry.' She bowed her head in shame.

'It's fine. They aren't exactly common to find, but I'm sure in good time with Adam Tideborne on your team, you'll find plenty. But you don't need to focus on that, for now just enjoy yourselves. Caesar will be leading you to camp early in the morning, and he's not one to slow down for the tired.'

Micholesh had pointed discretely at the person next to Gerard's empty seat who was calmly sipping from a goblet. He had short black hair, a thin face, and defined cheekbones with fair skin. He looked to be in his late twenties and sat upright with a rigid posture like a cross was nailed to him.

He wore a dark red doublet with beautiful embossing so deeply red it appeared black. The padded jacket fit Caesar's slim build perfectly and its silver clasps were open at the top, revealing a lighter red tunic shirt which had been loosely laced up to show off his collarbones but kept the rest of his chest from showing. Around his neck ran some black string that fell underneath his tunic, likely having some piece of treasure attached.

As Caesar stood up with his goblet to refill it, Adam was surprised to find that he wore two separate belts. One was a dark brown that went tightly around his body to keep his dark brown trousers in place. The other leather belt was double wrapped and jet black with a sword holster at the side, which – Adam realised upon looking around the room – contained the only sword inside the Pantheon.

Cautious about approaching Caesar, Adam left the view of the high table after thanking Micholesh. It had surprised Adam to hear how casual his leader was. With all the stories of his strength and power, Adam had envisioned he would act a lot more like how he looked, not like a laid-back teacher in a high-school movie that all the students liked.

Amelia and Adam moved over to the food where they started piling their plates with everything that was left on the table. Even though it was just the scraps of the feast, the food still looked and smelt extraordinary.

The two of them made their way outside, each carrying a large wooden plate stacked with food. By now most of the new students were outside. Some had already fallen asleep on the grass, and everyone else was yawning away, unwilling to sleep, far too entranced by the sky above them.

Kaya was devouring his food, barely stopping to breathe. Iosefka hadn't started eating yet, she wasn't praying or choosing what to eat, she was just sitting on the grass patiently. Adam wondered if she was scared to eat the food, but he realised after sitting down beside Kaya that she had been waiting for them to join.

The first thing that Adam ate was a piece of succulent meat that burst with so much flavour, he thought that he would never be able to stop eating, as if food this good was cursed so that the only thing he would be able to do till death was eat. This didn't bother him in the slightest as he devoured everything on his plate, barely stopping to breathe. Every time he ate something new, it was like a firework in his mouth, exploding with wonderous flavour that left him craving for more. In no time, their plates were empty.

Kaya had resorted to running his finger over his plate in the hope that when he put his finger in his mouth, he would still be able to taste some flavour. Being far too exhausted to even think about getting up and heading back into the Pantheon for more food.

Now that their hunger was satiated, they all started to feel the full force of the long day and they wanted nothing more than to sleep. Seeing that everyone was getting ready to sleep, Iosefka started her evening prayers. For praying, the followers of the Old

Ways spoke in an ancient dialect. It was a harsh language, one that sounded rough on the throat.

Adam's stomach was so full that when he moved too fast, it felt like he would throw up. However, seeing Bruce and Eddie Shark out of the corner of his eye sitting casually on the grass dissolved all of that feeling.

All he could think to do was get up and start heading towards them. With each step, he grew angrier, the image of a knife being plunged into his body flashing into his mind with each heavy exhale he took. Luckily, Kaya was fast enough to grab Adam's arm to stop him.

'Hey hey hey, this isn't smart. I know you want to get them back for what they did, but this isn't the place. If we start going for them with so many people watching, everyone will think we're the bad guys. It won't end well for us, especially if someone important sees us beating down on them.'

'We need to do something, look at them just sitting there!' Adam was doing his best to escape Kaya's clutches, but Kaya was persistent.

'Sit back down and relax. Have you tried feeling the grass? Adam, we've spent our entire lives dreaming of living here and I'm not going to let you throw it away over the Shark twins. Then they'll get exactly what they want. I promise we'll get our justice but now isn't the moment. Come on, I need you to trust me.'

Adam had stopped trying to push Kaya away. The rage in his body had started to fade with his touch.

'You're right,' Adam said, heading back over to feel the soft grass with Kaya.

As Adam sat back down, he glanced over to the twins to find that they had noticed him. Even with the cosmic sky above, the presence of life other than humans surrounding them, massive buildings and monuments all around, and the succulent real food below them, the thing that shocked the twins the most, to the point where their eyes shot open and their mouth dropped wide, was seeing Adam Tideborne alive and well in Elysium. This reaction from the two was enough to cheer Adam up a little, knowing that their day had been ruined by seeing him.

'What was all that about?' Amelia questioned the moment they sat back down.

As much as he didn't want to, Adam knew he had to retell the story and so he went over his day and how Bruce and Eddie stabbed him just to stop him from reaching the portal and how he sprinted for hours just to get to Elysium.

'I can't believe they are just going to get away with that,' Iosefka said once Adam had finished.

'We need to tell someone about this,' Amelia said, getting up.

'What! No, it's my problem to deal with!' Adam shouted, following Amelia as she walked back towards the Pantheon.

'No, it's now all our problem. I can't have those two constantly trying to interfere with us. They need to answer for their crimes.'

They had made their way into the Pantheon and Amelia showed no sign of slowing as she marched up towards the high table.

'Amelia, stop!' Adam demanded to no response.

By this point in the evening, the whole room was nearly empty and only three people sat at the high table. At the end, still wolfing down his food like he hadn't eaten for weeks, was the strange dirty man. There was then a long gap of empty seats until Micholesh who was talking with Disciple Maria.

Amelia waited patiently for Micholesh to notice her as she pushed away Adam's attempts to pull her back outside.

'Ah, Adam. Is everything alright?' Micholesh asked, his eyebrow slightly raised.

'Everything is perfectly fine, we just wanted to thank you again for the feast,' he replied.

'Actually, Micholesh, there is a small problem, and we didn't know who else to go to,' Amelia said.

'What is it?'

'Adam was attacked on Earth. Stabbed repeatedly by some twins in the hope that he wouldn't be able to make it through the portal. These twins are now in Elysium and sitting on the grass outside. I'm not certain about cross-world laws, but I feel like they must be reprimanded in some way. All signs would suggest that they would try and harm Adam and my team again.'

'Is this true?' Micholesh had risen from his relaxed posture, his face stern.

As much as Adam wanted to deal with the Shark twins himself, he couldn't lie directly to Micholesh.

'It's true,' Adam admitted.

'Very well.' Micholesh turned to Disciple Maria. 'You heard them and I believe them. It is your place to decide the punishment.'

Disciple Maria grabbed her staff that was resting on the wall behind her. She started to speak in a harsh language that sounded similar to the one Iosefka had used for praying, except it flowed together as a poem did. It was impossible to work out when one word ended and another started. That same glass-like material made from Enlightenment magic appeared again, but this time, instead of it being in the sky, it etched itself around her staff.

Within a few seconds, her staff had a small line of golden runes going down it. The strange dialect she was uttering sped up as she slammed her staff into the ground. All the markings glowed, burning until they disappeared into the wood, sending little golden specks of dust into the air.

'The twins will be seen to.' She sat back down, having nothing but disdain for the two on her face.

'Thank you. We appreciate it,' Amelia said.

'It is not a problem,' Micholesh replied. 'You need to feel as safe as you can in this world—there is enough to deal with other than the threat of other people on your mind. Now head back outside, I suggest you rest. There is a long day ahead of you.'

'I cannot believe you did that,' Adam said as the two left the Pantheon.

'It had to be done.'

'It was none of your business! You had no right to make that decision!'

'A good leader should never bring threats, they should only deal with them. Like I just did for you,' Amelia said.

'What are you talking about leading for?' Adam had slowed down to compute what Amelia was talking about.

'Well, we are a team of four, we can't all lead. I have spent all my life training to be a perfect leader.'

'Amelia, you're not the leader of this group.' Adam hadn't given the slightest thought to the fact that the team might need someone to lead it, but he certainly didn't want that person to be Amelia.

'Are you saying that because I'm short? Because I'm a girl? I'm stronger than you think. Come on, try and attack me!' Amelia raised her fists as people stared at them.

'Who said anything about you being short? You aren't going to lead this group because I don't want you to be in charge of me.'

'Oh, so you're saying you want to be leader?'

'I'm not saying –'

Before Adam could finish his sentence, two Disciples rushed across the grass towards the Shark twins, moving everyone's attention away from Adam and Amelia. Before the twins could do anything, the Disciples had restrained them, casting the golden glass around their wrists acting as handcuffs.

As they were led away, Adam could hear them yelling and shouting, doing their best to break the golden magic wrapped around their wrists. No matter how hard the twins tried to escape or break free, they could do nothing against the Disciples and their staffs, which repeatedly stuck them.

Whilst the twin's shouts and threats faded, the glowing golden text from the Pantheon started to intensify. It slowly disappeared, and the whole area grew dark. There were still some lampposts burning their embers in their glass cases, but otherwise, the only light that could be seen was from the dark colourful mists in the sky above them. Nobody had any concept of time at the moment, but it was clear that it was now lights out and that after the surprising scene with the Shark twins, they were all expected to go to sleep.

'That was quick,' Amelia said, staring at the street the twins had just been dragged down leading back towards Mount Ida.

'I wonder what's going to happen to them?' Iosefka wondered.

'It doesn't matter, they were my responsibility to deal with,' Adam argued.

'We can't do anything about it now,' Kaya replied.

'Oh, no, what a shame you don't get to ruin the reputation of my team.' Amelia scowled.

Adam wanted nothing more than to stay awake all night arguing with Amelia, but there was nothing he could gain from it. Everyone was trying to get to sleep, and she had already brought justice into her own hands.

Slowly, one by one, everyone laying on the grass fell asleep, the breeze soothing them as the noises of the world sang them sweet lullabies. A world full of life, possibilities and adventure no longer in their imagination.

7. Brown Fairies

Adam, like many others, had envisioned the first day he woke in Elysium to be wonderful. That when he opened his eyes, the hot sun would be burning down on him, with life all around. Birds flying in the sky, insects crawling on the ground, perhaps some magical creature resting beside him.

However, the deafening noise of a gong being repeatedly struck brought him back to reality. Everyone sleeping on the grass woke in shock at the noise and they all tried to cover their ears to stop the ringing.

'Everyone up! It's time to leave for camp, there is food in the Pantheon! Eat and be ready to leave in twenty minutes!' Caesar bellowed, almost as loud as the gong.

It was still dark out and the dew on the grass made Adam feel sticky and gross. He could tell that he smelled, everyone did. He was hopeful that the journey to the training camp wasn't too far away and that they would be able to wash and shower before they did anything else. Nobody stayed on the floor after waking. The day ahead of them was far too exciting to be able to get back to sleep.

Within minutes, everyone was walking back into the Pantheon. The tables within had all been cleaned from last night's feast, and now had an assortment of fruits, ready for breakfast. After eating his fill of new food that was divine in every sense, Adam realised that Iosefka hadn't come with them into the Pantheon.

Looking back outside he saw a small group of people kneeled on the grass, their faces painted with the same lines as Iosefka's, all in collective prayer. Adam had completely forgotten how much the Old Ways religion prayed.

Ever since the portal came into existence, almost everyone became some level of religious. It was impossible not to. There was only so much that could be done to disprove a miracle or a divine intervention. Being struck by lightning wasn't a punishment from God, but an unfortunate coincidence. Surviving a deadly disease wasn't a miracle, but the hard work of doctors and a strong will to live.

But the portal couldn't be explained with science and reason, at least not yet, and everyone believed it to be a sign of help from a greater being. When the results for science and reason came slowly, people were quick to grasp onto something that they could immediately understand. As a result, religion which had been almost non-existent throughout the war started to flourish once more.

The gong rang again as it was struck by Caesar. 'Everyone, follow me!' He ordered.

It seemed like the followers of the Old Ways wouldn't be able to enjoy breakfast, having only just finished praying. Adam still had an orange in his hand, which he wanted to try, it was such a bright colour, but he chose to save it. He would give it to Iosefka when he had the chance. They were meant to look out for each other after all.

A mix of students from Earth and those born on Elysium made their way out of the Capital. There were at least double maybe even triple the amount of Elysium students to the few hundred from Earth. They were all led over a wide stone bridge that passed over the flowing river, which Adam had seen from the top of Mount Ida.

Everyone was moving at different speeds. Those from Earth were spending time watching the water crash up against small rocks, throwing pebbles and weeds into the water to see the unique ripples it made in the stream. Whilst those who had been raised in Elysium led the group behind Caesar, trying their best to show him how good a soldier they could be.

Lined up on the left side of a dirt road that was just outside the city were a little over a hundred elegant horses, all connected to wooden carriages that could fit around eight people.

The horses were fascinating to look at. It was the first animal that the students from Earth had seen up close and they were remarkable creatures. Yet those from Earth couldn't help but keep their distance, wary of how large and strong the creatures appeared, and how weak and defenceless they felt without their nanobees.

Dozens of horses were pawing at the ground, wanting to start their journey, whilst others stomped their back hooves, wanting to be freed from the carriage they had been attached to, shaking their heads back and forth in an attempt to escape their harness.

It was like they had emotions. For the first time, Adam understood that they weren't just mindless animals like they had been taught, but creatures with a mind and soul. It was when a black horse closest to Adam let out a loud neigh as someone came a little too close to it that he truly realised how alive these horses were.

There was a whole spectrum of colours going down the road; grey, silver, white, and black, of all different shades and tones, each horse acting differently and independently. Almost all those from Elysium had immediately entered their carriage, eager to leave for camp.

Not wanting to spend too long looking, Adam started to wander down the path with the other members of his team.

'What is that?' Kaya pointed down the road. 'Some kind of Pegasus?'

Trotting up and down the right side of the path keeping all the horses in check was a creature that looked very similar to a horse except it was much smaller and thinner than any of its counterparts. In fact, whilst all the other horses had big strong muscles, this one had its ribcage pushing against its grey skin, and what set the horse-like creature apart the most was the set of pale thin wings attached to its sides.

'No, a Pegasus is always pure white, this horse is clearly not,' Amelia explained. 'I think someone has managed to tame a Chollima.'

'That is correct,' Caesar said, in a bored tone, making Amelia jump as he elegantly climbed atop the magical creature.

'Can I ask, sir, the Chollima are legendary for their swiftness. It was said that no human could ever mount one, how did you manage to do it?'

Caesar's face remained cold and unemotional. 'You have not researched enough. It is not written that no human could mount one, but that only a truly powerful human could tame the beast, and we are in a world where power is limitless.'

'Cool, how did you tame it? Did you use some kind of spell or an artefact?' Kaya asked.

Caesar gave the same blank expression he had been showing since the start of their conversation. 'Get inside a carriage or we will leave without you,' he said, riding up to the front of the line.

Of all the people they had encountered so far, Adam thought Caesar looked the most like a hero or some powerful prince. It felt like he radiated power, but something was wrong with him. He had all the right components to be someone special, but the way he spoke was like his spark had been extinguished. It was as if he had been waiting all of his life to be a hero, expecting a call to adventure than never came, and now he had lost hope of it ever happening.

The four climbed inside the closest carriage. Inside were two long wooden seats positioned opposite each other. The carriage itself seemed to be made completely of dark oak wood.

'I wonder how far away this training camp is?' Iosefka wondered.

'It can't be that far. We'll have to keep coming back here to take books out of the Bibliotech,' Amelia said.

'We'll also need to come back here so that we can become part of the community and get to know all the residents,' Adam added, already thinking of ways to find the greatsword.

'What's the Bibliotech?' Iosefka asked.

'Weren't you paying attention to Disciple Peter?' Amelia remarked with a scowl.

'I was just so interested in looking at everything.'

'That's not good enough. This world is dangerous and you have to make sure you are getting as much information as possible. It's bad enough that you have to pray all the time, you even have to pray before casting a spell. Do you know how difficult that makes things for me?'

'I'm sorry for not hearing what Disciple Peter said but I'm not about to apologize for my religion. That is who I am and I don't care if it makes your life harder.' Iosefka stared at Amelia.

'You shouldn't even have to apologize for not listening,' Adam added. 'I didn't hear about that either and that's fine, we were too busy appreciating the world.'

'Stop defending her! You're only saying that because you want to look good so that you can lead this team!' Amelia shouted.

'I never said that I wanted to –'

Before Adam could finish his sentence, the door to the carriage opened up, and Olivia stuck her head in. 'I thought I could hear you, Adam. Can we join?'

'Absolutely not,' Kaya said with a smirk, but he moved up to let Olivia in.

'Are you sure we aren't interrupting anything?' Olivia said, eyeing Amelia, presumably having heard her shouting from outside.

'Yes, you definitely are, come on in.' Adam held out his hand and helped Olivia and the rest of her group in.

Olivia was followed by their fellow schoolmate Max, then two people that Adam had never seen before. One had a small ratty face with a mole on the side of his nose and short blonde hair. He introduced himself as Jaiden. The other was a stunning tall girl with bright blue eyes called Rebecca. With all of them in the carriage, it became harder to sit comfortably. Adam was now pinned to the side with Amelia squidged next to him.

Outside they could hear some loud muffled shouting and neighing, followed by the horses trotting forward. Wanting to get a better view of the route they were taking, and to reduce the stuffiness of the small cramped area, Adam slid open the window on his side.

A calm breeze entered the carriage, cooling everyone down, but it did nothing to help with the uncomfortable silence and cramped bumpy ride. Every so often someone would try and wiggle into a less painful position, only to end up making it worse for themselves.

Iosefka's stomach started to rumble loudly, and Adam remembered that he had been holding onto an orange, except it had been slightly squashed in his pocket. Still, he offered it to Iosefka who would have no idea what an orange was meant to look like.

'Thank you, Adam, that's very kind of you.'

'Does anyone know what kind of stuff we're going to do at camp today? Is it just like orientation, or do you think we are going to learn how to use magic straight away?' Olivia asked.

'I don't know but I hope they let us have a shower soon, I've never felt so sticky in my life,' Max said, wiping some sweat from his forehead.

Everyone gave groans of agreement as Iosefka quietly prayed.

'I can't be bothered for any more of this admin stuff, we wait to get processed and move to another area to get processed. It's getting stupid. I just wanna learn something cool,' Jaiden whined.

'Hey, I noticed Bruce and Eddie getting taken away by those Disciples last night. I'm guessing it was something to do with what they did to you?' Olivia asked Adam.

'It had nothing to do with me. That was all Amelia,' Adam said, tensing up.

'It was not all me. You were the one to cause the problem, I was the one to fix it.'

'I didn't need you to fix anything. There was no problem to begin with, I've been dealing with those two all my life. I could have handled them here too.'

'Maybe, but it was a risk that as leader, I wasn't willing to make.'

'You aren't the leader. There is no leader. We haven't even got to camp yet.'

For a while, they all sat in silence, not wanting to say anything that might start another argument. As they travelled over the rocky terrain, Max started to go pale and made a loud groan after they went over a bump in the road.

'Are you alright, Max?' Olivia asked.

He shook his head slowly. 'Don't feel good. Got a headache, it's making me feel sick.'

Not wanting to get puked on, they all shuffled around so that Max could move over to the open window that now showed a view of a massive open farm. Flocks of sheep in one grassy area, hundreds of cows in the next, chickens wandering around freely, along with bouncing rabbits and fat pigs, it was like something from a children's book, each animal making their own strange and wonderful noise.

'We must be getting close,' Amelia said. 'This must be where most of the food is made, if I'm not mistaken. I can even see a few brown fairies.'

'Did you say fairies?' Rebecca asked.

But there was no need for Amelia to reply. Flying overhead like a swarm of locusts were thousands of little fairies, all in harmony singing some kind of melody. The sound made Adam want to be productive, flooding his body with motivation to work.

They swept through the fields, checking in on the thousands and thousands of different farm animals. The fairies had to be around the same size as Adam's finger, yet they still managed to keep the animals calm and in check. A small group flew over to the carriages to say hello to those inside, and one happened to land on the window that Max was faintly leaning against.

'Hello, everyone! My name's Daisy, what's yours?' Daisy had a sweet high-pitched squeaky voice.

She wore a dark brown dress, with tights and shoes of the same colour. Even her comparatively big eyes were a deep brown, along with her hair. It didn't take much effort to work out why they had been named brown fairies.

Everyone said their names all at once and Adam doubted if she managed to get anyone's name.

'It's great to meet you all. You're all going to love it here. Hey Max, are you doing, ok? You seem a little down.'

Max gave a small groan at the sound of his name, but that was about all he could muster.

'He's just feeling a bit travel sick, Daisy, I'm sure he'll be fine when we arrive at camp,' Olivia replied.

Everyone was staring at Daisy. She was so similar to a normal person, yet so very tiny. 'Not to worry. I can help with that. When some of our cattle get sick, we can help them get better.'

Daisy hovered over to Max's forehead, touching it with her pea-sized hands. A small amount of glitter seemed to crystallise from the air around her, and some of the colour came back to Max's face.

'Wow, I feel loads better, thank you so much,' Max said with much more energy than before.

'Don't worry about it. I might just be a brown fairy, but I still help whenever I can. Anyway, I've got to go now, but it was great talking to you. I hope you come over to help at the farm sometime, we could always do with a little help.'

They all waved at Daisy as she flew back over to all the animals, helping three other fairies to pick up some chicken eggs. Everyone kept on looking at the different animals and fairies until the carriage moved away from the farm and into a wooded area, where it became hard to see anything past all the thick trees.

'Why are all the worker fairies brown? Aren't there other coloured fairies that could help them out?' Kaya asked. 'It looks like a lot of hard work doing what they do.'

'No, Kaya,' Amelia immediately snapped. 'Brown is the colour of mud and growth, which is what those types of fairies have powers for. They are born to aid with crops and cattle. If they ever needed more help, which I am assuming they did when we built that farm, they would simply reproduce so that there were more brown fairies.'

'That's fine but you haven't answered my question. Why don't the other colours help them out?' Kaya repeated.

'It's not in their nature. Green fairies have control over nature, blue fairies are blue because – well, even you could work that one out, and so on. Colour is just how they were written in old tales and it's the changing variable to show the difference in what they are born to do and the difference in their species.'

'But then what if a blue fairy decides one day that she wants to be a green fairy and help the trees? Does it not get to live out its dreams?' Rebecca said, getting upset.

'That doesn't happen! Again, fairies are born with powers specifically adapted to what their species is responsible for. They evolved with those powers through survival of the fittest and by adapting to their environment, it is not in their nature to leave their life in search of something else!' Amelia started to raise her voice again.

'God, you sound like the bad guy in every children's story. What if one day someone like Daisy decides they want to go off on an adventure around Elysium? Are you going to stop them?' Adam argued.

'That is quite simply the stupidest thing I have ever heard. I genuinely can't believe the complete rubbish coming from your mouth. You can't compare stories for children with a society of living magical beings.'

'But these magical beings are only alive because they were in children's stories to begin with,' Adam retorted.

'I DON'T CARE IF –'

'Thank god, we're here.' Olivia opened up the door on her side and leapt out along with the rest of her group before their horses even had the chance to come to a full stop.

'Look what you did now, they're going to talk about us and then the whole camp will think we're stupid!' Amelia shouted to Adam and Kaya.

'What does it matter what people think about us!' Kaya shouted back.

'Please, could you all calm down? This is meant to be a magical day,' Iosefka pleaded.

'You're right.' Kaya calmed his tone. 'We're sorry. This is going to be a magical day.'

The two of them left the small wooden box, leaving Amelia alone with Adam.

Amelia leaned in close to Adam and pointed her finger close to his face. 'Don't think for a second that just because you have a friend in this team that I'm going to back down from being this team's leader. I deserve this. I have worked harder than you for it, and can achieve greater things with this team than you ever could.'

'Whatever.'

Before Amelia could get another word out, Adam left the carriage to join the others. Leaving Amelia, as usual, alone – having to process that her life's plan which had been so meticulously developed was being thwarted.

8. Hunted by a Monster

The Carriages had all stopped at the end of a dirt trail. Thick trees surrounded them, making the ground uneven from the arm-sized roots bulging out of the earth.

Caesar was nowhere to be seen. It would have been impossible to work out what direction they should go to find the camp without the help of the hundreds of tiny birds chirping away on a line of branches, forming a kind of audible path to follow.

Without any other indication of what they were meant to do – no signs or people to tell them what to do – the students all started to climb into the forest, following the noise that sounded like little trumpets.

The ground was covered in fallen leaves and odd forest debris that Adam couldn't come close to identifying. With no discernible visible route, everyone was going their own way. The mounds and dips all around made it feel like they were part of an obstacle course.

There were some points on the journey that required Adam to climb upwards as the dirt hills started to form almost vertically, only for them to drop straight down. Other sections made him go on all fours and crawl under a selection of vines, bushes, weeds, and branches.

People through the line of trees every so often and watched the less athletic ones fall down hills they had been trying to climb, scratching themselves on the way down. He watched someone push a thick branch to get through it, only to let it go, slapping their teammate behind them.

The trek down Mount Ida had been exhausting but it was just a lot of walking. So, for a lot of people from Earth, this journey through the harsh terrain was their first experience of real pain.

Most of them were taking their minor injuries well enough, but he noticed that a few found it a lot harder to cope without the help of the nanobees suppressing pain, having to stop and rest to deal with the pain from a few scratches and falls.

Adam assumed this was the reason for them having to go through this dense forest, to get a little hurt. It was good preparation for what the monsters and magic could do with ease. The few injuries Adam had accumulated weren't nearly as painful as the two hits Disciple Maria had given to his hand, or the agonizing run he had done on Earth. He found it enjoyable to push through the forest like it was an adventure.

Adam had looked around a couple of times for the birds when the chirping started to get farther away, but all he could ever focus on was that beautiful sky. Even with the dark green leaves blocking some of the view, light broke through all the cracks, glowing a deep orange as the sun rose over the mountains.

The sun's rays cut through the different colours of inky smoke way up high, causing them to become lighter and thinner, still with the same immense wonder that it had at night, but fading more into the background.

After a while, Adam ran into Kaya and Iosefka. It seemed like the three of them were farther than most of the other students, including those from Elysium.

Kaya hadn't received so much as a scratch but his blue clothes were brown from all the mud he had been crawling in. Iosefka, wasn't as agile as Kaya, and even with Kaya's help, her hair was covered in dirt, the yellow lines on her face had faded, and her hands had several cuts on them, with a cut on her leg deep enough to seep blood.

It was clear she was far out of her comfort zone. Her body clenched as they walked through mud, and each new scratch and cut made her recoil in pain and let out a quiet whimper.

Somehow, Kaya was keeping her sane, at least enough to keep her pushing through. He held her hand to keep her from falling, and carefully lifting her up so that she had an easier time going up some of the tougher inclines. With Adam now sticking with them, helping Iosefka out – like he knew he should have from the start – they continued to speed through the forest.

Slowly, the path opened up into a clearing. The sun, which had now fully come out, shone its hot rays down as they pushed through the last few bushes coming out into a large open field.

The noise of metal hitting metal filled the open area, as students practised their armed combat with swords, axes, and the like. Training dummies made from hay lined up around the large patch of grass, and arenas had been ringed off in squares and circles using rope for one-on-one and two-on-two fighting.

Adam had been uncertain if the forest he had just left was part of the Wildlands, but now it was clear that he had just been in an ordinary forest. At the other side of the field, an opening of massive trees half the size of mountains acted as the border to the Wildlands. Unlike the oak trees, which were a lovely brown, these trees were dark black and ashen grey, and many of the branches had thick thorns around them.

Caesar waited for them, looking immensely unimpressed.

'Are we one of the first?' Kaya asked, only seeing two other groups of students that had made it through, both from Elysium.

'No,' Caesar said bluntly.

'What do you mean?' Adam said in awe. 'We blasted through that.'

'You are the third to come through, but as you should be aware, there are four in a group. I only count three. It would appear that you have left the rest of your team behind. This is unacceptable, and should in no way be thought of as an accomplishment.'

'Dammit, Amelia.' Kaya scowled.

'We're sorry, sir, you're right. We'll head straight back in now and help her through.' Adam had already started to climb back into the forest. 'Iosefka, you wait here. Hopefully, she'll come through by herself and you can tell her to stay where she is.'

Caesar didn't indicate that this was what they should or shouldn't do. He did nothing other than continue to stand with his incredibly straight posture, staring back into the area that Adam and Kaya had just gone back through.

Heading away from the camp proved to be much harder than Adam expected. It felt unnatural to move against the sound of the birds and made the pair feel uncomfortable, as though they were doing something they shouldn't. Kaya pointed out several times that they had unconsciously turned back on themselves so that they were heading back towards the camp.

There were a few moments where the noise of birds completely died out and Kaya would joke that they would be lost in the woods forever. However, thanks to Kaya, they managed to track back to where the occasional slow group was still making their way through the terrain.

Eventually, after what must have been at least forty minutes of encountering dozens of people who weren't Amelia, they found their way back to the dirt trail they had started on. The horses and carriages were nowhere to be seen. Not being able to go back any farther, the two of them started following the noise again, shouting and searching, growing more resentful of Amelia by the second.

By now it sounded like the birds had grown tired from all the chirping, their music quieter and less magical by the minute. After a while, the two decided to split up. Kaya would sprint to the end and check if she had made it through, whilst Adam continued the slow walk searching for their teammate.

Adam couldn't see anyone as he moved through the forest. It was obvious that even though the rest of the students had struggled, they had all reached the end. Adam had just reached the obstacle in the forest he had struggled with the most, a dirt wall which he had to jump to reach the ledge of and pull himself over the top to pass when he spotted her. Covered in mud, sitting slumped over a particularly large root off to the side, was his so-called leader.

'Amelia!' He called.

'Oh, there you are,' Amelia choked, turning round, her eyes red and wet.

'Is everything alright?' Adam asked.

'Yes. Perfectly fine,' she said, wiping her face with a dirty sleeve. 'You see I was rather confident I could complete this simple obstacle, but it would appear that my height got the better of me. I've been sitting here trying to work out a plan to climb it and I'm sure it won't take long before I solve it.'

Taking a closer look at the dirt wall, Adam could see the many attempts that Amelia had made. She had made small holes in the wall to stick her fingers in when climbing, as well as a mound of branches to use as a pedestal to give her a little more height, and then there was what could only be described as the aftermath of a breakdown with everything structurally weak in the surrounding area being broken and snapped and stomped on.

'Hey, don't worry about it. We all have things we struggle with. Here, let me give you a hand.' Adam offered his hand.

'No. I don't need your help; I can do it myself. And just because I can't do this one simple thing doesn't mean you can lead this group. I'm not giving up that easily!'

'Look, there's no point focusing on that now, there will be plenty of time to work out who can lead the group later. For now, why don't we just enjoy ourselves? We can focus on burning our bridge when we get to it. In fact –'

Adam found a black velvet-leafed flower, a soft purple light emanating from its centre. As he tried to pick it up from the ground, it pricked him on one of the thorns he hadn't noticed on the stem. The thorn was a lot sharper than he ever expected a thorn could be, drawing blood from his finger, and as a few droplets fell onto the petals, it seemed to shiver and absorb it into itself. Not being too bothered about what happened, thinking that the flower had moved from the wind, Adam picked the flower from the ground, careful not to touch the thorns, and gave it to Amelia.

'Smell this.'

Amelia looked at him sceptically as if this was some kind of trick.

'Come on, just take a deep breath in, and smell the flower. I mean come on, we've both spent all our lives on a planet filled with nothing but pollution and waste. Here is a genuine living flower, something that could only be held whilst dreaming twenty-one years ago, and here we are in a whole forest of them.'

She still didn't seem too keen to do what someone else, especially Adam, had suggested, but she closed her eyes and took a deep inhale, causing the edges of the petals to flicker upwards. Amelia kept her breath in for a few seconds and then exhaled, opening her eyes with a smile on her face.

'That smelt great.' She stared into Adam's eyes. 'Thank you.'

'Don't worry about it,' he replied with a smile, getting back up from the floor. 'Right, come on, let's finish this. There isn't far to go.'

Adam helped Amelia up and they made their way over to the wall, ready to climb it together, but something didn't feel right. As Adam placed his hand on the wall, he froze, realizing what was wrong. The ground had been vibrating and now that he touched the wall, he could feel it trembling as if the ground was shaking in fear.

'What is it?' Amelia said, not understanding what was wrong, but Adam could barely hear her. His adrenaline was flooding as he spun around toward a barking noise, trying to work out if that is where the danger was coming from.

Then, confirming he was looking the right way, he started to hear the barking grow louder and – looking up through the gaps in the trees – he watched black birds fly up into the sky from afar as entire trees started to shake.

Adam realised the massive thing was making its way directly towards the two, and it snapped him into action. Grabbing hold of Amelia's hand, Adam ran as fast as he could to the wall and launched himself up it, dragging Amelia up as quickly as he could, ignoring everything she was shouting at him.

As he stood up, he saw the beast that was charging towards them. Its leopard body and legs sprinted at a ridiculous speed so fast that its snakehead – as thick as the tree roots it was weaving around – had to constrict and contort so as not to be crushed as it searched every crevice on its path for the thing that it hunted.

From its stomach came the barking noise as though it had swallowed a dozen dogs, their barks rumbling through the forest so loud that it terrified the singing birds away and made Adam's heart beat to its erratic rhythm.

Before the two could take more than a few steps, the beast spotted them and its head shot towards them, pointing like an arrow, its gaping mouth showing off its two dagger-sized fangs, as the body darted towards them too fast for them to think about running away.

In seconds, the monster leapt into the air. Adam grabbed Amelia and threw them both back down the wall. As the two fell, the monster's snake head followed them down, but before it could sink its teeth into either of them, its body carried it away to the top of the hill where it had jumped.

As Adam and Amelia crashed to the floor, the monster turned around in a flash and Adam knew there was no way he could get back up in time to defend himself. The two of them watched as the beast pounced into the sky again.

The great monster dove down towards them like a fallen angel, aiming to drag Adam and Amelia to hell, but just before the snake head struck them, an entire oak tree came flying through the air, slamming into its side, sending it crashing through another tree. Adam shielded his eyes as the explosion of wood came flying at them as the monster continued to roll across the ground.

From where the tree had been launched, Adam was amazed to see the feral man that had sat at the end of the high table in the Pantheon chase after the beast on his bare hands and feet.

'RUN!' He shouted as he continued chasing after the monster.

Adam had no intention of sticking around. He helped up a terrified Amelia and pushed her up the wall. They sprinted, with their lives depending on it, towards the training grounds.

As they ran, the noise of the barking faded and Adam thought he even heard a yelp before the forest turned eerily silent. Everyone stared at them as they bolted out of the woods and onto the grassy field.

'There's a monster in there!' Adam shouted to Caesar whose eyebrow raised.

'It was a Questing Beast. I can't believe it, you put a Questing Beast in that forest, I could have died!' Amelia screamed at Caesar.

'QUIET.' His voice boomed, silencing Amelia and everyone muttering around. 'I have no idea what you are saying, that forest is completely cut off from the Wildlands. There is no possibility that a monster would be able to get into it.'

Then from the forest came the feral man who was covered in mud and fresh blood that smelt so bad it made those around him gag.

'Caesar, come,' he said simply.

'Stay here, I will be back shortly,' Caesar commanded before heading into the forest.

Everyone stared at Adam and Amelia as they fell to the ground their bodies still in overdrive from the attack.

'Are you hurt?' Kaya asked Adam.

'It came out of nowhere,' Adam said, not blinking as he stared into Kaya's eyes.

'I can't believe you threw me down. That hurt!' Amelia whined, rubbing her elbow.

Adam shook his head in disbelief. 'Are you delusional? I saved your life!'

'You did no such thing! I am perfectly capable of keeping myself safe. You dragged me up the wall just to throw me down again when you realised you had made a mistake by making us so visible. You might as well have served us up on a silver plate.'

'Oh, like you had a better plan!'

'I was shouting at you to hide but you wouldn't listen to me!'

'Please don't argue. It sounds like you went through something really dangerous and thank God you survived. Be grateful that you are still both here,' Iosefka pleaded.

It was enough to stop the two from arguing. Amelia turned her back to Adam and walked away to sit on the ground alone. She had more scratches, blood and mud on her than anyone else.

About ten minutes later, Caesar returned, a few specks of blood staining his doublet and trousers. 'Pierre has explained the situation to me and I can now say that all is safe. The Questing Beast has been killed. It never should have made it into the forest and a thorough search will be conducted to discover how this has happened. Now everyone follow me.'

Without any further information or apology for putting them in such a dangerous situation, Caesar led all the new students around the outskirts of the camp. As they went, those who were training stared at them curiously, whispering and pointing at those who they thought could be powerful and important, and who would be dead by the end of the year.

'Think of this as your first day as a living person,' Caesar said, having led the hundreds of students into an open field of grass off to the side of the training students. 'My name is Caesar. I am in charge here at Camp Paragon. My say is final. My authority shall never be questioned. When I tell you to do something, you shall do it. Follow these rules and then you will never have to deal with my fury.'

'Is that it?' Kaya whispered to Adam. 'You could have died and he doesn't seem to care at all.'

'WHAT DID YOU SAY?!' Caesar made every single person jump out of their skin as he shouted at Kaya.

'N-n-nothing.' Kaya was just as terrified as everyone else.

'Do not ever interrupt me! Do you understand?'

'Completely understand. Won't happen again.' Kaya spoke as fast as he could.

'Good.' Caesar's voice returned to its slightly quieter volume that could still easily be heard by everyone. 'On the matter of the attack, there is nothing to be done. If you had died, you would have been given a proper funeral, but you all survived, even those that the beast attacked. This shows me that I have a competent group of students who may become great warriors in the future.'

This made a lot of students stand a little straighter in pride, acting as if they had done something special by doing what everyone else did every year but with a threat nearby that they hadn't noticed or encountered.

'Here in Camp Paragon, you have the opportunity to become great warriors. The spark of magic is the gift of Hope, but do not think that it is easy to learn. It will take months of studying for some of you to cast the simplest of spells. For others it will take days. Some of you may not have been deemed worthy at all. If you do not look for someone to mentor you, you will not learn how to fight, and you will not learn how to survive out in the Wildlands.'

Every single student was listening to Caesar intently. He spoke with such confidence and authority that they all hung on to each of his words, desperate to hear the next.

'As of this moment, none of you have permission to leave camp. You are less than the other students at this camp. You will spend your time learning and training for a month, whereupon you will all be tested in our coliseum stadium, to see how far you have come. Whether you fail or succeed at the challenge presented to you, you will become an official member of Camp Paragon, a true student. This allows you to leave the camp boundaries for the city and anywhere else you wish. This challenge is in place to show everyone, including yourselves, how far you have managed to come, and it will also be what determines your team totem.

'In exactly one year from today, no matter how much you have trained, each group will be sent on their own unique expedition into the Wildlands. This is your chance to be a true fighter and for me to see who is capable of venturing out into unexplored lands. This expedition should be taken with absolute seriousness. There has not been a single year where every group has come back alive. My students who have been here for a year have just recently come back from their first expedition. Thirteen have died. Make sure that this year you are not one of them.

'I do not doubt that you are all eager to start training.' Caesar pointed to a set of stone stairs that were shrouded by thick bushes and bright orange trees. 'Those steps will lead you to the Monastery, where many of our Elysium monks reside. Almost all of them are willing to teach. These monks are adept at the fundamentals of combat and magic. I would highly recommend you gain as much information from them as possible. As a resident at camp, you are given access to free food in the Food Hall and accommodation. You have Micholesh to thank for this.

'Those who make it back from the Wildlands will move onto their second year, where you will start to be assigned expeditions, going out into the Wildlands and the other monster-infested areas, searching for ruins that hold treasures, killing monsters that threaten to harm us, and adventure to where we have yet to explore. It should be noted that any treasure you find is the property of your team unless it is decided that an item is too powerful to be wielded. On that rare occasion, the team will be handsomely compensated and the item placed into the Mausoleum of the Gods to be kept safe. Also, any scrolls found will need to be given to a monk or disciple so that everyone can work to unravel their mysteries and gain from its knowledge. However, these are things to know for much later on in your time at camp. For now, feel free to explore, talk to the other residents and most importantly learn as much as you can in preparation for your coliseum task.'

9. The Cherry Blossom Tree

Immediately after Caesar's speech, hundreds of students ran over to the training grounds. They grabbed different weapons from the weapon racks and started swinging them randomly at the dummies. Adam and Amelia made a beeline straight for the steps that led up to the Monastery, wanting to get the best mentor monk they could find.

'What are these scrolls that everyone keeps talking about?' Iosefka asked, trying to keep up.

'Did they not teach you about scrolls in school? It was one of the first things we were taught.' Adam said.

'I've never been to school,' Iosefka admitted.

'What!' The other three shouted.

'My parents chose to home school me all my life.'

'You've got to be kidding me,' Amelia moaned. 'You don't know anything about this world at all?'

'No, sorry. I didn't think I would have to be a burden on others when I came here,' she said bluntly.

'Hey, you're not a burden,' Adam said to her. 'We've all got problems, and we can work through them together. Scrolls are how we discovered how to use magic. They are these pieces of coded parchment that have rubbish clues and riddles on them, and once you decode the scroll, it changes into a guide for casting a specific spell left behind by whoever the last race on Elysium was.'

'It's not rubbish what's written on them,' Amelia interjected. 'They are some of the most interesting puzzles and mental challenges someone can complete. I don't even know how much I care about the spell it unlocks when the process is so fascinating. I suppose you know absolutely nothing then?'

'Don't listen to her,' Kaya said firmly. 'Like Adam said, you're not a burden to us. It was just a surprise, that's all.'

'That means a lot to me, thank you,' Iosefka said to Adam and Kaya. 'I promise you won't have to carry me around all the time, I have plenty to offer. I just need some time to get used to everything. These scrolls do seem pretty neat, how do we find them?'

'They're all around the world,' Adam responded before Amelia could. 'They can usually be found in old ruins or temples, filled with traps, or even being protected by a monster.'

Adam had made the mistake of breathing and in that gap, Amelia stepped in. 'There are plenty of powerful scrolls containing magic that is incredibly challenging to conjure like Necromancy, which only Gonti ever learnt and he refused to teach anyone who followed him. Disciple Peter let slip to me about a body-switching spell that was incredibly complex but would allow the caster to switch bodies with someone, keeping all their memories and knowledge whilst gaining what the other person had known. I also overheard some people talking at the feast about a possible scroll that people think, when solved, will explain how to cast an entirely new vein of magic.'

After she was done explaining, Amelia walked ahead of the group with her head high, acting like she was the one leading the group.

The steps leading up to the Monastery were surrounded by orange leaves on thin trees arcing inwards, creating a tunnel that led up to the highest step. Hand-carved stone statues sat peacefully at the end of every couple of steps. Well-kept moss growing out from parts of the otherwise spotless figures, from the mouth of a phoenix, in-between the toes of a tiny troll and from the ears of elves and fairies.

The bright leaves were fascinating to them all. Not only were they a great opportunity to see a different kind of tree from the ones filling the forests, but it was also surprising to see that not a single leaf had fallen onto any of the steps. It was as if someone was prepared and waiting in the shadows, waiting to catch and clean anything that longed to touch the floor.

Once they had reached the top of the orange tunnel, the trees opened up and showed them a view of what felt like a different time. In front of them – like a perfect painting – was an immense Japanese Monastery.

A wooden floor led them to the entrance with a serene pool to the side, filled with water so clear, it looked like it wasn't there at all. Fat koi fish glided through the water in mesmerising synchronisation, their red and orange colours mixing with the trees that surrounded the borders around the building.

The Monastery itself was made solely from wood. All the structure and support beams were dark oak, and the walls were smooth white wood. It was strange to have seen the Greek-style Sanctuary guarding the portal at the top of Mount Ida yesterday, to head down into a city filled with all kinds of houses from the English Victorian era to fat mansions, to now be stood in front of a great Monastery. It was the kind of building that monks would have used thousands of years ago atop the peaks of the highest mountains where they lived in complete solitude.

The four of them made their way inside, taking in the hall's grandeur and grace. Along all the walls ran tapestries depicting different moments of importance in Elysium, similar to the doors into the Pantheon, but these were much more detailed and filled with colour.

Adam was immediately drawn to a tapestry that caught his eye. A blade being pulled from stone, a blinding light emanating from the tip, as though it were a holy sun. There was only one sword he knew depicted like that. Excalibur. That meant the woman pulling it was... It was the first time Adam had seen any kind of picture of his mother. It was a peculiar feeling.

He didn't find himself tearing up as he had been before at the thought of her. So much of his life had been spent resenting his parents for dumping him on Earth, but now hearing about them, and finally seeing what his mother looked like, how she had the same brown hair with a small streak of blonde at the side, humanised them.

It had been easy hating something he didn't know, but now as he stared at the small intricate depiction of his mother, he found that his old hate started to bloom into pride. He only wished that he would have been around to see his parents in action and to be part of their stories.

'Hello,' a calm voice said lightly from behind.

Adam turned around to find a short bald man in an orange robe that covered most of his body, exposing only his right shoulder and arm, had greeted them. The bright fabric seemed thick and durable and was carefully folded over and tucked in to stay tightly on the monk, who had thick bushy eyebrows and a wrinkly face. His hands were lightly clasping by his stomach and Adam noticed that his knuckles were hard and thick.

'Hello,' Amelia answered for Adam, who had been caught off guard by how quietly the monk had managed to get behind him.

'I can see a soup of emotions swirling within you. Can I help?' The monk said in the same calm tone without breaking his eye contact with Adam.

'Oh, no, it's fine. I'll be fine, I was just – it's nothing.' Adam found it hard to concentrate with the monk's unwavering focus on him.

'I understand. You have only just met me. You don't want to divulge your deepest fears and aspirations so easily, this is wise. There are many people who would use that against you, but I would recommend talking to someone about your emotions. Keeping everything enclosed within yourself is never good, especially when it can lead to anger. Anger clouds judgment and leads to recklessness.'

Finally, the monk broke his eye contact by blinking and slowly turning to face the rest of the group.

'My name is Papil, and should you want me, I will be glad to be your mentor. To teach you how to wield magic.'

'That would be great, thank you so much!' Kaya exclaimed.

'That's very kind of you, sir, but in the nicest possible way, how do we know you are the best-suited mentor for us?' Amelia asked.

Kaya scowled at Amelia, certain that she had just lost the chance to have a mentor.

'That is a good question,' Papil said, which made Kaya roll his eyes. 'I am the head of all the monks here in the Monastery, and I am one of the most knowledgeable in this camp.'

'That's fantastic,' Iosefka said.

'Then why have you chosen us?' Adam questioned. 'I'm guessing we are one of the first groups to visit. If you are one of the most knowledgeable monks here, you know that it's important not to rush into decisions. Why offer to be our mentor when you barely know us?'

'It's true that you are one of the first groups I have seen, but it is false to think that I do not know you. Actions can tell a lot about a person, and from watching you, I have decided that you are people that deserve my teachings, should you want it, that is.'

'Yes, yes, of course we want it,' Kaya pleaded. 'We would be honoured to be taught by you.'

'I did just survive an attack from a Questing Beast, after all,' Amelia said to herself as though this was the reason why Papil had chosen them all.

'A Questing Beast? It came after you?' Papil started to rub his hands against each other in thought like he was washing them without any water.

'It came after Amelia and I in the forest next to the training grounds outside,' Adam explained.

'That's wrong,' Amelia argued.

'No, it's not, that's what happened. The thing came sprinting at both of us and if I hadn't saved you, you'd be dead.'

'Firstly, I can look after myself, and secondly, it is Amelia and *me* not "Amelia and *I*".'

'Are you aware of the significance of a Questing Beast coming after *either* of you?' Papil asked.

They shook their heads.

'I don't know much about them, but I know they were a part of Arthurian legend,' Amelia added, not wanting to seem stupid.

'For the most part, they are the same as the old legends, but like most brought to creation in this world, there have been aspects of their nature that have changed. For example, it has been noted that the Questing Beast only hunts those who have the potential for royalty.'

'So, Adam's going to be king?' Kaya asked, nudging Adam in excitement.

'No, he means that I will be queen,' Amelia argued.

'I mean that one, or both of you, have the potential to rule this land, it does not make it your destiny, I do not believe there is such a thing,' Papil stated. 'You each decide your future no matter any prophecy that comes to light or what may be written in the stars. It is your actions that will lead you to the person you become and circumstance can only have so much of an effect.'

'But surely prophecies always come to fruition. It is God's way of acting from behind his curtain. People who can work out what is "written in the stars" are simply able to glimpse at God's master plan,' Iosefka said with a small frown.

'We are getting into deep philosophical topics, which are certainly interesting and important to have, but they can be had another time. Adam, Amelia, the Questing Beast has hunted many, especially during the war. It has gone after Gonti the Necromancer, Gerard the Unstoppable, of course Micholesh himself, and plenty of others, and only one has become what is as close to royalty as we have in Elysium. Do not let this experience get to your head, there is still much to happen before either of you will be able to lead anything. Now if you will all excuse me, I have a lot that I need to do. I expect you back here at dawn tomorrow to start our training.'

With that, Papil walked silently away, not making so much as a creak on the wooden flooring as he went.

As they made their way outside, they noticed several groups of new students talking to other monks, all dressed in the same orange robes. Olivia's group was speaking to one next to the koi pond, and she gave an awkward smile as they passed.

Even as they walked down the stairs, they found a group speaking with another monk. Adam wondered if they really had been hiding in the shadows, waiting to see what each group was drawn most to.

As they made their way back into the open area, they had a better look around the training grounds that was split into two sections.

The main area at the centre of the camp was all used for physical training with mostly steel weapons placed around on racks. It was filled with annoyed students struggling to get their daily practice in with all the new students watching them and getting in their way.

The other half was a few fields separate from anything else in the camp and it was where students practiced their magic.

Fighting rings were scattered around the large field. However, unlike the simple rope borders used for the weapons training area, these stages were made of the dark purple obsidian and were raised from the ground by a few feet.

The dummies were also made from obsidian instead of straw and were sculped to look like different monsters. At this time in the day, there was only one team practising against an obsidian cyclops.

One student was throwing fireballs at its eye, each time having to perform the same repetition of hand and arm movements to spark the ball of fire in their hand. As each fireball hit the cyclops's eye, the obsidian around the heat would immediately glow blue and the flame would be extinguished by the freezing cold the dummy made.

Whilst the student practiced their aim and speed with the fireballs, two other students in the team were on their knees, their hands planted onto the ground as they made grass grow around the cyclops's feet and wrap around it, keeping it in place.

In retaliation of the magic, the obsidian feet started to glow a deep orange from within, which then turned to a hot red that set the grass alight, causing it to break off and burn.

The students making the grass move at such an unnatural speed weren't muttering any words or moving their hands to cast the magic. Instead, their eyes were closed, and their skin appeared to grow whiter and sicklier the longer they willed the grass to grow.

Kaya gave Adam a nudge with his elbow. They both stopped so that Amelia and Iosefka wandered off ahead, towards what looked like a coliseum blocked from view by several lines of tall trees.

'Hey, you know how you said you wanted to find that artefact of Gerard's? Well, when you were in the forest with that monster fighting for your life, which is still insane to me that something like that can just happen and Caesar doesn't seem to care at all about how easily it got there, like it wasn't exactly quiet I could feel the earth shaking so it must have been massive –'

'Kaya, you're trailing like an actor that forgot their lines. Don't worry about the attack. I'm sure it's being looked into properly, and I managed to survive. I'm not going down that easily. Now, what were you saying about the greatsword?'

'Right, well, I overheard a group talking about a new student from Elysium whose parents were both Ascensionists.'

'That sounds like someone who would take the greatsword, Gerard said it was powerful enough to end the world. And if this person got their hands on it, they would do just that to try and open another portal to heaven.'

'That's exactly what I thought.'

'Fantastic, we can add them to the suspect list. Do you know what they look like?'

'Yeah, he's just gone up that hill.' Kaya pointed at a steep grass hill on the outskirts of the camp that had nothing surrounding it, except for a single cherry blossom tree at the top.

'Well, then I think we should go and have a chat with him.'

Adam and Kaya made their way over to the new student, leaving the other two members of their team behind. As soon as they made their way to the top of the hill, they were met with a vibrant explosion of pink from the cherry blossom tree's leaves, which managed to stand out from the cosmic sky in a way that nothing else had.

Planks of thin wood had been constructed into the ground, circling around the trunk of the tree so that when the pink leaves started to fall, they would go onto the sand that filled the wooden ring.

The sand itself was of two different colours, half white and the other half black, and had been raked in a way to resemble the yin and yang symbol. Two perfectly smooth round rocks of black and white had been positioned within the contrasting colour of sand to complete the symbol.

The student Kaya had spoken about was standing behind the tree at the edge of the hill which appeared to be a cliff face with a drop of several hundred feet down to the smooth beach below, forming the edge of the Ocean of the Damned.

Adam watched as the student stared off far into the distance where there was nothing but the open ocean and the wind blowing against their drawn face. They wore thick baggy trousers and an oversized hazel hoodie that covered the rest of their body, which would have done a good job of hiding how malnourished the person was if the wind wasn't pushing the fabric up to their chest. Adam noticed that the cuff on both the student's sleeves, that went over their hands, were burnt black.

Before Adam or Kaya could introduce themselves, the student turned around, hearing them approaching him. His Adam's apple protruded from his neck and his bony face tensed as he saw them.

'What do you want with me?' He asked, his voice deep for his young age.

'What's your name?' Adam asked, feeling sorry for him, even though his parents had been Ascensionists.

'Duke. Now leave me alone, or else.' Duke brought his fists out of the sleeves of his hoodie, ready to fight.

'We don't want any trouble,' Kaya said, stretching his hands out trying to calm Duke.

'We just want to ask a few questions,' Adam explained.

'About what? My parents? That's all anyone wants. Like I told everyone else, I never met them and I have nothing to do with them, they've left me in this damn world with nothing except for the people's hate.' Duke's bright blue eyes seemed to darken as he grew angrier.

'What do you know about Gerard's greatsword?' Adam asked firmly.

Duke's fists fell a little with the shock of the question. 'Who do you think you are? You think that you can come into this world and act like a Disciple. You're still wearing those disgusting Earth clothes! I've done nothing!'

'You're getting awfully defensive for someone who's done nothing,' Kaya said, getting ready for a fight.

'I may be one of the lowest bits of scum in Elysium, but anyone from Elysium is still superior to those from Earth, and you cannot talk to me like this!'

As Adam and Kaya had been expecting, Duke attacked them. But instead of running at them, Duke struck his fists in the air, and with each strike, the air around his hand seemed to shake. Then before Adam or Kaya had a chance to approach closer, a line of fire materialised from Duke's hands, which he used like a whip to strike just next to Kaya, making a loud cracking and then hissing noise as it struck the air, shooting off little flames that caught Kaya's shirt.

'Ow, ow, ow!' Kaya shouted as he patted his arm, putting out the small fire.

'Now leave me alone!' Duke was holding onto the fire like it was a toy, his hands completely unharmed from the line of fire.

Adam and Kaya slowly retreated back down the hill.

'This isn't over,' Adam yelled, staring at Duke, humiliated with how useless he felt.

'It never is.'

10. Team bonding

'Well, that sucked.' Kaya winced as he patted his arm where the fire had burnt the fabric black.

'Yes, it did.'

They had been stupid for confronting Duke so early. Now it would be all the more difficult to find out if he had any connection to the greatsword.

They found Amelia and Iosefka waiting in a long queue that led to another forest, separated from the Wildlands and more open than the one they had just been through.

Joining the line, Adam noticed a monk at the end of the queue, giving out a piece of wood to each group. The line backed up towards a large dark green tent, its canvas-flap entrance held open by a bamboo pole and thick rope. Inside were rows of beds with jars scattered around filled with all kinds of thick pastes, ointments, and herbs.

'What's that?' Kaya asked.

'The infirmary, obviously,' Amelia scolded.

The line moved quickly and the four soon found themselves at the front walking toward the young monk. She was huffing every time she moved and shoved a piece of oval wood towards Iosefka. 'Here, take this,' she grunted. 'When you find a cabin that doesn't have one of these on the front door, that will be your cabin for the foreseeable future. Place it on the front door and in a month, once you have received your animal to be your team totem, we will carve it onto the piece of wood for you.'

'Is there anything you can tell us about the different totems we can get? How are they decided? Is there some kind of scoring system?' Amelia questioned.

'I don't know, maybe,' the monk replied.

'Come on, let's just find our cabin.' Adam didn't want to bother the monk any more than they had to.

'Is everything alright?' Iosefka asked.

With a long sigh that made her long blonde hair fall across her face, the monk spoke again, still in the same frustrated tone as she moved her hair behind her ear. 'They're still not letting me be a mentor. I've been a monk for three years and they still won't let me do the one thing I want to do. To share one's knowledge with someone else is the highest level of understanding a person can achieve. For someone to know nothing about magic and to be able to teach them at the very least a basic understanding would be such an incredible feeling. But according to Papil, I'm not ready yet. It's so frustrating he won't so much as tell me why.'

'Hey, that's the dude who's going to be – ow!' Kaya shouted as Amelia stepped on his foot.

'Well, don't worry about it too much. There's got to be so much to learn before you can start mentoring someone, and you seem so young, I'm sure next year he'll let you.' Amelia stared into the monk's deep hazel eyes.

'That's very kind of you, but who knows? Anyway, I hope you four find a nice cabin.'

'What's your name?' Amelia asked.

'Theta,' she replied.

'Theta? Like the letter in the Greek alphabet?' Amelia responded as the rest of the group stood around waiting for the conversation to end. 'That's super cool, does that mean your parents were Hellenists?'

'Yeah, that's right. In the early days, like almost everyone, they believed in the Greek gods, but they barely did any research into it, I mean, my name means death. Not exactly the kind of name someone would give a baby if they were thinking properly. Then my whole family left the idea of Hellenism behind and moved over to a more agnostic view, which is one good thing they've done because otherwise I would have been forced to become a Charon's Disciple, and they're all so pretentious and self-loving.'

'I know, you should see the way they spoke to us when we came through the portal. None of them could be bothered to answer a single question I asked.'

'That sounds about right for them. But listen, if you ever have any questions about anything, come to me. Despite what Papil may think, I know a lot about what this world has to offer, and I would be happy to help you.'

'I'll be sure to take you up on that offer, I've got loads of questions, and it looks like it's going to be a while before I can access the Bibliotech.' Amelia unconsciously ran her hand through her shaggy hair, moving it out of the way of her face.

Amelia waved goodbye as they left, and Adam noticed that during their conversation, the line leading up to Theta had grown substantially.

As they made their way farther into the open forest, they found different cabins, each identical in appearance, made out of the same light oak. The only thing different about the design of each cabin was the animal carving on the piece of wood hung up on the doors, ranging from the fierce dragon down to a measly ant.

Whilst the cabins all looked identical, their location was completely different to each other. Some were high up on hills, some half-covered in bushes. They even saw one that had a tree going through the roof and another that was simply a tree house.

Amelia pointed at each team totem, talking loudly to Iosefka about them, whether they were a mythical creature or extinct from Earth.

'One thing I don't understand,' Iosefka started to say as Amelia finished talking about a griffin, 'is the difference between a creature and a monster?'

Amelia grinned as she got ready for her perfect monologue. 'A creature is like you and me. They are classed as something that, in their most fundamental state, has a will to survive above all else. This usually means that it will only attack when provoked or if they need to do so for food. Some humans have been known to hurt and kill others not to survive, but for personal gain. Whilst this makes them a bad person, they are doing it, at the very least, for a reason intended to aid their survival. Now a monster, in its simplest state, will always prioritise killing and causing harm over anything else. They will often put their safety below the need to kill. A monster cannot be reasoned with. For example, the Questing Beast, it would have...'

Amelia's assertive voice started to falter and she slowed her march through the woods, her face loosened just like how Mrs Blake's had in Kiwi High when she had thought back to old memories.

'That Questing Beast would have stopped at nothing to kill us. Papil said that its sole purpose was to kill one of us. It probably started chasing us the moment we came through the portal and only caught up with us in the forest. I could have died if that man didn't save us.' The reality of the situation seemed to have fully caught up to Amelia and she looked to be on the verge of tears.

'But he did save us.' Adam didn't care to try and explain again that he also helped save her life.

'Even so, we aren't ready for this. Everyone from Earth I spoke to, they all talked about the danger, but I didn't realise it was this bad.'

'I don't want to die here.' Iosefka's eyes were wide open as she started hyperventilating.

'Calm down, so we weren't told the full picture, and I'm sure there are other things we haven't been told, but it's worth it.' Adam was talking himself down from a panic attack just as much as he was helping the others.

'But in fairness, it's the second day and the two of you almost got slaughtered,' Kaya said, as they came to a stop, looking at each other as they started to realise the reality of Elysium.

'It's still worth it.' Adam was absolute now. He had chosen this path to go to Elysium and he was ready for all the danger and all the excitement that came with it.

'Yes – yes, you're right, for once. We were saved. It is safe enough in this camp, and soon, I'll be strong enough to protect myself.' Amelia's straight posture returned, and her voice reclaimed its fire as she continued leading the team farther into the forest.

'But what if it isn't safe?' Iosefka seemed seconds away from running back towards the portal.

'It is, and we are a team. We won't let anything hurt you,' Adam said placing his hand gently on her shoulder as they continued their search for a home.

Gradually, Iosefka calmed down with the support of Adam and Kaya telling her that she would be safe.

After almost ten minutes of searching the forest for an empty cabin, they started to find front doors without a creature drawn into their piece of wood and after a few more minutes of looking around, they found a nice cabin that wasn't too far off the beaten path.

To reach the cabin entrance, they had to steadily walk down a steep hill, which was the start of a long decline that would lead straight down to the beach Adam and Kaya had seen from the cliff face by the cherry blossom tree. An interesting aspect of the cabin was that it was planted into the hill they were descending, to the point where someone could slide onto the edge of the roof from the main path and dangle their legs over the entrance.

The four of them made their way to the entrance and, claiming the house as their own, Iosefka placed the piece of wood on the front door. It was a strange feeling, knowing that the cabin they were about to step into would be their home in this brand-new world.

From the moment they walked into the cabin, it was clear it had never been used. The entrance led into a large open area that served as both a kitchen and a living room, a layer of dust over everything. An old brown sofa along with a few worn armchairs of the same dark brown that would be cosy once cleaned up were positioned near a grimy fireplace.

The fireplace appeared to be the only way of keeping the house warm with four oil lanterns left on the wooden kitchen counter to use as a source of light in the night. They were the kind of lanterns that could be held by their steel handles as the old caretaker crept around the spooky mansion, the dancing flame from inside the thick glass barely breaking through the darkness, down the pitch-black ghost halls.

Adam didn't much like the look of those oil lanterns. They made him feel uneasy from all the old horror movies he had watched, and he hoped that he never had to walk in the dark with only the lantern as company.

The four bedrooms were almost completely barren, containing some thick black curtains for the windows, an oak wardrobe, and a small bed with a side table next to it. Amelia took the bedroom immediately to the left of the front door. Iosefka took the one next to it, with Kaya and Adam taking the ones across from the living room which, Adam only realised after opening the blinds, were at the back of the house – which meant that their window view was that of a dirt wall, blocking any natural light into the room.

Still, it would do, and neither of them complained about it out loud. They wouldn't be spending much time in there, as there was far too much to do outside. Whilst each person showered, the others worked to clean the cabin up a little, removing as much of the dust as possible, which made the showering feel pointless.

Having cleaned themselves up along with their new home, they headed back outside to see what else they could find around camp.

Cotton-white clouds drifted through the deep blue sky that mixed artfully with the cosmic colours above. By this point in the day, the new students seemed to have tired themselves out, swinging around the different weapons in the training grounds, allowing everyone else to get on with their practice.

Almost all of the ringed areas were being occupied by teams practising against one another, using blunt weapons. The group that attracted the attention of Adam was currently practising a three-on-one situation. A burly girl wearing thin leather armour, with long red hair braided down her back, fought with her fists against three other armed students, two wielding swords and the other a small axe.

Even at this massive disadvantage, she was holding her own exceptionally well, dodging and weaving around with near-perfect precision. Then noticing the slightest gap in the three's defence, she slipped past one of the swords and threw a punch that landed on the person's hand.

Adam had never seen a punch so powerful before. The sword fell to the floor as the sound of several fingers breaking cracked through the air. From there, she moved elegantly around the attacks of the other two, punching one in the leg, breaking their bone and dropping them to the floor.

The last attacker was the one with the axe, which proved useless as a shield as she tried to stop the flurry of punches that came their way. In moments, she too was down on the floor.

Victorious, the attacking student walked over to their teammate with the broken leg, pulled up her trouser leg, and gripped the skin with her left hand, making the young woman wince. The red-haired warrior then placed her right hand on the grass. Slowly the green grass started to turn grey as it withered away, and Adam watched as the student's leg started to mend, the bone snapping back into place.

At the same time, the one with the broken hand fixed his injuries, using the grass to heal themselves, and started to heal the other unconscious team member using the same kind of healing magic.

Exploring the camp a little more, they found where they would be eating – another massive building that looked similar to the Pantheon, except that it was made from wood and had been scaled down to populate a few thousand instead of tens of thousands.

Inside felt like the heart of the camp. Burning fireplaces scattered around the sides warmed the entire room. It felt like they were wrapped inside a thick cosy blanket. Sturdy wooden pillars held up the building from inside, and in the gap between one pillar and the next were tables filled with food that were constantly being replenished by the monks.

The ceiling was only half painted. One half was still the ordinary wooden ceiling whilst the other half was as detailed as the Sistine Chapel had been, painted elegantly with gorgeous art of the Greek gods. Zeus and Poseidon sat arm-in-arm, the sea and the sky connected as one. Smaller drawings of the other lesser gods like Dionysus and Hermes were dotted here and there, enjoying a splendid feast, as nymphs and demigods danced around each other. It made Adam wonder if Elysium was once inhabited by those Gods like the Charon's Disciples believed.

In the centre of the hall were several long tables, their edges worn down from so many people banging into them over the years. Bored students waiting on their friends to finish eating had littered the wood with chips and carvings. On each side of the tables were complimentary wooden benches that had received as much love as the tables.

At the top of the hall, like in the Pantheon, was a high table currently empty. This table paled in comparison to the quality of the one in the Pantheon but it was still bigger, grander, and finer than the tables the students sat at and each member who was important enough to sit at the table had their own fancy handcrafted chairs.

The hall was filled with mellow chatter that all clumped together to create a harmony of white noise. The taste of food was still just as fantastic as it had been yesterday. Adam spent his time trying everything he could, finding out what foods he liked and what he found disgusting. He had almost thrown up when he tried an avocado and had to discretely spit out a grizzly piece of bacon.

As they ate, Amelia lectured Iosefka on everything she would have missed out on having not been to school. Adam chimed in when he could to add some information, but Amelia was making a point of showing how much more she knew than him.

'Disciple Peter mentioned a small library around camp other than the one the monks use and I think that should be the next thing we go to. Apparently, the only books there are the ones in bad shape or the ones that don't have all that much useful information, but anything helps,' Amelia said.

'Really, a library?' Kaya whined. 'Have you not seen where we are? You want to go to a library?'

'It's the best way to get ahead of everyone if we learn as much as we can about what's been discovered so far.'

'Amelia's right. Don't worry, we won't spend long there,' Adam conceded.

It took Amelia about an hour of searching to find the library because it looked like a child's fortress, which needed a lot of imagination to come to life rather than something that held a wealth of knowledge.

The shack was so haphazardly built, it seemed like a big bad wolf really could blow on it to get to the little piggies inside. There was even a rancid smell coming from inside that Adam imagined was what a wolf's mouth smelt like.

The front door was battered and falling off its hinges. Amelia gave it a delicate push and the four of them all squeezed in. It seemed like nobody had visited the tiny shack in a very long time. On a dirty wooden table sat several piles of dusty books, covered in cobwebs and stacked so carelessly that several had fallen onto the floor.

The smell came from a book at the top of one of the piles closest to them and Adam thought about chucking it outside so that he didn't have to deal with the stench.

Amelia let out a small whimper as she picked up one of the books on the floor to find that its cover immediately ripped off. The crinkled thin paper within the book then started to split from the spine as she handled it.

'This can't be real,' Amelia whispered.

'At least nobody will interrupt you when reading,' Kaya joked.

'How could they treat these books with such little respect, there could be so much useful information hidden under all this dust and dirt.'

At that moment Kaya leant against one of the shelves. It instantly fell apart, bringing all the books crashing to the floor. For a while, Amelia just stared in silence at the new mound of books that Kaya had fallen down with.

'We need to take these back to the cabin,' she finally said.

'What?' Adam blurted.

'Here take these.' She found a pile of sacks and a gave a large one to each person. 'Fill them with as many books as you can, but be careful, we don't want to damage them more than they already are.'

The sheer determination in her voice ceased any disagreement. The four of them spent almost an hour attentively moving the parchments and books into their sacks, coughing and wheezing every time someone disturbed a layer of dust.

Getting all the books back to the cabin turned out to be much harder than any of them thought as the harsh material of the sack rubbed the skin off their fingers and the book edges stabbed their backs.

A few people glanced at the four of them as they made their way through camp, but quickly went back to training or with their conversations. They also passed Duke, his hood up as he walked through the training grounds. He smirked when he saw the small burn mark he had left on Kaya's clothes, but other than that did nothing to the two.

As they made their way down the slope to their cabin, Iosefka almost tripped over some weeds and would have tumbled down the hill if Adam hadn't grabbed onto her shoulder. Unfortunately, in doing so, he dropped his sack onto the ground. Its contents spilled out, covering them in dirt, with some pages ripping apart and flying away with the wind.

Amelia dropped her sack by the front door as she tried to grab the floating pieces from the sky, but she was far too short and the wind – whilst not particularly strong – made fine work of sweeping away the information that was so dear to her.

'I can't believe you, Adam! How could you be so reckless!' She shouted.

'Come on, I didn't complain once when you wanted us to take all of these stupid books all across camp, and now you're acting like I haven't just done you a massive favour.'

'Oh, thank you for being so kind as to help me out, and for not complaining at the impossible task I asked you to do, but excuse me for not being grateful that you've lost half the books you were meant to be carrying!'

'Just calm down,' Adam said.

'I will not calm down! This isn't just about the books anymore, it's about you and Kaya always ganging up on me, always belittling me and trying to make me seem like a weaker leader. I won't have it anymore. This isn't a fair way to decide who will lead this group.'

'What are you talking about, when did we belittle you? And I don't even know what we were doing in the first place to decide who was going to leader, but by the sounds of it, I was going to win, and you can't deal with it so now you're looking for some other invisible task to get your way!' Adam had done his best to be civil but this was the straw that broke his back, the cherry on top of this awful person the Disciples had put him with.

'That is not true! But fine, if you want to be this team's leader so bad then just try! You train Kaya, and I'll train Iosefka. We all get tutored by Papil but everything else we do separately. In a month, whoever is the better team during the Coliseum challenge gets to be the leader.'

'That's fine by me. Me and Kaya have been training all our lives for this, you've never even been in a fight.'

'And so, it will be all the more crushing when *Iosefka* and *I* outperform you in every single way,' Amelia boasted. 'Come on, Iosefka, we have a lot to learn.'

Amelia dragged all the sacks inside and into her bedroom with Iosefka who hadn't gotten a say in anything that had just happened.

11. Magic is Power

Wanting to get away from Amelia, Adam and Kaya left the cabin and made their way back to the training grounds. They spent hours testing out all of the available weapons, ranging from small blunt daggers and kunai all the way to greatswords that neither of them could lift.

They practised until the sun started to set. Adam spent the time taking out all of his pent-up pain and anger on the dummies, swinging at them with all of his strength over and over until his already blistered fingers started to bleed.

Just as Adam and Kaya were going to call it a day, the air filled with the ringing of a gong being struck in the distance, so loud that it echoed through the entire camp. Hearing the noise, all the students still training made their way towards it. Following the crowd, Adam quickly realised that they were going towards the Food Hall. Asking another student, he found out that it was time for the Fighter's Feast.

After having built up an appetite, Adam and Kaya ravaged their food once again, trying to ignore the pain in their hands every time they picked up a new piece of food. It was a miracle that neither of them had choked on any food yet. Being as exhausted as they were, the food tasted like it came from the hand of a god.

Along their table, people were chatting away about what they had seen throughout the day. All the new students from Earth had instinctively grouped together on one table in the centre of the room. When Adam had first been in the Food Hall, it was relatively empty, but now people were having to squeeze in to fit on the tables.

The high table now had all its seats filled. Caesar sat in the centre. Papil, their new mentor, sat reading a piece of parchment to his left, with two more people that Adam hadn't met to the left. To the right of Caesar, Adam was very surprised to see Gerard talking to a large muscular man with a brutish face, making him look like a rough prison warden.

At the very end of the table, Pierre devoured some meat from its bone, his clothes still ripped and shredded, his body covered in dried blood.

Once everyone had eaten their fill, Caesar stood from his chair and motioned for the hall to quiet, which it did immediately.

'Those of you who have arrived today, this is a feast in your name, to celebrate the potential you all have to be outstanding fighters. We also have the honour of welcoming Gerard the Unstoppable as a guest.'

The hall erupted with cheers and whistles as Gerard stood up from his chair and gave a big grin and laugh, waving at everyone.

Caesar didn't command the room to stop cheering and clapping. He waited – looking almost bored – for Gerard to take his seat before speaking again. 'As I am sure you have all heard, there was an attack this morning. A Questing Beast hunted two of my new students and attacked them in the forest where I have the obstacle course.'

Everyone looked over to the table where the first-year students sat and whispers quickly started. Adam watched students point towards him, look him up and down, and then go back to whispering. Adam tried to work out what they were saying but unlike the Pantheon, everyone's words melted together. But from the smirks and looks of dismissal, it was clear they all thought his destiny for royalty would never be fulfilled.

'I want you all to understand that this is not a common occurrence. Camp Paragon is safe and this is the first direct attack in over four years. As my older students should know, a Questing Beast hunts a specific person and doesn't stop hunting until it finds them. This is an unfortunate situation but even with the monster's determination, the two students only had to survive its attacks for mere seconds before Pierre the Devil Hunter managed to catch up and dispatch of the threat.'

A few people tried to cheer for Pierre the Devil Hunter but he was still wolfing down a pile of mashed potatoes with his hands, the fluffy white food turning a shade of grey with tinges of red as the filth and blood left his hands.

'Moving on, this Fighters' Feast is also in place to show you what can be achieved at the highest levels of magic we have uncovered so far.'

Caesar moved his hands with open palms. When he swung, he did so with precision and authority, like a martial artist bringing the side of their hand down onto a stack of bricks. It was slower and more thoughtful than how Micholesh and Duke had moved when casting a fire spell. Each time his arm finished its arc, a compressed gust of wind shot out from his hands, as though there was so much power being built up, some of it was leaking out of him.

Then with his final move, he clapped his hands together, perfectly symmetrical with the centre of his body. The clap sent out a shockwave of pressurized air all around the hall, blowing out every fire in its wake. The force of the wind pushed everyone backwards, sliding them down a couple of places in their seats, the people at the far end falling off of the bench entirely.

As the students slid back up the benches, Caesar knelt on the wooden floor where a hole showed the grass and dirt underneath, which he placed his hands on.

Adam could hear creaking coming from the ground, and then noticed some thin twigs poking out from the gaps in the floorboards. Then as the pressure against the wood increased, the creaking turned into a wailing noise as if the floor was in pain. It didn't take much longer before the floor could resist no more and thick roots started to break through the floorboards, snapping the wood as it escaped from underneath. One by one the roots came from the ground in front of Caesar, growing at an unnatural speed.

Then all of a sudden, a burst of green came erupting from below as an entire oak tree burst up from the ground, breaking through the planks, splintering them and sending them flying around in all directions. Students ducked and covered their faces with their arms to protect themselves from all the destruction as the tree continued to grow, its great trunk coming from the ground like a magician pulling a handkerchief from their sleeve.

The tree kept growing until it reached the ceiling, which seemed to hold it in place, like the painting of all the gods were fighting against the tree. Ares had his sword against the leaves as Zeus struck his lightning, trying to smite the tree back down to the depths.

The ceiling was resisting the tree as much as it could, the leaves and branches crushing together against the ceiling. But before long, the force of the tree became too much and it burst through into open air, bringing part of the ceiling up in its branches, and the rest falling to the ground below.

It grew so large that only the trunk was inside the Food Hall, the leaves going up to reach the heavens when it finally stopped growing. For a few seconds, the tree stood planted to the ground, immovable – like it had been there for a hundred years – blocking the view between all the students and the high table.

Adam watched as the tree's roots started to turn black. A few moments later, leaves started to fall, each one black and crisp. The rot that had withered the top of the massive tree now started to make its way down the bark and as quickly as the tree had appeared, it now disintegrated into a black powdery substance that fell back down the gaping hole it had created.

Black powder on the broken ceiling fell like ash after a devastating fire. Then in his loud clear voice, Caesar started speaking an incantation. A layer of golden glass formed on the floor like a layer of varnish on the wood. It moved upwards, bringing all the broken pieces of the ceiling with it, passing through all the students and chairs like they weren't there.

Adam felt no different as the material moved up him, carrying all of the ceiling pieces with it. He didn't get colder or warmer, nor did he feel a breeze or the hairs on his neck stand up. It was like the golden glass was only real for the broken pieces of wood.

The golden glass continued to rise like an elevator exactly the size of the Food Hall. When it reached the ceiling, all the pieces moved like they had a mind of their own back to their original places, like a self-completing jigsaw puzzle. Then the golden glass burned so bright, it looked like the sun had collapsed, and all the students had to look away and cover their eyes from the sudden brightness.

When the burning brightness of the golden glass finished and everyone looked back at the ceiling, they found that it had been completely fixed. Even the painting of the Greek Gods had gone back to exactly how it had looked before.

Having now fixed the ceiling, Caesar had stopped speaking the incantation and moved over to the hole in the ground, placing his hand firmly on the dirt. The ground shook as the hole flooded with dirt, filling it up so that it was safe to walk on again.

Then, almost lazily compared to everything else he had done, Caesar cast the same wind spell that he had done at the start of his demonstration, expelling all the dust in the air out of the doors that flew open from the force of the wind.

The monks who had been waiting at the sides, ready in case anyone was injured, relit the fires, and the room filled once more with that soothing heat. One monk moved over to the dirt floor with some new wooden planks, which they quietly added to the floor using the golden glass to bind the new wood with the rest. Students started to regain their composure from the demonstration. Even the older students were amazed by what had happened.

Caesar stumbled back to his seat, collapsing in it, his hands shaking as he accepted some food and drink from Gerard. As he ate, some of the strength and colour in his pale face returned, but it was clear all the magic had taken a lot of energy out of him. When he spoke again, he remained in his chair and his voice was uneven, not sounding nearly as powerful as it normally was.

'Twenty-one years ago, the portal opened into this world. In that time, we have already accomplished more than any man thought possible. The endless war started almost three hundred and fifty years ago, during which the human race destroyed everything in hope of getting what they wanted... Peace. After all this time, we have achieved almost perfect peace amongst ourselves. We must maintain this at all costs. Otherwise, this progress and all the progress we will make will fall to war and violence. Now that I have shown you what is capable in the world, I am sure you are all eager to start your real training. Go back to your cabins and rest, your future is nearing.'

With that, Caesar left the Food Hall, having regained enough energy to walk. Slowly students started to rise from their seats and made their way back to their cabins, talking about the incredible display they had just seen.

Adam heard a group asking Olivia and Max where they were meant to find their cabins. They sounded panicked. It was comforting to know that other groups weren't perfect – although the group trying to work out how to find their cabin was at least panicking as a group, compared to Adam and Kaya who sat without their other half who were nowhere to be seen.

As they left the Food Hall, Adam noticed Gerard speaking to the red-haired student who had taken on three armed students with her fists earlier in the day.

'Delilah, are you sure? You know I won't be mad or angry if you tell me you took it.' The relaxed demeanour Gerard had shown during the feast faltered.

'For the final time, I did not take your artefact. I do not know who took it. I will tell you if I hear anything,' she replied in a deep dry tone, her brooding face covered in freckles.

'Is everything alright?' Adam knew that he was probably overstepping, but he needed to find out more about the greatsword.

'Yes, everything is fine, this is none of your business. Move along,' Delilah ordered.

'Don't be rude,' Gerard said in a stern voice. 'Adam, this is my daughter, Delilah, and everything is not as well as it should be. Those useless Disciples still haven't found my greatsword. So, I'm trying to see if anyone has played a prank on me like Micholesh suggested, but just as I thought, that's not the case. Someone's definitely stolen it.'

'Can I do anything to help?' Adam offered, knowing he would be helping no matter what.

'Don't think so, kiddo. Gonna have to start looking at everyone as a suspect.' Gerard was looking grave as he spoke. 'This isn't good at all. In the wrong hands... but don't worry about that, you just focus on getting used to this world. And how are you finding everything so far? From what I've heard, you're already the talk of the camp, what with you being our new king and all.'

Adam started to fiddle with his streak of blonde as he blushed. 'Is Micholesh going to be mad that I might take his place?'

'Haha, of course not.' Gerard slapped Adam's back and he felt his organs jolt forward against his ribcage. 'Don't worry about it, kid, Micholesh doesn't care about the Questing Beast coming after you, he's more worried about it getting into Camp. I should have done something to prevent the attack, I thought it might hunt you.'

'Really? You knew the Questing Beast would come after me?'

'Well, only in hindsight, but your parents were both hunted by one, so was I. It's natural that those close to Micholesh will have the opportunity to become royalty, but I wouldn't worry about it now. Just be proud of yourself for surviving against the monster, that's no easy feat. Even for a few seconds. Now I'm guessing this is another member of your team.' Gerard looked at Kaya.

'Yes, this is my best friend, Kaya Marley.'

Gerard extended his hand and Kaya shook it. 'It's so cool to meet you, Adam's talked all about you and how we are going to help find your –'

'So, Gerard, I wanted to ask... what's your favourite... food?' Adam rolled his eyes at how bad the question was.

'Ooh, that's a good question. I think it's got to be steak, with some gravy, a few eggs, carrots, and a healthy pile of rice. Delilah, your favourite meal is my chicken soup, isn't it?' Gerard turned to where Delilah had been but found that she was long gone, having left the moment she could. 'But where are the other two students in your team?' Gerard asked, wanting to move on from the awkward moment.

'They're back at our cabin,' Kaya said.

'Iosefka was home schooled all her life and is a follower of the Old Ways, so we are just bringing her up to scratch on everything we know about the world,' Adam added, leaving out the main reason why they weren't all together.

'Wow, I'm surprised that her parents let her come through the portal at all. I know that the Old Ways can be ridiculously strict with its rules, even more so than Hellenists. Hey, I've got some time to kill before I'm needed back at the Capital. Why don't you show me around your cabin and I can help out with anything she's unsure about?'

Gerard was already striding towards the cabins, and Adam dashed over to catch up.

'It's fine, Gerard, really, I'm sure she's almost learnt everything anyway.'

'Don't be ridiculous, there's always questions people want answered. I get asked things daily from people who have spent their lives on Elysium. Would you lead the way? It's been a while since I've been through this forest, although if I remember right, there is a sweet beach close by.'

As they walked, Gerard waved and greeted just about every student that they passed, asking them how they were doing and giving pieces of advice, telling jokes that only the group understood.

'By any chance, do you know what happened to Bruce and Eddie?' Adam asked as Gerard waved goodbye to some older students that were getting ready to head into the Wildlands.

'Who are they?' Gerard said, following Kaya down the hill to their cabin.

'They're these awful twins that stabbed Adam on Earth to try and stop him from getting to Elysium,' Kaya replied, a muddy page on the floor as he turned off the main path towards their cabin.

'Oh, of course, it was you they attacked. That makes sense now. Yes, I was talking to Disciple Peter about them. He told me that they would be held in the Sanctuary at the top of Mount Ida for their crimes.'

'Oh, so, like, prison? For how long?'

'Five years.'

'Five years!' The two shouted.

Hearing the shouting, Amelia threw open her door. 'What the hell is going – Gerard, sir, what an honour it is to have you in our cabin.' Her temper switched as fast as lightning. She plumped the pillows on the largest chair, sweeping off some newly settled dust and offering it to their guest as she shook his hand.

'Thank you,' Gerard said kindly, setting himself down in the chair.

'Ah, Iosefka, wasn't it?' Gerard said as she also came out of Amelia's room. 'It is a pleasure to meet you, I hear that you need a little bringing up to speed.'

'It depends on how much boring stuff you're going to tell me.'

'Haha, no I promise to only talk about things that you want to know about.'

'Five years,' Kaya whispered to Adam.

'I can't believe it,' Adam whispered back, wanting to argue with Amelia but he realised that he was happy to hear the news that the twins wouldn't be a problem in his life anymore.

'I suppose I was wondering if you could tell me a little more about that man in the Capital?' Iosefka asked. 'The one that used to be a follower like me but is now blind and in all those chains.'

'So, you've met Rigby then.'

'Rigby?' Amelia repeated.

'In my opinion, he should have just been banished to Earth or executed for trying to overthrow Micholesh, even with the circumstances. Adam, it was your mum, Amber, or Disciple Amber at the time, who decided to show mercy.'

Adam felt pride hearing about his mother. How she was a good leader. He would do whatever it took to continue on her example.

'The devil's favourite jester, that's the best way I can describe him. Always trying to manipulate his way through life, taking advantage of anyone he can in any way he can. Listen to me carefully, if you run into him again, don't trust a word he says, and don't ever help with something he asks you to do, no matter how innocent the task seems.'

'But how could someone so weak and helpless ever do something evil?' Iosefka asked.

'You'd be surprised by what he is capable of. He's one of the people I suspect may have taken my greatsword.'

'You can't be serious? He can't see!' Iosefka argued.

'He learnt to be just as scheming without sight. But I still don't understand it, only the best swordsman in the world can wield my greatsword, otherwise the greatsword sets the wielder on fire. So, I have no clue how anyone, even Rigby, could have moved it more than five feet before turning to a crisp.'

'Are the Disciples helping at all? Are they interrogating the people you think are responsible?' Adam asked.

'They are very by the books, the Disciples. That makes them slow, and I need to find my artefact fast before something terrible happens. I am already putting strain on the small bit of love my daughter has left for me by getting her to help me.'

'We saw her fighting the other day. She's really good,' Adam said, trying to improve the mood.

'Yeah, she took three people out with just her fists,' Kaya complimented.

'She's an incredible fighter, there's no doubting that, but she refuses to use real weapons. It's like she wants everything to be a challenge, like she wants to feel pain. She grew up punching the bark of trees, then she moved onto stone. With how many times my poor girl has broken her hands, I doubt she can even feel them anymore no matter how much healing magic she uses.'

'Maybe she just wants to be as strong as you?' Iosefka proposed.

'I hope not... But enough about that, is there anything else any of you wanted to know?'

It was at this moment where Amelia chose to shine, bombarding Gerard with about a hundred questions, ranging from the different artefacts to combat strategies, from vivid details about the brutal war he fought in, to the properties of different plants and herbs.

Nobody else even bothered trying to get another word in. Amelia had trapped her prey and she would fight anyone to the death if they tried to eat from it.

Eventually, Gerard had to cut her off, so that he could leave.

'All great questions, Amelia, but I need to be leaving now. Adam, keep me updated on everything. If you need anything, just come to this address and you'll find me.' Gerard scribbled something on a piece of paper.

After saying his hurried goodbyes, he practically threw himself out of their cabin to avoid having to answer any more of Amelia's questions.

'Amelia, what the hell was that!' Kaya shouted at her. 'You chased him away with all your questions. You know I wanted to ask him things too.'

'It's not my fault that you're too slow to ask your questions, you could have spoken anytime you wanted.'

'Amelia, you were barely breathing. Tell me exactly where I could get a word in?'

'Back to my room, Iosefka, we still have a lot to learn!' Amelia declared, ignoring Kaya.

With a loud purposeful sigh, Iosefka dragged her feet back to Amelia's bedroom, waving to Kaya and Adam before mimicking putting a noose around her neck and hanging herself.

12. Flame Spell

Throughout the night, Adam kept on having the same dream. He would be watching an old classic film, and out of nowhere, he would experience a sinking feeling in his stomach as he realised that he was late for training with Papil. This startling feeling would then wake him up, and he would have to leave his bedroom to check that it wasn't dawn yet.

After several of these dreams, Adam simply stopped trying to get to sleep, not wanting to wake up again covered with sweat. To pass the time, he tried to have a shower in the pitch black, which turned out to be much harder than he expected. After having banged his elbows into the walls several times and taking a nasty slip that found his legs swinging upwards and his back plummeting to the ground with a loud bang, Adam felt very wide awake.

Somehow, nobody woke from his crash and, limping, Adam made his way over to the sofa where he found a book lying on the table without a cover and mud all over it. It was the book that had stunk when they first entered the shack, and even with all its new damage, the stench still remained.

He hadn't noticed it last evening or smelt it any of the times he had woken up and left his room to check if it was dawn. Adam guessed that at some point in the night, Amelia couldn't deal with the pungent smell and had moved it out of her room to rot in their communal area.

The night's darkness started to lighten as dawn approached. With nothing else to do, Adam picked up the book, and worked out the title on the first page: *A Compendium of Magical Herbs and Plants Vol III*. Just reading the title made Adam's tiredness return. Still, there was nothing else to do to pass the time and so he turned to a random page.

The pages were all damp, dirty, torn, ripped out, and in some cases burnt. Only a few pages were fully intact, and even those had been creased and crumpled. The page that Adam had turned to was about something called the Daphne Laurel. A rough drawing depicted a ring of thick dark green leaves tightly compacted together, with small blood orange berries tucked inside.

From what Adam could decipher from the blotched text, the plant only grew on the winter solstice, which he knew only happened once a year on Earth. When eaten with some extra ingredients, it would allow the person to speak to animals until the stroke of midnight.

As Adam turned the page, he felt that some of the paper was raised like it was crudely embossed, it seemed as if a pen with no ink had been pushed down hard on the other side of the paper to form the protruding lines. As he ran his fingers across the page, he realised the lines formed large letters. With a bit of work, he managed to work out the sentence that filled the page, '*Winter Solstice also on Elysium.*'

Wanting to see if there was any more of this hidden text, Adam turned to another page, depicting a detailed drawing of a fern, its leaves branching out from the stem getting smaller as it reached its top, reminding Adam of a Christmas tree that he had seen in classic Christmas movies.

The written description was near impossible to read, blotched beyond recognition, but running his fingers across the page, Adam found another hidden sentence saying, '*Too easy to cure.*'

He had just turned to a page titled '*Lotus Tree*' that was completely destroyed except for the illustration of the tree and another sketch of a flower that seemed familiar but he couldn't place it when the door to Kaya's bedroom started to open. In the heat of the moment, feeling for some reason as though he was doing something he shouldn't, Adam slid the book under the sofa.

'Hey,' Kaya said groggily as he scratched his head. 'What were you doing?' He asked, seeing how flustered Adam was.

'Oh, nothing, was just passing the time. I was about to wake you, by the looks of it, it's almost dawn.'

'Fair enough, I'd better start getting ready then,' Kaya said with a yawn.

Adam knocked on Iosefka's and Amelia's doors, telling them that it was time to get up if they wanted to make it to training. He had considered leaving Amelia behind, but even though they were now competing against each other, he didn't have it in him to be so dishonourable.

By the time everyone had dressed and washed and Iosefka had finished her daily praying in her room, streaks of red were bold on the horizon and had now infected the sky and clouds, burning an outline across the summits of the mountains. Amelia and Iosefka seemed especially tired. By the looks of it, they had stayed up much later than the other two.

The four walked past the Monastery to quickly grab some food. The Food Hall was empty except for a few monks and the camp had only Gerard's daughter Delilah and her group training in it. The air itself even felt a little different; each inhale was refreshing, like submerging in cold water.

They had no idea why Papil had requested their training to be so early, but when they climbed up through the orange tunnel of leaves leading to the Monastery and saw him waiting for them by the Koi pond, sprinkling some crumbs into the water, nobody asked. All four of them were far too excited to learn how to use magic.

'Good, you are here on time. Come, let me show you where we will train,' he said, scattering the remaining fish food.

Papil led them through the Monastery past dozens of detailed tapestries telling stories of Elysium until they reached a thin sliding door made of some kind of thick paper. The door slid open with ease and opened into a small dojo. Its floor was made from compact strands of straw that had been woven together to create the mat that was strong under the feet but seemed soft to land on.

The same opaque material as the door was also used for the windows at the height of the light oak walls. As it had just turned dawn, the orange and red streaks from the blazing sun broke through the windows, sending warm streaks across the pristine room.

The dojo was a perfect square. A scroll banner attached to the wall to the right of the entrance with bold black hand-painted letters read: *Not Phenomenally Skilled but Phenomenally Willed.*

'This is where we will be training for the month. All of our dojos are lined with obsidian. No matter how much magical damage you exert, the dojo will resist,' Papil explained, making his way to the front of the room.

'Will we be going to a different location after a month?' Amelia asked, taking her place in the room.

'No.'

'What do you mean?' Adam had taken up his position at the front of the room to the side of Amelia

'After one month, we will part ways. I can teach you enough to get you on your paths. From there it is your responsibility to continue down them. Every day, you will come here at the same time and we will train, and slowly you will improve, you will discover which strains of magic best suit you, and I will teach you how to learn by yourself.'

'We truly appreciate you taking the time to mentor us. We will do our best to be the best students we can be,' Iosefka said, suppressing a yawn and taking her place behind Amelia.

'Oh yeah, I can't wait to make fire come out of my hand!' Kaya had now taken his position behind Adam, forming a small square between the four of them.

'Well then, let us not waste any time. There are currently three strains of magic known. Elemental magic is the easiest to learn and it is what we will be starting with. As you seem to be interested in pyromancy, we can start there.'

'We're going to cast our first spell now?' Kaya couldn't keep his doubts at bay. 'I thought it was going to take weeks before we could do anything at all?'

'On the contrary, Elemental magic could have been done by any of you the moment you came through the portal, so long as you knew what to do. As I am sure you may have noticed yesterday, in Caesar's impeccable display of skill, each strain of magic requires a different sacrifice to use.'

'Caesar's what?' Amelia interrupted.

'Caesar's demonstration of magic during the Fighters Feast,' Papil reiterated.

'There was another feast!' Iosefka's longing voice made Amelia give a genuine frown as she turned to Iosefka.

'I didn't know about it. That one's on me, but now back to learning.' Amelia ignored Iosefka's death stare as she turned back to face Papil.

'Not to worry, there will be plenty of food and magic to experience in your futures,' Papil reassured, his eyes moving to meet all four sets of eyes. 'Now back to our sacrifices. Elemental magic asks the caster to perform a series of different movements usually with their arms and hands. These vary in style depending on what kind of element you are casting, and in what way you are using the element itself. For our first spell, we will try to simply set the tip of our index finger alight.'

Papil showed them the short series of movements needed for the spell. It was far less complex than any other spell they had seen, but as with the other pyromancy spells, the movements were harsh and fast.

'Now that I have shown you what is needed, you will all try. When you are moving, think of nothing other than what you want to happen. Feel each muscle move and experience the fire burning up within yourself. It is common to confuse this feeling with hatred or anger. Many think that the angriest people can control the element of fire better than anyone else, but know that this is a fallacy. When casting Elemental magic, you do not want your emotions to overcome you. Doing so makes the spell uncontrollable. When it comes to pyromancy, being over-encumbered with rage can make a person seem powerful, but in reality, these spells will always cause more harm than good. Keep this in mind and try, try until you succeed. There is no failing so long as you never give up.'

With Papil's guidance, the four got to work, trying over and over again to cast the simple spell. Iosefka had to spend the first five minutes of training praying to allow herself to use magic, whilst the others started their attempts. All of them had hoped to cast the spell on their first try but weren't surprised when they looked down to see their finger wasn't on fire.

Adam found that whenever he started the movements, his heart would beat faster and become hotter, but he couldn't help focusing on the peculiar heat instead of the spell itself, which would then cause the heat to disappear.

After an hour of non-stop trying, the novelty of the new sensation stopped being so overwhelming and Adam could feel the heat intensify as he made it further through the casting before the heat escaped him. He was certain that he was making progress, but every time he opened his eyes to see if he had been successful, he would waste a few seconds looking over to see if Amelia had managed to cast the spell before him.

More than he wanted to cast his first spell, Adam needed to beat Amelia to it. In his head, this was the first challenge between them, and it was clear that she felt the same. It wasn't that Adam wanted to be the leader of the group but he wouldn't let Amelia be in charge of him.

For several hours, none of them left the dojo. Papil had started meditating at the front of the room, somehow managing to find tranquillity even with the four teenagers grunting, sighing, and heavily breathing as they started to tire from the repetitive movements.

Adam was finding it hard to stay focused. Every time he failed, all he could think about was how Amelia would have another opportunity to best him. With all this pressure to cast the spell, Adam had made less progress in the last three hours than he had in his first.

Now the same thing would happen when doing the movements. He would reach the final gesture, which left his finger pointing outward, and he could feel the magic build up within him, but he was struggling to move it through his body and channel the fire to his finger.

Over and over Adam tried without any luck and his heart sank when he noticed Papil's eyes shoot open – breaking his session of uninterrupted meditation. Adam had never felt such panic when turning to Amelia, expecting her finger to be on fire, only to find that her hand was just as cold and ordinary as his own, to which Amelia seemed equally relieved.

'Cool,' Kaya exclaimed.

Adam and Amelia swivelled around to find Kaya inspecting his finger, its tip on fire. The flame was weak and seemed barely capable of staying on his finger without blowing away in the dormant air, but it was undoubtedly magic. Kaya had a mystified look in his eyes, staring at the light as a baby looks at its mother, moving his other hand around it, feeling its soft heat.

'Excellent work, Kaya. I now ask that you do the spell one hundred times, this will strengthen your casting of it and will solidify your hard work. Understand that the reason Kaya has managed to cast this spell first has nothing to do with natural talent, but is a result of hard work. I am confident in thinking that the three of you are close behind. Keep at it, do not give up.'

Kaya was smiling with glee as he looked toward his best friend. Adam couldn't muster a smile back, too focused on the fact that he had let Amelia cloud his judgement.

Giving an encouraging nod to Kaya, Adam turned back to the front, seeing that Amelia had already gone back to the movements, this time doing them even harsher and faster.

Kaya did the movements again, and again his finger was set alight. This time Adam turned back around immediately, going back to his movements as fast as possible.

Papil didn't try to meditate again. He seemed confident that it wouldn't take long before the next person completed the spell, and sure enough, by the time Kaya had lit his finger twenty-three times, Iosefka managed to cast the spell as well.

Eventually, both Kaya and Iosefka left the dojo, having completed their training for the day, saying that they would wait in the Food Hall for the other two. Adam had never felt so ashamed of himself. He was meant to be leading Kaya and the others to victory, yet he wasn't even capable of casting a simple spell.

After several more hours without Papil saying a word and many outrages that included the two of them stomping on the floor, shouting into the air, and screaming at one another, their mentor finally had enough and broke his silence.

'Stop!' He shouted. 'You are both far too concerned about things that do not matter. It is obvious that you two wish the other to fail, but I have no inclination as to why. You are part of the same team. In all my years of mentoring, I have never witnessed one let alone two people take so long to complete their first spell. I am exceptionally doubtful that you are without the spark, I have seen the kind that even Hope cannot see light in and neither of you possess such an evil. Leave this dojo now, come back tomorrow, and I hope for both of your sakes that you can conclude this hatred you feel for one another.'

Neither Adam nor Amelia knew what to say and left the dojo without a word. They walked in silence, the sun already falling behind the Wildlands, bringing night in its wake.

Amelia stormed off ahead of Adam, breaking down in tears. By the time Adam had made it to the Food Hall, it was mostly empty; everyone had finished their training and their dinner for the day.

Kaya was sitting alone, scraping his bowl of tomato soup with some bread.

'Hey, how did it go with the training?' Kaya asked as Adam sat down beside him.

'Neither of us managed to do it. This has to be the stupidest rivalry ever. You were the one who managed to cast the spell first, it should be you leading this group, not me, and certainly not Amelia.'

'Ew, no. Leading? Could never be me.' Kaya made a face like he'd tasted something sour. 'All that responsibility. All that boring effort I have to put into things I don't care about. Nah, I'm good, thanks.' Kaya put his hand on Adam's back. 'Hey, we haven't had a proper chance to speak about your parents. I know you didn't want to talk about them before but if you ever do, I'm here for you.'

'Thanks,' Adam said, smiling at Kaya. 'I just felt a little lost for a bit, but the longer we stay here, the closer I feel to them, and helping Gerard with his greatsword makes me feel like my parents are with me, like I am doing what they would if they were still alive. It feels good.'

'Good, and I'm here with you all the way. We'll find that greatsword, you and me. No problem.'

Adam gave a heartfelt hug to his best friend that he thought of more as a brother and then went up to get some much-needed food. Once he had shovelled his dinner down and Kaya had finished his fifth serving, they made their way back to the cabin. As they walked, Kaya made a point of talking about all the incredible things they had already accomplished.

'Follow me, I want to try something,' Kaya said, walking across the empty training ground that led up to the cliff with the cherry blossom tree.

'Where are you going, Kaya? It's late, we should get some sleep.'

'Stop thinking so much, would you? Come on, take another look out into the ocean.'

Adam did as he was told. There was no doubting the unprecedented beauty of the view, the sky above reflected on the still waters. Adam had never seen anything so intensely tranquil in all his life.

'Now close your eyes.'

Adam was only able to look away at the perfect sight to gawk at Kaya. 'Are you mad, we've come here to see this, and you want me to close my eyes?'

'We didn't come here for the view. We came here for something better. Maybe better. I don't really know if it's going to work, but let's find out. Close your eyes.'

Adam gave an exasperated exhale as he shut his eyes, looking forward so that at least when he opened them again, he could see the sea and sky once more.

'I want you to listen to the waves. They're not as loud as I was hoping but maybe this will work better.'

Adam did his best to listen to the soft sound of the water brushing up against the sand. Then Kaya carefully held Adam's hands and brought them up to the starting position to cast the pyromancy spell.

'You know the sequence better than I do at this point. Listen to the waves, and try and fill your head with what you've just seen.'

Adam's breathing had naturally slowed and his shoulders had loosened. He hadn't even realised they'd been tight to begin with. He started with the sequence of moves. This time he focused on the waves, imagining that the heat inside of him was linked to it. The water moved back and forth below and as it did, the heat intensified with them.

As he finished the last move, he felt all the warmth shoot from his heart, turning at his shoulder, past his elbow, and he felt the heat flow out of him like his finger was a gun. As he opened his eyes, his focus was not far in the distance, but on what was right in front of him. A bright glowing flame that acted as a candle on the cliff, illuminating the pink of the tree leaves above.

13. Confessions

A month went by in a horrible flash. Every day before dawn, Adam and Kaya left their cabin in the dark to go to the Food Hall, with Amelia making a point of always going ahead of the two. They would then meet up with Iosefka in the Monastery where she had found a quiet place to pray.

No day of training took as long as the first day, with their sessions usually lasting four to five hours. Amelia had been furious when Adam had shown up for their second lesson to see that she was now the only one unable to cast a spell, which only put more unnecessary pressure onto herself to the point where she had to be moved to a separate room because of how distracting she was when shouting and yelling at herself.

It had taken her four days of non-stop trying before she could finally cast the simple spell. By that point, the other three had already learnt how to form a marble-sized orb of water in their palm and had been making progress on splitting a pebble in half.

A month in and they had now all learnt a large chunk of basic elemental spells. After a few weeks of Elemental magic, Papil had moved them on to Life and Death magic. This required the caster to drain their energy instead of doing unique movements.

The only spell that they were able to fully learn at the most fundamental level was holding an almost dead plant that had turned crispy in one hand and a healthy flower in the other and managing to transfer the life from one plant to the other.

At the end of each of these Life and Death lessons, everyone in the group would have to head back to the cabin to sleep for a few hours, due to how much energy trying to cast the spell drained.

After they had spent some time with Life and Death, Papil moved them onto Enlightenment magic. This turned out to be far too complicated for Adam's liking, and although he no longer worried so much about Amelia outperforming him, it didn't make him feel good when she managed to immediately create the golden glass material, which Papil had explained was called desert glass.

To create desert glass, they had to speak different incantations. Getting the slightest pronunciation wrong would stop the glass from appearing or would cause the spell to malfunction, but when done correctly, the desert glass had plenty of valuable uses like forming letters to create bright messages, mending things together using the magic as a binding substance like glue, and creating a layer of protection in the form of a shield or dome. Every month, there would be a new discovery for one of the strains, usually Enlightenment magic, either found from someone decoding a scroll or through research from what was already known.

After a few sessions with enlightenment magic, Iosefka could create the desert glass with ease, unlike Adam and Kaya who had decided to focus more on the other two forms of magic that they were more comfortable with.

Amelia was easily the best at creating desert glass, reciting whole paragraphs perfectly as she changed the shape of the glass at her whim, forming different symbols in the sky, mending small objects, and creating a small barrier strong enough to stop a swing of a sword.

Their last week of training was spent on improving all the magic they had managed to learn, and with only four days left until the coliseum challenge, the four wanted as much practice as possible.

For their current lesson with Papil, Kaya and Adam were paired together to fight against the other two. As they duelled, Adam could tell that Kaya was pulling back his spells to be kind to Iosefka who was shaking after each attack was thrown her way, barely managing to block the simplest spells with her desert glass makeshift shield. Adam gave Amelia no such courtesy, coming at her with everything he had.

He started by shooting dozens of embers through the sky in an attempt to make Amelia's clothing catch on fire, but as each flame came close to her, she sent back a thick mist of water shooting from her palms, extinguishing them with ease.

Adam then created a small fireball in his hands. The sensation of not feeling any pain or heat from the fire still amazed him. Papil had explained that 'only until the spell is released from the caster will it become fully realised within the world'.

Amelia quickly shook her hands to make her water mist evaporate, knowing it wouldn't be strong enough to stop the ball of fire. Adam then attempted to throw the fireball at Amelia. However, she had already anticipated what was coming, and had created a large shield out of the desert glass, which blocked the fireball from hitting her.

Amelia wasn't strong enough to keep the shield up after the collision, and her protection shattered into tiny little pieces that then disintegrated into the air like fire, and made her take a few steps back from the force of impact.

In retaliation, Amelia created a handful of tiny desert glass balls the size of peas, which she blasted towards Adam with the aid of a weak wind-based spell. The poor casting of the Elemental magic didn't matter as the desert glass was so light, they shot through the air at a deadly speed. Adam had barely any time to react and managed to dodge most of them but the little projectiles were so small and scattered that one clipped his cheek, shattering on impact and cutting into his skin like broken glass, drawing blood.

'Well, that was an interesting display,' Papil noted before Adam could retaliate.

'Yeah, Iosefka, that was a good spar,' Kaya said encouragingly.

'It was awful, I could barely defend myself against your weakest attacks, and I was too scared to retaliate.'

Iosefka had been struggling with fear since they started training to fight and it had only grown worse as the coliseum challenge approached. In practice, she was just as good as the others, even better in some aspects, but when it came down to fighting, she kept on buckling under the fear of getting hurt.

'Do not fret, you have all come far. I expect great things from all of you. Although I suggest you practise teamwork,' Papil said, looking at Adam and Amelia.

'I know it's still before the challenge and all, but would you be able to bend the rules a little and show us the library? It's just that I've gone through all the books I have access to,' Amelia asked, trying to mask how keen she was to see the room.

'My answer has not changed, Amelia. I will be more than happy to give you the full tour the moment after you have made it through the challenge,' Papil answered in earnest.

Amelia seemed disgruntled but not surprised by the answer.

When the lesson was over and they made their way outside, they noticed Theta, the blonde monk who had given them the piece of wood for their cabin, tending to the bushes by the staircase.

'Hey!' Amelia called out, a little more loudly than necessary, blushing instantly.

'Ah, Amelia,' Theta said. 'How have you been? It's been some time since I've had the pleasure of your company.'

'Aw.' Amelia's face turned even redder.

'We've been good, where have you been this month? We haven't seen you at all,' Iosefka asked.

'I had some work to do in the Capital,' she said, her head held high.

'Sounds like Papil is giving you more responsibility. See, I'm sure you'll be able to mentor next year,' Amelia said.

'It is starting to look that way,' she replied with a smile. 'The coliseum challenge is in a few days, how are you feeling?'

'Very confident,' Amelia said, giving Adam a dirty look. 'You wouldn't be able to give us a quick look around the library, would you, or even the room where you keep all the scrolls?'

Theta ran her hand through her hair as she pondered what to do. Amelia was batting her eyelids at her as best as she could, but it just looked like she had something stuck in her eye.

'I'll show you the scrolls, but we have to be quick and silent.'

Not wanting to miss out on the opportunity, Adam and Kaya followed along. They were led back into the Monastery past the dojo rooms, down several corridors where they had to stop and hide behind pillars to make sure the monks walking around didn't see them. Eventually, Theta stopped in front of a wide wooden door that had dozens of different symbols carved into the wood.

'Those are all symbols meaning knowledge, aren't they?' Amelia whispered to no response as Theta pressed the different symbols in a specific order. They then glowed with the same golden aura that came off of desert glass.

'It's empty. Quick, get in, before anyone sees us.'

Inside was what Amelia's mind might look like. Cabinets lined the room with hundreds of scrolls slotted in each cubby hole, going so high that ladders had to be used to reach the highest parchments and scrolls.

Most of the holes were empty but all the ones being used had a label above, giving a brief description of what each scroll had been deciphered to teach. A handful of labels were blank as the scrolls still needed to be deciphered.

The right wall was filled with all the Enlightenment magic scrolls, with Elemental magic to the left. Both sides had around the same number of scrolls, however, the right wall had papers and parchments shoved inside with the protruding scrolls struggling to fit inside the small gap. The back wall was thinner than the sides of the room and held the few dozen Life and Death magic scrolls.

All through the centre of the room, fat tables with boards, stencils and other mechanisms were evenly distributed with drawers at each desk filled with parchment and even more tools to help decode newly found scrolls.

'Life and Death magic was only discovered a year and a few months ago. I remember when Caesar found the first scroll in the Wildlands, it was all anybody wanted to learn. Now you didn't hear it from me, but when I was in the Capital, I conducted some research in the Bibliotech and overheard talk about a possible fourth strain of magic that a new scroll is seeming to unravel.'

'What was that type of magic, do you know?' Amelia asked, having delicately removed an Enlightenment scroll.

'Yes, it's thought to be –'

'That is enough!' Papil shouted as he entered the room, causing everyone to jump. 'Theta, you know better than this! You four should be ashamed. After all I have taught you, you go and show me such little respect.'

'I'm sorry, Papil, we just wanted –' Iosefka started to say.

'I do not want to hear it! You can consider my mentoring with you finished! All four of you out now!'

None of them challenged Papil and after Kaya picked up the scroll he had dropped onto the floor and haphazardly shoved it back into the wrong hole, they all rushed out of the room without another word. As Amelia stepped outside, she glanced back at Theta with a sorry expression but she was too busy enduring Papil's ridicule to notice.

'I don't know why you followed us in there. If it was just us girls, we wouldn't have been caught,' Amelia hissed.

'Hey, you were the one wanting to break the rules. I don't know why you were so desperate to see those scrolls anyway. After the challenge, once I've shown how much better a leader I am and have heard you admit defeat, I'd still be happy to go to the scroll room with you. There's a lot of useful stuff in there that I wouldn't want *my* team to miss out on.'

'Don't you dare!' Amelia pushed Adam hard on the chest as they reached the bottom step, making him stumble as he reached the ground. 'Just you wait, by this time tomorrow, you won't be so confident. Follow me, Iosefka, we need more practice!'

Iosefka's kind face sunk as she rolled her eyes at the thought of doing more so-called practice, which was just learning more from books rather than any physical training.

On their way over to pick up the blunt weapons they wanted to train with today, Adam and Kaya nodded to the students they had started to become familiar with. They had quickly found that teams trained at the same time, including Olivia and her team which they often worked next to. They would even spar alongside the four every so often.

Adam had made sure to ask for as much advice as he could from the older students and they were almost always happy to point him in the right direction. He wanted to be one of the very best fighters in all of Elysium like his parents and so he made a point of trying to start his training with Kaya before anyone else had, and would always finish after everyone else had left.

As per usual, after a long day of training, the moment Kaya came back to the cabin, he showered and collapsed onto his bed where he fell asleep in an instant. Adam would normally do the same thing, except tonight he found himself having trouble sleeping.

As much as he tossed and turned in his pitch-black room, he couldn't get comfortable, all of his troubled thoughts swirling around his brain so fast it made him dizzy and nauseous.

At first, he had started thinking about how he failed Papil, then how he had failed Kaya, having spent all their time in Elysium training and not enjoying themselves, then his mind revolved around Amelia, and then onto his parents. After several hours of his downwards spiral, he decided to head outside to try and clear his head.

To his surprise, as he opened the front door of the cabin, careful not to wake anyone, two feet were dangling from the roof hanging over his head.

'Iosefka?' Adam whispered, closing the door behind him.

'Oh, hey. I thought everyone was asleep. Did I wake you?'

'No, no, I was already up. I just wanted to get some fresh air.' Adam went around the cabin up the hill to join Iosefka on the roof. 'So, what's keeping you up?'

'It's nothing, you don't have to worry. What about you?'

'I'm not saying if you're not saying.'

'That makes sense, I suppose. I guess we will just have to sit here and stare at the sky.' Iosefka reclined against the roof.

For a while the two said nothing, staring up past all the branches and leaves toward the magical sky together, watching the universe move around them.

'I thought that when I came to Elysium, the hard part would be fighting against monsters and learning magic,' Adam finally said. 'It's taken me off-guard that the hardest part of my story has been feeling like I don't belong. I've told Kaya that I'm fine and that I've found purpose again but the truth is I haven't. All those years I spent on Earth, the one thing I wanted more than anything was to be with my parents and be part of a real family. When I found out that couldn't ever happen, I just felt so hopeless. I'm trying to do what I think would make them proud because it makes me feel like they are beside me, but it's only barely working enough for me to keep moving forward. I have Kaya, and he is everything to me. Without him, I don't know where I would be, but I don't know... I just can't properly explain it.'

'You've explained it just fine. There is an old saying that grief is simply all the love you didn't get the chance to give spilling out of you. You have spent so much of your life filling up your cup with love and now with that cup so full, you have found out that the people you have been saving it for can't drink it, and you're standing here in this unfamiliar new world watching everyone fill their cups with so many new beautiful emotions and you want to do the same but you can't.

'You have so carefully squeezed out your love and filled so much of your cup with it that there is barely any room to add anything else, but you can't just throw away the love to make more space. It's far too valuable. Yet you also don't want others to fill their cups with your special love because you didn't spend all that time making it for them, you made it for your family. Now as the days pass, you are experiencing so many incredible new things and your cup is starting to overfill, that precious love is spilling and it's burning like acid into your heart.'

Adam closed his eyes and took several deep breaths before replying.

'But then how can I get rid of it, because it feels like I'm going to burn a hole straight through my heart?' Adam was glad that Iosefka was still looking at the sky and not at him.

'You accept that sometimes things don't go how you need them to go. God's plan for us is unpredictable. You give people your love. Those that deserve it at least. They will know it isn't pure love, but love bittered with grief, and although it isn't love that they can fully appreciate it will be enough for you to start healing. It will give you a chance to finally empty your cup.'

'But I can't give all of my bitterness to Kaya, it will kill him.'

'You don't have to, there are others you can talk to. Remember this team is meant to act as a family.'

Adam couldn't help but chuckle at this. 'This team? A family? We're split in half. This is the first proper conversation I have had with you in weeks because I have somehow agreed to this stupid competition to become leader. Now, we've only got a few days till the whole world finally sees how broken our team is, and nothing I do will ever stop that.'

'On some level, you are right,' Iosefka said with a sigh. 'I've spent all month with her and we are so deep in that she's lost all reason. All she is focused on is being this group's stupid leader. This will just have to be one of those times where it gets ugly, but when it does, I'd like to believe you will pick up the pieces and use all that love of yours to put us back together. That's what a family does.'

Adam extended his hand. 'You've got a deal.' She shook it with a smile. 'At least one positive of her relentless want to be a leader is that you're as ready as you'll ever be for tomorrow.'

'That isn't even slightly true. She's trained me for nothing of value. I can't fight, I can't even defend myself properly, but I can tell you the five uses of hydra blood by heart. Not like that's ever going to do me any good. I'll be dead in less than a year on that expedition, if not in the coliseum.'

'Don't say that. You won't die. You're stronger than you think, and no matter what happens, we all have your back. We all have strengths and weaknesses, and I would much rather have you on my team than someone else.'

'Adam, I can't cast a spell without praying first. I have to pray in the morning and at night, and before I eat, and there is so much more I have to do, all because of my religion. It would be so much better for the team if I weren't a part of it.'

'That couldn't be further from the truth. Not everyone can be incredible, but anyone has the potential to be, and I like to believe that it's the people who have the most obstacles that end up being the ones that do the impossible because they've fought harder for it than anyone else. Maybe that will be you, maybe it won't, but you are who you are, and I wouldn't ask you to change that for anything.'

'That's nice. Thank you.'

Again, they fell back into silence, a darkness in Adam's soul growing lighter as his cup started to empty. Throughout the month of training, Adam had barely looked further than whatever he was trying to hit, always trying to make sure he was doing more than Amelia. It was nice to just relax as he had on his first days on Elysium, feeling the grass with Kaya.

'I ran away,' Iosefka said all of a sudden.

'What?'

'From Earth. I had never had any real intention of going to Elysium. Sure, I would fantasize about what it would be like, but I never thought I would muster up the courage to go through the portal. I lived in the town where the portal gates were, so I'd seen them open and close every year, and I'd watched everyone go through. Last month on the morning that the gates were going to open, I got into a bad argument with my parents. I threatened to go through the portal and leave them forever. I didn't mean it, I just wanted to say something to hurt them, but then they said that if I went through the portal, I would no longer be a child of theirs. I don't know what happened, hearing that they would disown me, after all the time I had spent with them, memorising all the old testimonies, that they would cast me out with such ease... It just made me snap.

'I left my house, and I kept on running. I wasn't paying attention but I found myself in front of the portal. I don't understand why I did it, but I went through. It was just a stupid fight, at the wrong time, and now I'm all alone. Alone in a world where I have to wait a year just to be with my family again. They are the only people I have ever spent time with, and I am so afraid that I'll never get to see them again. I'm so afraid of never getting the chance to apologize.' Iosefka couldn't keep it together as tears fell down her face, and she made no attempt to stop them.

Adam held her hand as they lay on the roof. He was never good at these situations, and Iosefka squeezed his hand tight as she continued to cry.

'I'm confident that your parents haven't disowned you. I'm sure they know it was just a stupid fight. They are probably worried sick about you and will hug you tighter than you could ever imagine when you see them again. And you *will* see them again, I'll make sure of it.'

The two stayed holding hands for a little longer. When Adam turned to look at Iosefka, she was smiling a bright wide smile wiping the tears from her face. The yellow lines on her face smudged, breaking the symmetrical patterns.

'It's getting late. We should try and get to sleep before Amelia catches us out here, and screams at me for trying to sabotage her chances of being leader.' Adam smiled as Iosefka laughed.

The two made their way back into the cabin, but before Adam went back into his room, he looked back at her. 'It's going to be ok,' he said, and she nodded, both of them believing that it could be true.

14. The Qiqirn

On the day of the challenge, all of the new students were down at the training grounds early in the morning, panic practising. They were terrified that they had spent the last month relaxing when they should have been training. This desperate attempt at improving didn't last for long, as the monks took the weapons away to be moved to the coliseum.

Adam had found out that the coliseum was on the very outskirts of the camp, several fields away from the main training grounds, where there was nothing except for a few lines of trees to separate the fields and an area to train magic with dummies and raised arenas made from obsidian, which Adam and Kaya had used the last few days, having lost Papil as their mentor.

They had tried to go into the huge circular stadium made of a light white stone, but all the entrances were heavily locked and they couldn't find any clues for what the challenge would be.

Having already spent several hours on their magic casting for the day, the two made their way into the relaxing Food Hall to try and clear their heads for the challenge. The aching of their muscles started to melt away just by smelling the steam that floated around the comfortable air. Whilst the Food Hall did wonders to their muscles, it did nothing to help with their stomachs, which were so knotted they could barely swallow a slice of toast.

It seemed like everyone participating in the coliseum had received as much sleep as Adam and Kaya, by the waves of yawning that flowed around the tables like the food was poisoned to make them all fall into an everlasting slumber. People rested their hands on their foreheads to support their drowsy heads whilst others splashed cups of water over their faces.

After Adam and Kaya had finished eating what little food they could, they decided to join Amelia and Iosefka who were sitting in the very corner of the hall. Amelia was whispering things to an uncaring Iosefka who seemed far more interested in tracing patterns on the table with her finger. She smiled at Adam and Kaya as they sat down.

After a few minutes of silence where Adam could do nothing but stir with his thought about what the day would bring, he found that it started to become a struggle to breathe and the once soothing atmosphere had turned overwhelming. The thick warm air now made Adam choke. The world was spinning too fast for him to focus and Adam ran out of the hall into the fresh air.

'Hey, what's up?' Kaya asked, having followed Adam outside.

'We're so unprepared for this. We could have done so much more. If I hadn't gone along Amelia's stupid competition, we would be working as a proper team like everyone else.' Adam shook his head in disappointment, doing his best to take deep breaths as his heart tried to break free from his chest with how violently it thumped.

'There's no point beating yourself up about it, it's done. No matter what would have happened, we would be struggling in some way or another. How many teams have you seen train as hard as we do? Even divided, I reckon ours beats others because you have pushed Amelia and she has pushed you. I won't lie, it could have done with a little less pushing when it came to Iosefka and me, but we are all so much stronger than we were when we first came through the portal. Remember what Caesar said, even if we fail, we can still go out into the Capital and do some proper digging for that greatsword. It really doesn't matter how well we do.'

'It means everything how we do!' Adam said. 'Everyone will watch us together and they'll see what a joke of a team we are. Even if we can fight individually, we can't function as a team. If I do badly, everyone will think I'm nothing but a failure, that I'll never be like my parents. I have to prove them wrong!'

Adam had been doing his best to deal with his grief the way Iosefka had suggested, but in the moment of his panic attack, that conversation now seemed so far away and that feeling of reassurance she had given him was being ripped away.

'In all our time together, I've never once known you to care about what someone else thinks about you.'

'That's because nothing mattered on Earth. It's different here.'

'Why?' Kaya asked.

'You don't get it. I have to continue my parents' legacy. I have to be a hero.'

'Adam, I've been your best friend, all your life. You are so much more than that already. I've been there when you said stupid catchphrases when we started a fight against some bully twice our size. I was there to see you defend the kids that couldn't fight back, and I know how selfless you are when someone needs help. You are already the person you want to be. You are a hero. We both are.'

'But then you have to understand why we need to be the best in this challenge, nobody will ever think I can be anyone if we fail here.'

'Give me one time that a single hero in any film or show, or just any main character of anything you've seen, has ever needed to give a damn about what someone else thinks, to be who they are?' Kaya waited, but Adam didn't have an answer so he pressed on. 'A good person does good things, not because it makes them look good in front of others, but because it makes them feel good within themselves. That has always been you.'

'I –er –well.'

'You think too much about how bad things can be.' Kaya took a seat on the ground, running his hands through the cool blades of grass. 'I know there is a lot going on, but you should try and enjoy yourself a bit more. You don't have to explore the world and find the rarest most powerful artefacts to be happy, you only need to live in the moment.'

'Like sitting on the floor and feeling the grass?' Adam sat down with his friend, as his heart calmed down.

'Now you're starting to get it,' Kaya exclaimed.

Adam and Kaya sat there on the grass, their breathing slow and relaxed. They were unaware of the students pacing around them, frantically reading from books aloud to try to find some hidden piece of information. Then, in that moment of living, the gong that hadn't been struck since the Fighters' Feast on their first day at the camp started to ring inside everyone's ears once more.

'Looks like it's time,' Adam said, looking in the direction of the coliseum just visible over the line of thick green leaves in the distance.

'I hope you've lost your nerve,' Amelia remarked as she came outside and stood next to Adam. 'It'll be even easier to outperform you in every way. I have trained Iosefka as best as I can and you will see what we can both do. I very much doubt you can do anything better.'

In those few moments of clarity, Adam had come to a decision. 'Amelia, I'll be honest with you. I don't want to be leader. If you want it, you can have it. I just want to be a family.'

Amelia didn't think about it for a fraction of a second. 'Yeah, nice try. I'm not stupid enough to fall for something like that.'

'I'm being genuine.'

Iosefka made a gesture to Amelia to show that she should take the victory, and it made her think about the offer for no more than a second.

'No, you're lying, it's a trick,' she said with certainty. 'Now let's get a move on.'

'I tried,' Adam said with a shrug to Iosefka as they followed the line of people all heading towards the coliseum.

Two lines led into the coliseum, the shorter one was filled with nervous teenagers all waiting to be told where they needed to go. The other line was filled with anyone else who wanted to watch.

Even people from the Capital had come down to see what kind of potential this intake of students had to offer. Adam noticed that a few of them were taking bets on how many students would fail and if they thought a specific group would do well.

'Hey, guys,' a familiar voice called once they had come to the front of the queue.

'Theta!' Amelia shouted in excitement. 'I'm so sorry about what happened. I hope you didn't get into too much trouble.'

'Don't worry about it. It was my fault for letting you into the room. Most of my punishment is doing this all day so it could be worse.'

'So, where should we go?' Adam asked, not wanting to stand around as the two made each other blush.

'What?' Theta replied hazily, staring into Amelia's eyes. 'Sorry, what you need to do is just head through those doors to the left and it'll lead you through into the waiting area.' She leaned in so nobody else would hear her. 'Now I can't tell you what you'll be doing when you head out onto the stage. If Papil finds out I told you, my punishment will be worse than you could ever imagine. However, as I'm in charge of the order that people go in, when did you want to go out?'

'First,' Adam and Amelia said together.

'Are you guys sure? Maybe we should go last then there won't be so many people watching,' Iosefka pleaded.

'There is no point in going later. If we go now, we can get this over and done with, and have a clear victor,' Amelia said matter-of-factly.

'I'll be glad to do that for you. Just head through, it won't be long until you're called to head under the stage.'

'Thank you so much, we won't forget this,' Amelia said.

The four made their way to the left, down a set of wide stairs that led to a large underground holding room lit only by candles attached to the thick rock walls surrounding them.

The room was filled with a few hundred students anxiously waiting. Some were huddled in their groups planning, others walked around talking to themselves absentmindedly. On the wall that would lead directly underneath the stage of the coliseum, a tall muscular monk stood guarding a wooden door.

As he took a seat on the cold floor, Adam's nerves started to return. He found the only thing that helped him stay sober from his anxiety was to focus on every group walking down the stairs, recalling how often he saw them in the training grounds, knowing he had been there more.

Everyone was as nervous as Adam. Olivia and her team had made their way down not long after they had. Max looked as pale as Iosefka if not worse and Adam did his best to boost the confidence of both of them by explaining everything Kaya had comforted him with.

Not long after, Theta came down with the last group and the hundreds of people all huddled as closely towards her as they could, not wanting to miss out on what she would say.

'Now that you are all here and accounted for, I have randomly selected the ordering of who will go when.' She turned to Amelia with a quick wink. 'Amelia, Iosefka, Kaya, and Adam will be going first. Please make your way through the doors and get ready. You will be sent up in a matter of minutes.'

Just about everyone else waiting had been holding their breath, praying to whomever they believed in that they wouldn't have to go first. It seemed that almost everyone praying had their pleas answered, all except for Iosefka, one of the most religious people in the cold dungeon-like room. Hearing her name caused her to chuckle as she hyperventilated, as though it was some kind of sick joke.

'Hey, hey, Iosefka, look at me, it's going to be fine. We will get through this.' Adam helped her past the strong monk to where they could choose their weapons.

'I... am... scared,' Iosefka muttered, her throat dry.

'I know, so am I,' Adam conceded, grasping her hand tightly.

'Really?'

'Oh yeah, and to make it worse, it's just hit me how many people are going to be watching us. I'm not that great with crowds.'

At this Iosefka started to panic even more, and her grip on Adam felt so strong that she would never let go. 'I had not even thought about how many people would be watching. God, please give me strength, I do not know if I can do this.'

'Sure, you can. Come and sit on the floor with me.'

Iosefka had been oblivious that they had already walked through into the area under the stage. Kaya and Amelia were arguing over what weapon was best to use, as Kaya retrieved a pair of daggers and Amelia grabbed a spear. A large square podium made from stone was positioned in the centre of the room with a trap door above.

Thin slivers of light from the gaps at the edges of the trap door were broken up by pieces of fine powdery sand wedged between. The noise from the crowd grew louder as older students and residents of Elysium filed into their seats, ready to witness the hours of carnage that would be taking place.

'Iosefka, come down here with me, we haven't got long,' Adam said, as he sat on the floor.

She collapsed where she stood.

'I know this is incredibly difficult for you, but we'll only be out there for a couple of minutes, and either we will do well or we'll do awfully. Try not to care because in the big picture, it won't ever matter. Also remember, we are all in this together and whatever happens, we will still be here at the end of it. It'll be even better because we can finally be a real team.'

'Thank you,' she replied, still shaking and her voice uneven, but with the belief that she could get through it.

'Ah, don't worry about it. Now I'm going to have to quickly grab a sword and shield. I'm guessing you're gonna be using magic out there?' Iosefka nodded in response. 'Then I'd recommend you do your prayers quickly because it doesn't sound like we have much time.'

From above, they could hear the crowd start to quiet as a booming voice started to speak, giving a muffled introduction. Feeling slightly better, or at least well enough to think properly, Iosefka started to pray for casting spells and spent an extra thirty seconds saying a prayer for all their safety.

'Are you all ready?' Theta asked, coming through the door.

'Oh, I'm ready, I don't know about Adam though. I think he needs a couple more years for that,' Amelia snarked as she climbed up onto the stone podium, spear in hand.

'I'm good, it's shorty over there that could use a few more years to grow.' Adam made a point of getting onto the podium without having to climb, lifting his knee as high as it would go and stepping up like it was nothing.

'You're not even that much taller than me,' Amelia argued.

'Ok then, well, there's about thirty seconds until I bring up the podium, so make sure you're all as prepared as you can be.' Theta scratched the back of her head, trying to ignore the situation.

Kaya gave Iosefka a leg up onto the stone, and then quickly jumped up to join them. Caesar's booming voice stopped, and the crowd's hungry cheers swarmed the air.

'Good luck, Amelia,' Theta said. She performed a few lazy hand movements and sent the trap door flying open as the platform started to move upwards.

The four of them had to shield their eyes from the sun with their hands as they came out onto the stage.

After the stun effect of the light had dimmed and the platform came to a stop, Adam started to take in the thousands of people that were all cheering and shouting at them. The stage itself was much larger than it had appeared from the outside.

Dozens of rock pillars going as high as the top seats in the coliseum with the same width as a thick oak tree were scattered around to act as cover. These pillars were made by crushing orange and brown rocks on top of each other, the floor below covered in a thick layer of dark orange sand.

They all left the platform and started to carefully inspect the area around them. Then without any warning, a loud scraping noise started to fill the open air. It was coming from the back area of the coliseum, which wasn't visible to any of them from the pillars blocking their view.

Instinctively, the four of them all huddled together, then shuffled closer to the noise to see what was happening. The scraping noise was coming from a huge gate made of obsidian, now fully opened.

The crowd had turned silent as they waited to see what would be coming from the darkness. The four of them waited like everyone else to see what would happen.

Adam noticed something blue streaking out onto the stage, so fast he barely noticed it.

'Did anyone see that?' He asked, unsure if it was just a trick of the light.

'I saw it too. It was like a fox but blue,' Kaya said, turning around to try to spot it again.

The group started to fall back to the centre, scared that whatever it was would catch them by surprise.

The four of them waited back on the platform, looking for anything blue in the stage of orange. Different sections of the crowd made noises of shock and excitement mere moments apart, like they could see the monster going all around the stadium, as if the thing was circling them.

'There!' Iosefka shouted, pointing at one of the pillars around its midpoint. 'It's jumping from the pillars.'

Adam stared at the pillar Iosefka had been pointing at and noticed a misty blue substance growing from it. 'It's turning whatever it touches into ice!'

They heard a loud patting noise on the sand behind them and, turning around, they saw a line of ice going across the ground only a few pillars away.

'Maybe we just need to help it.' Iosefka had been sticking as close to Adam as possible.

'Iosefka, have you not noticed that whatever it touches turns to ice? What happens if it manages to touch one of us? I can't risk it.' Amelia was frantically trying to spot the monster.

Adam had his sword sheathed and a fireball waiting in his hand. 'I don't think it's very strong. If I land a shot, it might be enough to take it down. I just need it to stay still.'

As if hearing Adam, the monster made itself known as it jumped to the top of one of the shorter pillars. The thin canine-like monster's ice-blue skin stretched tightly across its body. As it snarled at them, a cold mist filled the air around it, growing in density the harder the monster exhaled. Its snout was one of the only parts of the skin with fur, which was a snowy white, short and wiry. Its paws, the tip of its long tail, and its pricked ears were the only other parts that had any fur on them.

'There it is! Shoot it!' Iosefka screamed, desperate for the fight to be over.

'No, it won't work.' Adam put out his ball of fire by slashing his hand and closing his fist. 'The thing makes ice wherever it goes, and it's super-fast. There's no way a fireball would ever manage to hit it.'

'So now what?' Like everyone else, Kaya couldn't take his eyes off the monster, scared that at any moment it would try and pounce.

'I know what it is,' Amelia said with absolute confidence.

'What is it?' Adam asked.

'Perhaps if you had prepared better, you would know. Let's split up, Iosefka with me. I have a plan. We can finally prove who the better leader is.' Amelia grabbed Iosefka's arm, dragging her backwards.

'No, I'm staying with the team,' Iosefka retorted, yanking her arm out of Amelia's clutches.

'This is not up for discussion. I know exactly how to defeat the monster and you will come with me. We will wait for the other two to fail and then I will come in and save them.'

'No, I'm not leaving them behind.'

'Fine, then I'll just wait for all three of you to fail to prove that I am the best out of you all.' Amelia walked away from where the monster was still growling at them, going back towards the obsidian gate.

The hot sun was doing nothing to impair the progress of the cold that had now grown to consume about a third of the entire stage. Even the crowd rubbed their hands together or cast fire in the air around them. Their noise and cheers had also increased, and at this point, Adam wasn't so sure about who the audience was rooting for.

'We have to do something before all the floor is ice, otherwise, we'll just slip and fall,' Kaya said.

'You're right. Iosefka, back off a little and get ready to cast some barriers of desert glass for us. Kaya, you throw a quick spell at it and when it drops, I'll go in for a hit.'

The two did as they were told and when in position, Kaya launch a slice of pressurised wind up at the monster. As expected, it managed to dodge it with ease and pounced to the ground between Adam and Kaya. It held its head low, growling and biting madly, revealing a row of sharp teeth made for ripping through meat.

Adam crept toward the monster, his sword and shield raised. When the beast was just out of swinging reach of the sword, it took the opportunity to lunge towards Adam, shooting off with its powerful hind legs like a bullet, completely unaffected by all the ice.

Thankfully, the month of practice hadn't gone to waste as Adam's reflexes brought the shield up in time to block the monster's body colliding with his own, landing instead on the shield making Adam slide back from the force of impact.

The beast pushed back against the shield, using its hind legs, bouncing back the way it came, the power of which made Adam lose his footing. He dropped to the ground. Iosefka shot sharp pieces of desert glass, but it completely missed the monster, colliding into the icy pillar behind them.

Adam's shield had completely frozen at the touch of the monster, and the ice had already reached his fingers, making it impossible to let go. Thinking of Adam as less of a threat, the monster moved towards Kaya, a few paces away.

Once again, the monster lunged toward its target. Kaya stabbed both his daggers into its side as it jumped on top of him. The pain from the daggers made the beast run away, but it had managed to scratch Kaya on the leg as it retreated, which was now slowly starting to freeze faster than his shoulders, which the monster had also made contact with.

Iosefka had no ice on her at all, yet she was completely frozen in place. But as Adam lifted his sword, in the hope of fending off the ice hound that was gunning for him once again, a dagger still stuck in its side, something inside of Iosefka snapped. The same drive and determination that pushed her to go through the portal came flooding back.

Running as fast as she could, she used the ice to slide on her knees over to Adam, his entire left side frozen. As she slid, Iosefka shouted an incantation without fault and created a small dome of protection out of desert glass, which covered the two of them just in time to stop the monster from making contact.

Its white claws scraped away at the golden dome trying to break it down, pushing all of its weight on it, trying to shatter it, ignoring the pain it felt from the two stab wounds in its side, the blood freezing as soon as it escaped its body.

Eventually, the monster managed to make a hole in the glass and, seeing this as the opportune moment to strike, Adam swung awkwardly at the beast with his sword, just as the dome shattered. The monster barely managed to evade the sword, but it was startled enough to run away.

'How the hell are we going to break this ice before that thing comes back!' Adam shouted to Kaya who was almost completely frozen from the neck down, stuck to the ground.

'Maybe someone should tell a joke?' Kaya said, wincing at the pain from talking.

'Kaya!' Adam shouted.

'Right, bad timing.' Kaya said as Iosefka used Elemental magic to blow a boiling mist from her hands to melt the ice.

'Thanks for that protection, Iosefka, it came at the perfect time.' Adam dropped his sword to the sand so he could use his unfrozen hand to cast a ball of fire onto the floor below him, hoping it would melt the ice encapsulating him.

'I may be afraid but I am no coward runaway, not anymore.'

Gradually Adam managed to melt away all the ice. Once it was all gone, no more started to spread. However, Kaya's scratch wouldn't stop producing layers of ice around the skin no matter how much heat went against it.

By now, the monster had finished its retreat and had built up enough courage to run back towards the group huddled together. Adam made a few swings at it whenever it came close, as Iosefka kept up a desert glass barrier and Kaya threw out a constant stream of wind spells, and for a while, it seemed to be going well. The monster was too injured and afraid of getting hit with the sword to try and pick off one of the three.

As they worked to ward the enemy away, none of them noticed the new layer of thick ice slowly creeping towards them. It was only when the monster tried to bite and Adam tried to step forward to swing his sword that he discovered his feet had been completely frozen to the floor. Before he could do anything to react, the horribly sharp teeth pierced Adam's skin like butter. Immediately, his arm burst into agonizing pain, and he experienced a temperature so cold that it burned.

He didn't know how badly he was injured, but the pain would have brought him to his knees if his body hadn't already started to freeze over. Kaya's scratch had now frozen all of his lower body, with Iosefka's feet also frozen to the floor. They were helpless as the monster broke through the desert glass barrier Iosefka had hastily created, making one last leap towards them.

Having been hiding behind a pillar, Amelia came sliding between the monster and the rest of her team. 'QIQIRN!' She shouted.

The very second that she had spoken the monster's name, the Qiqirn wanted nothing more than to flee, but still shooting through the air, there was nothing it could do to change its course and came crashing into Amelia like a bowling ball.

Just before the ice fully consumed him, Adam watched as Amelia's unconscious body skidded off across the ground, knocking into all of them. The Qiqirn whimpered as it dashed back to its obsidian cage. Without any way to break free, Adam became fully encased in ice.

15. Two Beings at the Start of It All

(*Ascensionist's testimony to the creation of magic, the universe, and everything.*)
At the start of everything, there were two. We can call one Ira. It fed on chaos and calamity. The other can be named Pax, which fed on peace and joy. Neither being good or evil – they simply existed – completely unaware of the other's presence.

Light was the first creation by Pax, and all was good for it. Having a reservoir of food, Pax felt no hunger. However, in this happiness, Ira started to dwindle. Starving. In a fight for survival, it created darkness to feed on. And all was good for it.

Unfortunately, the dark had destroyed half of Pax's light; there was still plenty to feed on, but Pax craved more. It tried to create an atom within the dark and the light, wanting to consume harmony. Although, Pax was still young and naive and made the atom with only the proton and neutron. Alas, it was too unstable to consume.

Finding this failed creation, Ira believed that it had been rewarded for birthing darkness. So it started to devour on the atom's volatile state.

Both entities were now older and wiser than when the atom was created.

Ready to be rewarded once more, Ira easily created the electron and completed the atom. Pax, who had for all this time been trying to solve the mystery of the atom, believed that the universe itself was taunting it, solving the problem for it.

Desperate to overcome its enemy, Pax tried using the now stable atom for joy, and so the entity made a cosmic explosion, one so chaotic and spectacularly joyous that both Pax and Ira fed greedily on it, experiencing a perfect wondrous state.

After this big bang had concluded and one atom shredded into many, both were left insatiable. Refusing to suckle on such microscopic things and desperate to reach that euphoric sensation once more, Pax and Ira started creating as much as they could.

As time passed, each entity remained ravenous. Before one could feed, something would be created by the other that diminished its source of food. When Ira created raging fire, Pax created the serene water, now both believing that it was the universe itself they were fighting against.

These cunning entities continued to starve the other in more elaborate ways. Ira, creator of darkness, made weaker beings, instilling these things with a will to survive. This led to conflict of all mannerisms which Ira attempted to feed on. But before long, Pax instilled these organisms with a will to live, dawning resolution and rest.

For all of time, these two entities fought in a never-ending battle; blinded by greed, barely managing to survive.

16. A Bakunawa in the Cosmic Sky

By the time Adam woke up in the infirmary, it had already gone dark. Every single bed was occupied by other students. He could hear muffled arguing between two people whose silhouettes were outlined on the closed entrance like in a children's show. Adam was surprised to find that Iosefka was the one waiting by his bed and not Kaya.

'How are you feeling?' She asked, passing him some water.

Everything that had happened on the stage all seemed blurry.

'What happened?' He found that when he spoke, his teeth were chattering.

'It was all Amelia's fault. Kaya's outside now shouting at her for leaving us to fight alone when she knew exactly how to win the fight from the start.'

It all started to come back to him now. He swung his legs out of the bed and as his feet touched the grass, he shuddered with how soaking wet it was. Then he remembered how he had frozen like a popsicle and must have been thawed out by the monks – which also gave reason for why the bedsheet were so damp.

Iosefka helped Adam to his feet, but he found that he was mostly back to normal except for a cold groggy feeling and an aching in his arm where the Qiqirn had bitten him. Adam rolled up his ripped sleeve to see that a thick cloth had been tightly wrapped around it, and when he tried to poke the area where the teeth had pierced him, he found that his skin was rock hard.

'They put an antidote onto it,' Iosefka said. 'The monster's bite made ice grow from inside your body. Apparently without the antidote, which they had at the ready, it would have been fatal. No magic would have been able to stop the coldness reaching your heart if you had run into one of those hell spawns out in the wild.'

Iosefka helped Adam for the first couple of steps but he managed to walk by himself, and they made their way to the exit. Adam noticed that the students on the beds had all kinds of injuries. Groups were covered in burn marks and had a green ointment applied over them. Several buckets were filled with large brown spikey quills, their tips red with blood from impaling those that rested next to them. Clearly, the Qiqirn was not the only challenge that the students had had to face.

Opening the fabric doors, Adam watched as Kaya screamed at Amelia. 'You are a disgrace to this team! You should be ashamed of yourself! There is no way that any kind of leader would leave their team to fend for themselves. We may have been beaten by that dog, but at least Adam was there to help fight!' In all the years Adam had known Kaya, he had never seen him this angry. Spit was flying from his mouth and there was a big vein popping out from his forehead.

'I know, I'm so sorry, I am a terrible leader. All I cared about was proving that I was better than Adam and I ended up getting everyone hurt.' Amelia had tears rolling down her eyes as she pled for Kaya's forgiveness.

'This isn't even about being a bad leader anymore, Amelia. You're just a terrible person for letting that happen to us.'

'I know... Tell Adam I'm sorry,' she whimpered before running off.

Neither of them had noticed Adam and Iosefka loitering by the entrance and only after Amelia had gone out of sight did Kaya turn around and notice them.

'Adam! You should stay in bed. That bite did not look good.'

'I'm fine, Kaya. Let's just head back to the cabin so I can sleep in my bed.'

Kaya insisted on helping Adam as they made their way back to the cabin. Trotting through camp, they could hear the celebrations of all the students that performed well in the coliseum, cheering and dancing as they went to the Food Hall, which seemed to be having another feast in celebration.

When they stumbled down the hill to their cabin, they found their new team totem carved into the wooden plaque on their front door. The small wart-covered rodent barely managed to stand on its four feeble trembling legs. The carving had gone into extra detail showing the pathetic thing to be crying, its tears streaking down its ugly face, its wrinkly body shrivelled up in fear. Nobody said a word about the miserable totem they had been given. They would now have to live with the pathetic thing for as long as they were at camp.

It was several hours later, after sitting in silence around the living room, when the three of them heard something fall down the hill and smack into the cabin wall. Adam ran outside and found Amelia lying on the leaf-covered ground, not bothering to pick herself up, as though she had given up on everything.

'I guess you'll be the leader then,' she said in a dry monotonous tone. 'We technically drew with the Qiqirn, but you were always with the team, I hid away, and did nothing to help. Not until it was too late.'

'Come inside. It looks like it's about to rain again.'

Amelia gave a long exhale as some droplets of water fell onto her forehead, slipping past all the branches and leaves just to fall onto her. 'Fine, I guess there's no point in trying to argue with the leader.'

She slowly picked herself up, and like a zombie, she stumbled towards the front door.

'Ah, a Squonk. How fitting,' she said bitterly looking at their front door.

'You know about this creature? Is there anything good about it?' Adam asked.

'As you can see in appearance, the Squonk looks like a shrivelled potato. Hunters are easily able to track a Squonk by its tear-stained trail, for the animal weeps. Constantly. When cornered or surprised, it can dissolve itself in tears. It's written about in an old book by William T. Cox, called *Fearsome Creatures of the Lumberwoods*. Although, if I'm not mistaken, it may be the least fearsome, most pathetic creature to ever exist.'

Several more hours passed as the rain poured more heavily than they had experienced so far. None of them were in any kind of mood to be around other people, and so chose not to attend the feast. Amelia had conceded that Adam should be the leader, but he felt nothing like someone who should lead. If anything, Iosefka and Kaya had proven to be better leaders than he had.

Eventually, they made their way to their rooms. Adam knew that he was the one who needed to bring the team together but he didn't have it in him tonight.

At some point during the night as the storm continued to bring down its wrath, Adam slipped into a fever-like dream, so incredibly vivid he thought it impossible that it was anything else but reality.

He was standing on the roof of the cabin. The forest was completely ablaze. Smoke polluted the air with such blackness and grittiness that it was even worse than the atmosphere on Earth. The rain was pouring down so hard that it almost seemed like the world was made from television static.

The water falling from the clouds couldn't reach anywhere near the burning trees before evaporating into an icy blue steam that started to freeze the grey clouds above. The fire raged on, unaffected by the freezing mist. Somehow it hadn't consumed his cabin. Everything else in all of Elysium had now burned to a crisp yet here he was standing on top of the cabin, completely fine. Adam leaned over the side, curious if anyone else was below, and was amazed to find that the Squonk was alive.

The ugly thing was cowering by the front door in a pool of tears. 'Waaaa– Waaaa,' the Squonk cried, making the puddle of tears grow.

The puddle became so large, soon it was no longer a puddle but a pond, which then quickly turned into a river flowing down towards the beach with its now blackened sand, and then it became a full ocean that filled all of the world. The Squonk had saved Adam and he wanted nothing more than to show it his gratitude, but he found that the moment he leapt from the roof to the ground, a bolt of lightning struck the Squonk, killing it.

Adam wanted to mourn but he knew there was no time. A second strike would be coming soon, he could feel it. Sure enough, another bolt of white light came running through the sky down into the cabin, causing the roof he was just on to explode. However, something was different about this lightning... something was riding it.

The fear of what was in the lightning was enough to scare Adam awake. He was back in his comfortable room on Earth. Everything was fine, he was safe. Nothing could hurt him, his nanobees would make sure he was protected.

All of a sudden, the door handle of his room started to twist back and forth, and Adam pulled his sheet up close over his face. Whatever was trying to get into Adam's room gave up twisting the door and started to knock, calling out his name in a dry raspy voice.

As the monster continued to knock, Adam walked over to the door, trying not to make any noise, a rusty sword in his hand, ready to slay the monster.

He was right in front of the door now, the wailing of his name still repeating. Building as much courage as he could, Adam took a deep breath as he swung it open.

'Adam, could you open the door please?' Amelia knocked on the door again.

Adam was back in his bed on Elysium, covered in sweat from the dream. His breathing was heavy as he slipped out of bed, trying to check if he was still asleep as he plodded over to open the door.

'What is it? Is everything alright?' Adam was certain he was awake now. He could feel the wooden flooring pushing against his feet, and the cold air brushed against his skin as the rain and thunder continued outside.

'I know you're the leader now, but could we please all go somewhere, there is something I want to show you all.' Her eyes were red but she had stopped crying, and her voice was strong with new determination.

Adam had no intention of falling back asleep, knowing what kind of things were waiting in his dreams. 'Show me the way.'

'Could you tell the others to come with as well? I don't think they will listen to me.'

The other two turned out to be wide awake.

'What's up?' Kaya asked.

'We're going on a quick adventure,' Adam said in the most positive tone he could, looking out the window and realising they were about to get soaked.

'Sweet! Where to?' It was obvious that Kaya was faking his excitement.

'I'm not sure, where are we going, Amelia?'

'Just to the cherry blossom tree.'

'Why is she the one making decisions? She abandoned us,' Iosefka snapped. 'Why does she get to choose what we do?'

'I know I don't deserve any respect from any of you but please follow me. I know you will all love it, I'm almost certain it's going to happen.'

Trying to take the initiative to invite them all to follow her, Amelia opened the front door. The wind was so strong that the moment she pushed the door slightly, the entire thing flew open, and Adam had a flashback of his nightmare. The door smacked against the outside wall repeatedly from the force of the whistling wind carrying all kinds of nature in its wake. Amelia stepped out into the storm and started to climb up the hill, slipping as she did.

Adam and Kaya followed with Iosefka grudgingly joining from behind. By the time they had all clambered up the hill, everyone was drenched with so much rain, it felt as though they had fallen into the ocean. There was no point in keeping his bandage on now that it was falling apart so Adam ripped it off, exposing his hard skin to the harsh weather with Kaya doing the same to the bandage he had on his leg.

As they moved through the forest, their wet hair flew across their faces like hundreds of tiny whips. Walking past all the cabins, Adam saw the aftermath of a night of partying and celebrating. The lights in all the cabins were off and there wasn't any sign of anyone, but food and drink were littered all around the cabins. Kaya barely managed to duck as a wooden plate flew through the sky, speeding past all of them into a tree, which snapped the plate in two.

After this incident, Amelia made a dome of desert glass around the four of them, which helped stop the rain and dry leaves from slapping them in the face, but it was still impossible to see farther than a few steps ahead of them.

Even with this dome, Adam, Kaya, and especially Iosefka were all in a worse mood from having to leave their comfy cabin to walk to the cliffside, where the cherry blossom tree's pink leaves swung madly.

'So now what!' Iosefka shouted over the storm.

'Just keep your eyes on the sky. It should be coming any time now if my astronomy calculations are correct.'

Adam thought about questioning this. Amelia's skills in astronomy were surely terrible, considering she had only been in Elysium for a month, during which time she had her head buried in books, not staring aimlessly into the sky.

'There, look!' She pointed at the sky where they could barely make out a cloud of blue smoke floating through the sky.

'What are you pointing at? That's just a bit of the sky!' Iosefka seemed close to pushing Amelia off the cliff.

'No, wait!' Kaya had cupped his hands around his face. 'It's some kind of dragon!'

Emerging from the inky smoke was an impossibly gigantic sky serpent.

The deep sapphire snake-like dragon was larger than anything Adam could ever imagine. Its ash whiskers could fill the largest of canyons, and as it flew around their solar system with silky ease, like a shark in water, its sheer presence pulled millions of meteors with it.

'What is that?' Iosefka asked with an open mouth.

'That is the Bakunawa. It only comes into our sky once every five years and it tries to destroy our world,' Amelia said casually.

'What!' They all gawked at the thing that travelled galaxies, its immensely long body covered in different shades of blue scales twisting around the cold space, dispersing the perfect clouds of colours with the slightest of movements.

'You can't be serious?' Kaya gave a short laugh, assuming Amelia was joking.

'Don't worry about it, just keep watching.'

The Bakunawa seemed to be searching for something as it spiralled. It contorted its sapphire body in loops, as though it couldn't tell where it was, colliding with hundreds of thousands of meteors – a single one being capable of destroying most of Elysium – without showing any signs of pain.

Adam's eyes were as open as they could be. Even with the water getting through the desert glass onto his face, he couldn't blink – too afraid that he would miss the end of all the worlds.

The sky serpent moved impossibly fast. Adam felt like he was an ant watching a questing beast cross distances in seconds that would take him several lifetimes to traverse.

Across the left side of its face and down the side of its head was a planet-sized burn mark, blackening the deep blue scales as though it had flown too close to the sun and had tried to eat it at some point in the past.

Iosefka was saying her final prayers. She was down on the floor kneeling in the wet mud, her hands tightly gripping one another as her head dropped, too afraid to see this devil spawn.

Kaya seemed to still be in disbelief, his mouth open, almost smiling, certain that this was some elaborate prank from Amelia, with hidden cameras recording to catch his reaction.

'Guys, trust me, we will be fine, it's not after Elysium,' Amelia encouraged.

Having found the thing it was looking for, the Bakunawa darted in a straight line towards the glowing moon that orbited Elysium, which had been hidden behind a cloud of red smoke.

Nearing the target, the Bakunawa blocked the moon from their sights like a solar eclipse. It opened up its mouth, revealing a line of jagged black teeth – each a thousand times bigger than Mount Ida – and, in one gulp, it swallowed the moon whole.

Everyone gave gasps of shock and fear that their only moon had been snatched from the sky, all except for Amelia who was waiting for something to happen.

From the very depths of the Wildlands, all mannerisms of noises started to emerge, from howling to wailing and shrieking all the way to roaring so loud, the air itself started to vibrate.

'What in all the heavens is that?' Iosefka, like the other two, thought she was hallucinating as she shakily rose from the ground.

'The Bakunawa tries to eat our moon, and so every single living thing makes as much noise as they can to scare it into letting the moon go. It doesn't matter if it's a monster or a creature, hunter or prey, everything stops and works together to defeat the Moon Eater. Arguments, rivalries, fights, they all stop to deal with the bigger problem.' Amelia said all of this whilst staring straight at Adam.

'AHHHHHHHH!' She screamed at the top of her voice, dropping the protective barrier.

Desperately wanting to help get the moon back, the other three all shouted, screamed and yelled up at the Bakunawa, that tossed and turned in confusion from noise that, shouldn't logically be able to reach it.

'BEGONE, FOUL DEMON!' Iosefka cried.

'GIVE BACK OUR MOOOOOOOON!' Kaya howled like a wolf.

'AHHHHHHHHHHH!' Adam screamed at the Bakunawa, and as he did, he could feel all of his frustrations escape his body.

Trying to be as loud as possible was great for letting out all their rage. Once they had started, they couldn't stop, going as loud as their voices allowed, fighting against the Moon Eater the only way they could.

The ocean creatures and monsters started to join in with the noise, jumping as high as they could and smashing back down with as much force as they could, creating massive tidal waves. The very sky itself brought down bolts upon bolts of lightning that boomed around the world.

Everything in the Wildlands continued to make as much noise as they could. No matter where on Elysium, whether it was the depths of the Ocean of the Damned or in the deepest crevices in the mountains, this united stentorian noise could be heard. And by some miracle, it even appeared to crack through the silence of space to pierce and discombobulate the Moon Eater.

The Bakunawa became so confused that it started to heave, recoiling its godly body as it spat out the precious moon exactly where it had found it. Frantic to get away from the noise, the Bakunawa swam through the cosmic sky until it found the spread of blue inky smoke it had entered through and disappeared back into it.

With the attack on the moon over, all the monsters and creatures returned to their normal life routines, silently stalking their prey or falling asleep in their nests. The storm started to ease, the wind coming back down to a mellow chill and the rain reducing to a drizzle.

The only things that had continued to make notable noise were Adam and Kaya, who were yelling the lyrics of their favourite songs as Iosefka did her best to scream along with them.

'Adam!' Amelia called.

Adam fell back towards the cherry blossom tree where Amelia stood.

'I have let this competition blind me from the bigger picture for far too long,' Amelia said as Adam came close. 'I want you to know that I do not have any resentment towards you. I know that you wanted this as much as I did, but when it came down to it, your priorities were better than mine. We are safer in your hands. I just hope you can forgive me for everything I have done over this past month.'

Amelia appeared genuinely unsure as to whether Adam would forgive her. She had looked him in the face throughout speaking and he could see that it pained her to do so. That admitting to her mistakes was something that she would rarely do.

'I don't want to lead you,' he replied.

Amelia's face fell and she finally let her head drop, after trying so hard to seem strong. 'I understand; I can see about getting a cabin for me to live in tomorrow'

'No – no – no, that's not what I mean. I don't want to lead at all.'

'I don't understand. You deserve it, you won.'

'I told you I don't want to be the leader. I only wanted to lead because I didn't want to be told what to do by you.' It felt so stupid to say it now.

'So, when you said that I could be leader if I wanted to, you really meant it? As in, it wasn't some joke or ruse to get me off my game?'

'I thought you would make a great leader.'

'I thought so too, but the truth is, I don't think I would be. I find it hard to accept what others say if I think differently, and I guess, similar to you, I only wanted to lead so that people would respect me, and so that they would have to listen and agree with whatever I said.'

'So, now what?' Adam asked as Kaya and Iosefka raw in the throat came strolling over.

'Iosefka,' Amelia said, 'you showed so much bravery in that coliseum, you deserve to be the leader of this group.'

'What! Me! You're mad!' Iosefka had her hands up as if physically trying to push back the idea. 'I know nothing and need to spend my time learning not leading.'

'Are you sure? You're stronger than you think,' Amelia complimented.

'I'm certain. Perhaps you're right about me being strong. I couldn't believe I did so well in the coliseum. But leading is too much pressure for me, it's not something I was made for. Kaya would be much better, I think.'

'Nope,' he said immediately. 'Not a chance.'

'What does that mean? None of us are leading this group?' Iosefka asked.

'Or all of us are leading it.' Adam put his hand in the centre of the little circle they had formed. 'I know it's a little corny, but I say we make a deal. Nobody and everybody leads this group. No decision is ever made by one single person, always as a group. As a family.'

'Sweet,' Kaya said, putting his hand on top of Adam's.

'Sounds like a plan,' Iosefka added with an encouraging nod to Adam.

'Thank you,' Amelia said, placing her hand on the pile. 'May the Squonk team be the mightiest of them all.' They lifted their hands into the sky, all shouting the name of their awful totem.

The story of the Bakunawa's coming had always had a way of making people come together back on Earth, and as the four of them made their way happily back to their cabin, excited for what the future would bring, it seemed that when brought to life, the Moon Eater had a similar effect.

17. The Perfect Mentor

On their way back to the cabin, soaking wet, the group worked out how their team would function.

'It's time I was honest about my capabilities,' Amelia said, her shoes squelching as they walked through the muddy grounds covered in fallen branches. 'You weren't there to see it, but when the Qiqirn came away from you, it found me and... I just froze. I couldn't do a thing and it only ran away because it heard you destroying some of its ice.'

'Well, I'm glad that us desperately trying not to freeze to death was useful to you,' Iosefka snarked.

'I'm sorry I wasn't there to help, and I'm sorry that I dragged you through all my problems and then tried to make you leave the rest of your team to get hurt. I wish I was as brave as you, but I'm not.'

This stopped Iosefka from making another remark.

'As a result, I don't think I should have any real responsibility in the heat of the moment,' Amelia said. 'At least not until I learn how to deal with real situations that are truly dangerous. However, if possible, I would like to spend time planning things. I know I shouldn't be asking for anything, and of course, nothing would be done without the majority of you all agreeing, but we will have to divide our time. We can't have everyone focusing on the same thing, otherwise nothing will get done and we'll all just get in each other's way.'

'I think that's smart,' Kaya agreed. 'I don't know what I want to do to help this team, but I know I don't want to sit around planning things. So, yeah, I like that idea.'

'Sounds good to me,' Adam said, his body shaking from the cold. 'You know more than me, there's no point pretending you don't.'

Once they had all dried their clothes, using a few heat spells and the burning fireplace, the four of them sat down in the living room together. Even though their performance in the tournament, which felt like weeks ago, was mediocre at best, it was done and they were now able to leave the camp boundaries.

'Now the best kind of teams are the ones where each member brings something of value to help,' Amelia said as soon as everyone had sat down. 'It doesn't make much sense to me if we all practice Elemental magic, for example, as we will only be as strong as the weakest caster, and if a situation arises where Elemental magic is a crux for us, we put ourselves in a bad spot. So, I suggest that we each pick several things that we want to focus on for the next year or so. You don't have to work out what it may be straight away, you can even look into different areas of study to find the one you want. After this awful last month, everyone should just do what they enjoy and not what they are being forced to do.'

'What do you mean, areas of study? I refuse to do any more reading.' Iosefka pointed her finger at Amelia.

'No, not if you don't want to do something that has reading involved in it. I mean we will all need to learn how to fight to at least an advanced level with both magic and physical combat, but we should all have a speciality of some kind. Learning how to make traps, skills in tracking for when we go on long expeditions. I am personally going to try and learn how to decode the scrolls so that when we start finding them, I can help us discover what knowledge it has for us. You could specialise in monsters or artefacts. Knowing cartography would be useful. Even something like making food and learning about herbs and meats can come in handy in situations that you may never expect. Do we all agree?'

Everyone gave nods of agreement, but whilst all four of them were exceptionally excited for what the future would bring, it had been over twenty-four hours since most of them had taken a proper rest, and their tiredness was starting to catch up with them.

'Tomorrow, I say we get up as late as we want,' Adam said with a long yawn, which then copied its way around the room. 'We can take our time with the day and take it easy. We've got eleven months till we have to go out into the Wildlands. I think we can take our foot off the accelerator a little.'

'What's an accelerator?' Iosefka asked before they all slowly made their way to their beds.

# #

The following day, the sun rose as it always did and for once the Squonk team were resting peacefully whilst it did so. None of them were concerned about training today and all made their way merrily towards the Food Hall, as if the soggy mud-filled path were a yellow brick road.

'Has everyone given some thought about what they want to try and do today?' Amelia asked, trying her best to sound casual and relaxed as everyone ate.

The Food Hall was emptier than it was before dawn. Adam assumed that the feast had been filling, or everyone was still sleeping after a night of partying.

'I've given some thought about what you've said and it's completely stupid and illogical,' Iosefka stated.

'What!' Amelia quickly dropped her casual demeanour, sitting forward, ready to challenge Iosefka.

'You're just expecting us to find something that will make us valuable because apparently, we aren't good enough as it is. Then once we've found whatever it may be, I still don't understand how we are meant to find out if we like something without anyone to show us what it properly is. We are then expected to become skilled in it without any way of knowing how to progress.'

'You raise some good points,' Amelia said through gritted teeth.

'I know what we can do,' Kaya said, tapping Adam on the side to get his attention as he pointed towards another group eating their breakfast. 'Isn't that what's-her-name's group, you know Gerard's daughter's group?'

'Delilah,' Adam answered.

'That's the one! Why don't we just go over and ask if they could show us some of the skills they have and how they learnt them?'

'Can't hurt to ask, I suppose.' Adam rose from his seat.

Delilah, like the other three members of her team, was eating oats and porridge.

'What?' Delilah said, not looking up from her food.

'We are very sorry to interrupt you, but you are one of the strongest students at camp, and we were just wondering if you could help us learn some new skills.' As Amelia spoke, her confidence declined. The more she saw Delilah's uninterested face, the more she worried that she had offended her.

'What would be in it for my team?' Delilah asked.

'Whatever you need,' Adam replied.

'Except we don't have any money, artefacts, or knowledge that you don't already have unless you want to know about the twelve-act hero structure or anything to do with T.V and film,' Kaya said with a forced smile and his thumbs up.

Delilah stared at the four of them for some time. Her cold eyes amid all of her fiery hair made Adam feel like he was staring into the cold heart of a burning sun.

Just before Kaya made some joke to break the silence, Delilah made her decision.

'For one day, my team will give you a basic amount of knowledge spanning the different skills we have learnt over the years, along with instructions on how to progress alone. You are fortunate that we are heading into the Wildlands tomorrow and are taking this day to rest and pack our supplies, and that if I tell my father I have helped you, he may ease his relentless questions.'

'Thank you so much –' Amelia started to say.

'In return,' Delilah interrupted, 'each of you four are indebted to this team. In the future, I will ask something from every one of you. It may be to give me an item, to assist or aid my team, or something else entirely. Whatever I ask, you will do it without any questions asked. Once you have completed the request, your debt will then be paid. Those are my terms.'

They all thought hard about the offer. 'Is it alright if we quickly talk it through?' Adam asked.

Delilah gave a slow nod and went back to eating her porridge.

'Do we ask someone else?' Iosefka wondered as she started to look around at the other teams.

'No, we've seen Delilah fight. She's got to be one of the best and she only uses her fists,' Adam responded.

Kaya kept looking back at Delilah. 'But what will she ask us to do? Couldn't she tell one of us to kill someone else? Would we have to do it?'

'I'm not sure. I would need to go to the Bibliotech so I can understand the exact laws of the land.'

'Well, we don't have time for that, Amelia,' Iosefka complained. 'I think we should go through with it. I can't imagine they are the kind of people to take advantage of others.'

'I think I know what we need to do,' Adam said, having thought hard about what was best for the team. 'Amelia, you already have a good idea of what skills you want to learn, right? Books, planning, Enlightenment magic, that kind of stuff?'

'Yes.'

'So, there isn't as much point in you making the deal with Delilah, and I already have an idea of the things I want to practice and get better at. It's more you two that need the help finding what you want to do.' Adam looked at Kaya and Iosefka. 'But you wouldn't be struggling if you hadn't spent the last month being bossed around. So, I'm suggesting that we offer for just the two of you to get the help from them, but it's me and Amelia who are in debt to them.'

'Are you sure?' Iosefka asked, looking more at Amelia.

'I think that is a great idea, allows the chance for me to repent a little,' Amelia replied.

'We all agree then?' Adam checked, and the other three nodded.

Delilah considered the offer and decided to accept. The moment the deal was done, all of her team rose slowly from their seats like they were in the army, doing everything in perfect synchronisation.

'Let's get started,' Delilah said as she made her way out of the Food Hall, beckoning Kaya and Iosefka to follow.

'Guess I'll see you later then, thanks for this.' Kaya gave a wave as he left with Iosefka.

'What did you want to learn?' Amelia asked as the two of them sat back down to finish their breakfast.

'I'm thinking about learning how to cook, seems like it could be fun but that's not important now, seeing Delilah has given me an idea. I think we should go to the Capital. You can go to the Bibliotech and I can try and get Gerard to mentor us.'

'Whilst I love that idea, and Gerard seems like a great person, he is one of the highest-ranking people in all of Elysium. Why would he spend his time on us?'

'He was close with my mum and dad. I'm pretty sure that if I ask for his help, he will have a hard time saying no. They dumped me on Earth and he feels responsible for not being there for me after they died.'

Adam had never properly opened up to Amelia before. 'I'm sure your parents left you on Earth to make sure you were safe,' she said carefully.

'That's what Gerard said. Look, I understand now that they did it because they thought it was best for me, but I can still use the connections they had to help us grow. So, are you ready to head to the Capital?'

'Yeah, sure, sounds like a plan,' Amelia replied.

It didn't take them long before they found themselves on the large open path where the carriages had brought them down from the Capital. They could see the end of the path where they had gone through the forest on their first day at camp and made sure to walk the other way, assuming that the carriages were only used on rare occasions and that normally they would have to walk the journey to and from the Capital.

It took about forty-five minutes to make the trip, throughout which the two did not stop talking, going over battle tactics, scrolls and spells that would be valuable to learn. It was as if they had never been at the other's throats.

The two found an older resident throwing bread over the bridge that led across the river at the entrance to the city. As the small pieces of dough fell into the water, a couple of ducks and their fluffy ducklings would scramble to try and eat it, quacking away as they did.

He told them that the Bibliotech was in the opposite direction to where Gerard had said he had lived. So the two separated, agreeing that they would split up and meet back up later.

It wasn't hard to find Gerard's house. Being someone of his power and rank had its clear benefits. Gerard had only needed to give Adam the street name when he had visited them at their cabin because there was only one house along the street at the edge of the city.

The house had a timber frame and oak plank walls that gave it a Medieval Viking era mixed aesthetic. A large turret erected from the tiled roof, scaling over the chimney that was billowing black smoke from the other side of the house. The turret was tall enough that if Gerard would climb to the top and look out of one of the many little windows going around it, he would have a clear view of the whole town in one direction, and over the meadow fields in the other.

Shields of all sizes and styles hung on the walls around the entrance, as though they were decorations. The grass was so unkempt that it covered the slabs of concrete that were made to act as stepping stones leading to the front door. The house opened up to the outside with a low roof.

Coming from this add-on to the house was a rhythmic clanging noise, one of metal against metal, and as Adam made his way closer, a great waft of fire blew from inside like the house was breathing fire.

Gerard was arguing from where the fire had come from, but it was hard to understand with who. Gathering a small bit of courage, Adam made his way around the corner, where he discovered a blacksmithing shop built into the house.

Barrels of weapons lined up around the walls, with a large anvil pointing outside so that as Gerard furiously hammered onto it, causing sparks to come flying off, he could see out into the beautiful meadows. To the side of the anvil was a forge covered in ash, which currently had many red-hot blades resting in the fire. Even with one wall missing, all the forging made the surrounding area incredibly stuffy.

As Adam thought about making himself known to Gerard, thinking that he must have been arguing with himself as he worked, a stern voice came from the corner of the room. 'Like I have explained to you before, we cannot risk going any deeper into the Wildlands.' Micholesh's tone was harsh.

'I don't care about the risk!' Gerard was hammering the metal with such force, it was amazing that it didn't break. 'You aren't doing enough to find my artefact. You know how dangerous this is for our world. It could be out there!'

'It isn't as dangerous as the risk of what might be out in those unexplored lands. And how do you suppose your greatsword—what is believed to be the very weapon used by the horseman of war—managed to find its way out there?'

'The Ascensionists.'

'The Ascensionists are dead!' Micholesh shouted with such fury that Adam retreated a few steps out of utter fear. 'We wiped out those horrid people that infected this land long ago. There are none left.'

'You can't destroy a belief. All it takes is one person to believe that ending the world will create a portal to heaven to have the Ascensionists return.'

'Enough, I will hear no more of this.'

Even Gerard seemed to be fearful of Micholesh as he chose not to pursue that line of discussion any further. 'Then what have Maria and her Disciples discovered? Anything?'

'They are working as hard as they can, but there is a lot they have to deal with. However, they have a few clues that they are confident will lead them to the culprit.'

'What are they?'

'I think we both know it is not a good idea for me to say. Although the Disciples do seem confident in their assessment. It will only be a matter of time until their work is done. Now, if that is all, I have other matters to attend to.'

'That is all that matters. Tell me the instant something happens.'

'Of course.'

Not wanting to be caught eavesdropping, Adam retreated, but in his haste to leave, he tripped over something bright white that he hadn't noticed in the long grass and he fell to the ground with a thud, which made him panic and sprint away before either of them came to investigate.

From what he could tell, nobody noticed he was there and by the time he had done a few laps around the area, Adam could only hear the noise of metal cooling and sizzling in water.

'Ah, Adam, my boy! How can I help you?' Gerard said in a stiffly cheerful way.

'I'm good. How's everything going with you?' Adam asked, wanting to see if he could get any more information than what he had already overheard.

Gerard huffed as he wiped his hands on his loose greasy shirt. 'Nobody seems to be giving me any real answers. Micholesh is doing what he can, but he can't be seen playing favourites. Even if I am his third in command. Soon I will have to take matters into my own hands when the Disciples fail.'

Adam only now started to wonder why Gerard was making so many weapons. 'Are you going to kill the people you think took your artefact?'

'Of course not,' he said as though thinking such a thing was stupid, moving over to a sack filled with different grey and silver ores.

Adam was surprised by how organized everything was. All of his tools were neatly hung and his workspace was incredibly clean. Even with all the smoke, it looked like he even scrubbed the floors.

'Then what are you making all of these weapons for?' Adam asked

'I do it as a hobby, calms me down. I've been doing it for years, on and off. It was my job way back when on Earth and then on Elysium for some of the war. I'll tell you what though, it is an entirely different entity blacksmithing here.'

'I'm guessing it's harder?' Adam said seeing all the different pieces of equipment hanging on the walls and the rows of jars, each containing different ores and items that had magical appearances; glowing, sparkling, and mesmerizing.

'More can go wrong. What makes it special is that the worse it can go, the more spectacular it can be. I could never build a dagger with an enchanted frozen blade on Earth. There was nothing new I could build on that dull chunk of rock. I just made sure those ugly machines worked to make pointless weapons.'

'If they were pointless, why would anyone want them made?'

'Come on kid, you lived on that planet, you know there was no point in using anything back then. Nothing was powerful enough to kill someone. Didn't matter what those machines made. No matter how technically perfect, it wouldn't ever be good enough. All that mattered about blacksmithing on Earth was that it meant I was the one to make weapons when the war moved to Elysium.'

'That sounds cool, being able to make weapons nobody else had ever used before, but no matter how good a blacksmith you were, how did you get to be Micholesh's third in command?'

Gerard had taken a seat on a tiny little stool as he washed his face and beard with a wet rag. 'First, I became fourth in command, in charge of all explorations trying to find points of vantage and any loot.'

'Isn't being in charge of all explorations the complete opposite of being a blacksmith?' Adam found that with each question he asked, three new ones popped up.

'That was the point. I hated being a blacksmith. Reminds me of my time on Earth. I'm still fighting with myself if I hate it or love it. I'd been forging some incredible weapons for people that they would name and treat like an extra limb, just to watch them spend all their time using magic instead. Then they would die to some monster, or to an Ascensionist that was smart enough not to rely on something they didn't properly understand. 'Specially when their life hung in the balance. I knew I could do better. I went into a territory that had just become occupied by some Ascensionists and took each person down one by one with my own blade till nobody else was left standing. I had mastered the sword and they had spent all their time on too many things to be good at any of them. When Micholesh heard about what I'd done, he came to the territory himself. Immediately promoted me, he did. Was just my luck that he'd lost his fourth in command at the time to a bunyip of all monsters.'

'Who were the second and third in command?' Adam asked, thankful that Gerard's mood had completely flipped. He was speaking almost fondly of the Endless War.

'That's a good question.' Gerard wiped down his tools and hung them back up. 'Third in command was Maria, course this was when your mum was still leader of the Disciples. Maria was responsible for training everyone, she was meant to teach both physical and magical training, but I always knew she favoured magic a bit too much. She was relentless, but there was no doubting that she was effective.

'After a year of her teaching, our side of the army could beat any Ascensionist in a one-on-one fight. It's a shame really, she never taught another person to fight after that night we killed Gonti. Something changed in her. I guess something changed in all of us the night your mother died. You should have seen Micholesh, he thought of all four of us as a family. He was like a different person when she died.'

'Is that when Maria became leader of my Disciples? After my mum died?' Adam wanted to know about his parents, but he didn't want to learn too much at once and be overwhelmed.

'No, that happened about six years before. As soon as your father died, she passed down the role to Maria. Struggled to believe in a god after Casper's passing and she thought it would be enough to be allowed to visit Earth, but she was still second in command. She would lead multiple divisions in attacks when Micholesh had to be positioned somewhere else and came up with a lot of the battle strategies that helped win us the war. Of course having Excalibur did her plenty of good as well. There was no person better for the job than her, she was the best leader I've ever seen, other than Micholesh, and maybe Gonti. When she died, Maria took her place as second in command, I moved to third, and Caesar became fourth.'

Gerard realised what he was talking about and decided he shouldn't say any more, looking at the sorrow on Adam's face. Adam was smiling at the memories but the rest of his face was pained and his eyes were shining a reflection of the furnace's fire as he teared up.

'Anyway, enough about the past, how did the tournament go? I've always wanted to see them, but it technically breaks the oath, and I had a lead to follow.'

'I've broken the oath?' Adam had completely forgotten all about the oath he had taken before entering Elysium.

'Well, it's debatable. It's non-optional for you. You are required to do it, so you shouldn't worry about it, but it's a bit of a grey area when it comes to trapping a monster and then using it for entertainment.'

'Oh, is that why there weren't any Disciples there?'

'Exactly but go on, tell me how you did.'

'It could have gone a lot better, we ended up kind of drawing. Had to fight a Qiqirn.'

'Ooh, I remember those things. Nasty bit of work, before we discovered its name at least.'

'Yeah, we fought it off for a while, but it ended up biting my arm and freezing the rest of my team just as we called out its name.'

'That's a pretty good result, at least you managed to defend yourself enough and had the knowledge to know that saying its name makes it retreat.'

'I guess so.' Adam wasn't sure how to get to what he wanted, so decided the best way was to just ask. 'We definitely could have done better, and I was just wondering, with a bit of your help, our team would have a better chance of surviving when we go on our expedition.'

Gerard turned his muscular back to Adam. 'I don't know if that's such a good idea, kid. I've not got a great track history when it comes to mentoring. The last person I taught was Delilah and... I just don't think it's the best idea.'

'You don't have to mentor us. We could just come to the Capital every so often and you could give us a few pointers.'

'It's just, I have to get my greatsword, and the path I might have to go down... I don't want you to have to see it.'

'I know, I'm sorry I shouldn't have asked. I only want to be as good a leader as my mum was and I thought you would be the best person to help.'

Adam turned away to leave, but as he expected, like in the movies, Gerard called out to him.

'Fine,' he said with a sigh. 'But only because your mother was so kind to me. And we will only train once a week, I'm a busy guy. Every Monday, come here at mid-day. I don't like waking up early. I'll advise your team on what could be useful to you.'

'Thank you so much, you won't regret it.' Adam shook Gerard's hot sweaty hands, then left straight for the Bibliotech before he changed his mind.

18. Storytime

Adam had spent hours with Amelia in the Bibliotech, which was filled with thousands of books made from both Earth and Elysium. He had expected the library to be something immensely massive like the Coliseum, Sanctuary, Monastery, or seemingly any named building in Elysium, but was surprised to find that the Bibliotech was the size of any other shop in the town's square.

There was a small seating area with some tables similar to the taverns but with leather chairs instead of wooden stools, and nobody went around serving food and drink. In fact, you weren't allowed to take anything inside the Bibliotech that could damage any of the books.

All the lighting was done through desert glass so as not to run the risk of burning any books and it made the whole shop glow, especially the parchment used for the book pages, which seemed to almost shine as if the knowledge inside of it was something holy.

Amelia had taken out the maximum of twenty books and then had made Adam also sign up as part of the Bibliotech so that he could also take another twenty books, making the long walk back to camp even more tiring.

'How was it at the library?' Iosefka asked when they returned.

'It was fantastic, I've written down so many different spells that we can practice, and Adam managed to get none other than Gerard the unstoppable, the fiercest warrior in all of Elysium and third in command to Micholesh, to be our mentor!' Amelia was electric with excitement as she moved all the borrowed books into her bedroom.

'That sounds great!' Iosefka replied.

Adam smiled at Iosefka, seeing how much happier she appeared.

'We are only going to be seeing him once a week, but it will be enough to help all of us,' Adam said.

'Oh, and guess what...' Amelia gave Iosefka less than a nanosecond before answering her own question. 'We've also managed to get us all a job helping out at the farm.'

'What do we need a job for?' Iosefka replied.

'So, we can earn some drachmas and finally get out of these clothes. We ran into that brown fairy Daisy on the way back, and she asked if we wanted to help and we know that we are meant to make all the decisions together but it was too good an opportunity to turn down. I hope you don't mind? If you and Kaya are against it, we can always not do it,' Amelia asked, concerned that she had overstepped.

'No, it's fine. That works pretty well because I could do with some money for getting some ingredients and equipment.'

'Ingredients, oh, did Delilah teach you how to cook?' Amelia asked as she came back from her bedroom to collect Adam's books.

'Not quite, Delilah taught me about potion brewing. I think it's what I want to do. We tried cartography first, but then Kaya found out that it meant drawing maps and he lost all interest and I can't draw very well. Then we tried to learn to cook but I couldn't do it. Delilah had us skinning a rabbit and I could barely hold the poor thing without feeling like I was going to throw up, and then Kaya did throw up halfway through trying to skin it. We spent quite a few hours going over different skills. It is truly amazing how much Delilah and her teammates know. You were right, Adam, it definitely is a good idea to have us specialise in different things.'

'I was the one who suggested that,' Amelia said, coming to take a seat with the two in the living room.

'That doesn't matter, but it turns out I have a real skill for potion brewing, I find it deeply therapeutic. It's very similar to making food except it is done predominantly with herbs and things that weren't recently alive, like powdered bone and rotten apples. We were shown by Grainne how to make a potion using just honey, crushed eggshell, and some herbs that we easily found around the forest.'

'Who's Grainne?' Adam asked.

'The other girl in Delilah's team. I think she's the one that uses an axe, she's nice. She taught us that those items that ordinarily do nothing special can be mixed in a specific way, using exact amounts in a small bowl over a fire, and will turn into a deep red liquid. Then when you drink it, all the colours that you can see become inverted for a minute or two. Black turned to white, blue to red, and the grass turned all shades of purple. It was so fascinating seeing the world through such a unique lens.'

'That's fantastic!' Adam encouraged. 'Did you make any other potions?'

'Yes, one second, let me get it for you,' Iosefka said, matching Adam's excitement as she rushed off to her room. She returned with a corked vial containing a bright sparkly green liquid. 'This should help to reduce the energy you lose when casting Life and Death magic. It only reduces it a little bit though, it's just a basic potion and it took me all day to get it right.'

'Iosefka, that's perfect!' Amelia studied the swirling liquid with immense interest.

'So, what happened to Kaya? It's getting late. I'm guessing he wasn't a fan of making potions?' Adam said, looking at the darkening sky.

'No, he didn't like any of the things we tried. When I started to focus on potions, he went off by himself to see if he could find something he liked.'

'Do you think we should go and look for him?' Adam asked Amelia.

'I'm sure he is more than fine. Hopefully, he found something to learn and he is just spending all of his time soaking in all the information. That reminds me, Iosefka, you'll want to sign up with the Bibliotech so that you can take out any potion brewing books.'

'There's no point in that, it's one of the best parts about me doing potion brewing, there are next to no books written about them yet! I have already been taught near-enough everything there is to know from books, and now I get to experiment with everything. Only a few people have ever been interested in the skill and they either died during the war because they weren't great fighters, or they turned to work with Enlightenment magic. Which means there are so many different potions that I can create and I will be the first person ever to make them!'

Hearing that there was almost no written documentation about something made Amelia's eyes widen in bewilderment.

'What kind of stuff are you going to start with. Do you just mix loads of things and hope they do something?' Adam asked.

'Kind of. It's a little more complex than that. I know a general idea of what can go together to make the ingredients do something, different things have their own base properties that can be brought out with other ingredients. I have a list of every known ingredient written down in my room, but I do think it's just going to be a lot of trial and error.'

Amelia had fallen a few inches down the sofa, shocked from hearing that something would have to be done without any real research and just pure guesswork.

After a few hours of talking and waiting for Kaya to come back to the cabin, Amelia decided to grab a book to read from her room.

'Iosefka,' Amelia called from her room.

'Yeah?' Iosefka replied, looking at Adam, who was twirling his streak of blonde hair. Her face had scrunched-up like she afraid she was about to be lectured again.

'You mentioned that you would need to document things, didn't you?' Amelia emerged, holding a leather-bound notebook with a light green edge around each page.

'What's that?' Iosefka asked.

'I found it when we collected all those books on our first day here and I wanted to keep it because it's a nice notebook, but now that you are going to find all of these incredible discoveries, I thought that you should have it, as you deserve it.'

'Oh.' Iosefka blushed as she stood up and took the book from Amelia. 'Thank you,' she said quietly, examining the empty pages.

'I want you to know that I am sorry for how I treated you before, and I hope that we can be friends in the future.' Amelia shifted her weight back and forth.

'That sounds… nice.' Before she knew it, Iosefka had been pulled into a hug and had to act like it didn't hurt to have the book pressed into her rib, wincing as Adam smiled at her.

'I'm sorry,' Amelia said softly in Iosefka's ear.

'I believe you.'

Then just as the two started to pull away from each other, Kaya came through the door, looking like he had just been in the Endless War.

His face was covered in mud along with all of his clothes, which had been ripped to pieces. He had bruises and cuts around his face, and as he walked towards the sofa, it was with a small limp.

Everyone stared at him shocked as he collapsed onto the sofa beside Amelia. 'I found the bear!' He said triumphantly.

'Kaya what – what on Earth happened to you?' Amelia couldn't help but brush as much of the dirt off Kaya as she could while looking for serious wounds.

'Oh, have I got a story for you three. There I was walking around camp, not having a clue what I was going to start learning, and I mean I appreciate what you did for me to help learn with Delilah and her squad but damn, it was all so boring. So, I'm walking around and I see something move a little funny towards the Wildlands. It was Pierre... the Devil Hunter. And he was walking like this.'

Kaya fell to the floor, having covered the sofa in filth, and then demonstrated walking on his hands and feet, his back arched upwards as he ran like an animal around the room.

'And I thought he was up to something odd, because – well, he looked it, and I thought it might be something to do with Gerard's artefact so I followed him into the Wildlands.'

'Kaya, what were you thinking, you could have gotten yourself killed!' Amelia screamed in worry.

'And I almost did.'

'You almost died!' Adam shouted, like a father catching their son doing drugs.

'Shhhh, no spoilers, I'm getting to it.' Kaya put his finger to his lips as he sat back down. 'So, I'm sneakily walking through the Wildlands trying not to get caught on any of the thorns or get attacked by some monster and I can't see Pierre at all. He's vanished into the spooky abyss.'

'That sentence doesn't make any sense. How can the Wildlands be an abyss?' Amelia critiqued.

'Shhhh, stop interrupting the Story Master.' Kaya was filled with so much adrenaline that he couldn't stop moving and shaking his leg.

'All I could think to do was follow these bent spiked leaves and splintered black branches that led off to the side of the kinda beaten path. And as I'm going through these harsh terrains and the sunlight disappears, I catch a glimpse, through some massive dark leaves, of slow movement that I was sure were Pierre, and I'm creeping towards him and I started to notice how spookily quiet everything was. Then bam!'

Kaya had smacked his hands together, making everyone jump.

'I go into the clearing to find that I was not sneaking up on Pierre but a big fat brown bear hunched down devouring this dead deer, just ripping the things to shreds, and it was terrifying to look at.'

'Great God above, please tell me you ran,' Iosefka pled on the edge of her seat.

'I wanted to, but I couldn't. The beast's eyes shot up at me, blood running down its mouth, and I could tell it wanted to eat me. As I took a step back, this massive bear jumped up onto its back legs and let out a growl so loud, it started sending all the birds in the area flying away. Now in my panic, my foot got caught on a bit of tree root. I scrambled as far back as I could but it was no use, this bear was on top of me in a flash. It pinned me down. I didn't dare move, terrified of what was about to come.

'There it stood, great slobs of red drool hanging from its mouth, taking these deep raspy breaths. I can still smell the stench of dead deer on its breath, that's burnt into my nostrils forever now. Now I know what you're thinking, did I survive?'

'No, I'm wondering how on earth you managed to survive it, we know you survived, otherwise you wouldn't be here,' Amelia criticized.

'For all you know, I'm a ghost brought back to haunt you for not going along with my epic tale. Lucky for you, I was saved. Just as the bear was about to rip into me, I heard a high-pitched whistling. Something came screeching through the air, piercing the bear's side. Then, I watched as the light in those dark black beads it had for eyes faded, and it fell over onto its side. Dead. A long arrow pointing from the side.'

'Oh, what a relief.' Even knowing he was fine, Adam felt more scared than when the Questing Beast had run at him.

'I managed to get out from under the dead bear and clambered to my feet and out of nowhere came Pierre, holding a bow the size of himself. He asked me why I was in the Wildlands and I thought I was in more trouble than when the bear was on me, but he turned out not to care as much, he seems like a pretty cool guy. He spoke in an odd way, like he misses out words, I remember he said, 'You follow me?' and stuff like that, never spoke more than a sentence, but yeah, he was more amazed that I'd managed to follow him or at least the bear more than he cared about me going into the Wildlands.'

'He should have told you off then you wouldn't be tempted to go back into the Wildlands again. You know how dangerous it is,' Iosefka scolded.

'But that's the thing, he didn't even send me back into camp. He kept me in the Wildlands.'

'What, why?' Adam asked.

'Well, I told him I was trying to find a skill to learn and he said I already had the skill to track and he wanted to test if it was just a fluke – and can I just add, the dude doesn't blink, it's really weird.

Anyway, he dragged me even deeper into the Wildlands and would like spin me around constantly so I didn't know where I was and then he told me to find my way back to the bear.'

'Surely, he can't do that. That's putting you in so much danger. He's part of the high table, both at camp and for the Capital, he should know how stupid doing that is,' Amelia sputtered.

'Yeah, but he's not like all the other higher-ups. He told me that he's in charge of keeping all of the Wildlands clear from any dangers. Dude's super powerful with Life and Death magic. I think that's why he's always barefoot, so he can have a constant connection to plants and stuff.'

'But then what happened, he just left you in the middle of somewhere incredibly dangerous alone?' Iosefka sounded scared at just the thought of it.

'Yeah, pretty much. It was so cool, he was keeping an eye on me in the shadows, but I never saw him. So, I spent hours trying to find my way back, climbed all the way up a tree to get my bearings, managed to see the top of the Monastery so I worked my way back there. Ran into a couple of wolves and other animals that tried to kill me but a few arrows shot from the abyss and killed them so I could focus on tracking the bear. I finally managed to find some footprints big enough to be the bears and I knew the footprint pretty well because it made a big mark on my shoulder from when it was on top of me, and from there it was easy enough work to find it again.'

'Haha, great work, always believed you had it in you to find a dead bear in a random deadly forest.' Adam gave Kaya a high-five.

'And what's even better is that he is going to give me private sessions every single day to help improve my tracking.'

'Kaya, that's incredible!' Amelia said, ecstatic that he would be learning from one of the best.

Iosefka hadn't seemed too happy for Kaya and was still worried about the story he had told. 'But wait, where are you going to be learning? Surely not –'

'That's right, I'll be heading into the Wildlands every single day. Isn't it exciting!'

19. Learning from the Best

Almost everyone had taken the day off after the coliseum challenge, either relishing in their triumph or hiding from the pain of defeat. So, the following day, all those students were surprised as they watched Adam, Amelia, Kaya, and Iosefka bringing the daily stock from the farm over to the Food Hall – relishing in their pain.

They had all woken up before dawn without much difficulty, having grown used to it from Papil's lessons. Before the first students had made their way down to the Capital, the four of them had already spent hours bringing the food from the farm over to the Food Hall.

After completing all the hard labour for the day, they received their payment of ten drachmas from Daisy. Having money for the first time in their lives was exciting; they could finally buy things. It didn't take more than half a millisecond for them to all agree on what they would be purchasing first.

It had been a long sweaty tiring month, throughout which they had been wearing the same blue clothes from Earth. They had been doing their best to clean them with elemental spells and in the shower but the fabric on them was falling apart from being poorly sewed back together so many times, and after Kaya's adventure into the Wildlands, he had barely any material left to call clothes.

It turned out that ten drachmas was a decent amount of money to make for about four hours of work, allowing them all to get a couple of outfits from one of the cheapest tailors at the edge of the town square in the Capital.

After realising that they hadn't had a chance to have any breakfast in the Food Hall, they decided to go around the market to find some food with their last drachma. They found stands selling fresh orange and apple juice, thick wraps filled with meat, and a selection of unique fruits and vegetables, all of which they had never seen in the Food Hall. In the end, they decided on getting a massive bowl of curry to share on the way back to camp.

As they ate away, Amelia explained that they should come up with a daily schedule. Being as tired as they were from all the heavy lifting, it sounded like a good idea to do something that didn't require as much physical effort. This is where Amelia tentatively put forward her idea to give them lessons about whatever she felt was important for the rest of the team to learn.

The second Amelia said this, Iosefka fought against the idea as hard as she could. Amelia promised it would be interesting, and Adam agreed it would be useful. Kaya had the deciding vote and he grudgingly sided with Adam and Amelia.

So, against Iosefka's pleas, the four of them found themselves back at their cabin. Whilst the other students started their practice out in the training grounds, they listened to Amelia talk about how they should approach an artefact if they found one in an obsidian treasure vault.

After Amelia had finished, Kaya realised that it was time for his first lesson with Pierre, and so everyone decided to spend the time working on their individual skill. This put Iosefka in a much better mood as she went around the camp gathering herbs and what the average eye would perceive as junk but which she thought might be useful for potions.

Kaya had decided to stay in his Earth clothes when going out into the Wildlands with Pierre as when he returned, there was more brown and black dirt on him than there was blue.

'How was it?' Adam asked once Kaya had changed into his new clothes.

'It was so cool, I followed him as he went around doing his normal hunting and it was crazy to see how much goes into tracking a single animal. I'm pretty sure he was going slower than he normally would and didn't use any magic to help track to make it easier for me to learn.'

'Did you run into any monsters? Are you injured at all?' Iosefka asked, her palms green from the leaves she had been crushing with her hands.

'No, don't worry, I'm fine, and unless a monster goes far from their lair, I shouldn't run into any. Pierre explained to me in that simple way that he speaks that we would only hunt in places where monsters don't live, and where all the ruins have been explored and cleared, but that's still plenty of miles worth of land to cover.'

'So, what did you do in the Wildlands?' Amelia asked.

'Well, I mostly just watched him work. The Devil Hunter, such a cool name. He killed different animals to take back to camp. Every animal he killed was with a single shot to the heart. Before they even knew they were being attacked, they were dead. It seems like the most painless way for them to die. I helped take the smaller stuff like rabbits back to the camp, I even had to carry a deer over my shoulders at the end.'

'I still don't think it's safe for you to be going out there with just one other person to protect you, what if something happened?' Iosefka sounded like a concerned mother.

'It's fine, you should see how powerful Pierre is. I was right when I thought he didn't wear shoes and walked with his hands to use Life and Death magic constantly because whenever he moved, he would immediately cover the tracks behind him. Like he would warp the plants and dirt back to how they had been, and a few times he even cut off the path we had gone down by growing thick thorn-covered bushes behind us. Even though he was doing that for hours, he didn't look tired.

'He only started to overwork himself at the very end when he killed another bear, and to move it back to camp, he made the grass go all around it like it was mummified. Then he raised the ground into a hill and when the bear started to roll down it, he moved the hill forward like it was some kind of wave. He moved all the trees out of the way, and he rode the wave all the way back to camp. It was insane. I had to run after him to keep up. After he did all that, I thought the dude was going to collapse so we called it there, but I'm going straight back in the same time tomorrow!'

With Kaya back, they made their way over to the training grounds to work on their magic and weapons combat. Adam and Kaya were now skilled at weapon fighting, and took the lead to teach the other two the very basics, like how to hold their weapons properly.

It felt strange teaching Amelia, after having spent so long working against her. She picked up the basics pretty quickly and decided to work with a shortsword.

Wanting to be as far from any kind of violence as possible, Kaya had the bright idea of giving Iosefka a crossbow to use as her weapon.

This would allow her to keep her distance in a fight. It didn't need much strength to use, and she could even dip different potions onto the arrowheads to aid them. Once they had practised with weapons, they then moved over to training magic for a few hours, and finally headed into the Food Hall for dinner when it had long since gone dark.

By Monday morning, the four were all relatively comfortable with their routine, and as they headed into the Food Hall for their breakfast, having just been paid by Daisy, they couldn't wait to start their first lesson with Gerard.

Iosefka had made incredible strides with potion-making. She had already concocted every single potion that had already been discovered and spent her division of their wages on ingredients and equipment.

They had been having breakfast around the same time as Olivia and her team. It was like they were back on Earth, the way that Kaya and Olivia would bicker with each other. On Earth, they would argue about absolutely nothing, and now in Elysium, a world filled with everything one could imagine, beauty and horror all around, where there was so much to talk and argue about, the two would still argue about nothing.

Today it was about how loudly Kaya chewed his food when sitting next to her. Olivia's team had performed exceptionally during the coliseum challenge, having fought off a young minotaur without so much as a scratch. Even Max had managed to help when sticking close to Jaiden.

Having done so well, none other than Micholesh gave them a job for their performance, paying twenty-five drachmas a day to deliver messages around the Capital. Yet, it was only the chewing sounds that Olivia wanted to talk about.

'You're doing it on purpose!' She shouted.

'I don't know what you're talking about.' Kaya replied, his mouth wide open as he continued chewing obnoxiously loud.

'So, how's the farm?' Rebecca asked Iosefka.

'It's not too bad, hard work, but we are used to the early wakeups,' she replied.

'Hey, give it back!' Kaya reached over the table to grab his plate which Olivia had stolen.

'Only when you swallow your food before talking!'

'I'd hate to wake up that early,' Max said. 'It's so much easier just staying up later, and there's something peaceful about training in the dark with no other groups around.'

'Since when did you train at night?' Adam asked.

'We've always practiced our magic at night.' Olivia had given Kaya's plate back now that he had stopped chewing with his mouth open.

'Well maybe we can join you some time?' Amelia, like Adam, had thought their team was the one who trained the hardest.

'Oh, yeah for sure, that sounds like it could be fun,' Jaiden responded.

'That does sounds nice, we can plan something later, but for now we've got to get to the Capital. See you all around, except you Kaya, I hope you choke.' Olivia gave a tiny smile at Kaya as she left.

Once the other team were out of earshot, Amelia smacked Kaya in the arm.

'Ow! What the hell was that for!'

'Why were you being so mean to Olivia? She's not done anything wrong, it's important for us to have good relations with the other groups. We may need help from them in the future. And she has got a point, you do chew very loudly!'

'Don't worry about it. He's been acting like that for years.' Adam lent in towards Amelia to whisper loudly so that everyone could still hear. 'He's got a crush on her.'

'I SO DO NOT!'

'It all makes sense now!' Amelia laughed.

'Why would I like her, there's nothing to like, she's just a girl.'

'Oh, just a girl, is she?' Iosefka acted like she was offended.

'No, not like that, I just mean...'

'Kaya and Olivia, sitting in a tree,' Amelia sang as Iosefka and Adam laughed.

'Whatever,' Kaya said, shaking his head and rubbing the back of his neck.

Adam led the group over to Gerard's house. They found him waiting outside, packing a couple of barrels full of weapons and equipment, all of which were of much higher quality than the selection they had had for the coliseum fight.

'Perfect timing.' Gerard picked up the barrels with ease and started to lead the group over to the meadow outside the city. 'Kaya, are you the one that Pierre has been teaching?' He asked as they walked.

'Yeah, that's me,' he responded, surprised that Gerard knew.

'You should be very excited. He may seem a little dim, but he has loads of knowledge when it comes to hunting, and he is one of the most skilled Life and Death casters I have ever seen. Wouldn't want to be hunted by him, that's for sure.'

Once they reached far enough into the meadow so that nobody could watch and gawk at them, Gerard dropped the barrel onto the ground.

'Right, I want you all to try and attack me. Don't hold back. Whatever you throw my way, I can take it.' Gerard retrieved a blunt greatsword with parrying hooks at the base of the blade.

'Are we allowed to use magic or do you just want us to use our weapons?' Adam asked.

'Use anything you like. Go through the barrel and use whatever you want. Don't worry, they are all blunt, or at least not sharp enough to cause serious harm, and I have forged them all myself so they aren't going to break on you.' Gerard had the greatsword over his shoulder as he put himself some paces away from the group, giving them a chance to plan an attack.

Searching through the barrel, they found many interesting weapons – like a zweihandler, which nobody bothered to try and lift, a katana, mace, and flail, all of which were in pristine condition.

Gerard was waiting patiently, the cross-section of his sword resting on his shoulder blade as the four picked their weapons. Kaya found three pairs of gorgeous daggers. One pair was like the kind he had grown used to using and another had a chain attached, but he chose to use the pair made from obsidian.

Adam went for an ordinary longsword that was most similar to the swords back at camp and strapped a shield to his left hand. Amelia decided to use a shortsword and Iosefka couldn't find any projectile weapons so Adam suggested that she simply focus on casting spells to take Gerard off-guard.

'Now before we start, who here can cast healing spells?' Gerard called.

Only Kaya and Iosefka raised their hands, having both spent the most amount of time practicing Life and Death magic. Gerard pointed at Iosefka. 'Iosefka, I won't harm you as much, as you're going to be responsible for healing your teammates. It is important to learn how to cast healing spells in the moment when your team is relying on you, so whenever anyone needs mending, you will be the one to help.'

It was like a Bakunawa's weight had been lifted from Iosefka's soul after hearing she wouldn't be attacked. The other three didn't seem to care in the least that they were about to get battered, or that they were about to try and attack the fiercest warrior alive.

'Adam, what are you thinking?' Amelia whispered as they all huddled up, having put on some lightweight armour.

Adam explained his plan for how they might be able to attack Gerard. They nodded and took their positions. Before they started, Iosefka quickly prayed and was half expecting Gerard to attack them whilst she did, but he stood steadfast waiting until she was finished.

Seeing that they were all ready, Gerard swung his sword from its resting point and, holding the handle with both of his strong hands, he moved into his fighting stance, pointing the greatsword at the group.

All of them huddled close together with Amelia at the front as she brought up a protective barrier using desert glass large enough to cover them all from the front. As they ran towards Gerard, Iosefka started throwing different spells at him.

Kaya was also trying to cast spells but every time he tried, nothing would happen, and then he realised that his obsidian daggers were working against him, stopping him from using magic at all. With the plan hinging on his ability to use magic, he threw the daggers into the ground and started throwing out different Elemental spells.

It was difficult to aim when they were so huddled up, and everything they threw at Gerard, as expected, did nothing to hurt him. Gerard dodged fireballs with ease and swung through the rocks getting hurled at him, his greatsword breaking them apart like they were nothing more than bubbles.

Once they were slightly out of reach from Gerard's attacks, they split off, with Amelia pushing up, her golden shield protecting her. Iosefka had broken off and walked backwards, keeping the pressure on Gerard, while Kaya and Adam ran to the right in a pretend attempt to catch him off guard from behind.

Gerard pounced and hit Amelia's protective barrier, shattering it with ease. Amelia only just managed to back step out of the way from the follow-up attack and would have been hit with a swarm of swings if it weren't for Iosefka sending a wave of dust in between them, which made Gerard spin around to avoid being blinded and so that he was facing Kaya and Adam.

Kaya pretended to start casting a wind spell to knock Gerard backwards, but as he held his guard up, Kaya switched targets. A strong explosion of wind sent Adam flying into the air.

The impact of the hit made Adam much more disorientated than he had expected as he soared through the sky. Whilst airborne, he managed to regain some form of grace and swung his sword down towards Gerard's head. Even with the surprise, Gerard brought his sword up in time to collide with Adam's.

Having never practised being airborne with a heavy sword, or being airborne at all, Adam twisted his ankle as he hit the ground. Luckily, he had landed close to Iosefka who ran over to help.

Amelia and Kaya carefully fended off Gerard's attacks. Amelia created protective shields that shattered after every hit but did enough to protect the pair, with Kaya shooting Elemental spells to reduce the power and accuracy of Gerard's swings.

Iosefka grabbed onto Adam's ankle a little more forcefully than she meant to, causing Adam to wince from the pain. She slammed her other hand down onto the lush grass, willing its life to transfer through her body. The grass started to slowly lose its colour, and Adam could feel the energy coursing into his body. In less than a minute, Adam stood up completely healed. But there was no time for celebrations as by now, both Kaya and Amelia were down, with Gerard approaching.

Adam did his best to defend himself with his sword and shield, but the sheer strength he had to produce to stop his sword from escaping his grasp made him run out of energy fast.

With no real way of getting around Gerard to heal the others, Iosefka resolved to stay with Adam, putting up protective barriers where needed. Her spells weren't nearly as powerful as Amelia's, as Iosefka's voice was shaky and she stumbled over some of her words. Her protective barriers would only work to slow down the swings instead of blocking them.

Gerard wasn't giving it his all. If he had, Adam would have been beaten from the first strike. It was clear that he was just feeling them out to see what each person was capable of, and Adam was determined to show how strong he had the potential to be – pushing far past the point of exhaustion. But Gerard's swings never relented and as hard as Adam tried, the attacks kept on slipping through his defence. If it weren't for Iosefka's quick spells of protection to reduce the blow, they would have struck him down.

The moment that in Adam's head he knew it was about to be over and he wouldn't be able to block another attack, Gerard noticed, like he could read minds, and swept his leg, dropping Adam like a stack of pebbles.

With practice over, Gerard gathered everyone around. Iosefka healed Kaya and Amelia, whose injuries were significantly worse than Adam's. Still, Iosefka managed to heal the two enough for them to stand and hobble over to Gerard, but in doing so, all of her energy had been drained and she had to sit down, her legs unable to support her.

'Amelia, your desert glass is strong, but it needs to be stronger. Focus on learning how to turn a defence into something that can swing the fight in your favour. Having a simple shield is great when you don't know what to expect, but you had plenty of knowledge beforehand about the weapon and force of what would be coming at you. I would highly recommend using something that has more layers of defence and once you've improved, add some kind of immediate counter-attack. Almost like hitting you would spring a trap. You and Kaya fought smartly together. However, there is still plenty of room for improvement.

'Kaya, your skills in Elemental magic are strong but don't feel like you have to rely on them so much. I noticed that you left your obsidian daggers behind. You need to understand the limitations of a weapon before going into battle with it. Making a mistake like that out in the Wildlands will result in death. You should try and work more Life and Death magic into your fighting.'

'Iosefka, that was a lot of great quick thinking. Throwing the dust to try and blind me was smart, and of course, the more you heal others, the better you'll get.'

Gerard then turned to Adam. 'Can you tell me what gave you the idea to go flying through the air?'

'Well, we worked out before that you would easily be able to defend against anything that had been done before. You have more knowledge about battle tactics than all of us combined and have real hand experience. Even if we tried something that you didn't know about, I'm sure you would have been able to react quick enough to block it.'

'Ha, and so you thought that by doing something ridiculous, I wouldn't be able to think quick enough to respond.'

Adam was feeling awful. 'That's what I hoped, but it didn't work.' All of his nerves were burning with shame and he wanted to get back to fighting to prove he was better.

'But it did work,' Gerard stated.

'What?'

'Not in the way you were hoping. I managed to block the attack, but what you should always think about is what your opponent might be thinking in the heat of battle. In doing this, I knew when each of you were about to slow down, and so chose those opportunities to give a proper strike. When I saw you flying in the sky and over my head, I was taken out of the fight. I couldn't think properly as I was too focused looking at the incredible sight before me. In that short bit of time, Kaya or Amelia, you could have capitalized and very well might have landed a hit on me. Don't underestimate the importance of what your opponent is thinking. If you can learn how they are feeling in the moment, a lesser opponent can pull out a win.'

'But how could we ever plan to surprise our opponents so much they lose sight of what they are doing? We only did that bizarre plan because we had no other viable options,' Amelia said.

'It all depends on the situation. I remember Gonti managed to execute one perfectly when we were fighting on the barren planes. Throughout the fight, he was nowhere to be seen and we thought that this was the final battle to end the war. We believed he had run away and left his army to die. We all got a little too confident and overstepped. Then from over the hill, the ground started to shake like a whole army was marching towards us. Turned out that Gonti had furthered his skill with necromancy and had managed to puppet a twenty-headed hydra. In the shock of seeing one of the most dangerous creatures in Elysium under Gonti's control, most of us froze, and the Ascensionists took full advantage of this, killing far too many.'

'How did you manage to recover from that?' Kaya sat with Iosefka, listening intently.

'We didn't. It was the biggest loss we had ever seen since the war moved into Elysium. If it wasn't for Micholesh's leadership, we might not have been able to regain a holding in the war. But enough of that for now, it's time to get back to fighting!'

For the next several hours, Gerard ran them through different drills like the one they had just done, two-against-two, free-for-alls, using weapons, using only magic. After every fight, Iosefka would heal everyone, and Gerard would talk them through what went well and what could be improved, whilst she regained her energy.

By the end of the training, all four of them desperately wanted to sleep for the rest of their lives. With all the information Gerard was giving, Adam was thankful to have Amelia next to him, memorizing every word.

'How's the search for your Greatsword of War going?' Adam tried to ask casually as they made their way back to Gerard's house.

'More dead ends. Wait, Greatsword of War? How did you know that it was the weapon from the horseman of war?'

'Oh, erm –'

'Didn't Duke let it slip, we asked him about it because we thought he was a little suspicious?' Amelia lied.

'Duke? Is that what Deucalion is calling himself now? The one whose parents were Ascensionists?' Gerard said.

'That's the one, have you had a chance to look into him at all?' Adam asked.

'Couldn't if I wanted to. Micholesh has banned me from interfering with the investigation, I'm meant to just sit on my hands and wait for nobody to get anything done.'

'We can look into it for you, see if we can find out if Duke knows anything?' Adam offered.

'I don't know. I don't want to get you lot into trouble.'

'Please, it's the least we can do for you taking the time to teach us,' Amelia added.

Gerard turned his head to all of them with a smile through his bushy beard. 'That's good of you kids, I appreciate it. Just check he's not up to anything, and don't get yourselves into trouble over me.'

'So, how did you manage to get away from the hydra?' Kaya had been waiting to hear the end of the story.

The proud smile Gerard had quickly dropped as he started to bite his lip. 'That was the work of your dad, Adam. Casper sacrificed his life that day so that those of us who were still alive could escape. I wanted to stay with him, but he wouldn't have it, said that they needed me. When I turned my back to let him die, I never forgave myself. He was married to Amber, and you were on Earth, waiting to be brought back home. He had his whole life ahead of him. I shouldn't have let him go.

'I thought that day would be the last time I would ever see Casper, but Gonti had a trick that he loved to do. See, surprise can make you weak for a few moments, but when you see someone close to you brought back from the dead to fight those you love, now that's enough to break one's spirit. That'll leave a person weak for life.'

Nobody said anything. They all walked silently back to the house and when they parted ways, Gerard's sullen face gave a very weak smile as he said his goodbyes.

20. Crux of Life

With Gerard's approval to look into Duke, the four started to follow his movements, which turned out to be surprisingly difficult. After looking around camp for several days, they found no sign of Duke at all. It turned out – after asking different students at the camp over two weeks – that he didn't live in a cabin with his team but off in his own makeshift home.

It took them almost a month to find Deucalion's home out in the wilderness past all the cabins. At first, Kaya had thought that the little dirt igloo was an animal's den, considering it was barely larger than a person, but he had spotted Duke emerging from within it.

After bringing the other three to the house, they started taking shifts in their free time to watch Duke and see if he would bring out the Greatsword of War from some hidden area. After spending a few days observing Duke, they discovered that he didn't eat from the Food Hall, but got all of his food from fish he caught in a nearby stream.

After Adam found the other three people in Duke's group, he discovered that they didn't train with him, eat with him, or even speak to him if they could help it. The only time they had fought alongside him was during the coliseum challenge when they had to and even then, they fought separately.

The three students made it clear to Adam how much they didn't want Duke in their group, saying that they would have preferred only three people in their team than the son of two Ascensionists, as he was bound to sacrifice them to appease his gods.

Adam had spent a while watching Duke train by his dirt house alone without any guidance – using predominantly fire spells – and thought that the only reason someone would be solitary to such an extreme extent was if he was hiding something valuable.

None of the four had caught Duke doing anything suspicious, and it was hard to watch him when they had to remain so hidden. Knowing that if any of them were spotted as they watched from behind thick bushes, Duke's response would involve a lot of fire.

As the months passed and they entered the winter season, the world grew colder. This did nothing except make the Squonk team work harder. Iosefka's room was now filled with potions – ones to heal, weaken, boost, and disorientate, all ready for their expedition, which was only six months away.

Whatever the expedition was, there was a chance one or all of them could die. It would require them to go deep into the

Wildlands, much deeper than Kaya had gone with Pierre. It weighed constantly on the minds of every student. It felt like time was passing them by.

Over their many lessons in the Wildlands, Kaya was now adept at tracking. He still struggled with things like skinning animals, not yet able to do it without throwing up, but his Life and Death magic was stronger than even some older students.

When everyone else in his team spent time honing their skills, Adam continued to follow Duke's movements. But nothing had changed. His life was miserably boring and isolated. Adam never saw him do anything wrong and he had even managed to get inside his dirt igloo house when Duke had gone to catch some fish and found nothing that could lead to the stolen greatsword. So, as the four approached Gerard's house, ready to start another lesson, Adam was ashamed that he had no new information to give.

Adam knocked on the door a few times, but there was no response. They waited for a few minutes to see if he was hiding from them as some kind of test, but nothing happened, and they guessed he was busy, his blacksmithing area cold and unused.

As the four walked around the Capital, not sure if they should ask someone if they knew where Gerard was, Adam spotted the familiar dark hoodie of Deucalion walking down a thin alley. Adam had rarely seen Duke leave his home to go into the main part of camp and here he was in the Capital. Adam was certain something was about to happen.

Duke was speaking in a hushed voice to someone else. In his eagerness to eavesdrop, Adam stepped on a branch making it snap loudly.

'What was that?' Duke said, cutting the other person off.

'Would you calm down? It was a twig snapping,' the other person said.

'That's not something to be calm about. If it snapped, someone has to be close by.'

'And? We are in a town. The only town in all of Elysium. That means people walk down the streets, and some, if not all of them, don't look where they are going.'

'But somebody could be listening?' Duke responded.

'HELLO!' The other person shouted. 'If anyone is listening, do feel free to continue although I will have to disappoint you in saying that we are debating how much we should pay the butcher across the street. Feel free to join in if it so pleases you!'

It was then that Amelia decided to pull on Adam's shoulder to get him away from the alley.

'What did you do that for? They could have been talking about something important.'

'They aren't going to say anything if they think someone's listening,' Amelia reasoned.

'They might have just been talking about the prices for the meat,' Iosefka added.

'Come on, that was obviously a ruse,' Adam said, wanting to go back before he missed something.

'I don't know, have you seen those prices, two whole drachmas for a bit of fatty deer meat? I could hunt an entire deer in less than an hour, I'd make a fortune if Pierre let me sell what we hunted,' Kaya said.

'Even so, we should still listen just in case.' Adam made his way back to the corner but found that Duke had gone. 'I can't believe it, the first lead we've had in months and it's gone!'

'Adam, I think now's a better time than any to bring it up, but you are in too deep looking for this greatsword. Even Gerard has learnt to let go,' Amelia said, her eyes watching Adam carefully.

'He hasn't let go. He isn't allowed to interfere with the investigation.'

'But the investigation is over, the Disciples have concluded that someone tried to steal it and was burnt to death at some point, leaving the weapon safe and hidden,' Amelia repeated like she had several times over the last few weeks.

'But then where is the greatsword! How has nobody found it?'

'Maybe it's time to move on,' Kaya said. 'Let's go get some food whilst we're here.'

Adam hated to admit it, but he knew they were right. 'Fine.'

After they had eaten and spent some time shopping around the market, they decided to go back to Gerard's house to see if he was home. Once again Adam found someone who distracted him.

Rigby was struggling to move a heavy wooden box up a cobbled hill. His face was red and his chains pressed harshly against his body as he pushed with his entire right side in a desperate attempt to move the box.

Iosefka was very aware of what Gerard had said about him. She knew not to make any deals with him or trust him. But seeing a blind person struggling so much without anyone to help them was enough to make her go over to offer her help.

'Oh, is that the lovely Iosefka I hear?' Rigby asked.

It had been a long time since Adam had heard Rigby speak but it was now easy to connect him to the voice Duke had been talking to a few hours earlier.

'Look, we don't want any funny business, but if you want, we can help take this stuff up to wherever you need it,' Kaya offered, also recognizing the voice and nodding at Adam.

'No. No funny business at all. I would never think to do something like that.' Rigby had moved away from the box, letting it slide down the few feet he had managed to push it. He felt around for the wall next to him to get a sense of his space.

'Can I ask, Adam Tideborne, are you also here?' Rigby said.

'Yes.' Adam was thinking to stay silent, but he was almost certain Rigby already knew he was there.

'What a pleasure it is once again to meet you, thank you for this help. I deeply appreciate it.'

The box turned out to be no heavier than the stock they would bring down from the farm to the Food Hall every morning and so Kaya was fine with picking it up and walking up towards what they assumed was Rigby's home.

'This is very kind of you all. Nobody else ever offers to help me. Not that I would expect them to.'

'What have you got in the box?' Iosefka asked.

'Just different ingredients for something that I've been wanting to make for a while now. It has been quite a challenge to get them all. See, it's coming up to the anniversary of my father's passing and, back when I had my sight, I read a recipe that my father made. I've always put off trying to make it, but I decided that enough was enough and that I would give it a go.'

'That's sweet, what is it that you are making?' Amelia asked, her hands at the ready as she walked behind Rigby, scared that he would fall down the wobbly streets he had spent so much of his life wandering.

'Ooh, can't say I'm afraid. It's one of those things that's better as a surprise, and if you want, you're all more than welcome to swing over to my place and try some if you ever get a chance.'

'I think we'll pass,' Adam answered for them.

After a few minutes of tense conversation, they made it back to Rigby's house, which was even less of a home than Duke's dirt igloo. Down the end of the darkest grubbiest street on the complete other side to Gerard's house, tucked far away from the town square and out of sight of the Pantheon and Mausoleum of the Gods, was a small little rodent den. Three thick slabs of wood made up the walls, held together with some kind of make-shift black glue, with a large piece of rusting metal acting as a roof.

Inside there was barely enough room to fit a small sleeping bag that, like the rest of the items lying around in the little space, appeared to be made by hand with very little skill. To the right of the sad home, a grimy cooking camp had been set up. The small handmade firepit, which had to be lit with some flint lying next to his sleeping bag, would allow Rigby to heat whatever nasty meal he had in the metal pot, a chunk missing from the rim.

Kaya dropped the box onto the floor with a thud as Rigby reached into his little den and started touching everything there, checking that he still had all his possessions. Adam had to close his nostrils with his fingers. The stench from the home was so strong, it made everyone's eyes water. None of them had ever experienced such an overwhelming selection of awful smells all at once. Adam realised that each one of Rigby's items had a distinctive potent odour, presumably to help him find where they were.

'Is this where you're living?' Amelia had almost collapsed the metal roof onto the floor after giving it a slight nudge.

'It has been since I received my punishment; seventeen years in a few months. Nobody will let me get a proper house, and I can't leave the Capital for more than a few days. Otherwise, they think that I might devise some cunning plan to get these chains and my sight back.'

'This is horrible.' Iosefka couldn't understand why anyone would not only be allowed to live like this but forced to live like this.

'It can be tricky sometimes, but there's nothing to be done. Adam, I'm sure someone has told you by now that it was your mother that decreed my punishment, and since she died, it appears that there is no way of changing her decision. Nobody, not Disciple Maria or even Micholesh, is willing to overturn her final punishment as a Disciple. This is how I will live the rest of my life.'

'I'm not sorry for what my mother did, you tried to kill Micholesh, and this is a much better punishment than death,' Adam replied.

'During my bad days, I would very much disagree with that; one thing worse than death is to be forgotten and left behind to fade into the dirt.'

Rigby opened up the box and took out his different herbs and ingredients that looked as though they were gathered from the dirt or found in bins, carefully putting them in a pile at the foot of his sleeping bag.

'Again, thank you for this kindness,' he said once he had put everything away.

'Don't worry about it, we were happy to help,' Amelia said, looking at the filthy man with pity.

Rigby rubbed his dirt-covered neck, acting like he was trying to work up some courage. 'Well, I was just wondering, now I'm sure people have said not to trust me, but I was just wondering if you could get the last few ingredients for me.'

'I don't know if that's such a good –' Kaya started to say.

'It won't take long at all,' he added quickly. 'It's just a few things that I can't get myself.'

'We really shouldn't,' Iosefka responded as if it hurt to say it.

'I'll pay you!' Rigby said desperately, diving into his den as he scavenged for a couple of drachmas. 'Here take it, it's all I have.' He reached around the air until he found Iosefka's hand and dropped the money into her palm. 'I just want to feel like I have my father by my side again, please.'

'It's not about the money, Rigby, I just don't think it's the best idea to help you.' Adam felt bad saying it.

'Please, everyone, It's just a few things.' Iosefka bent down to where Rigby was kneeling on the floor begging for them to help and clasped her hands over his. 'What do you need?'

Against their better judgment, Iosefka convinced them to help. Amelia had seen all the ingredients and items in Rigby's den and she was sure that none of them would be enough to do anything dangerous. Iosefka also confirmed that everything she had seen from the box were all used for types of healing and growth, nothing that could harm someone.

Grudgingly, Kaya agreed to collect some seaweed down by the beach next to their cabin.

Iosefka was asked to get a bag of drupes – a bright yellow stone fruit from a stand in the town square where the only person who sold them refused to give any service to Rigby.

Amelia was then asked to retrieve a small red fruit called jujube, which were slightly larger than grapes and grew naturally on bushes near the farm.

Then lastly, Rigby wanted Adam to retrieve a type of lotus plant. To which he was surprised to hear that nobody, not even Amelia, had heard off. He then started to describe the flower, with its black velvet leaves, and a purple light that came from its centre. By chance, Amelia remembered the plant as the one Adam had picked for her when they first arrived at the camp and had gone through the forest.

It didn't take Amelia long to find some jujubes growing on the bushes along the road opposite the farm, chatting away with one of the fairies that had come over to say hello as she picked them.

Rigby had specified that only Adam should touch the flower as they were incredibly delicate and their leaves could fall off easily. So, on reaching the camp, Amelia split up with Kaya to get some seaweed whilst Adam headed into the overgrowing part of the forest to find the black lotus flowers.

The only reason Adam had agreed to do this was because he would be expecting something in return. It was clear how much

Rigby wanted these ingredients and that meant Adam would be able to get some real information about the greatsword from him.

It was strange going back through this part of the forest, remembering how it felt to sprint through it with Kaya and the life-threatening encounter with the Questing Beast. The encounter that still gave him the occasional nightmare that led to the daydream of what it would be like to be king.

After ten or so minutes of wandering, Adam found himself in front of the vertical climb where he and Amelia had been attacked. Off to the left, he found the fallen tree trunk where she had been crying alone. Now she would have no problem getting over the vertical climb that Adam could now tell was clearly made with magic.

Dispersed around the ground around the fallen tree were a few dozen of the black flowers. The purple light coming from them filled the cold air, making it look like they were breathing.

He was careful not to touch any of the thorns coming from the stem, yet as he yanked it out of the ground, he still managed to be pricked and once again, the flower drew blood from his index finger.

Immediately, he started sucking his finger like Amelia had taught them to do in case he had been poisoned, but he already knew he would be fine, having been pricked by it long ago. Still, he liked the idea of giving help to Rigby even less than before now that the flower had taken in his blood.

Once they all returned, Rigby couldn't stop sputtering out his thanks, and although they had been warned against helping Rigby, they couldn't help but feel good seeing him so happy.

'Now before I give you this flower, I want something from you.'

'Whatever it is, I will give it gladly.'

'What do you know about Gerard's Greatsword of War?'

'Now that... is a good question,' Rigby said with a hint of a smile.

'That means you do know something about it,' Amelia deduced.

'I suppose you have done something of great value to me so I will share with you what I know. I happened to be around the area when the Greatsword was taken.'

'Is that because you were the one to take it?' Adam interjected.

'No, I was around there because I know it is not wise for me to be at home when the Capital gets drunk, and considering it was the night of the anniversary of the war's end, I thought it best to make myself scarce, so I was heading towards the meadow to relax and forget about my troubles. It was as I went past Gerard's house that I smelt something burning, I couldn't feel much heat but I was worried that something was on fire, and then I heard something coming from Gerard's house.

'Its stride was like a drunk man's and so I hid, but I could hear the fire following the person and I could smell burning flesh. It was as if the person was completely on fire, yet I heard no screams, just the shuffles and groans of someone who had too much to drink.'

'Where did they go? Through the meadow?' Amelia asked.

'No... no, oddly enough, it went up the street towards Mount Ida. I didn't know what to do and so I ran away back to my home, which was stupid as sure enough, a group found me an hour later, drunk out of their minds, and beat me till I lost consciousness.'

'Are we supposed to believe that?' Kaya said. 'The way you've put it makes it sound like a Drunk Disciple took the greatsword back to the Sanctuary.'

'I am afraid that is my truth, and it is all I know and I have shared it willingly. Please, I ask that you hold up your side of the deal and give me the lotus flower.'

Grudgingly, Adam gave Rigby the flower. He believed that Rigby was telling the truth, but it did nothing to help work out who took the greatsword or where it was hidden. Still, it was definite progress and so they all went straight over to Gerard's house to tell him but found that once again he was not home.

Not knowing who else to trust with the information, the four of them made their way back to the cabin, discussing what Rigby's story could mean and how someone could have survived being on fire without being noticed by anyone.

As they walked, their discussion came to an abrupt end as they all stared, amazed that the sky was producing little snowflakes. They had grown accustomed to all the different types of weather and temperatures in Elysium, from the rain to the blistering heat that made training miserable, but until now, they had never seen snow.

They all reach out so that the snowflakes fell onto their hands, which they inspected as though they had the mysteries of the portal locked behind them. By the time they arrived back at camp, the snow had started to fall heavily, a thin layer of white everywhere they looked.

All the students had stopped training, choosing instead to make snowballs to throw. Adam wanted to celebrate, but he knew that Amelia would have none of it, she always put bettering themselves over having fun. He then very quickly realised how wrong he could be, as Amelia dropped a handful of snow down his back, running away with Iosefka, laughing.

The four of them spent hours in a free-for-all, throwing snowballs at whoever they could hit. Each of them had built a makeshift cover to protect themselves as they launched snow around.

Not a single bit of training was done that day, as the four of them blasted snow around with magic, seeing how high they could get it or how much they could get onto one person. They grouped together to make a fat snowman the size of a giant, and as the snow kept on falling, the games they played only became grander, as groups of students came together for a massive snowball war.

Their noses turned bright red, and their bodies started to shake, so everyone made their way into the Food Hall to warm up and eat some hot food. As they ate, the gong struck four times, silencing everyone. Nobody had any idea why the gong had been struck and made their way outside to find out.

Standing by the gong was Caesar. Every other person of importance at camp stood beside him, along with Delilah, whose face was red and clenched. All of them looked defeated. The crowd waited in silence as the last students made their way over to the announcement.

Then finally, after it appeared that everyone had arrived, Caesar stepped forward and spoke in his booming voice. 'Gerard, the Unstoppable, third in command to Micholesh himself, the fiercest warrior this world has ever seen, has been killed.'

21. A Heroes Downfall

The student next to Adam let a piece of bread slip from her hand. It moved towards the snow so slowly that it felt like it would never land. Adam watched the fires inside the Food Hall wave around in such a sedated way that it felt fake. It was as if the whole world had screeched to a stop. It felt like they were about to be attacked from every angle. Gerard was the protector of Elysium and he had been killed.

Caesar waited to let the dreadful news sink in before speaking again. 'We believe that Gerard had been searching deep in the Wildlands for a greatsword that had been stolen from him. A few hours ago, Micholesh was sent a direct message and proof of death from what can only be Ascensionists.'

Those that weren't too stunned to listen looked around at each other in awe. The Ascensionists had all been wiped out.

'Micholesh is certain that this is no folly and that there are still Ascensionists alive. It is assumed that throughout all of these years, they have been cowardly hiding in the Wildlands. As we speak, Micholesh is readying his forces to find them and remove them from this world. If you are in your final year of training, you are allowed to join the hunt, should you wish.'

All the older students were resolute in wanting to help. It didn't appear that a person would be staying behind.

'As this camp is one of the main entrance points to the Wildlands. You will be seeing Micholesh's forces enter in the coming days. We do not know if we will ever be able to retrieve Gerard's full body and so there will be a hero's funeral tomorrow in the Capital. Immediately after, we will find those responsible and make sure they pay for their crimes. Those of you who want to assist come into the Food Hall now. If not, I expect to see you all tomorrow at mid-day.'

First to follow Caesar into the hall was Delilah, who had been clenching her fists so tightly that her nails dripped blood from digging into her palms. As all the older students went up the steps, Adam started to follow them, believing that if he joined in the fight, the crushing sadness within him that made it hard to breathe would go away. That if he killed those who killed the closest thing he ever had to a father, Gerard would come back.

Amelia grabbed his arm as he separated from the group, but he quickly ripped it away, turning back to look at her as he tried his best not to break down into tears. 'I'm going. You can't stop me.'

'Adam, they won't let you join. Please, I know how you're feeling.' She was speaking in the kindest tone, but it wasn't enough to stop Adam's facade of anger that veiled his pain.

'No! No, you don't!' Adam had to scrunch up his face to stop the tears from coming out. 'Without him, I never would have been here, he has helped me through so much, and now... and now he's gone.' As hard as he tried, he couldn't hold back the tears anymore as Kaya pulled him in for a hug.

As they walked back to their home, Adam saw Duke scurrying to get back to his house. Something inside of Adam snapped as it had when the Shark twins stabbed him.

'You!' Adam shouted, storming over to Duke.

Duke had just enough time to try and throw a punch, which Adam dodged. He landed one of his own, dropping Duke. Before Duke could cast a spell to defend himself, Adam jumped on top of him and wailed on him with unrelenting fury.

'Tell me! Tell me what you did to Gerard!'

'I... didn't... do... anything,' Duke said in-between punches, his hands up to protect himself.

'Liar!' Adam shouted as he picked up a large stone.

Before Adam could hit Duke with the stone, Kaya pulled him away. Adam tried with all his strength to break free so that he could go right back to beating the life out of his enemy, but Kaya was stronger and managed to pull him back.

'What were you talking to Rigby for then!' Adam shouted, giving up on trying to get back on top of him.

Duke had pushed himself against a tree, using it as support so that he could stand back up. 'I check up on him when I can, he's all I have! He's the only person that doesn't see me as a monster!'

Before anything else could happen, Duke used the break in getting attacked to quickly cast a line of fire between him and Adam. As the line of fire grew to a wall, Duke fell from the pain. When he stood back up, he was clutching his stomach.

'You can't get away from me, I will get you back for what you've done to Gerard!' Adam screamed as the other three dragged him back to the cabin.

'What was that!' Amelia shouted at Adam once they were back in the cabin.

'We all saw it! He was in the Capital today with Rigby, and we helped them! After what they've done!' Adam sounded like he was going to vomit from how revolted he was with himself.

'Adam, they didn't do anything! It was the Ascensionists that killed Gerard,' Iosefka reasoned.

'He is an Ascensionist, his parents were.'

'Come on, man, you've been watching him more than anyone, does he look like he's proud of who his parents were?' Kaya said.

'He spends all of his time alone, why would he do that if he wasn't up to something?' Adam argued.

'The kid's been brought into this world a villain!' Kaya retorted. 'Obviously he's given up trying to live with everyone. You've spent all this time watching him and he hasn't done anything wrong, he isn't a bad guy. This isn't what a hero would do, this isn't what Gerard would do.'

Kaya had put his arm on Adam's shoulder and once again Adam found himself crying as he came to terms with what he had just done. Looking at the blood on his knuckles, he wanted to be sent back to Earth for how he had acted, he wanted punishment for disgracing Gerard.

'You're right. I'm so sorry. I don't know what I was thinking.'

'You weren't thinking,' Amelia said. 'None of us are in our right minds. I just – I can't believe he's dead.'

The four of them dropped down onto their sofa and chairs. It felt like they were waiting for something. As if Gerard was going to come bounding through the door at any moment, covered with battle scars but alive. That he would sit in the largest chair, which they had unknowingly all left empty, and recount the epic story that led him to evade death once more.

However, as the soft snow calmed from the heavens and the moonlight reflected on the white sparkly surface around the camp, the front door remained closed.

As the hours slipped by, they all started to realise that their mentor would never come into their cabin, or be a part of their lives again. Adam's head had been spinning with unanswerable questions. How could Gerard fall to Ascensionists? Why did he think his artefact would be out there? How could he have been so reckless?

Nobody went to their room that night, they simply sat by the fireplace, recounting all the Mondays they had spent with Gerard. It was a strange thing, talking about him. For those few hours, it felt like he was still with them. Amelia went on for a long time about all of his accomplishments during the war, how he managed to single-handedly take over an entire territory as a mere blacksmith. She recounted how he found some of the first Elemental scrolls, and how he was the one leading the group that discovered the Capital ruins. His name was littered across the history of Elysium and his legacy would be remembered for as long as there was someone alive.

#   #

The following day, the world felt just as empty. The snow had remained untouched and acted as a blanket of emptiness over the world. The birds were chirping less than normal. Nobody was training. Nobody was even talking. The whole camp was in a cold mourning.

The four of them didn't show up at the farm, they didn't give any message to Daisy, the other fairies or anyone else that worked there. None of them had thought to do so. All they could think to do was to make their way to the Capital and even that felt like a challenge.

Expecting the vast number of students, the trail of carriages had been brought back to the camp. All the horses had been draped in a thick black cloth around their faces and down their bodies, for the occasion, as well as to help them with the freezing temperature.

The four of them slowly climbed into a carriage with Olivia, Max, Jaiden, and Rebecca. They exchanged a few words, and Olivia offered her condolences, knowing how close Adam and the rest of them had gotten to Gerard. The short journey was spent talking about unimportant random things, words that none of them would remember.

To keep him grounded, Adam focused on Olivia's two silver rings, which hovered above her palm through wind magic. He watched as they floated around like they had no gravity, swirling around each other like little planets.

The Capital was in an even deeper state of grief than the camp. Adam noticed that every single house was without light, not a single fireplace blazed nor was any streetlamp lit. There was no light, for today there was no hope. Desert glass had been forged above the entrance of the Pantheon reading: GERARD THE UNSTOPPABLE. Even the desert glass was dimmer than normal.

All those attending gathered around in the park outside, standing on the crispy grass that crunched when stepped on. At the top of the steps looking over everyone were all the highest-ranking people in Elysium. Pierre was standing at the far end, for once not covered in dirt, having cleaned himself. He had even covered his feet with shoes and had thrown on a black shawl to try and blend in with everyone else.

Down the line were other camp leaders, with Caesar being closest to the centre, Disciple Maria between him and Micholesh. Micholesh was the one and only person sitting, a small grubby wooden stool supporting him. His face and body were controlled. He sat casually but with an expression of deep sorrow, and that aura of peace around him had disappeared like vapour in a storm swept away by the harsh wind.

Resting on his shoulder, gripping onto Micholesh tightly, was Patches. The sentient white glove had another black glove over the top of it, blending in with Micholesh's black blazer. It was doing nothing at the moment, as though it were frozen, and to someone who hadn't seen the artefact before, it looked like an ordinary glove filled with sand.

To Micholesh's left, there were people that Adam had seen around the Capital, but had never spoken to. Disciple Maria stood forward once it was clear nobody else would be arriving. Not that it seemed like anyone was missing. Everyone alive had come to give their respects.

The streets were tightly packed with mourning people, as was the grass field. Kids sat on the rooftops of buildings and the elderly were leaning out of their windows. Not a single point of view that could see Micholesh was unoccupied.

'Gerard the Unstoppable. The Viking Warrior. Son of Hercules. To me, he will always be the blacksmith that wanted more from life. He could be idiotic, reckless, and a fool that made poor decisions because he could never see farther than he could swing. He hated when people used magic over their physical strength. So naturally, when he first met me, he hated me as well. I was the living embodiment of what he hated about Elysium. My pioneering into the art of spellcasting and my teachings of all that I had learnt was the polar opposite of what he thought would be the way to win the war. To him, I was a bigger threat to winning than all the Ascensionists combined.

'However, after a great deal of resentment, arguments, and displays of skill, we started to respect one another. Our relationship has been far from mundane. We were unable to agree on the simplest of things, and over the years, there have been long stretches where we have hated each other. Yet, through all of that, I would consider him my closest friend. We pushed each other to be better and it is one of the hardest things I have had to accept, that I will never be challenged by him again.'

Disciple Maria had held herself together like an obsidian statue throughout her speech, but as she stepped backwards, Adam noticed her stumble, ever so slightly losing her balance, which she quickly regained. She did it so naturally that barely anyone noticed out of the ten to fifteen thousand people watching.

Now Micholesh raised himself from his chair, Patches falling to the floor so that it could pull the seat back out of sight with a screech.

'Gerard was the finest warrior Elysium has ever seen. I am sure you are all aware that his legendary artefact—what is believed to be from the second horseman of the apocalypse—a mighty greatsword wielded by the horseman of war, was stolen. This weapon was like no other, and could only be wielded by the fiercest strongest warrior in the world. Anyone else who touched it would burn where they stood. It is clear now that the Ascensionists—whom I have believed dead for a long time—came up with a plan to steal it. I believe that the only reason they took the greatsword was to lure Gerard into a trap. Whether this is correct or not, it does not matter. Either way, we will be storming the Wildlands in search of Gerard and his weapon and invoke revenge on those who deserve it! Today we grieve, and tomorrow we start our righteous work!'

Adam had never seen Micholesh speak like this. It was scary. He was acting and sounding like how the king of a world would be expected to act.

As leader, whatever Micholesh did, people followed, and that was the same with how he was feeling. If he was happy, even the weather would be bright and happy. When he was in mourning, there would be snow. It seemed now that the whole world would start burning.

The entire crowd cheered so loud, the noise would be enough to scare away a dozen Bakunawas. Micholesh didn't sit back in his chair but remained standing for the rest of the ceremony. There was no body to bury, nor ashes to scatter, and so there wasn't much left that they could do.

Towards the end, all those lined up beside Micholesh cast a powerful bolt of electricity back up into the clouds. As the lightning shot from their hands, the booming thunder also escaped, sounding like the blast of a cannon.

After that, the doors opened to the Pantheon and everyone was invited in for a great meaty feast to celebrate the life of Gerard. Adam didn't plan on staying very long as the building was packed with so many people speaking about their mentor that it quickly became too much for him to handle.

The four of them chose to eat outside in the cold park, to move away from all the noise and claustrophobia. Then, for some strange reason, Disciple Maria started to approach them. Adam and Kaya immediately assumed that they were doing something that they weren't allowed to, and tried to hide their plates of food behind their backs.

Disciple Maria had a look of deep regret on her face, which only grew after seeing the food Kaya had dropped onto the floor, but she took a deep breath to compose herself and hold back the urge to scold.

'Gerard had decided to mentor you. He had done so because he saw greatness in each of you. I don't know how, I look at you four and see nothing but weakness. However, I am indebted to him. I still owe him one favour and he made a promise to you; now that he is gone, I will honour him and make us even by keeping his promise to you.'

'What do you mean?' Kaya asked with a groan, knowing what she was meaning.

'You will refer to me as Disciple Maria when addressing me!' Her polite demeanour escaped her the moment it could, but she took another deep breath as if speaking to the four of them nicely was the hardest thing she had ever done. 'I am saying that once I come back from the Wildlands, I, who have sworn off teaching for over ten years, will teach the likes of you.'

'You don't have to... Disciple Maria,' Adam said.

'Are you saying that I should dishonour Gerard? He almost certainly chose to help as a result of who your parents were. They were good fighters, but they were impolite and thought the world revolved around them, something that clearly has been inherited by you.'

'I don't think the world revolves around me!' Adam had overstepped, and he knew he was in trouble the moment the words left his mouth.

Disciple Maria moved so fast, there was no way to block the staff colliding against his hand.

'Do not raise your voice at me! You forget your place. Gerard might have treated you like you were his friends, but believe me, I will not be giving you the same luxury. You will all treat me with proper respect or else you will be punished. I must return to

Micholesh to help plan. Once I return, I would expect that you four would have all learnt some manners.'

'The bad news just keeps on piling up, doesn't it,' Kaya whispered with a sigh, after turning his back to Disciple Maria, once she had re-entered the Pantheon, afraid she would hear him.

22. Charon's Disciple

Micholesh and his hundreds of warriors had been searching for the Ascensionists for about a month. Adam had watched Micholesh enter with his army into the Wildlands. His armour was made from thick black leather, each piece marked by a sharp blood-red line around it, making his arms, chest, and legs look like dragon scales. His helmet consisted of the same colours as the armour, with red spikes coming from the sides forming two large horns, making him appear like a demon.

Caesar had led the charge, riding his Chollima, holding a massive shield that covered almost all his body, Pierre at his side, showing the path and tracking for any signs of Ascensionists. Delilah had, of course, joined in with the hunt and had asked Amelia to tend to all of the plants and flowers her team had in their cabin, clearing the debt she had with Delilah and specifying that it was still Adam that was indebted to her, which didn't bode well for him.

Since Caesar had been gone, Papil had been given a temporary position as leader of the camp. With this new power and lack of older students, all remaining members were given important responsibilities normally done by the older students.

After recovering from his beating, Duke had gone to the Monastery, not to report Adam like he had been expecting but to get a mentor, and none other than Papil had agreed to teach him. This was a surprise throughout all of camp, as now that the Ascensionists were back, everyone was looking at Duke with even more disgust.

Yet Papil refused to see him this way, training him to be stronger so that he could defend himself against the likes of Adam, who knew that there would come a time where Duke would get revenge. He had accepted that he deserved it.

Adam and the rest of his team had been hoping that Papil had forgotten all about how they had broken the rules and gone into the scroll room, but as they were forced to spend hours hand washing all the bowls, plates, and cutlery in the Food Hall kitchens, it became very apparent that he was still disappointed in them.

One morning, Kaya and Olivia were having yet another heated argument in the Food Hall. This time it was about how he had spent so much time in the Wildlands and Olivia hadn't.

'It just doesn't make any sense that you should get rewarded for going into the Wildlands in the first place. It's against the rules!' She shouted, even though they were sitting next to one another.

'Sometimes you have to bend the rules, to improve. They're only there in the first place because people aren't strong enough to survive out there,' Kaya stated, matter-of-factly.

'Oh, and you think you're strong enough to be out there without help. I'm so much stronger than you. You should see how powerful my wind magic is. We have all been practising our spells, whenever we aren't helping Micholesh with his *important* deliveries and messages. He even said himself how good we are at fighting! I don't hear any of the pigs complimenting you when you're shovelling their poo.'

'That's not what we do!' Kaya retorted like a child.

'I mean, I'd expect nothing less from a team whose totem is a squonk, what would people think seeing us mighty phoenixes talking to you?'

'They would probably wonder more if you're asking about what it's like in the Wildlands.'

'Oh yeah, we'll show you how strong we are, just you watch.' Olivia stormed off with the rest of her teammates following behind, cut off from finishing their conversations with Adam, Amelia, and Iosefka.

Amelia tried to smack Kaya in the arm, who managed to dodge it but was then hit on the back of the head by Adam. 'Ow! Would you two stop hitting me every breakfast!?'

'We only hit you because you need to stop treating Olivia like that, she seemed really upset this time,' Amelia scolded.

'She's fine,' Kaya said, waving his hand.

'And I only hit you because you still didn't take the opportunity to ask her out,' Adam joked.

'You little!' Kaya shouted, jumping from his seat running after Adam who had sprinted outside laughing.

Before Kaya could retaliate, they both stopped running, and watched the older students emerge from the Wildlands, looking tired and injured.

None of them were happy or had the slightest look of victory on their face. As they walked towards the Food Hall, taking off their armour as they went, the lower-year students came over to them asking about what had happened.

'Didn't find a thing, only monsters. Lost some good people. Barely went into uncharted areas.' Was all one person could say as they made their way over to all the food.

Thankfully, Adam didn't know anyone who had gone into the Wildlands, and as sad as he was to hear that there were casualties, his heart didn't sink like it had when Gerard had passed. Like it still did when he thought of Gerard the Unstoppable.

Micholesh was the last to leave the forest. Adam was surprised to see that both he and his jet-black horse were as clean as they had been when leaving, compared to how even Caesar looked with dents and dirt on his armour. His large shield, however, was still in perfect spotless condition.

'We ran into some tough monsters out there,' another tired student said as she looked over at Micholesh. 'A fully grown manticore caught one group off guard, and that was that for them. Then Micholesh went in alone to fight it, and came out without so much as a fleck of dirt on his armour.'

Wanting to hear more about all that happened over the month, the four of them started to make their way back into the Food Hall before a stern voice called, sending a shiver down their backs.

'What are you four loitering around for? Get down here, I don't have all day!' Disciple Maria shouted, her white garbs only slightly dirtied.

'We didn't realise you were going to be teaching us so soon, don't you want to rest a bit?' Kaya asked.

Whack.

'Ow!' He whined.

'So, you have spent no time working on your manners then! What is my name?'

'Disciple Maria,' they recited.

'And you will do well to remember it. Now follow me over to this field, so we can train. My time is valuable and I will not have you ungrateful children wasting it.'

Adam had only told a few people that Disciple Maria was going to mentor them, but word had spread like fire. As they marched over to an open field, a crowd wandered in their direction to watch.

'What are you going to teach us, Disciple Maria?' Amelia asked in the politest way she could.

Whack.

It didn't seem to matter how polite Amelia was, it wasn't good enough. Disciple Maria swung her staff at the same inhuman speed, slapping Amelia so hard on the hand, she whimpered.

'Don't ask questions. That is rule one. Do not question my authority. That is rule two. At the start of each lesson, you will all line up in silence and wait for me to greet you. You do not come up to me so casually and ask about what you will be gaining from your time with me.' In the distance, they could hear the students laughing at seeing Amelia getting hit. 'And I see you've also told the whole camp about this. I guess I should not have expected any less. Boasting to anyone who will hear it. Well, I do not allow onlookers when I train so you will have to do without the audience.'

As if she was as young and limber as the students, Disciple Maria performed a few movements with her staff and then jumped into the air, slamming her staff into the ground, creating an immense circular ripple as though the grass and dirt were water, which continued to grow in height and momentum as it moved outwards like a growing wave. She lifted her staff once the hill that surrounded them like a crater was high enough so that nobody could see over the top.

After stumbling and almost falling over from the ground's wave rolling under them, the four quickly lined up in silence.

'Acceptable,' Disciple Maria said looking at the four. 'It appears that even idiots can follow basic instructions. Now today, you will show me what little magical abilities you may have.'

They had expected to be asked something like this, and so had planned a routine. Adam showed off his Elemental magic and Amelia weaved some desert glass to form her name and then turned it into a protective barrier, covering her like a dome, which she then condensed to make into a thick shield.

Kaya, whose skill with Life and Death magic was unmatched by any other student at camp, touched the ground and made the grass all around him wrap and contort to his will, growing in size at an incredible speed. He then ripped a few blades of grass up from the ground and threw them with the aid of a wind spell to send them whistling off into the distance at a deadly speed with enough force to stick into someone and draw blood – something that they had discovered when Kaya had been messing about in the cabin and had shot a bit of grass into Amelia's arm.

Not having had the chance beforehand, Iosefka had started to pray whilst the others showed off what they could do, getting ready to show off how skilled she had become at healing with Life and Death magic, and how effectively she could expedite the life cycle of plants, barely feeling tired after.

Whack.

Disciple Maria brought her staff down onto Iosefka's outstretched hand whilst she was down on her hands and knees praying.

'You can't do that, she was in the middle of praying!' Kaya shouted.

Whack.

'I do not care what she was in the middle of doing. What is rule two!' Disciple Maria commanded.

'Do not question your authority,' Iosefka said quietly, tears in her eyes.

'And by ignoring what I have asked of you, and doing something completely different, you have questioned my authority. I told you to demonstrate your casting skills, not how well you could talk to your fake god.'

'You can't talk about her religion like that!' Adam shouted.

Whack.

'I can talk about her religion however I wish. You are under my authority. You are all forgetting your place!'

'You aren't being fair, just because you don't like us.'

Whack.

Kaya put his hand outwards, taunting the hit after speaking out of turn.

Before anyone could say or do anything else, Iosefka stood up, having taken the time they were arguing to finish her praying and healed her red hand. She then went to her other teammates and healed them as well.

'That took you long enough. In future, get all your silly rules out of the way before my lesson starts. Do you not realise that there will inevitably be a time when you need to use magic to stay alive and you will not have the chance to pray?'

'That's why she will always have us to protect her whilst she prays,' Amelia stated.

'You can fool yourself into thinking that will work, but I am not so idiotic. There will be a time when you will need to cast a spell without prayer, if not today then sometime soon. Now let's check your accuracy.'

Disciple Maria made four stone pillars appear from the ground, near the edge of their crater. She then shot four beads of water from her hand. They dented the stone just below its peak, maintaining a perfect orb.

'I want each of you to cast a fireball and put out those orbs of water. To make sure you take this seriously, for every throw you miss, I will strike you,' she instructed.

The pillars were barely in their throwing range. It would be impossible for the four of them to hit their mark on their first throw, so they were already preparing themselves for pain.

Adam threw first. He overestimated how hard he needed to throw, causing the fireball to sore past the pillar and hit the newly made hill.

Whack.

The moment the fireball passed its target, Maria had brought her wrath down on Adam's hand.

Too focused on not wanting to get hit, Amelia didn't throw nearly hard enough and only made it three-quarters of the way to the pillar.

Whack.

Kaya had watched Pierre shoot a lot of arrows after their months of daily practice and had practised his aim plenty. With all his skill, he managed to hit the pillar on his first attempt, just not on the water.

Whack.

Iosefka was their best shot at getting it first try. She had trained solely with a crossbow and her aim was exceptional. Seeing the others try gave her a good idea of how much power she would need, and so with a deep breath, Iosefka threw her fireball into the sky where it collided at the top of the pillar, just missing its target, but through her praying or just dumb luck, the embers from the collision fell and brushed against the water, extinguishing it.

She turned immediately to Kaya, throwing herself at him with uncontrollable excitement as she jumped up and down. 'Did you see that? I did it! I did –'

Whack.

'Ow!'

'What did you do that for?' Kaya argued. 'She hit the target!'

Whack.

Expecting the hit, Kaya had tried to move his hand away to no success.

'You do not ever question my authority! And you do not ask questions! You may have hit the target, but you would have died the moment you took your eyesight away from the enemy as you so childishly celebrated. Now the three of you go again, and hit the target this time.'

Not daring to say anything in retaliation, they all continued casting their fireballs, as Iosefka silently prayed for them to hit their mark. Kaya managed to hit the water on his second try, smirking and winking to Adam when Disciple Maria wasn't watching. Adam extinguished the water on his fourth attempt.

The problem was Amelia, who, after seven attempts, was only throwing worse. Her hand had now started to bleed from how many times it had been hit and with each strike, her eyes would water enough to cloud her vision so that the following attempt, she could barely see the target.

Disciple Maria had refused to let anyone heal her, she was enjoying the physical pain she was inflicting along with the emotional pain it gave to the others. On her eighth throw, Adam had had enough and discretely did the movements to cast a wind spell to guide the fireball towards the pillar. Although in his anger, he had overcast the spell that was meant to be subtle and ended up making the fireball gather so much speed that it obliterated the stone pillar.

'What was that?' Disciple Maria rounded on Adam, her staff high in the sky, ready to bring it down on him.

'We are a team. If I can help my teammates, I will,' Adam said simply, staring straight back into her piercing eyes.

It seemed certain that she would punish Adam, that she would do much worse than give him a sore hand. Yet, to their surprise, she slowly lowered her staff.

'Adam has just said the first smart thing that has ever come out of any of your mouths. I said that each of you had to hit the target. I will not ever allow you to heal yourself or another whilst in the middle of a task, there is great skill to be unlocked through pain, but I said nothing about having to stand and watch without helping.' She turned to face Amelia. Her face that, for a moment appeared to almost tolerate the group, fell back to its normal disappointed look. 'You are a terrible aim. Let's hope your life doesn't ever depend on it.'

The painful lesson continued for several more hours, with each test getting gradually harder. Their hands endured so much agony that they started to reach the point where they would involuntarily make noises when getting hit.

The only reason their day with Maria came to an end was because none of them could take the pain anymore. Dropping to the ground in defeat, Iosefka was too exhausted to heal them anymore. After they had given up, Disciple Maria placed her hand on the grass and pulled the crater back in, the field appearing just as it did before, except all the spectators had long since moved on.

After the lesson had finished, they all continued to stay miserable. Their hands had gone numb even after being healed, and it ached to move them. The moment they got back to the cabin, Iosefka pulled out some of her ingredients from her room and concocted a thick liquid which she put into four bowls to soothe their hands. For a good hour, the four all sat around the living room, complaining about how much they hated Disciple Maria and how much better Gerard was.

23. Another Funeral

It took no less than a day for word to spread about what exactly happened out in the Wildlands. Micholesh and his army travelled deeper into the Wildlands than anyone ever had and Pierre couldn't find any sign of Ascensionist life.

In total, seven students died. A funeral for them was scheduled by the cherry blossom tree. As the smallest of positives, throughout their travels, they managed to find plenty of undiscovered ruins, leaving the less dangerous ones untouched to be used for the expeditions for the first-year students.

Micholesh had deduced that the Ascensionists had to be hiding somewhere other than the Wildlands, and so had started to gather a team of only the strongest fighters to bring up to the mountains with the intention of going to the Devil's Bog after if they found no sign of their enemy. As hard as Delilah tried, Micholesh wouldn't allow her to go with them, and – refusing to stay put – she had gone straight back into the Wildlands with her team in search of her father's murderers.

The sky outside was a dreary grey, black clouds covering the sky and blocking any view of the cosmic colours floating through the universe. It was a perfect fit for their second lesson with Disciple Maria, who had them making sculptures of themselves to show their accuracy and finer skill.

Adam had made a statue of himself out of rock using elemental magic, but apparently, his face wasn't nearly ugly or detailed enough and he had failed to show the streak of blonde on his hair with the stone, and so was hit five times on his hand.

Amelia had created a perfect mirror image of herself using desert glass but was still punished with ten hits for taking too long to make it.

Iosefka had made her model out of grass, moulding it and making it move as she did, which also earnt her ten hits as it wasn't a sculpture but a mirror image.

Kaya had been hit fifteen times for having the only sculpture that looked nothing like a person, let alone him. He had been too concerned about Olivia to focus on what he was making. Nobody had seen anyone on their team since everyone had come back from the Wildlands and he was getting worried.

As the four of them made their way back to the cabin to apply some more of Iosefka's ointment, they found Rigby wandering down the dirt path towards the cabins calling out for Duke.

'Is everything alright, Rigby? Are you lost?' Amelia asked.

'No, not at all. It is so very good to hear your voice again, Amelia. Is the rest of your team with you?'

'Yes, we are all here. What do you want with Duke?' Adam asked, eyeing the large pot Rigby was holding.

'Ah, Adam Tideborne. I was just trying to find Deucalion so that I could see how he was doing, it has been some time since he has come to visit me, but no matter. Now that you are here, I also have something for all of you. I wanted to thank you all again for your kindness towards me when you helped obtain those ingredients for me. I managed, with a lot of difficulty, to recreate the dish that my father used to make and I wanted to give some to you all.' Rigby carefully gave out the large pot, making sure not to wrap his chains around it.

'Sweet,' Kaya said, taking the pot. 'Thanks, man.'

'Would you mind eating some of the dish with us?' Amelia asked, placing her hand gently on Rigby's shoulder.

'Thank you, but I made it for you. I've already had my fill.' He tried to step back but Amelia's grip hardened so that the blind shackled man couldn't escape the four of them.

'We insist,' Adam demanded, certain that something was wrong.

'We aren't far from our cabin. It won't take long at all. You've come all this way from the Capital. That couldn't have been easy, rest with us. It will give us a chance to tell you how good this food surely is,' Iosefka offered, doing her best to remain kind.

Amelia had opened the lid of the pot, checking inside to find some stew.

'Well, when you put it like that, I guess I am rather tired.' Rigby chuckled anxiously.

The four of them escorted Rigby back to their cabin and led him down the dirt stairs that Kaya had long since formed over the hill so that they didn't have to climb up it every morning.

Iosefka and Adam showed Rigby to the sofa where they both sat beside him, as Amelia helped Kaya dish up the stew into five bowls. Rigby couldn't see it, but he knew that all four of them were watching him, waiting for him to try it first.

Rigby started to eat the stew filled with all kinds of meat, herbs and vegetables. Bite after bite, he continued to eat as they searched for any signs of poisoning or foul play, but to their great surprise, Rigby ate every last drop of the meal.

'This does bring back memories. Thank you so much for letting me have some more, but please, I really should be getting back to the Capital before they think I've done some evil thing. If you see Duke, do ask him to visit.'

Astounded that nothing bad happened, they let Rigby get up from the chair and fumble around, feeling for the door, which he found, opened and left through, leaving no evidence of any wrongdoing. It seemed like he had truly only come to give them all a nice meal.

'So, we can eat this stuff now, right? That's what that was all about? Checking to see if he was trying to turn us into a frog or send us into an eternal sleep?' Kaya said, lifting a spoonful of the stew to his mouth.

'Something like that,' Adam said, staring at the doorway that Rigby had just left through.

'Wait!' Iosefka shouted, making Kaya drop his spoonful of food onto his lap.

'What did you have to shout for!' He shouted, wiping the mess from his clothes.

'I have an idea of why he did this. Everyone, give me your bowls.'

'But it looks so tasty,' Kaya whined as Iosefka took everyone's stew and moved into her bedroom.

The others followed her into her room after being invited in. Nobody ever went into someone else's room, to allow for some privacy, and the three of them were shocked to see what had become of the bedroom. It looked more like a madman's mind than a place to sleep.

Jars with all types of strange items lined her shelves, labelled things like bouncing worm juice and full-moon redberry. The dark wooden desk she had bought months ago was now covered with stains and splatters from unknown liquids. Papers and parchments were filled with her lists of potion ingredients, while notes and drawings covered her floor and any small crevice she was able to shove them in. The notes were written in the cheap black ink that sat in its pot on her desk, along with all the other measuring equipment she had made and found.

'How long has your room been this messy?' Amelia sounded like a disappointed parent.

'Yeah, I've been meaning to clean up.' Iosefka was rifling through her papers and drawers, moving bottles of potions and clinking them against each other. 'Doesn't matter now I just need to find – ah, there it is.' She retrieved a vial from behind her curtain that contained a thick grey liquid that had little chunks of some brown rock floating around.

'But, how can you sleep with all this clutter? Doesn't it bother you? It bothers me,' Amelia said.

'Not really. Adam, would you mind passing me one of the bowls.' She pointed to one of the stews she had stacked haphazardly on the small morsel of space she had left on her desk.

'What are you trying to do?' Adam asked, passing the stew to her.

'I want to try and revert the meal to its original ingredients, then we can see exactly what he put in it.' She placed the bowl on a metal stand, having cleared away all the flammables around it. 'Amelia, could you cast a small orb of fire under the food so I can bring it to boil, please.'

Amelia did as she was asked, and once the stew started to boil, Iosefka sprinkled some white powdery substance onto it.

'This is all so cool! You're turning into a real Witch with all this double trouble boil and bubble stuff.'

'God forbid I would ever be a Witch! No, no, no, no, no, I am a Wiccan. Wiccans heal others, they are helpful, kind and decent. They do not abuse the powers of the earth but work to help mend and grow. Now, I need you to drink this.' Iosefka gave the grey liquid to Kaya, who drank it without question.

'Firstly Kaya, it's *double, double toil and trouble. Fire burn and cauldron bubble.* And Iosefka, I'm surprised you have even heard of Wiccans, they came into existence after all the Old Ways texts.'

'Oh no, I never learnt about Wiccans through anything my parents thrust upon me, I saw it once on the screen. A long time ago, my parents left our house for the hospital when they were giving birth to Joseph, my brother, and apparently, I was too young to stay alone so they left me with one of our neighbours. They put on a film and to this day, it is the only one I have ever watched. I don't remember what it was called or really what happened in it, except that it wasn't with real people, they were like coloured drawings, and that there were Wiccans in it that were good and helped others, and there were Witches and Warlocks that were evil.'

'But Iosefka... that was just a film. A cartoon by the sounds of it. Real Wiccans, they are –' Amelia was cut short after seeing the stare Adam was shooting at her, eying her to stop speaking.

'Oh, and I remember that someone in it had a similar last name as me. Ravencroft, I think it was, when mine is Ravenscroft.'

'That's a pretty neat coincidence,' Adam said. 'Well, it is great how good you are getting at this, Iosefka Ravenscroft, the Wiccan.'

Iosefka blushed from a mixture of embarrassment and happiness as she added another vial to the bubbling stew.

'Now, Kaya, what I gave you should allow you to use Life and Death magic without having to make direct contact. It only works for a couple of centimetres but it works nicely here because I need you to put your hands over the stew and age it backwards, please.'

'But that only works for a single thing like a tree and when I know what it is. I don't know what the ingredients are and there are bound to be dozens of them. You're better at this stuff, you should do it.'

'It's too late for that now, you've already drunk the potion. There shouldn't be a problem with ageing it backwards, I don't think at least. Just put your hands over the stew and focus on making the life cycle of the stew go backwards.'

'Ok, if you say so.'

Holding his hands out to the side of the bowl, as he stared into the stew, Kaya started to work his magic. Like some strange kind of mitosis, the stew started to split and divided itself into smaller sections. Then the different shades of liquids started to harden, some sections shrunk and shrivelled whilst others grew and darkened in colour. It was like they were experiencing a real hallucination. After around a minute, the bowl contained strips of each meat stacked on top of each other, herbs in a pile as if freshly picked, and cubes of vegetables as colourful as when they had been cut in preparation for the dish.

'That's great. I had no idea if that would work. Would you all mind separating and checking the ingredients in the kitchen while I note all of this down?' Iosefka said, already getting out a blank piece of paper and dipping her quill in some ink.

It didn't take them long to go through all the ingredients; carrots, rabbit meat, beef, spinach, onion, drupes, seaweed, and jujubes. Nothing that would cause any kind of immediate or delayed illness. In every single aspect, it was just a family recipe stew, just as Rigby had presented it.

'I don't understand. How can it be just normal stew?' Adam said.

'Nothing normal about this,' Kaya said as he wolfed one of the bowls down. 'I think it's one of the best stews I've ever had.'

'So maybe he was just being nice?' Amelia suggested as she ate her portion.

'But Gerard said we shouldn't trust him.'

'And we didn't. But even the worst people can do nice things,' Iosefka said, eating her stew as well.

'What about the lotus flower?' Adam finally said.

'What about it?' Amelia responded with a full mouth.

'It isn't in the bowl.'

'So what?' Kaya shrugged.

'So why did Rigby ask me to get it for him?'

'Maybe he just didn't need it in the end, he is blind after all. Maybe he didn't remember the dish correctly,' Amelia suggested.

'He said it was his father's special meal, how could he possibly think there was an extra ingredient, especially one so specific?'

'Adam, you're overthinking it. Even if for whatever reason he wanted the lotus for something else, he can't use magic, and he can't see. It's fine. We have enough to worry about, we don't need to add more to our plate,' Kaya said, eating the strips of rabbit meat, having finished his stew.

Whilst that was true, Adam didn't feel good about what was happening, but then he thought, how much harm could Rigby do?

After eating all of the stew and the ingredients that Adam had noted down in case he ever wanted to try and make it, Kaya made his way straight into the Wildlands for his lesson with Pierre. After having returned from the Wildlands, Kaya had asked if he could bring Adam for a lesson, to which Pierre had allowed.

As was expected, Pierre was filthy, but his clothes were completely shredded and his entire left arm was covered in leaves he had wrapped around like a bandage, with a lot more bruises and deep cuts than he normally had. What made it stranger was that Kaya had spoken to Pierre the day before and he had been completely fine.

'Good to see you,' Pierre said quietly, his movements less sporadic and animalistic as he looked at the two.

'Do you want to skip today's lesson? You look pretty beaten up,' Kaya asked.

'No. Is good to get out. Come, need to show you, my failure.'

'What do you mean?' Adam said as they travelled into the Wildlands.

'Am ashamed to speak. I am meant to be protector of forest. I failed, failed, failed!'

Adam was scared at would could have happened as Pierre brought an entire tree hurtling towards him just so that he could snap it down the middle, letting out his rage as he threw each half into other trees. It created so much noise that all the wildlife ran and flew away, trying to escape the destruction.

'Hey, everyone makes mistakes,' Kaya said, trying to be supportive. 'You've been out helping Micholesh, and haven't been able to stay here.'

Pierre didn't respond to this and just kept on crawling.

'This doesn't feel good,' Kaya whispered to Adam. 'Pierre is normally so chill, and I don't have any idea where we are, everything looks so different. I'm pretty sure the army moved all the terrain around so that they could all go through easily.'

Even without knowing where he was, Kaya effortlessly kept up with Pierre, dodging past all the thorns and rugged terrain, whilst Adam cut himself several times just trying to keep up with the two.

They stepped out into a large open area, where the aftermath of a spectacular battle had taken place. Trees splintered in all directions as if they had been hit by cannonballs. The grass was burnt and charred in areas, and then as tall as Adam in others. Chunks of bark and piles of leaves were scattered all around the ground, which was itself pulled apart, rugged like the effects of an earthquake, leaving rips in the earth itself, deep enough to bury a building.

Trying to follow Pierre through the battleground was a struggle. They jumped and leapt through the carnage. As they traversed, large arrows from Pierre and thick stingers from some gigantic monster littered the battlefield, stuck in the ground or in the bark of what were once massive trees that were now split into thousands of pieces.

In the centre of all this carnage was a fully grown manticore. Its head and body was like a lion's, a full mane of scarlet red hair against its golden fur. Starting at the back of the head and coming down the spine came thick spikes much larger than its piercing canines, with even more spikes protruding from within its mane.

Between the spikes running down its back were a set of thick wings, red like the mane and folded over the monster lying motionless on the ground, like a death blanket. The long scorpion tail covered in the same stingers that littered the area was cut off from the rest of the body, lying some distance away.

Adam heard Kaya choking up, and looked where he was staring to see a single silver ring on the grass.

'You said you failed.' Adam was staring all around him. 'You weren't the first one to find the manticore, were you?'

'Believe it followed us back. After Micholesh killed other.'

'Pierre who – who ran into the monster before you?' Kaya asked.

'One survived. Took him to Micholesh. Name was Max. Was terrified. Could barely speak, but told me one of the other names. Olivia.'

At that moment, Kaya looked as though he would drop down the deep holes next to him. To just let the world swallow him up.

'No, no, no, no, no, not Olivia. You're wrong! You're wrong!' Tears fell from his face as he slammed his fists over and over into the ground. 'There has to be something we can do. Come on, you're one of the strongest casters of Life magic. You can bring her back. You can bring her back.'

Pierre did not respond, but just stayed where he was, frozen. As if Kaya wouldn't see him if he didn't move.

'Bring her back.' Kaya grabbed onto the little material Pierre had around his chest. 'I know you can do it. I need her back.'

Pierre still said nothing, only shaking his head as Adam tried to get Kaya to calm down. Slowly, Kaya let go and fell to the ground again.

'Aaaaaaaah!' He wailed. 'It's my fault, it's all my fault.'

'Kaya, it's not your fault,' Adam said.

'I shouldn't have – I kept on – I was really stupid!' Kaya ripped a massive chunk of earth from beneath him with the aid of magic and launched it high into the sky. As it came crashing back down, it cracked into several pieces, each one making mini-craters in the already annihilated area.

'They must have been so afraid, and I'm the reason they came here. She wanted to prove me wrong... she should have known I was... I was...'

For a long time, Kaya did nothing but sob as he grieved the loss of Olivia. Adam put his arm around him and mourned with him.

Next to the manticore were several light brown sacks, all empty except one. Pierre reached into it and retrieved two large saws. 'Take,' he said, holding out the sharpened weapons. 'This the best way to feel better.'

There was something in the way that Pierre seemed as miserable about what had happened that made it all feel slightly less painful. Both of them took a saw and started to grind away at the monster's legs.

It was gruelling work that required more effort than either of them had expected. Adam was sure that Pierre could have taken the manticore apart in seconds, but didn't mind. Like Kaya, he was relishing in the hard work.

'I wonder what it was like for them in those final moments,' Kaya said, sweat soaking his face as he cut into monster. 'I hope it was over quickly. I know she would have been brave.'

Adam didn't want Kaya to feel as defeated as he had been with Gerard. 'Olivia would have stood her ground well, and she made sure that at least one of them escaped.'

'You're right. She would be glad that Max survived.' It seemed that Kaya was close to smiling, and then he stopped cutting. 'But how can he live with what he's seen? He's always been so quiet, and Olivia brought out the best in him. What's he going to do now? If I had to see what he has, I don't know if I could...'

'But you don't have to experience that, and Max is a strong kid. He'll pull through.'

After several hours, they were finally done with the work. Pierre cut the tail up into small chunks within the space of four seconds, using the blades of grass around the tail to slice away as fast as a propellor, proving that Adam had thought right.

Before they left the area, Pierre realigned all of the ground to be the same even level, sealing all the cracks and making all the debris from the fight get absorbed into the ground. He then picked up several of the stingers still on the floor and placed them in a sack.

'Take. You said your other friend makes potions. This is all good for potions. But do not let stinger poison you. If it does, use this.' He showed Kaya and Adam several large thick leaves, the same wrapped around his arm. 'Make cream, then wrap around.'

'Thank you,' Kaya said simply, still thinking that this was all a sick dream.

'Go rest. Take few days to be sad,' Pierre said firmly to them.

A poster had been nailed onto the front door of the Food Hall, explaining what had happened to Olivia, Jaiden, and Rebecca and that their funerals would be held at the same time as the other seven students.

For those following days leading up to the funeral, the four of them didn't show up to a single one of Disciple Maria's lessons. They didn't care how much trouble and pain it would cause them. They needed the days off to grieve.

#   #

As the day of the funeral came, everyone from camp gathered around the cherry blossom tree, Caesar standing at the very edge of the cliff. Caesar, whose voice always boomed so loudly, now spoke with a quieter tone.

'This week we have lost many warriors. We have lost those who served Micholesh and fought for Gerard's honour, and we have lost three who died because they broke the rules. They thought that they could survive in the Wildlands once we had returned. They thought the rules were there to impede them and not protect them. Let this be a lesson that even the outskirts of the Wildlands can be exceptionally dangerous. Now just because this group broke the rules does not mean that they deserve any less of a burial than the rest. From what Max, the only survivor of the group, has told me, these three fought valiantly till the very end.'

Max sat to the side on a small chair facing the crowd, lined up next to many other students, looking dishevelled and defeated. He had surpassed the point of extreme sadness and had allowed himself to drown in it. He sat there with an expressionless face like his soul had left him.

Caesar circled to the back of the crowd, and by chance stood next to Amelia as Papil walked up with a stack of wooden boxes. 'I have here the ashes of the fallen. We stand here, to send their spirits to be at peace.'

The sheet of black clouds above started to cry with little drops of rain. Papil opened each box slowly, saying their names and then emptying the grey dust into the wind. The ashes flew calmly far away from the cliff, off to a place where all was safe and beautiful, a mix of Earth and Elysium, where the dead could rest.

'Those aren't Olivia, Rebecca, and Jaiden's ashes, are they?' Amelia asked Caesar when Kaya was out of earshot.

He gave a heavy sigh. 'No.'

'Then why pretend they are?'

'Because this way people can believe that they are all at peace.'

'But then why not do the same for Gerard?' Adam asked.

'It gave those who needed it a reason to fight.' Without a word more, Caesar marched away from the group as the last of Olivia's fake ashes were scattered.

Adam opened his mouth to speak but Amelia answered without hearing the question. 'The manticore's stinger is imbued with a paralytic toxin. The moment it enters someone's bloodstream, the person is unable to move. Once this happens, the manticore will then eat its prey alive. It's an awful way to go, and there would be nothing left of the three to make into ash.'

People started to leave the hill, giving kind words to those still sitting. Wanting to do the same, Kaya made his way over to try and give his condolences to Max. However, the moment Max saw Kaya, he jumped onto him and started to punch him.

'This is all your fault!' He wailed, striking Kaya as Adam had done to Duke, except Kaya made no effort to defend himself.

A group of students pulled Max off of Kaya and he sat back down in his chair, not taking his eyes off Kaya. 'I hate you, and I hope you die a horrible death! My friends would still be here if you were never born!'

24. Adventure Time

After a long exhausting year in Elysium, the time was finally at hand for the first years to go out into the Wildlands. After thousands of hours of training, Adam was confident that he and his teammates could deal with anything thrown their way. However, not all the other teams were so confident. Many were even questioning whether they would go back to Earth when the portal gates opened in a week.

Throughout months of searching, in every dangerous and known area around Elysium, except for the Ocean of the Damned, there was still no sign of any Ascensionists. Twenty-four people that had fought in the Endless War and had spent years training had died trying to find them.

This did nothing to help with the nerves of those preparing to go out into the Wildlands. The thought of what happened to Olivia, Rebecca, and Jaiden burned into every student's mind. With the added threat of an Ascensionists' attack at any moment, students were hoping for the expeditions to be cancelled.

It was the day before they were expected to depart. Everyone had gone to the armoury and were given a handmade set of armour and requested weapon, their totem etched into both weapon and chest piece. A spell fell over those who felt that they were not ready, where they were fixated on the idea that they would be walking into their death.

Duke had no choice but to join his teammates for the expedition and even though they all bore the same hedgehog totem, they were not a team. Adam had probably spoken to Duke more than his teammates had and even though they would be putting their lives in danger, they still chose to ignore him and look at him as the villain.

That night, not knowing what to do, every student had found themselves sitting in the cosy Food Hall – a place that had the best chance to calm them down, as they all fidgeted and panicked at the thought of what the following day would bring. Too anxious to eat anything, even when a lot of them were starting to believe it could be their final meal.

Max, who still hadn't recovered from the death of his friends, had been thrown into the leprechaun totem group, making them the only team of five. At first, they were more than happy to have another member help, but they quickly realised that Max would be slowing them down more than anything.

He wasn't sleeping, eating, or even talking. There was no light in his eyes, and he seemed like a shell of the teenager he once was. Still, Caesar had refused to let him miss the expedition, and the team had given him the role to carry as much as he could, like a mule.

Amelia had been pacing around the living room of their cabin, mumbling to herself whilst the other three tried to focus on cramming in any last morsels of information from the piles of books she had taken out from her room when Theta knocked on their door. Amelia sprinted the few steps to the door and immediately was drawn to the pieces of parchment the monk was holding.

This time she had no interest in chatting with Theta, shutting the door on her the moment she had handed over the parchment, cutting the monk off mid-sentence as she tried to wish Amelia good luck.

'It has been one year since you arrived at Camp Paragon,' she read from the parchment. 'It is now time to prove your skills here by embarking on a mission in the Wildlands. Your task is to explore a newly found ruin. You will search for its treasure, most likely held in a room with obsidian walls, and bring it back to Camp Paragon. The ruin can be found in grid G6 on the attached map.' Amelia unpinned a detailed map of the Wildlands, which she handed to Adam. 'It is yet to be properly explored, but a griffin is known to be protecting the ruins. It is not a requirement to kill the griffin as it is not classed as a monster, but you are expected to defend yourself should it attack. You are expected at the edge of the training grounds at sunset tomorrow to start your journey. Good luck to the Squonk team, Caesar.'

Adam took a deep breath. 'We can do this.'

Iosefka was doing her best to stay calm. She had come a long way from the scared runaway she had once been. She was stronger than she had ever imagined, but the time of safety had flown by and now her fears had caught up with her.

Adam passed the map around the group. 'Amelia, tell us everything you know about griffins. By the sound of it, there might be a way for us to drive it away instead of killing it?'

'Well, I'm sure we all know the basics.'

'Body of a lion, with a head like an eagle and wings like a massive eagle as well,' Kaya recited, passing the map to Iosefka.

'Exactly, now it can obviously fly, which makes it harder for us, and depending on the species, it could have talons or claws, but either way, we don't want to get scratched or grabbed by them, and of course, we need to be careful about its teeth. And I think you're right, Adam, we should be able to find a way around killing it.'

By the time all of them called it a night, they were far too tired from planning for the following day to spend the night lying awake, but all of their dreams were filled with nothing but terror and action.

The next day Adam woke with extreme excitement, finally ready for some real adventure. Not having their expedition until the end of the day, the four of them all decided to train to warm themselves up.

As the hours passed, the four of them went over some of the more advanced spells they had learnt from scrolls in the Monastery, watching as groups met Caesar at the entrance to the Wildlands. Almost everyone was shaking in their shiny armour, having to hold onto their teammates to stop themselves from stumbling and throwing up.

Adam noticed that a lot of people did a scan of the camp, taking it all in for what could be their last time. Some groups walked into the Wildlands alone. Others had their mentors by their side, a monk or someone from the Capital. Each mentor had as grave a look as their students, giving as much last-minute advice as they could think to share.

As though the sun itself was taunting Adam with how minutely it moved, minutes turned to hours and hours turned to days. Eventually – after what felt like an eternity – sunset arrived, and it was time to leave.

They had each packed a bag filled with food and basic items that could be useful. Adam carried pots and cooking items. Amelia had packed books for ancient runes and a book that had information about griffins. Iosefka had carefully stacked all the different potions that could be needed over the next few days, and as many crossbow arrows as she could carry. And Kaya had brought the rest of the cooking items that Adam couldn't carry.

Each bag also contained a sleeping bag and a map in case anyone got separated from the rest.

To their great surprise, Disciple Maria was waiting for them at the entrance, standing next to Caesar in silence.

'Disciple Maria?' Amelia said as if she wasn't sure it was her, having lined up like they had done every day of their torture with her.

'Yes, it is me. Whilst I have made it clear you are not anywhere near my favourite students, you are still my students. You have all learnt a great deal from both me and Gerard, Zeus rest his soul. I have had a look at this task of yours and it is perfectly completable, but do not make the mistake of being overconfident. I am aware of how easily you can get flooded with emotion. Stay true to my teachings, and you should be able to get back here in one piece.' Her voice was harsh and strict as usual, but for the first time, it sounded like there was a morsel of warmth seeping out from her icy shell.

'Thank you, ma'am,' they all said at once.

'You all appear prepared. I have trained you well.'

'Well, at least we know whatever's out there won't be as bad as your staff,' Kaya said, flinching his hand out of habit as soon as the words came from his mouth.

But from Disciple Maria came something that they never thought could come from her. A slight flicker of a smile. Just a small one, but somehow, she was smiling. 'Yes, I suppose you are right. It is quite the force to be reckoned with. Good luck, the four of you.'

Hearing Disciple Maria speak as though she almost liked them made their spirits grow tenfold. The jitters they were trying to keep back stopped, replaced with only the thought of making their mentor proud.

'You all understand the task?' Caesar asked.

'Yes,' they responded.

'Then head into the Wildlands. If you do not return to us within five days, we will send a search party for you. If you are still alive by that point, they will bring you back.' Caesar gestured for them to start their journey and so they all took a deep breath and stepped into the Wildlands.

With one last glance back, Adam saw Maria staring at them. When she caught Adam's eye, she gave a small nod and walked away.

Kaya had been delegated to the front of the group, guiding everyone to their destination, his daggers sheathed at his sides, manoeuvring through the thick trees and harsh terrain with ease.

Before long, they had caught up with a group completely lost – jumping at every slight noise, including Kaya who moved almost silently. Kaya gave the group some directions, then four of them were back on route to where the ruins were said to be.

Nobody said much of anything as they traversed the wilderness. They were all too focused on not letting their guard down, listening for anything.

After only a few hours of travelling, night approached and they decided to set up camp. They were already farther in than Kaya had ever gone and the deadliest monsters were likely to search for something to kill when it was dark.

Iosefka and Kaya worked together to grow a dome of grassy dirt that encircled the four of them into a kind of earthy igloo, an idea Kaya had suggested from seeing Duke's home. Amelia then cast some orbs of desert glass to light up their camp, whilst Adam unpacked all their cooking equipment.

The dirt mound around them was then given an extra piece of support to hold it up, with a circular dirt beam that Kaya raised from the ground in the centre of their circle. With some difficulty, Adam managed to hollow out the beam and turned it into a makeshift furnace, with the smoke billowing up like a chimney out from the top of the mound.

As Iosefka prayed to eat, Kaya prepared some rabbits he had managed to catch earlier and gave them to Adam who made dinner for them. Having half a rabbit was a drastic change from the camp's ready-made, endless supply of food so tasty it was a miracle everyone wasn't plump, but it was enough to keep their strength up.

Once they had all finished eating, Amelia dissolved the balls of hovering light above them, submerging them all into complete darkness. They wanted to leave the moment the sun rose over the mountains, so knew how important a good night's sleep would be. However, having not done much training during the day, none of them were the slightest bit tired, and although none of them spoke, it was clear that they were all still awake hours into the night, trying their best to get comfortable on the hard ground.

None of them had any idea how long it took to fall asleep, but they all remembered waking up with a fright as something started scratching against their dome. Not knowing how long it would take for whatever was trying to attack them to break through their weak walls, which were meant only to camouflage, they decided to use the element of surprise whilst they still had it.

Iosefka quickly retrieved a potion from her bag and covered the tip of an arrowhead in the slimy red substance. When she was ready, Kaya opened up the dome like a sliding door in the direction of the noise. Despite how fast he had opened it, they only just had enough time to see a terrified stag run away, dirt falling from its antlers onto its head.

After that scare, none of them had any intention of going back to sleep, and as their camp defences had already opened up, and the dark black sky was starting to become a greyish blue, they decided to continue their journey.

As the team packed everything up, Iosefka recited her morning prayers along with her prayers for casting spells, which she was doing at any moment of reprise they had. All four of their hearts were beating far too fast for something as simple as tiredness to get in their way, as they marched farther into the somewhat unknown.

By around midday, they had entered the grid section on the map where the ruins were, without having encountered a single monster. Everyone's emotions started to rise as their goal was in sight, which meant the most dangerous moment any of them had experienced so far approached.

They found that the grid they were searching in was much larger than what they had been anticipating, due to how rugged the terrain was. It would take them hours or even days to find the ruins they needed. At least that would have been the case if it weren't for Iosefka who spotted a feather covered in dirt which Amelia identified – using her book – as an unmistakable griffin feather.

Kaya used a piece of magic he had learnt to track the feather back to its owner. It took what felt like no time at all before they started to see chunks of rock and rubble littered on the ground. It turned out that what Caesar and everyone else called ruins were nothing like what Adam had pictured in his head. To him, ruins were a few old dilapidated stone walls that would fall over with a strong kick, which was nothing like the fortress Kaya led them towards.

They had come to the ruin from its side where they were met with a large stone wall, a guard walkway running across the top made from old wood that was, except for some broken pieces and clumps of moss, in good condition.

They could have destroyed the wall if they wanted, but it had been decided from the start that they would play it silently for as long as they could. Plan A was to sneak past the griffin, get any treasure, and leave. All of them hoped this would go exactly as planned and that they wouldn't have to reach Amelia's plan T.

Since they couldn't scale the tall wall quietly, they tried to go around the left side, as the trees to the right were so clumped together, they would have had to leave their backpacks behind to get through them.

After a few minutes of awkward climbing over thick tree roots, their surroundings opened up into a wide path that bathed in the warm afternoon sunlight. The stone path led towards an arch, runic symbols etched into the entrance.

'Can you read that?' Kaya asked Amelia.

'Yes, I think I can.' She dropped her bag to the ground, excited as she extracted a thick book from its depths. 'Let's see.' She turned through the pages, her finger running across the paper. 'Beware... The... and that must be griffin.'

'We already know there's a griffin here,' Kaya moaned.

'Even though we already knew, it's nice to know that we're in the right place,' Adam said, looking inside the ruin.

'And it's reminding us to beware,' Iosefka added.

'Exactly, so let's make sure we make as little noise as possible,' Amelia said, following Adam into the ruin.

Four walls went around in a square, each one with a walkway, and each having an entrance in the centre point. There was no roof. Instead, the trees hung over it, shedding their dark green leaves onto the hard stone floor. A large water feature created a mini-waterfall off to the side, but it was covered in grime and moss like the walls, with barely enough dirty water to flow properly.

On the other side, a giant nest made from small trees was currently unoccupied. The threat of the griffin coming back to its home at any moment made all of them move with great urgency. Iosefka pointed next to the nest, where a set of narrow stairs led underground.

It became some consolation that when they went down into the tight tunnel, they wouldn't have to worry about the griffin following them inside– although there was still the fear of getting trapped alive, or finding some monster lurking in the darkness waiting to pounce on them.

'Well, doesn't that just look lovely?' Kaya said in a higher tone than normal.

'We could always just lie and say that there wasn't anything down there,' Iosefka sputtered as they prepared to continue their journey underground.

'Calm down, Iosefka,' Adam said, placing his hand on her shoulder. 'Remember, this is what we have trained for. We have more training than anyone else, and you are more than capable of doing this. Keep your crossbow at the ready, I believe you can do this.'

Iosefka stared down into the seemingly endless staircase. 'You're right. I can do this.'

25. Honour and Treasure

As the sunlight behind them started to fade, Amelia, who was positioned at the back behind Iosefka, cast the same desert glass light orb from the night before. Kaya – who was at the front with Adam – had a fireball in his hand, ready to throw at anything that attacked.

Carefully, they worked through the cold tunnels, inspecting every crack they could find. Eventually, the group found themselves in front of another set of stairs going down even farther than they already were. With all the different turns and crossroads they had come to, Adam could tell it was going to be a struggle to find their way back out, so asked Iosefka to leave a trail as they went.

She took out a bright white potion in a syringe and ejected a few drops onto the ground, which shone and sparkled like wet coins in the blazing sun.

The moment they reached the bottom step of the lower level, they had their first scare. Spooked by the sudden light, a bat came flying at them from the ceiling. Whilst it made the four of them jump, they were quick and had trained for much worse. Kaya hit the bat with the fireball before it could get anywhere near him, killing it instantly.

'Did we have to kill it? It was just a little harmless bat,' Iosefka whispered.

'Bats can be far from harmless. They can spread diseases like rabies, histoplasmosis, and salmonellosis, which are all lethal,' Amelia whispered back as they slowly crept forward.

'Plus, they might turn us into vampires,' Kaya added.

'There is yet to be a single case where someone has been changed into something else by a monster. So, nobody is going to be turned into a werewolf, vampire, or some kind of superhero in these ruins.'

'But nobody has ever been in these tunnels before, have they? We don't know what the bats down here are capable of?' Kaya joked, recasting the fireball spell.

'Are vampires monsters, Amelia?' Iosefka asked.

Adam had grown used to Iosefka starting random conversations when she was scared, it helped keep her mind calm.

'If vampires were to exist in this world, which they don't, there would be a mix between those that are monsters, and those that are creatures. A vampire has to drink blood to survive. If that is the only reason it hunts, I think it's fair to class it as a creature, like how we humans need to hunt other animals to survive. But then once a vampire starts hunting for the thrill of it, they can turn into a monster. I've read old stories where this can even change their physical properties.'

'Guys, focus, we need to be quiet,' Adam said as they kept on moving.

Other than a few more encounters with some sleeping bats, nothing stood in their path as they kept on journeying deeper down the tunnels. After what felt like an hour of careful tiptoeing around, checking for traps and monsters around the labyrinth, Kaya's fire cast its light on an obsidian door at the very end of an especially long tunnel – so long that even the light from Amelia's orb couldn't reach the other end of it.

Amelia came to the front to examine the obsidian. Delicately she ran her hand across it. There were no markings or symbols etched in or coming out of the door, nor were there holes, levers, or contraptions to open it.

'How do we open it?' Iosefka asked.

'I don't know,' Amelia conceded. 'Maybe all we have to do is lift it.'

'What?' Adam shook his head. 'No secret message, no unique pattern, you just want us to lift the door? Have you ever tried to lift obsidian? It doesn't exactly look light.'

'I don't have any other ideas so unless someone else has a way to get us through, then I'm all ears.'

'Why don't we look for a book that's actually a lever? That always does the trick,' Kaya teased.

Since there were no other working suggestions, Amelia left her orb of desert glass hovering in the sky to shed light as they all felt around, trying to find a good grip on the jagged stone.

'On three,' Adam said once they had found a good grip. 'One, two, threeee!' All four of them pulled upwards with every bit of strength they had in them, but the door wouldn't budge, their grip slipping on the obsidian the more force they gave.

'Well, that worked great,' Kaya said, frustrated, as he picked himself up from the ground having slid down the door.

'I don't know what to do. There's always some kind of test to get through, but for the life of me, I can't work out what we need to do.' Amelia was pulling her hair in frustration. 'Often the clues will be what has happened to get to the room, but we haven't had anything to deal with except for a few bats that probably weren't even meant to be here. They most likely just flew in because it was dark and quiet.'

'I think I know how to get the door open,' Iosefka sputtered.

'How?' They all asked.

'You just said that it's a clue. The bats only liked it here because it's quiet and dark. So shouldn't we do the same?'

'Of course! How could I have been so stupid?' Amelia smacked her hand against her forehead. 'Everyone stay silent. Don't move.'

Amelia destroyed her orb of light and as it shattered into little pieces, they delved into the pitch-black void. Not being able to see anything and with nothing to be heard, within seconds, their minds started to exaggerate reality.

Adam couldn't help but think that there was some massive horrible monster at the other end of the tunnel. That it was creeping towards them under the veil of darkness. He had to hold his breath to keep silent, certain that he was seconds away from death. The hideous monster could now be inches away from him, so close he was sure he could smell its horrid breath.

The smell of rotting flesh filled his nostrils, but he kept telling himself that it wasn't real, it wouldn't matter if he turned to his other friends, he wouldn't be able to see them. And like him, they weren't making any noise. Then, just as he thought the monster in his head would strike, the obsidian door started to rise, and as it did, a spark was triggered, giving a flame to the torches attached to the obsidian walls, bringing light into the empty tunnel.

'Thank the heavens,' Amelia said with a sigh of relief.

'God, I thought you had all disappeared for a moment.' Iosefka seemed a lot calmer than Adam would have expected, and then he noticed that she had been holding Kaya's hand.

As the four of them entered the small treasure room, they couldn't help but celebrate. It wasn't a room filled to the brim with scrolls and artefacts, nor did it have so many riches that they would be able to swim in it. The only item in the small fortified room was a wooden chest, but just seeing it, knowing that whatever was inside was theirs and that they had earnt it, was a feeling of achievement like no other.

The four of them awkwardly huddled around the little chest and pushed the lid open together. From within, they retrieved two scrolls rolled up with lace, a beautiful silver chalice with small green gems encrusted around it, and a small leather pouch that held a selection of little crystals.

Not wanting to waste any time examining the items when they still needed to get back to camp in one piece, they carefully placed the four pieces of loot in each person's bag and made their way back the way they came, following the trail Iosefka had made for them.

'I can't believe we found two scrolls! I wonder what strains they will be for?' Amelia was bouncing with excitement as they carefully made their way toward the surface.

'Ooh, imagine if we found a scroll for that new strain Theta spoke about. Amelia, did you find out what kind of magic it was in the end?' Kaya asked.

'No, they're keeping it all secretive, I don't even think Theta was meant to know what it is expected to be. But enough of that, now we need to focus.'

The second Adam made it back to the surface, he was attacked. The griffin had been waiting in its nest and pounced towards Adam, its sharp talons screeching at him as it swiped.

Adam had been just fast enough to throw himself out of the way of the massive eagle-lion, but the griffin managed to hit his shield-wielding arm. Without the armour, it would have been severed from his body completely. Blood poured from his wound, leaking down onto his shining armour as he backed away from the creature.

The other three had sprinted up to help Adam, but none of them could get near him with the griffin screeching and flapping its wings at them, attempting to ward them off.

'Iosefka! The sleeping plan!' Adam screamed over all the noise of the mythical creature.

Iosefka backed off as much as she could and threw off her bag, frantically searching inside it. To give Iosefka as much time as possible, Kaya and Amelia attacked the griffin at a distance.

Amelia did her best to keep the griffin stunned by throwing pieces of sharp desert glass towards its face, which exploded into a blast of blinding light like a grenade after impact, disorienting the beast. To keep the beast where it was, Kaya held his hands to the ground and was causing the grass to wrap around the griffin's talons, locking it to the ground.

By now, Iosefka had dipped one of her bolts in the manticore venom and shot it without any difficulty at the massive magical creature. The bolt soared through the air and hit its target but barely pierced its thick skin, falling almost immediately.

Wanting to escape from the its attackers, the griffin flapped its wings with such power, it pushed Amelia and Kaya backwards, scattering the thin trees that made up its nest. In the few moments Kaya's hands left the ground, the griffin used all its force to break free of its grass binds, and started running towards Adam, who was already feeling faint from his injury. As the creature ran towards Adam, he stood holding his sword, swaying left and right, trying to think of a plan to survive.

'Iosefka, I'll give you a mark to shoot! Kaya, boost me!' Adam screamed to make sure they heard him as the griffin outstretched its wings so that Adam couldn't escape its attack.

Iosefka had dipped another bolthead in the paralysis venom and readied herself for the opening, her heart beating too fast to count. Her nerves burned with fear, but her breath remained steady and her bones were solid as stone.

Like they had practiced, Kaya performed the movements and launched Adam into the sky just as the eagle head dove forward, its yellow beak snapping madly. Adam's stomach jolted from the sudden movement. The extra weight of his backpack and armour and the dizziness from his wound made it difficult to orientate himself, but as he soared through the sky, his sword swung down across the side of the griffin, opening a large gash in its side.

Before Adam had even landed, Iosefka pulled the trigger and sent her bolt driving into the open wound. Adam collided hard on the ground on his injured side and let out a cry of pain.

The griffin turned around, furious that Adam had managed to escape it, and saw all four of its enemies huddled together. But as soon as it took a single step, it found that it couldn't move another part of its body. It collapsed, the paralytic manticore venom taking over.

Iosefka sprinted to Adam, healing him with Life and Death magic whilst Kaya applied a lotion Iosefka had made to help with pain. Once Adam's wound was healed, he felt strong enough to stand and they all walked over to the griffin lying defenceless on the ground. Its yellow eyes darted around, trying to work out a way to escape. Iosefka pulled the bolt from its side and gently stroked its fur, trying her best to soothe it.

Looking down at it, Adam thought about how easily they could finish it off. How it had tried to kill him, and how it came incredibly close to doing so. He had his sword in his hand. All he would have to do was plunge it into the griffin and then they would have another valuable item to take back to camp.

Adam locked eyes with the creature. He could see its emotion and intelligence, just like any person Adam had met, and as it closed them shut, it could not have been clearer that it was waiting for its life to end. But they had used the manticore venom and not a lethal potion for a reason. The griffin wasn't a monster, it was only defending what it believed needed defending.

'Let's go, the venom won't last forever,' Adam ordered, walking back towards the entrance.

The others followed, happy, knowing they were victorious without taking an innocent life.

On the way back, they slacked on their hyper-vigilance, talking, laughing, and assessing how they could have done better. It wasn't that they were casually meandering about, far away from each other with their eyes closed. They were still checking for possible threats, but they had become comfortable manoeuvring around the Wildlands.

As they set up their camp, in the same way they had done the night prior, they all took out their treasure. After everything was secure, with the dirt dome up around them, and with Amelia's lights illuminating the dark, they gathered around as she picked up the two scrolls, ready to unravel them.

'Now remember everyone, we won't know what spells we have discovered straight away. I will need to spend some time with them and I think I've managed to learn enough to at least crack one if not both tonight.'

'Yeah, yeah, whatever. Just open the things,' Kaya said.

Since she was the most eager and the one who would be spending the most time with the scrolls, they decided that Amelia would be the one to open them. That was what they would later say to people asking about their first adventure, when in reality, Amelia slapped, pinched and threatened to seriously injure anyone who so much as tried to open them.

After pulling on the white lace holding the first scroll, a light glow started to emanate from the yellow parchment, identical to the glow that came from desert glass.

'That is what happens when you open a scroll for the first time after it was sealed,' Amelia lectured as though the other three weren't smart enough to work that out.

As she opened the scroll, symbols in all the colours of a rainbow were scattered around like the colours of smoke in the sky. Immediately, Amelia started to ramble about all the possible things the symbols could mean. She must have been speaking at the speed of sound as everyone else quickly stopped being able to understand her.

'Why don't you open the other one?' Iosefka suggested.

'That's a fantastic idea, I wonder if there could be a link between the two. This is going to be so much fun.'

The second scroll was just as uninteresting as the first one to everyone but Amelia. To Amelia, it was even more fascinating. All across the scroll were black ink lines, some curved, some thick. All of them appeared to be nothing special.

In the end, they left Amelia on one side of the dome as she disappeared into her own world, using her finger to draw on the dirt ground as if it were a chalkboard in an attempt to work out what the symbols and lines meant.

Next, they took out the silver chalice and spent a little more time looking at all the gems encrusted on the sides. Four large green gems that could have been emeralds were placed at equal distances apart, little white gems wrapping around them.

Adam decided against trying to drink water out of it, uncertain if the chalice was some kind of artefact or cursed object, or if it was just a fancy cup to drink from. Whatever it was, he thought that it wasn't worth the risk to test out in the Wildlands.

Finally, Iosefka opened the little pouch and emptied the small crystals onto the ground. 'What do we think these are for?' Kaya asked, picking one up and turning it around in his hand. Each one was unique with different colours, transparent and opaque. Most were smooth, but one was sharp enough to be used as an arrowhead.

'Do you think it's some kind of sorcery magic? Like you put the crystals in a circle and draw a pentagram whilst sacrificing a chicken and they all start glowing and then something appears?' Adam wondered.

'I'm pretty sure they are just used for potions. I've seen these types of crystals at the shop I like going to and they sell them for about five drachmas each?' Iosefka said, looking closely at a light rose stone.

'Are you sure?' Kaya scrunched up his face, thinking that he would have to swallow one to find out what they did.

'Yes, if I am correct, I believe you are meant to wait until moonlight to grind them up and sprinkle them over a flame to change the effect of the flame in small ways to work better with certain advanced potions.'

'Ok well, that sounds super boring. Should I just eat one to see if it does anything to me?' Kaya joked.

There wasn't much more that they could learn so Adam, Kaya, and Iosefka attempted to sleep now that the adrenaline of the day started to dissipate. Amelia had no intention of sleeping, the light above her head staying on throughout the night, as she did everything she could think of trying to reveal the spell on their scrolls, with seemingly more adrenaline than when she had been fighting a deadly griffin.

26. Let the Dead Be Forgotten

The following morning, all four of them were running on fumes, having barely rested the night before due to Amelia's incessive mutterings and scribbling on the ground.

Now, as they stumbled through the Wildlands, Amelia still had her head buried in the scrolls. Occasionally she stopped the group so she could retrieve a book from her backpack. Everyone had grown to love Amelia, and whilst she was a valued member of the team, they all wanted nothing more than for her to go somewhere far away from them. Finding the scrolls was starting to feel more like a burden than a reward.

With her slow walking and constant stops, the group was taking much longer to get back than what was expected, but after hours of walking, Kaya confirmed that he was in familiar territory and that they would be back at camp within the hour. At this moment of happiness, Amelia stopped dead in her tracks. The black lines on the second scroll had started to move and rearrange by themselves.

'I can't believe it!' She screamed and to everyone's surprise, she threw the scroll into some mud.

'What did you do that for!' Shouted Adam, puzzled.

'I've decoded it,' she said as if this was the worst thing to possibly happen.

Amelia was kicking everything around her. Small stones, twigs, and flowers all received the full force of her foot.

'That's good, why are you acting like someone just corrected you?' Kaya asked.

'I don't act like that when someone corrects me. Go on, tell me one time someone's corrected me and I've acted like this. See, you can't.' She said, having given Kaya less than a nanosecond to respond.

'Amelia, what's wrong with the scroll?' Adam picked it up and started to wipe the mud from it. 'Oh,' he said after reading the new diagrams that had been revealed.

'See, this sucks!' Amelia yelled, ripping a branch from a tree and launching it off into the wilderness.

'Could someone please tell me what's going on, I don't understand?' Iosefka urged.

'It's a spell that's already been discovered,' Adam explained.

'You're kidding, I didn't know there were duplicate scrolls,' Kaya said.

'There aren't, but these scrolls are just slices of knowledge from whoever has been here before us, and they had to discover this stuff through trial and error. People have managed to discover spells the same way, and look, it's the spell in the Life and Death vein to rot something and reduce it to a black dust.' Amelia grabbed the scroll from Adam and shoved it at Kaya.

As said, the scroll showed a flower in different stages rotting until it was nothing but a pile of ash.

'Which is exactly what Caesar did to that massive tree that came through the Food Hall floor when he was showing off his skill,' Adam explained to Kaya.

Anyone else would have been demoralized and would have taken a break from decoding the other scroll, but for Amelia, it only made her more motivated. She was now at the front of the group with Kaya, trying to go as fast as possible back to camp, caring very little about any possible threats around them.

With this speed, only twenty minutes later, they started to hear a crowd of noise in the distance. Thanks to Kaya's excellent tracking and navigation skills, he managed to take them back to the exact point that they had entered. As the four of them moved the last few branches and bits of shrubbery out of their way, they could hear two people arguing loudly.

'I don't care how dangerous it is! We need to go deeper into the Wildlands. That's where the Ascensionists are hiding, they can't get away with what they've done!' Delilah shouted.

'Micholesh is working out a safe way to find those responsible for killing your father, but we can't lose any more warriors than we already have,' Caesar replied.

As Kaya came through into camp, the crowd all moved their attention from Caesar and Delilah to him. The moment the crowd of older students and Capital residents saw all four of the group back and safe, the silence changed to cheering.

The tables from the Food Hall had been moved to the entrance and were set with food. As they walked through the crowd, people congratulated them, shaking their hands as though they had just saved the camp.

'Well done.' The four of them turned around to see Caesar, his face as expressionless as ever, Delilah having stormed off.

'Piece of cake,' Kaya replied, already stuffing his face with a chicken leg.

'For verification that you have completed the task, show me the treasure you managed to obtain from the ruins.'

Everyone gathered around as they dropped their backpacks onto one of the benches and retrieved all the items they had found. As they took out each item, the crowd would 'ooh' and 'ahh' like children watching a magic trick. Amelia, Kaya, and Iosefka were lapping up all the attention, but Adam could tell that the crowd was overexaggerating how interested they were.

These were all the students who had done this exact adventure at some point in their life, along with many more adventures far more dangerous than their first. They were only giving them this much attention because they knew what it meant to the four of them. To feel like what they had done was of incredible value – to feel like they were heroes.

The reality of it, which Adam hated to admit to himself, was that the two scrolls they had were unlikely to yield anything of real value – they already knew for a fact one didn't. The silver chalice was nice, but it probably wasn't worth much, and he already knew what value the crystals had. It wasn't like they had gone to the ruins to save a princess or slay a dragon, they were ultimately grave robbers, taking the treasures from someone long dead.

Still, Adam did his best to ignore this and basked in the admiration he and his team was getting. There would be no value in shattering the moment for everyone, he was content to just ignore the truth and enjoy himself. After all, it was no easy feat that they had completed and he deserved to be proud of himself.

'Good,' Caesar said, after watching silently. 'You are one of the first to return. The only group to come before you is the team with a hedgehog totem.'

The four of them were incredibly surprised to find Duke sitting at one of the tables, his team talking happily with him, speaking to him like he was their friend.

Their armour all seemed pretty badly damaged, and Adam noticed that one person's chest piece had melted by the shoulders. Their faces were marked and bruised, but they appeared to be without major injuries.

'Apparently, Duke saved them all. Risked his life to keep them safe. Someone who does that can't be all bad, I guess,' a student added as everyone's attention moved towards Duke.

'Come on, tell us what happened,' another student surrounding them probed, bringing the attention back to the Squonk team.

Kaya happily took the lead, providing his normal enthusiasm when telling a story, explaining how they opened the obsidian door and how they managed to get away from the griffin without having to kill it.

'That sounds like quite a story, it is a good job I was able to train you so well.' The crowd parted immediately for Disciple Maria. As she walked, people made sure not to look her in the eye, afraid that they would get hit by her notorious staff.

'Couldn't have done it without you,' Kaya mumbled, mouth full of food.

Kaya had made the mistake of thinking that just because Disciple Maria had given them the smallest of smiles before they left, she was now their best friend.

Whack.

A mistake that he was quickly reprimanded for.

'Ow!' It was a surprise that he could still be hurt by the staff, considering he had been struck by it more than anyone else in all of Elysium.

'How many times do I have to tell you?'

'Right, right, sorry.' He rubbed his hand and swallowed all the food that he was close to choking on. 'Couldn't have done it without you, Disciple Maria, ma'am.'

'Now with any luck, that will be the last time I ever have to discipline you. I have honoured Gerard as I promised I would, and now I am no longer burdened by you four every single day.'

'Oh, I don't know, I reckon I've still got a few more in me, ma'am,' Kaya smirked as he stood behind Amelia, using her as a human shield.

'Very well,' Disciple Maria said, turning away and walking back towards the Capital.

'Everyone quick! I can hear someone coming through,' someone shouted.

The camp gathered around the entrance, and Adam waited eagerly to see who else would come through so that he could hear all about what kind of adventure they had to go on. But something felt off...

It was too quiet. The team coming to the entrance of the Wildlands was moving at a worryingly slow pace. Everyone moved to the edge, ready to heal whoever came through, believing that something had gone wrong. However, what appeared from the Wildlands was so much worse than what anyone could imagine.

Emerging from within came the withered corpse of Gerard the Unstoppable. His armour had now become part of his skin over months of decomposition, and his stomach had a wide gaping hole going all the way through it, revealing his rotting insides and black dried blood.

The whole of the camp went into a frenzy. People pushed and shoved others in an attempt to run away, not having the slightest desire to try and stop his steady approach into camp, a greatsword dragging across the floor as the corpse stumbled forwards.

'What do we do?!' Kaya shouted at Adam, but he never answered. All he could do was stare into Gerard's dead eyes and hard gaunt face, stuck to the ground as if he had turned to stone.

The screaming of students filled the area, along with their feet pounding the ground to run away as Gerard's corpse crossed the threshold into Camp Paragon. Not knowing what else to do, Kaya threw an arc of compressed air toward his old mentor, but the thing approaching them menacingly wasn't some zombie from the films they had watched. Those zombies wander around, barely able to hold themselves upright as their body parts fell off. They are braindead and can't defend themselves.

Gerard's corpse had been approaching them as a warrior walks into battle, steady and certain. So, as Kaya's spell came close to it, the corpse dashed aside so fast, the fallen leaves around it blew up into the air as the slice of wind came soaring past. Seeing Kaya as a threat, Gerard's head snapped to face him with a horrible crack. The legendary greatsword burst into flames as the corpse pointed it toward Kaya.

A strike of fire rushed through the air like a bolt of lightning coursing through the sky, as Gerard's body dashed towards Kaya, ready to kill. Seeing his friend in danger snapped Adam back into reality, and he raised the ground between the two to form a thick wall, proving useless as Gerard the Unstoppable smashed through it, using his massive body as a ram.

Then as the blazing greatsword swung across to hit Kaya, Amelia created a thick wall of desert glass in an attempt to deflect the attack. The magic shields proved futile as the sword smashed through it as if it wasn't there.

Kaya had been just fast enough to dodge back but his shoulder was burnt from the heat of the fire, the pain so strong that it dropped him to the already smouldering grass. Iosefka was desperately trying to find a safe space to pray, but there wasn't the opportunity to and all she found herself doing was watching as her teammates tried to survive.

Gerard's corpse stepped forward, its greatsword high in the sky, ready to deliver the final blow to Kaya.

That second stretched out for Adam as time slowed just like it had when he heard about his great mentor's death.

He watched as the man who was so close to his parents prepared to kill the only family Adam had left.

In that moment, Adam realised that there was nothing he wouldn't give to keep Kaya, Amelia, and Iosefka safe.

The flaming sword came dropping down like a guillotine, but it was not Kaya it found in its path, but Adam.

His shield was raised in defence with his sword, but it would not matter. Adam knew that his flimsy pieces of metal would be sliced through like they weren't there and then he would be dead.

Out of fear of his imminent demise, Adam found that he could not look at the burning greatsword, and so turned his head back as much as he could to get one last look at his best friend. As he felt the heat build in his hands, he knew that his life was about to end and closed his eyes, accepting his fate.

Death never came.

Seconds crept past, and yet all Adam could feel was the burning heat from his sword hilt and shield. Opening his eyes, he saw that Kaya was just as amazed and stunned. Gathering some courage, he turned his head back to Gerard's corpse and found that he had stopped, the greatsword resting on top of his shield, slowly melting it.

As much as his mind wanted him to keep his weapon and shield in his hands, the metal had grown too hot and he was forced to drop them both to the floor. Still, the greatsword stayed where it was, floating a few inches above Adam's sweating head.

Adam stared at Gerard's cold dead blackened eyes. It seemed as though the corpse was deliberating, its head tilted to the side. Adam had no idea what was going on, and then he heard a fresh scream.

'Dad!'

Turning its attention away from Adam, Gerard's corpse bounded towards Delilah, who was too overwhelmed to move or defend herself and the greatsword cut through her side. As soon as the greatsword touched her skin, the fire latched onto her and grew in size. She cried out from the pain, dropping to her knees as her entire body burst into flame.

Before the corpse could finish Delilah off, Caesar blasted into its side with his enormous shield, flinging him far off into the distance and slamming into a tree, which collapsed under the impact.

'Run!' He screamed as he raised the shield, blocking the swings already coming from the massive flaming greatsword. On impact of the shield, the Greatsword of War created an explosion of fire that singed Caesar's clothes with every hit.

The two were locked in battle. One had a seemingly impenetrable shield, and the other was already dead with a weapon that allowed for no error to be made against it. It seemed as though they would be fighting forever.

Adam wanted to help Delilah, but he first needed to get the rest of his team out of the area, so he helped Kaya to his feet, his shoulder covered in burn marks, and passed him over to Iosefka and Amelia who carried him away. Once they were a good distance away, Iosefka recited her prayers so fast that the words wouldn't come out properly and she had to repeat herself over and over, as Adam sprinted towards Delilah, whose yells still pierced the air.

As Caesar fought Gerard's corpse, the surrounding area went up in flames from the embers and spurts of fire that came with every hit against the shield, which remained as Caesar's only defence.

By the time Adam reached Delilah, she was no longer screaming and Adam was terrified that she had died. He performed the movements as he dropped to the ground, causing water to burst from his hands like heavy rain, putting out the fire that had consumed her. He then desperately started to heal her unconscious body.

Caesar had found the smallest opportunity to best Gerard's corpse and dodged under one of its swings – manoeuvring around the burning ground – and drove his sword through the rotten back, striking slightly above the open hole.

Caesar then tried to pull his sword out, but the corpse turned round in an instant, the sword still protruding out of its body, going right through what was once Gerard's kind heart.

It was poetic that in death Gerard had been reunited with his precious artefact, the Greatsword of War – a weapon that can only be wielded by the greatest swordsman in the world.

It didn't matter that Caesar's attack didn't kill Gerard's corpse, the greatsword could tell that its owner was no longer superior, having just a fragment of the skill that the real Gerard had.

As Gerard's corpse lifted its arm, ready to unleash another flurry of fiery attacks in the hope of breaking through the impenetrable shield, the fire that covered the blade crept down to the hilt. It spread to the hand and then the arm, and within seconds, Gerard's entire body was ablaze. Caesar then managed to get some distance away and made some quick hand movements, and the flaming body turned to stone.

Disciple Maria had come back to the camp. 'I don't believe it,' she whispered as she watched Gerard's almost skeletal hand drop the greatsword, the flame going out as soon as it hit the ground.

Without the greatsword holding it back, cracks started to form in the rock surrounding the corpse. Like a shrapnel bomb, stone flew off in all directions as the corpse broke out. Caesar had fought incredibly well but he was burnt and exhausted and wasn't fast enough to bring up his shield to stop the chunks of rock crashing into his head, knocking him out.

Before the corpse had a chance to attack again, Disciple Maria recited an incantation and chains made of desert glass came from the ground and latched around it. The corpse was doing as much as it could to escape, but the dozens of chains weren't letting go. Disciple Maria continued her incantation as runes started to appear all over her staff.

Her wording was elegant and without fault, but her face failed to stay strong as tears ran down her face. The more she cried, the louder she shouted the incantation until the runes had turned her staff completely golden.

She slammed her staff into the ground with a shriek of agony at seeing the person closest to her in such a hideously evil state. A golden circle burned radiantly around Gerard's corpse as it was lowered into the ground.

It was doing everything it could to escape and break free, but as it dropped lower, all Gerard's corpse could do was stare at Maria, until finally the ground swallowed it.

Everyone waited cautiously to see if the corpse would escape from below, but it seemed like the fight was over. Iosefka rushed over to Delilah and applied some lotion she had from her bag for burn marks and did her best to apply it to her waist and chest, which had received the most damage.

'What the hell was that? Why did Gerard attack us?' Adam shouted.

'That wasn't your Gerard,' Caesar explained, having been brought back to consciousness by Kaya. 'He was being puppeteered through necromancy magic. And there is only one person who could ever do something like that.'

'Gonti... He is not dead.' Disciple Maria was still staring at the spot where she had locked eyes with Gerard's corpse.

'How can that be?' Adam asked.

'It doesn't matter how it has happened,' Caesar said. 'What matters now is that he's telling the world that he's coming back. That he is going to take over Elysium.'

27. The Fourth Strain

There was meant to be a whole feast in the Capital after all the teams had returned from their expedition, as a celebration for the students' first adventure and a welcome for those entering the terrifying world. Instead, once the three groups that had casualties had been found and mourned – including the group of five with Max Aglet being the sole survivor once more – every resident on Elysium found themselves outside the Pantheon listening to Micholesh's speech.

'The portal gates on Earth will be opening in a matter of hours. We will explain the situation to everyone there as well. Those who want to come through into this world may now choose to stay on Earth, and I do not hold anyone to disappointment if you decide to move to Earth for safety. Those who have served in the war are well aware, Gonti is the only person to ever learn how to use necromancy magic. He never showed even the other Ascensionists how to use this form of magic. Now, after the incident that took place just days ago with Gerard's corpse being puppeteered like so many others have been— desecrating his body— we have no other option than to accept that Gonti is still alive.'

There was a wave of shock that rode through the thousands of people standing in the streets and on the grass outside. Since the fight, people had been speculating that someone else had learnt the powers, that there was no chance Gonti could ever come back.

'I know what you are all thinking. I myself found it a struggle to come to this conclusion—I killed him myself—but let us not forget that this is a world where we understand very little. We have to accept that there were Ascensionists that managed to hide away all these years and have managed to bring him back from the dead. I would like to believe that there is any other explanation, but I still believe this is the most likely. Therefore, I am not allowing any student, or resident of Elysium, to go any deeper into the Wildlands, out of fear that they will never return.'

This news did not go down well. The expeditions had cleared out the few remaining ruins and monster-infested areas that were in the searched sections of the Wildlands.

'What are we meant to do then!' A bold older student shouted.

'We should be fighting to find Gonti and take him out before he gets too powerful!' Said one of the residents of the Capital.

'I know this is frustrating, but we must remain careful.' Micholesh's voice was level and calm through the outrage, Patches the glove resting on his left shoulder. 'We have already lost so many; I can't lose any more. We must be ready for the coming attacks. That is all I have to say, please remember that it is not necessary to progress when we are already happy. As we have seen on Earth, progress for the sake of progress will only lead to destruction.' Micholesh then turned away and left to plan for another war.

After arguments among themselves, the crowd slowly dispersed into smaller groups, ranting about how they couldn't go out into the world, or staying silent, worrying about Gonti's return.

'At least we managed to go on one expedition,' Kaya said as they started to walk back to camp.

'Everyone, there's something that I need to tell you all and you're not going to like it,' Iosefka said suddenly.

'What is it?' Amelia replied.

'Since the very first day that I came here, I've been debating whether to go back to Earth or if I should stay here, but after a lot of thinking, I have concluded that it's best... it's right... for me to head back home.'

'What?' Kaya frowned like it was a bad joke.

'That doesn't make any sense, you should stay here. This is where you belong.' Amelia's lip started to quiver.

'But I don't belong here. I belong with my family, where I don't hold others back.'

'You don't hold us back,' Kaya said angrily.

'You could have died because of me! All of you could have. Gerard came and I couldn't pray and so I couldn't do anything to help you! I was useless. Disciple Maria was right, it's only a matter of time before I get someone killed. Delilah is barely alive and maybe she wouldn't be burnt for life if I was able to help protect her. When I go, you'll get someone new to your team and you can trust them to protect you.'

'But... we are your family.' Amelia held Iosefka's hand as if it would keep her with them.

'We are. And I'll never forget a single day of this, I promise. This is just what I have to do, I can't run away from my parents all my life, it's time I go back to them. I didn't want to have to tell you all, goodbyes are so hard, but I couldn't run away from you all too.'

'So, this is it?' Kaya found that he couldn't look at Iosefka, staring at a twig on the ground instead.

'I think so. I'm going to head up Mount Ida now before I change my mind again. I'm so very sorry, everyone, but I want you all to know this has been the best year of my life.'

Adam had been expecting this for some time. 'Iosefka, wait,' he called as she started to leave them.

Before she could give a reply, Adam pulled her in for one last hug, which the others quickly joined. None of them knew how long they stood there, holding the other like a child trying to keep their snowman from melting in the sun. Eventually, Iosefka worked her way out, tears falling down her cheeks and running past her yellow patterned lines.

'It has been an honour, to train, to fight, and to live alongside you. I hope our paths cross again, Iosefka, the Kind Wiccan,' Adam said with a bow.

They all waited and watched as Iosefka faded away, chasing her ever after.

The hours trickled by as the three of them sat around on their sofa, not knowing what to do with themselves. 'Have you had any luck decrypting that other scroll?' Adam asked, pretending like everything was normal.

'Oh.' Amelia barely reacted to the question at first. 'No. No, I was told to hand them both into the Monastery. They wanted to document a copy of the spells.'

'So, then what's that scroll on the table?' Kaya said, pointing at what he very well knew was the second scroll.

'It may have escaped my mind to give them the other one,' she said casually.

'Escaped your mind!' Kaya shouted, making her jump. 'Do you know how much trouble we can get in for doing that? Seriously, because I have no clue.'

'I only kept it because I think that there's something suspicious going on.'

'What are you talking about? Surely not, the all-powerful necromancer that is threatening to wage war on the Capital with their inevitable first stop being this very camp?' Kaya said, sarcastically.

'I think it's odd how Micholesh is completely against going out into the Wildlands.'

'I think it's exactly what I would do,' Kaya argued. 'How many people has he seen go out there trying to help him, only to die a horrific death? He's only doing what's best for us.'

'Maybe you're right and maybe I'm just being paranoid but something feels off. So, I've decided to work on the scroll alone. I just gave the monks the one I solved and said that was it. I think the reason this one is such a challenge to decode is because it is not one of the three strains. I think we have been lucky enough to find one from that fourth strain that they are still trying to decode.'

'What?' Kaya walked over to the parchment and carefully picked it up, examining all the strange holes Amelia had put through the parchment, which had moved the coloured symbols around.

'I'm thinking that if we manage to crack it first, we will become some of the most powerful people in Elysium, and then –'

'And then we can get justice for Gerard,' Adam finished. 'Do you have any idea what kind of magic it is?'

'If I'm not mistaken, I think that this scroll could very well be some minor form of Reality magic.'

28. Epilogue

'Oh. Hey, Max, how are you doing?' Iosefka had just climbed up Mount Ida. They sat in a room almost identical to the one they had waited in a year ago except smaller.

'I just – I can't do this anymore. I don't even know why I'm alive. I'm the weakest person in each of the teams I've been in, probably the weakest in the entire world. I don't deserve to be here.' He spun Olivia's silver ring around his finger.

'You did the best you could, you just ran into some really bad monsters,' Iosefka reassured.

There were a good few hundred people in the waiting room for Earth, a couple of first-year students, older students, and even people who lived in the Capital, some alone and others with their families, all choosing to retreat to Earth out of fear of Gonti.

'Why are you here? You're one of the strong ones?'

'I left my family on Earth, and I need to be back with them. It's where I belong.'

Max gave a nasty chuckle. 'Where you belong? I thought I belonged with Olivia, Becca, and Jaiden. Now they're dead, thanks to Kaya. Do you think that's it for me? Are you saying I should just end it all so I can be back with them?'

'No, don't do that, you can't. You still have so much left to live for.' Iosefka put her hand on his knee, which was shaking violently as he bit his fingers.

'And you still have so much you can give in Elysium. You belong wherever it feels like you're not lost, and it seemed to me like you were happy here.'

Before Iosefka could respond, Micholesh entered the room, surprising everyone. Conversations ended and heads turned all to focus on him. He looked tired, but he still gave a sweet smile to them all.

'Hello everyone. I hope that this is not a final goodbye and that you all come back to Elysium one day. When you come back, each of you will be welcomed and treated with respect as always. I do not condemn your choice to go back to Earth, there is a great threat coming, and I wish you all to stay safe.'

Everyone gave murmurs of thanks and an applause. Hearing these words seemed to make a lot of people feel guilty and almost everyone found it difficult to look at him. For some strange reason, Micholesh made his way over to Iosefka and Max.

'Max Aglet. It is good to see you again, I want to say again how sorry I am for your misfortune. It was always a pleasure having your team help deliver letters and packages. If you would allow it, I would like to have a word with you in private.'

Max looked starstruck. He didn't know what to say, and so stood up and followed Micholesh who gave only a small nod to acknowledge Iosefka.

Without anyone to talk to, she sat there in her chair thinking about her future – how far behind she would be on her readings. Trying not to think of Earth, she thought back to how proud she was. She had climbed up Mount Ida with ease. It had been such a challenge to go down it a year ago, but today she barely broke a sweat. She was proud of how much she had uncovered about potion brewing, and above all, she was proud to have found friends and another family along the way.

After about twenty minutes, a Charon's Disciple came into the room and announced that the portal gates would be opening soon and that they were to be led back to Earth. Max still hadn't come back from talking to Micholesh and she was now starting to worry that something had happened to him. However, as she followed the others out into a long hall, she noticed Max walking to the other end.

'Max!' She was shocked to find that there was a wide smile on his face.

'Iosefka, I've just been given a fantastic opportunity. Micholesh offered for me to stay in the Capital and continue delivering his mail. I get paid a lot, and I never have to step foot into the Wildlands again. What's even better is I will spend all my time in the Capital as a citizen without having to do the rest of my years at camp!'

'So, you're not going back to Earth?'

'Nope, Micholesh convinced me how much worth I have here in Elysium. But I hope you enjoy yourself back there. If I'm being honest, part of me was hoping something like this would happen, I didn't like the idea of going back there. Micholesh explained it best when he said that I've just been through so much recently that my vision is clouded. Best of luck on Earth though, I hope your parents are glad to see you.'

And with that Max left Iosefka, who found herself looking around in the small hope that Micholesh was going to walk up to her and change her mind. At this point, she was looking around for anyone to tell her to stay, but all she was told was to continue following the others to the portal.

Going through the portal felt like the last piece of adventure she would have, the last drop of her rollercoaster before it evened out to a long flat straight track. As soon as her feet landed on Earth, she was given a breathing mask and told to wait to the side of the colossal gates that were currently closed.

Once the last person came through the portal, the Disciple opened up a fortified box and took out a remote, which they pressed. The gates started to grind open. As the filthy air came into the Box, she noticed how sticky and thick it was. All she could see were different shades of grey, and once the gates had opened enough, a splash of dark blue from all those excited people desperate to start their new life.

The gates finally stopped their gross deafening grinding as they fully opened. It was like the Disciple had forgotten about them as he welcomed those from Earth and brought them towards the portal. Everyone in the line with Iosefka shifted their weight awkwardly as they tried to get used to breathing through their mask, expecting to be told when they could go.

After a few minutes of waiting, Iosefka got fed up and walked straight out of the Box back into the streets that she had grown up around. After her, the others started to follow, except they did as they had been told on Elysium and made a left for the hospital so that they could be given their nanobees. Iosefka, on the other hand, kept walking forward, heading back home.

She hesitated before knocking on the door, but her anxiety was beaten by the desire to get inside where the air wasn't as sickly. It was her mother who opened the door to her, her face wrinkled and bitter.

'Iosefka,' she said as a hero speaks to their villain.

Iosefka had known that she wouldn't be ecstatic to see her, but was expecting her to be relieved at the very least.

'Mother, I have come home.'

'This is not your home.'

'I know I ran away and went to Elysium, and I am so sorry for disobeying you, but I am your daughter.'

Her father now came to the door and also showed no sign of love as he looked down on her. 'You are no longer our daughter.'

'Don't say that. I'm sorry, I shouldn't have left. It was just a stupid argument. I want to be with you.'

'You have brought shame and dishonour to this family and to our religion.'

Iosefka dropped to her knees, begging to be let back inside. 'Please! Mother! Father! I'll do anything to repent.' She tried to reach for their shoes but they stepped back as if her touch was poison.

'Pray then,' her mother ordered.

'What?' Iosefka looked up at her parents.

'You disgraced yourself and us for a year. Pray on this doorstep for a year. Recite all that you have learnt from us, all our laws, beliefs, everything. Do that for a year and when the gates take away the wretched like you, we will allow you back into this home,' her father said.

'But I haven't got my nanobees yet, let me just go to the hospital and get them and I will pray. I will pray for as long as it takes.'

'No,' he said. 'You start now. Abraham, Jesus, Muhammed, they lived without the help of such technology. If you wish to repent, you will pray as they would.'

'But – but I'll be in so much pain. I could die.' Iosefka was still on her knees.

'If you are weak, perhaps. If you are strong, you will survive.'
Her father closed the door on her as she was left on the ground.

It's a trick, she thought. *My parents would never do that to me, they just want me to suffer for what I have done.* So, wanting to prove to her parents that she was sorry, she started to pray.

She had been there for almost two hours, non-stop praying. Her throat was dry and it hurt to talk. She needed water but still, her parents hadn't opened the door.

Then the ground started to shake, and moments later, she could hear it. That brutally loud grinding of the portal gates coming to a close. At first, she hadn't noticed that the front door had opened, the noise around her was so deafening.

A small soft hand touched her shoulder and she looked up to see her younger brother. 'Joseph.' She stood up and hugged him. 'It's so good to see you again.'

He was hugging back but he was withdrawn. 'They don't want you here,' he whispered in her ear, scared that even over the noise, their parents would overhear him.

'They will. I just need to repent.'

'I've heard them, they are never going to let you back into the family. When you left... they were happy.'

Iosefka pushed her brother away and stepped back a few paces. 'No... No, they were angry at me, they were very very angry and disowned me. But I just need to show them how sorry I am and then I'll be back in the family!'

Their parents came to the door to see if she was still praying and shook their heads with a frown, seeing that she was standing up. 'You have failed!' Her father shouted.

'You are weak! Another year of praying!' Her mother attempted to slam the door but Iosefka dashed to it before it could be fully closed, sticking her foot in the way.

'I am not weak!' She shouted, entering the house.

'Prove your worth to us then.'

'Prove my worth! I am your daughter! I may have made mistakes, but you are acting like you don't even want me!' Iosefka walked up to the people who raised her and brought her into the world with more anger in her than she had thought possible.

'Start praying,' they both said trying to maintain their power over her.

'No.'

'Then leave.'

'I don't understand! Joseph said you were happy when I left. Was I such an awful daughter that you want rid of me? You would rather I die than have me in your life?'

'You are a burden, a nuisance who questions too much, a thorn in our sides. Leaving was the best decision you ever made, and now you have returned, grovelling, like a peasant. You are no child of mine,' her mother said with disgust, having backed away into the corner of the room.

'Then fine. I'll leave you, not because I am some runaway, but because you are the cowards, who cannot love their daughter! I may have flaws, but in Elysium people accept me. When it causes them so much hardship, they still accept me. You cannot even deal with the thought of me and for that, God will never forgive you. It won't matter how much you abide by his laws and pray to him; you have lost sight of what our religion means, and you will not be met by him when you die!'

With her parents too shocked to say another word, Iosefka sprinted out of the house, her feet slamming on the ground with such force, it felt like with each step she flew. All the way back to the portal gates, she ran, understanding finally where she belonged.

There was the slightest gap still left in the gates and she slipped through it to the outcries and rage of the Disciple as she dove through the portal back into Elysium, sprinting towards her real family.

The End

Adam Tideborne and the Greatsword of War
Copyright © 2022 Joshua Steven-Shachar

All rights reserved.

No part of this publication may be reproduced, stored in a retrieval system, stored in a database and / or published in any form or by any means, electronic, mechanical, photocopying, recording or otherwise, without the prior written permission of the publisher.

Printed in Great Britain
by Amazon